BOOK ONE OF THE ETERNAL TALES

RHIANNON'S TALE

BARBARA ELDER

Barbara Elder

FIRST EDITION

ISBN: 9780996207409

Editors: Roz Spafford & Ruth Schneider
Proofreader: Esther Kennedy
Cover design: Mallory Rock
Interior Layout & Formatting: Mallory Rock

Special thanks to Krysta Hunt and everyone at MuseFish Press

MUSEFISH PRESS
in conjunction with
WITCHSCRIBE PUBLISHING
WITCHSCRIBE@GMAIL.COM

For Philip
&
For Dr. A. Wood,
who taught me how to Travel.

ONE

Family History No. 7564
Rhiannon's Tale: The Lost Sister
AS TOLD BY Neo's'lai *Historian G.V.*

It was hard, remembering her own death.

The memory was always in the back of her mind, stuffed down in the darkness, where she could almost pretend it wasn't there.

But now the wound was ripped wide, the memory brought to the forefront.

There was a man, a man with a horrifying dark aura. He stood halfway up the block on Grand Boulevard in downtown Kansas City, his body limned with a shifting black mass, churning to reveal bloody red gashes.

He was stalking her. He'd been stalking her for two lifetimes.

Just staring at him, Rhiannon cringed inside, recalling every detail. Dying all over again. The hardest part of remembering her death wasn't so much the remembering itself, as it was reliving the fear.

1

Now, more than two decades afterward, Rhiannon could see the blood unfurling through the bathwater like crimson ribbons, the pain bright and keen, her breath ragged, echoing in the stillness of the tiled bathroom. Another lifetime, another body, unquestionably her own.

She'd thought death was a cloak, concealing, safe and warm.

Looking at the man with the black aura, she knew she'd been wrong.

Rhiannon remembered more than just her death, but an entire past life, beyond her current existence. It wasn't like a series of New Age visions, all lotus petals and a connection with the divine. Instead, her previous life had been rife with mundane details, like any other existence — the sunshine-yellow dollhouse she got for her 10th birthday; the afternoons with her grandmother at the Impressionist exhibit at the Met, her footsteps echoing on the gallery floors; the faded blue tattoo on her grandmother's forearm.

It had been a life temporal, worldly. Yet even then — as now — she'd borne a multi-layered shining aura that no one else appeared to see.

And there was always the man with the caliginous black aura, hunting her, a monster burning with a horrible darkness.

Rhiannon spent two lives terrified and angry, wrapped in fear and self-doubt, sometimes even wondering if she was only imagining her stalker. But he was real, after all.

And once again, he was going to kill another woman, while Rhiannon watched. He would do it to torture Rhiannon, remind her who he was, what he was capable of. How vulnerable she was. He wanted her to know he could find her any time, over decades, lifetimes.

It was just like last time, 24 years before. Back then, Rhiannon lived in San Francisco, wearing another face, another name. But the moment, the murder, were the same. Standing on a sidewalk in downtown Kansas City, more than two decades later, she'd had the Feeling again, a sensation of something impending, terrifying, a Feeling that followed her all her life, and the lifetime before.

Rhiannon had turned slowly, drawn inexorably toward the source of the Feeling. Like a sleepwalker, a drunk, an unholy man's vision, she moved helpless, silent, facing up Grand Boulevard.

A half-block away was a large bank. From the sidewalk, a red canvas canopy arched over marble steps leading to wide glass doors, laced with the bank's name in gold.

One of the doors opened, a man holding the glass with one hand, to allow a blonde woman to pass. She was young, in her early 20s, close to Rhiannon's age. She was lovely, all big eyes and high cheekbones, looking back to her companion, laughing, her lipstick shiny red. He'd followed behind, his dark hair crisp and short, his collar snowy against his black suit and his horrible dark aura. Laughing, too, he guided his companion down the stairs, holding her elbow solicitously. At the curb, a chauffeur exited a Town Car and came around to open the rear passenger door for the couple.

It was all so normal, simply one of a thousand moments people have in their lives, inconsequential, insignificant.

But no one could see what Rhiannon saw. She knew what was coming. Knew what the consequences would be, for her, for the lovely blonde.

She'd seen this before, this moment, a breathless, terrifying scene of control and death. And she was helpless to move, her muscles utterly unyielding, betraying her. Rhiannon could only watch with a horror so profound that she detached herself from it – though not quite entirely numb to it. Her back began to ache, a terrible pressure just below her shoulder blades. The pain was familiar, too, but she didn't understand it, couldn't explain it. She only knew that watching this man brought with it a terrible agony, physical, emotional, the vestige of some moment she couldn't recall, just out of her reach.

The man's glowing aura was strong and wide, with multiple layers like Rhiannon's own, though where his was dark, Rhiannon's radiated light. But no one else could see his seething glow, rendering the moment mundane to passersby – but in truth, a nightmare, meant for Rhiannon's eyes alone.

Almost at the car and the waiting chauffeur, the man halted abruptly. The woman bumped to a stop, her face registering surprise. He turned slowly, stopping when he faced Rhiannon, a huge grin seeping across his features. He simply smiled and stared, his dark eyes fathomless, glacial, unblinking. His companion, following his gaze, turned to stare at Rhiannon, too, reflecting a mixture of boredom and polite curiosity.

The man simply watched Rhiannon. He seemed to wait until he'd seen her thoroughly appraise the blonde woman, and then his smile deepened, sickened somehow. It was the darkest smile on Earth, filled with glee and the joy of devastating cruelty, death, and the black-red raw meat of violence. Rhiannon flinched at that terrible smile, desperate to run, frozen helpless on the sidewalk.

Still watching Rhiannon, he took the blonde woman's arm again, and she turned to him, smiling. Rhiannon saw the moment when the woman found herself unable to look away from him, her smile fading, her eyes widening.

He began to glow brighter, the light around his body a dark corona, glimmers of grey shining in a black, roiling sky, like lightning amidst midnight clouds. A silvery light flowed from the blonde woman's body, into his hand. With every passing moment, her light faded, and the seething haze around him grew stronger, more vivid. Her face had lost all expression; she looked unreal, a doll, her skin waxy pale. His handsome face was a mask of dark pleasure.

Her luminescence faded, extinguished at last, and he released her arm. She sagged to the pavement at his feet, as though she were kneeling. Her red lipstick was bright against the pasty ashes of her skin.

No one saw what Rhiannon saw, rooted cold and undefended on the sidewalk. No one else could see anything more than one of a thousand inconsequential moments – perhaps 30 seconds, perhaps a minute, surely no more. It wasn't until the blonde woman collapsed on the pavement before anyone turned. People rushed to her aid, shouting for someone to call 911, someone else crying out that she was dead. And all the while *he* stood by, staring at Rhiannon a half-block away, offering her his knowing, stygian smile.

Rhiannon's whole body vibrated, aching with shock, dread. He'd killed that blonde woman. He'd wanted her to see it. He was hunting her, teasing her, playing with his prey. But worst of all – far worse – was the hideous knowledge that she'd seen him do this before.

Twenty-four years ago in San Francisco, Rhiannon had run from him in a blind panic, making it back to her tiny, cheerful apartment, her lungs burning, her mind screaming. She'd been certain there was only one way to make sure he couldn't find her again, her only chance for deliverance. She'd sliced her wrists in the too-hot bathtub, and Rhiannon remembered how it felt to drift, the opaque bloody water carrying her into the sanctuary of Lethean darkness. Dying had been easy, her escape complete.

You can't get me now.

Rhiannon always thought death was the ultimate exit; the final chess piece removed from the board; dandelion seeds blown into the vehemence of the oncoming storm.

But the exhilaration of escape was Rhiannon's delusion, valiant, pathetic. He'd shown her his horrific power, and she'd run, run all the way into another life. But now he'd found her again, and it was all happening the way it did before. Another woman had died, reminding Rhiannon that she could never run far enough, or die too often.

Rhiannon gasped and opened her eyes, shaking, her body clammy with sweat. She stared baffled at the sickly green paint on the wall. This wasn't her room, her home. She rolled over in the narrow bed, looking around the room. Daylight seeped around the edges of the closed curtains hanging in stiff, blue folds. Polished grey linoleum shone dimly. A sink stood in the corner, surrounded by yellowing Formica, next to a door leading to a room with a solitary toilet. And everywhere, the smell of disinfectant and fear.

She remembered now.

She could still see the ghastly dark man, and the dead woman on the sidewalk, kneeling at his feet, as though in supplication. Rhiannon was screaming, screaming, unable to stop, and all the while he smiled at her, that hideous black smile. There was an ambulance; she fought the paramedics wildly, howling, arching her back, finally strapped down in five-point restraints. They brought her here. A hospital psychiatric ward.

5

What had she said? How much did they know? How crazy did they think she was? She rifled through her memories, trying to sort through vague recollections of screaming, babbling, begging. Pleading for protection. Warning them.

He'd watched it all. She felt an icy stab in her chest. He could find her here. It would be so easy.

The main door to the room was cracked slightly, three inches revoking solitude. Beyond the door, Rhiannon heard a woman's voice from some distance, speaking under her breath. As she approached, her words gradually became clear.

"No, no, no, no. It's the bad thoughts. It's the bad thoughts. No, no, no. Everything's fine, everything is going to be fine, everything's fine. No, no, no, no."

The unseen woman continued her quiet babble without ceasing, until her words slid into mumbles, quieting as she passed Rhiannon's door and continued on her way.

In the silence that followed, Rhiannon sat up and swung her legs over the side of the hospital bed. The linoleum was cold and smooth against her bare feet. She sat like that for awhile, hunched over her knees. She was acutely aware of the gaping door to her left, the windows to her right. Exposed. Vulnerable.

The dark man probably knew more than she did at this point. Where was she? Which hospital was this? Glancing at the partially open door, she closed her eyes and began breathing with careful deliberation, inhaling through the nose, exhaling through the mouth. She struggled to find a sense of calm that normally came easily, when she used her "Feeling" gift, as she called it.

Focusing intensely, she turned her vision inward to warm darkness, shimmers of scarlet and gold, alive, a universe vast contained within her body.

Breathing deeply, she began drawing energy from her center, white and gold coalescing into wisps of vapor, becoming clouds glowing with power. Rhiannon allowed the energy to flow now, her limbs conduits, pulling the energy through her body, into her chest, there to expand and pulse, before she finally permitted the power to slide down her left arm, into her hand.

6

She opened her eyes, utterly calm, and looked down at her left hand. A nimbus of gold radiated from her palm, her fingers. Slowly, she laid her hand against the blanket on the bed.

Francisco Alvarez making the bed, hurry, irritation, the head nurse is such a bitch, annoyed, Sonia's baby could come any day, why didn't she quit smoking she'll make the baby sick, love worry love, buying a lottery ticket at lunch, hope, yearn, maybe Jerry will go in on it with me, St. Michael's is so crowded, parking sucks, bored, going to apply at Lutheran, be closer to Sonia, love love Sonia, I'm good at beds, pride, fast and crisp corners, they should appreciate me more.

Gasping at the rush of emotions and thoughts, Rhiannon pulled her hand free of the blanket, releasing the energy to dissipate into the air. She took several deep, calming breaths. She was in St. Michael's, the main hospital in downtown Kansas City.

Wrapping herself in a carefully constructed mantle of confidence and calm, she got up and went to the sink, where she found pajama pants, a T-shirt, and a new pair of fuzzy socks with rubber strips on the soles. Rhiannon smiled at that. The only good thing about a visit to the psych ward was getting free non-skid fuzzy socks.

She dressed quickly. Standing in front of a polished metal mirror – no glass here – brushing her thick black hair, she fought down panic, trying not to notice her distorted image in the warped metal, her tawny olive skin, her body enveloped with bands of golden light.

Rhiannon first remembered her prior life when she was 13. She'd spent her entire life believing, filled with a *knowing*, an understanding of herself and the world that just didn't fit with anyone or anything else. Throughout both her lives, she'd borne a shining aura of her own. In her current incarnation, she'd had dreams like memories, dreams that taught her to use her surprisingly powerful gifts.

For almost all of her 24 years, she'd tried to convince others, to justify her beliefs and understanding – only to be rejected, even locked away, medicated. Eventually, she'd stopped trying, resigning herself to her solitary views, beliefs.

But now, suddenly, everything was different. Immediate. No longer just a nightmare from another life, it was clear that at least part of what she'd always believed was true. The worst part. The dark man was back, and he was hunting her. She was in terrible danger.

Nobody could help her. Why would anyone believe it now, when they never had before? Her life might have changed, but the rest of the world had continued on its way, oblivious.

She had to get out of the psychiatric ward immediately. She wasn't safe anymore. Not now. She couldn't stay here, exposed, defenseless. He'd watched them take her away. He probably already knew where she was. Would he come here, or would he wait, toying with her?

Rhiannon had been through this before. She reflected how easy it was, to think you're insane, when you remember a past life, or discover some disturbing psychic ability. While, in other circumstances, the psych ward might be a nice place to visit – it was rather relaxing, having no real responsibilities – it was, in truth, a kind of jail. Getting in was much easier than getting out.

She needed to get sane in a hurry.

Rhiannon opened her door carefully, taking in everything beyond.

She hadn't been in St. Michael's before. Looking in either direction, she decided the common area and nurses' station would most likely be to her left. Walking down the hall, she affected a deliberate casualness, seemingly relaxed, but hyperaware, tension seething tight just under her skin, fear coiled icy within her chest.

She was used to hiding who she was, hiding her emotions, pretending she was someone else. She'd learned to suppress her fears, half-imagining they weren't even real. She hated being wrong, hated the terror that even now left her feeling weak and alone. No, she reminded herself, while she may be alone, she wasn't weak. She was strong. She had to be.

The hall opened into the large common room. Three old beige floral loveseats and a few chairs created a circle around a low table, strewn with magazines. A television blared, attached high on the wall with indestructible powder-coated metal.

Across the room was a small kitchen, two tables, and some chairs. Everything was made of blond wood and Formica, the edges rounded and blunt, like outsized furniture for children. Rhiannon imagined having a tea party there, with giant fluffy insane teddy bears.

"I don't want to watch this!" A man in a disreputable blue bathrobe stood screaming at a petite dark-skinned nurse, who sat at the heavily fortified and defended nurses' station on the west wall.

The man in the bathrobe gestured toward the television. "There's poisoners and thieves on this show! Temptresses! Demons!"

Rhiannon looked back at the television. It was airing "Fox and Friends." Currently, the hosts were learning how to make a cherry pie in the shape of Israel.

"Mr. Atkinson," the nurse was the soul of reason. "If you can't calm down, I'm just going to have to turn the TV off."

"Turn it off then!" Mr. Atkinson bellowed. "Keep those demons out of here! That succubus! They feed on our brainwaves!"

The nurse held up a remote and the television went dark and silent. "There. No more demons. Maybe you should go lie down for awhile, Mr. Atkinson. Meds in an hour." She looked pointedly toward the hallway.

"Yeah, maybe I should." Mr. Atkinson ran a hand through his sparse hair, adjusted his raggedy bathrobe, and shuffled past Rhiannon, down the hall.

Watching him, the nurse caught sight of Rhiannon. "Ah, Miss Byrne. You're up. Well done."

Only in a mental ward do they appreciate how difficult it can be to get out of bed, Rhiannon thought.

"Thank you." Rhiannon studied the nurse's face, her aura brightening slightly as she focused on the other woman's eyes. A wave of pale blue kindness, orange boredom, and red-grey harried stress washed over Rhiannon. Flicking a glance at the nurse's nametag, she smiled into the woman's eyes. "Roberta, isn't it? Please call me Megan."

Rhiannon had three names.

She was born into this life in Kansas City, Missouri, christened Megan Byrne, born to Rosa Gonzales, once of Bogota, Columbia, and David Byrne, formerly of Boston, good Irish stock. Both deceased.

9

But in Rhiannon's previous life, she'd carried the name Katania – Kat – Weiss. Raised in Brooklyn, she'd eventually moved to San Francisco – where she was destined to die at the tender age of 19 – at her own hand, escaping the man with the black aura.

The third name? Or was it really the first name, the primary name. Rhiannon, the name that sang to her in her dreams over two lifetimes, the name that hovered fragile on the lips of nocturnal dream lovers, glowing men and women who knew her soul, the name that felt true and real and right, ineffably *hers*.

But she gave Nurse Roberta the name she was born with, in this lifetime. Megan. The name on her driver's license. The name that never felt right.

"It's too early in the morning for 'Miss Byrne'." She forced a smile, disarming on the outside. Terrified on the inside. The nurse laughed.

Clinging to her composure, Rhiannon clenched her fists behind her back. "I guess I'm scheduled to see an intake nurse or doctor, at some point today?" Some things were routine, regardless of the hospital.

The nurse smiled. "Both. The psychiatric nurse does a kind of triage, and then the doctor will see you this afternoon. I'm expecting Ms. Applegate – that's the nurse – around 10 a.m. Dr. Gates does rounds after 2."

"I see," Rhiannon's mind raced. She had two people, figuratively, between her and the door. She only had to stay safe a little while longer.

"Breakfast will be in 10 minutes in the kitchen," Nurse Roberta continued. "You were just brought in last night, so you didn't get to order what you'd like. So it's oatmeal for you." She grimaced. "It's not the best."

Rhiannon smiled, the picture of calm. "That's okay."

Nurse Roberta waved toward the couches and the thick glass windows beyond. "There's a courtyard out there, if you'd like some fresh air. Oh, and Ms. Applegate can help you make a phone call, if you like."

Rhiannon sat down in the kitchen to await breakfast. And to think. To form a plan.

In this life, Rhiannon had grown up in Columbus Park in Kansas City, raised by her single mother. Her father had died when she was very small. It had been a hard childhood, but she clung to the moments of magic, dreams that felt real, like memories, filled with a family she'd never known; dreams that taught her how to use her gifts.

In the life before that, Rhiannon remembered Kat Weiss falling and skinning her knees wearing her first pair of roller skates, wobbly plastic wheels strapped to her tennis shoes. She remembered her bat mitzvah, standing next to the rabbi as she spoke aloud the words of the Torah, awestruck in the very presence of the fragile sacred scroll.

But even back then, she remembered the feeling that she was being hunted. That someone was out there, looking for her, hungry for her. Someone unbelievably evil. Her grandmother, her Bubby, was the only one who believed her. "You got the *Dybbuk* after you, *kindella*," she said. "A dead, evil soul, walking around in a man." Her grandmother would fold her into her generous body, holding her close. "Strong, that's what you have to be."

Kat had moved all the way across the country, away from her parents and her grandmother, thinking she could hide 2,600 miles away, in a city as big and welcoming and anonymous as San Francisco.

And for two years, it had worked. Until the dark man found her.

Being in the psychiatric ward is something like being in prison, a bit like being in the waiting room of a motor vehicle office, slightly like being in the military, and somewhat akin to being in an emergency room or maternity ward. Waiting is the primary focus, the chief inactive activity.

Little moments become major events, looked forward to and savored. Patients mark time, measure their days by these precious moments. Two hours until lunch. Half an hour until snack. Meds at 6 o'clock.

In between these major events are the minor ones, little triumphs and tragedies, both personal and social. Taking a shower, washing your hair, changing into clean pajamas and your fuzzy socks

11

with rubber strips on the bottom. ("No, you are not allowed to go barefoot. Please go back to your room, and put on your socks.")

Rhiannon had seen, for some, the simple act of taking a shower is a nearly insurmountable challenge. Being naked and exposed in a strange place, even a private shower stall, is humbling and strange. Being alone in a tiled box, with only your own madness for company, can be terrifying. Thoughts, voices, and memories constructed within the misfiring synapses of one's own mind constitute a mental assault, bruising, crushing.

Interactions with others – nurses, doctors, orderlies, patients – seem fraught with consequence, the outcome emotionally uncertain and perilous. One wrong word, one bad thought voiced, can determine whether you stay or go, whether you watch television, or are bound in restraints.

The first time Rhiannon was hospitalized, when she was 13, she could feel the people around her, the other inmates. Many felt as though they were bruised emotionally, mentally. With every contact, a nurse, another patient, that inner bruise was touched, rubbed, pressed deeper. Some touches felt harder than others. Some bruises were really wounds.

It had been terrifying, being surrounded by so much pain, confusion, anger, and grief. Rhiannon felt insane herself, bearing the weight of it.

Now, she'd learned to buffer herself from others, to shield her own emotions and feelings from those of others. But when such emotions were strong, she could still feel them dimly, an echo in her skin.

After breakfast (the oatmeal had, in fact, been inedible), Rhiannon sat in the kitchen with the other patients. There were three, besides herself: Mr. Atkinson in his grubby bathrobe; a woman named Carol, who was always hugging herself, rocking; and the glowing one.

Apparently, no one else could see glowing people. While everyone had a little glow, a thin haze around their bodies, the glowing people were surrounded by a nimbus of light, shimmering strata, rich with color and depth.

Rhiannon looked down at her hand, her own glow a thick band of luminescent gold layers, rings around rings of light. Seeing that aura, in herself or others, caused an inexplicable yearning so sweet it ached. But almost immediately, she would think of the dark man's black aura, and a deep dread would seep into her heart, congealing cold and dark.

She'd seen perhaps a dozen glowing people in her current lifetime. They'd all looked right at her, yet never approached. Two had nodded, as though to say hello, but then walked on. She wished she had the courage to speak to them, more than a little afraid to know the truth. *Are you real?* She'd ask. *Are you really glowing? Am I? Or am I really crazy after all?*

Would the glowing little man talk to her?

Rhiannon watched him surreptitiously. He was around 60, deep wrinkles attesting to much time in the sun, his skin leather-tanned. His hair was a frowsy cloud of white around his head, sticking up in all directions. He was a little person, perhaps only 3-feet tall, his hospital-issued pajamas hanging loosely on his meager shoulders. His hands were constantly in motion, shaking, incessantly turning around and over one another in his lap. Faded blue eyes darted in all directions but hers.

She'd never been confined with a glowing person before, neither able to truly escape the other. She'd been nervous when she first saw the little man, four thin bands of light surrounding his body. Part of the light was shadowed somehow, a smear of dark wiped carelessly into the gold.

But like all the others she'd seen before, he didn't speak to her. Didn't approach her. Didn't even nod. In fact, the man seemed almost frightened of Rhiannon, and she didn't know why. She focused, using her gift to study his face – and was suddenly gripped with a bright red terror so profound and absolute that she cringed in shock.

The man scrambled away, down the hall, his little legs churning in his effort to get away from her.

"Wait!" she cried, all at once finally wanting to try, mortified she'd frightened him. "I won't hurt you," she whispered. *I'm not scary.* But he was gone.

Rhiannon always thought that maybe one day she'd get used to rejection, to people being frightened of her. But it still hurt, leaving behind an unalloyed loneliness. Unable to bear the common area any longer, she shuffled past Mr. Atkinson and Carol without looking at them, feeling their eyes on her, imagining accusation and loathing. She went to her room, curling up on Francisco Alvarez's well-made bed. Only one more hour until the psych nurse came to evaluate her.

Sitting in the psychiatric ward's beige meeting room, Nurse Pamela Applegate favored Rhiannon with a tight-lipped smile. "It seems you had a rather difficult night, Miss Byrne." She tapped Rhiannon's file with her pen. "When you were admitted, you were in a state of serious agitation. You said that there was someone trying to kill you."

"I realize that," Rhiannon replied carefully. "I had a traumatic experience."

Nurse Applegate raised one perfectly tweezed and penciled eyebrow. "I see. What exactly happened?"

Rhiannon looked down at her lap, willing her hands not to shake. She'd rehearsed in her head how she would describe the events of the previous day, but the act of recounting a sane and edited version, on some level, would require reliving the real thing. And thinking about what really happened was so terrifying — could she maintain her calm façade? She had to.

"Can you talk about it?" Nurse Applegate prodded, frowning.

"Yes," Rhiannon looked up. "I was downtown. I saw a man and a woman together. The woman seemed all right one moment, but then suddenly she fell down, and she was dead."

He'd killed her. Just like before. She'd watched him kill her. He'd wanted her to see it. Again. *Stay calm!*

"Then he turned and looked at me." *Her back hurt, just remembering. It hurt so much. Stay calm stay calm stay calm* "And he looked just like my stepfather. He molested me when I was a kid." *Nice touch. Total bullshit, but a nice touch.* The dark man looked nothing like her stepfather. "He died when I was 10," she added.

Rhiannon offered a wan smile. "Anyhow, it was all so horrifying, I guess I kind of just ... lost it. I'm feeling much better now."

14

Nurse Applegate pursed her lips, tapping the file with her pen again. "Hmm, that does sound difficult," she said, in a tone of unbelief. She flipped open the folder. "According to the police, it seems the woman you saw did indeed die. A heart attack, they said."

Unlikely. She wasn't even 30. "Oh." Rhiannon shook her head, fighting a wave of sadness and fear, not having to feign grief. That poor woman. *She died for me ...*

"Still," the nurse continued, riffling through the pages in Rhiannon's file, "you've been hospitalized before, always showing paranoid tendencies and delusions – like last night."

Rhiannon focused for a moment, her aura glowing slightly, and looked directly into Nurse Pamela Applegate's eyes. Muddy green and black suspicion, irritation, and dislike assailed her. She looked away. *Swell. If I could just touch her ....*

"I haven't been hospitalized in several years," Rhiannon pointed out. *Everyone thinks you're crazy when you see glowing people.* "I've been doing quite well."

"Yes, well, it seems you've backslid a bit," Nurse Applegate smiled coldly. "I think it's best if you stay here for the full 72-hour hold, and we'll re-evaluate then. Perhaps send you over to West Pines Behavioral Health for awhile."

Fear danced icy down Rhiannon's spine. She was helpless here. The dark man had always been a memory from another time, another life. Now he'd found her again. Small wonder she'd fallen apart, broken down.

She fought back panic. Remaining calm was her only hope. "I really would like to go home." But when the nurse frowned, Rhiannon added hastily, "But if you think that's best, I'm sure I can get the help I need here."

"Yes, indeed," Pamela Applegate closed the folder. "You'll be seeing the doctor this afternoon. I make my recommendations to him. I'll include a course of medication." She stood, glancing at the door. "If you'd like to make a phone call, there's a phone in the next room. I'll unlock it for you."

"Yes, thank you." Smiling placidly at the nurse, Rhiannon

followed her out of the room. Behind her back, she clenched her fists, until her nails dug into her palms.

The afternoon was glorious, hot and moist, the air redolent with the chlorophyl breath of growing things and loamy earth. Rhiannon stood barefoot in the manicured grass in front of the hospital, breathing deep, feeling jubilant in spite of her underlying fears. The earth was cool beneath her feet, solid, reassuring.

A battered, red pickup truck pulled up to the curb. From behind the wheel, a blond man with a crooked grin waved.

Rhiannon slipped on her sandals and ran to the truck. "Greg," she said, part sigh, part laugh. "I knew I could count on you."

"Always, little *ved'ma*." *Little witch.* His accent was thickest when he said her silly nickname, syllables evoking czars, KGB spies, and endless snow-frosted onion spires.

She climbed up onto the truck's worn bench seat, an old, olive-brown army blanket covering frayed upholstery and lumpy springs. She pulled the door shut with a satisfying heavy slam, not once looking back at the hospital. Greg threw the truck into gear.

"We need to get on the Turnpike." Rhiannon twisted to look back into the cab. Her old purple duffle bag was there.

"I got what I could. I don't know from what girls need." Greg glanced at her. "We're going into Kansas?"

"Topeka. I figure I can catch a bus from there tomorrow."

"You can catch a bus from KC a lot easier."

"It's a long story, Greg." A long, long story. A horror story.

The big man laughed, watching the road. "It's at least an hour to Topeka. Plenty of time for stories."

Rhiannon rolled her eyes, smiling in spite of herself.

The world streamed past her window, the trees emerald and shimmering hazy in the humid air. Sometimes the road cut through layers of rock, brown and tan flinty strata, naked beneath the soft, lush curves of soil and summer grasses. The sky felt bleached pale blue in the heat, stretched forever, pulling the earth wide in the sun.

16

Rhiannon leaned back against the seat and closed her eyes. Every mile away from Kansas City eased the weight hanging heavy in her bones.

Greg kept sneaking glances at her, then looking back at the road. He flipped the visor down to shade his eyes from the afternoon glare, made worse by the glittering, badly pitted windshield. He dared another look. Her eyes were closed, her olive skin smooth and glowing in the sunshine. Her hair was a dark silk waterfall, flowing in waves, pillowing her head against the back of the seat. She was achingly beautiful. He wished he could tell her so.

They drove another 10 minutes in silence. Finally, Greg nudged her, his eyes firmly on the road. "What's wrong? Why are we going to Topeka? What's happened?"

She opened her eyes, but didn't look at him, staring instead through the windshield. "There's someone after me. Stalking me. Someone evil." Her tone was flat, an emotionless statement of fact.

Greg felt a wave of panic. He believed her instantly. He always did. She could never know why. "Who? How do you know? What happened?"

Rhiannon saw it all over again, playing again and again in her head, a loop of horrific memories that never stopped. Everything that had happened in San Francisco, all over again, now fresh and raw. The pain below her shoulders, like in all of her nightmares. The way the blonde woman's light, her life, flowed so easily from her body, into him. His dark glow pulsing and expanding. And that smile. How could a smile contain such sick joy, all the evil that ever stained the world?

She turned toward the window, looked down at the white stripe on the side of the road, speeding by in a blur. "I don't know if I can talk about it," her voice was low, strained.

Greg gripped the steering wheel tightly, overcome by frustration, concern, anger. His jaw clenched as he steeled himself against the jumble of confusing emotions. Feeling out of control was not familiar, and he shifted in his seat uncomfortably.

After a moment, when she didn't speak again, he asked, "So, how did you get out of the hospital? It sounded like that nurse meant to keep you." He strove to sound casual, but his voice came out discordant and strained.

17

Rhiannon turned to look at him, wary, beseeching. "The doctor. I *touched* him." Rhiannon had used another of her gifts. Greg's eyes widened for a moment, brow raised in surprise, only to immediately drop in a scowl. "Just a little," she explained in a rush. "You know I can't nudge anyone in a direction they aren't wanting to go anyhow."

Greg didn't say anything.

Rhiannon reached out, touched his sleeve, entreating understanding. He looked down at her hand, disapproval stamped on his broad features.

"I'm not doing anything to you!" Rhiannon huffed, yanking her hand away. She crossed her arms protectively over her chest and glared unseeing out the window. "I only reminded him of stuff he already knew. That nurse is overly suspicious. Zealous. And the hospital needs to keep beds open for people who are truly insane. That's all."

Greg remained silent, stoically watching the road, his shoulders unyielding stone.

Rhiannon felt tears prickling behind her eyes. "Dammit, Greg, I know it's wrong to manipulate people. But I had to get out of there. I'm in danger, and no one but you even believes half the crap I say and do." She scrubbed her eyes with the back of her hand, like a child. "Please," the plea was whispered, hollow, and heartfelt.

He didn't say anything for a long while, his silence damning. She sniffled and turned to the window, giving him her back. When she wiped her eyes again, he couldn't bear the guilt, couldn't punish her any longer. He touched her shoulder, sighed heavily. "Don't cry, little *ved'ma*. I know you did what you had to do."

Such a strange relationship, Rhiannon reflected. When she was younger, their eight-year age difference had seemed vast, and he'd been like a big brother and friend all at once. But things had changed as she matured. One moment he was close, funny and sweet, his body strong and so male, trying to get him into bed – *why won't he sleep with me?* – and the next, she was 15 years old again, and he was the neighbor with the funny accent, teasing, comforting, making her cry – her best friend.

She focused her energy, then looked into his face. Nothing. No flow of emotion or thought. It was like trying to feel the grimy dashboard, the wind, a boulder. Like he wasn't even there. How did he do that? Once in a while, she caught a whisper of emotion, a ghost of some feeling that evaporated before she could even define it. She was always forced to study her enigmatic Russian's tone, his body language, his expressions. With him, she was like everyone else in the world, determining meaning by rudimentary guesswork and observation.

Her chest felt open somehow, soaking in his familiar face, warm, tawny eyes and lopsided smile. That slightly crooked nose, broken in a fight with Tommy Ayles when he was 23– defending her.

And all at once, it came pouring out of her, the whole story. She told him about the man in Kansas City, the way he killed the woman with a touch, absorbing her light until she was cold ashes, crumpled empty on the sidewalk. About how he'd wanted Rhiannon to see it, watched her with a horrible dark pleasure that felt like pain and ecstasy all at once.

Rhiannon told Greg all of it. And then she told him how it had all happened before, in another life, another place, to another woman. Her. It had all happened to her. Again.

Eternal Tales: The Three Sisters

Once upon a time, there were three Sisters who lived together in the wild wood.

The Sisters were magic, and they carried the pieces of the world between them.

Together, the Sisters could right any wrong, weave all things to their desire.

The first Sister was wise. She held the Story in her head, and could read it everywhere. She could speak to fire and feel it in the hearts of others, lighting the darkness of the waning moon. She could dance with rivers and oceans, and talk to the creatures of the sea.

The second Sister was kind. She sang beneath the full moon. She could hear the stories whispered by the wind, sing truth, create with words. She could talk to the birds.

The third Sister was clever. She hunted beneath the waxing moon, and could spin magic from the earth and trees. She could talk to the beasts of the land.

The Sisters took turns carrying the Song of the Soul, for this most powerful magic was both a gift and a heavy burden.

A demon, jealous of the Sisters' power, sought to weaken their strength. Being immortal, the Sisters could not be killed, but he could divide their lives into the cycles of mortals and beasts.

With each new cycle, the Sisters would have to come together again, to reclaim their power – only to lose it, and each other, with the ending of every Season.

For all time, the Sisters must find each other again and again, so the pieces can form the whole.

It is said that whenever the Sisters reunite, the earth sighs peace.

And they lived ever after.

TWO

For most of us, our innocence doesn't disappear all at once. Instead, it suffers a thousand tiny lacerations, quietly bleeding to death.

This was almost true of Megan Byrne, later known as Rhiannon Elektra, of the Sisters *nahyin* of the Family. Stories have been told for thousands of years about such people – stories so old they evolve into legends, fables, myths, and fairy tales; lore passed down from one generation to the next, embellished with each retelling. Only great joy, passion, and insatiable curiosity could keep such beings from becoming utterly hardened. Most first lost their innocence at the beginning of time, so long ago that even Those Who Do Not Forget could barely remember.

But it is also true that these people are always given innocence again, for a short time. Forsaking innocence once is painful enough. Doing it a hundred times, a thousand, is much harder.

For young Megan Byrne, most of her innocence was ripped away at the age of 10. But she'd always been a strange child, laughing and playful one moment, frighteningly adult the next.

She grew up in the early 21st century in Columbus Park, a working-class neighborhood in Kansas City, in the United States. She lived with her mother in a small, run-down house on Forest Avenue.

The house was built in 1890, and had gone through several low-budget remodels in more than 100 years. The kitchen floor was a dense linoleum from the '50s, sprinkled with gold starbursts, barely visible beneath decades of ground-in grime and discoloration that no amount of determined scrubbing could remove. The dining room was paneled in cheap faux-wood sometime during the '70s, and it always felt dark and small inside. The living room was disgraced by mottled green shag, marred by years of dubious stains.

Megan's was one of only two rooms relatively untouched by time. The original hardwood floor was dark and smooth, perfect for imagined figure skating championships in bobby socks. Rosa Byrne, Megan's mother, had found a large round rug at a thrift store, stiff scarlet synthetic fibers adorned with tan flowers and vines. For a little girl, such a rug is an island, or a ship in a stormy sea, a castle, a cloud floating high over distant hardwood fields, a magic circle no demon could cross.

The old window frame and walls had been painted over so many times that the paint was thick and dull-edged, yellowing. On the inside of the window frame, a bit of paint had chipped off, revealing aqua-green paint beneath. For years, Megan absently picked at the paint while she stood at the window, revealing layers and layers of paint beneath, green, white, yellow, blue. She imagined going back in time, touching the walls of her room, wondering who had lived there then, what their lives were like.

Her father, Robert Byrne, had died in an industrial accident when she was two, and while she could barely remember him, Megan had taken to imagining him as a perfect parent who loved her no matter what, who listened to her every thought, who played with her when she was lonely and sad. She talked to him late at night, when she was supposed to be sleeping, sitting in her pink twin-size bed under the window.

She loved her mother, but sensed instinctively that Rosa kept her at a distance. As though she was afraid of her, just a little. And it was true. Rosa Byrne had a superstitious fear of her own daughter. There was something not right about the child. And while she would never say it aloud, Rosa imagined her daughter had been hexed. It was *brujeria*, witchcraft.

At 3 years old, Megan wanted to know why she "glowed big," and Rosa didn't.

At 5, splashing in the fountain at Crown Center on a humid July afternoon, Megan suddenly cried out, pointing to a man across the street. "He 'glows big,' too, Mama!" Rosa flushed with embarrassment. The man stared right at them; Rosa was relieved to see an indulgent smile light his features. He nodded gravely, not to Rosa, but to the child, and walked away.

One afternoon, when Megan was 6, Rosa began to be truly frightened. She had to go to the hotel where she worked as a housekeeper, to pick up her paycheck. School was out for Thanksgiving break, and without child care, she was forced to take Megan with her. Bundled up in their secondhand winter coats and boots, they waded through the snow to the bus stop, and made their way downtown to the Hotel Royale.

Clutching Rosa's hand, Megan was wide-eyed as they entered the hotel's service entrance from the alley. Everything was huge and new and interesting to Megan, and by the time they got to the manager's office, she had begun talking. And talking. Exploding with the questions, thoughts, and observations of an intelligent, imaginative child. "Did you see the big dryers, Mama? What if we had a dryer like that? We could dry all the clothes at once. Those ladies are wearing nets on their heads. Why are they wearing those? How big is this building? How much does it weigh? Do you come here every day? Can I come with you to work?" And on. And on.

As they were ushered into the manager's office, Rosa shushed her daughter. "Now be quiet, Meg. We're going to see my boss, and I need you to be a good girl." Megan was practically bouncing in her chair, trying to contain her excitement. Rosa narrowed her eyes. "Now calm down. Close your eyes and breathe. Think about your breathing, and nothing else." To her surprise, the suggestion worked. Megan calmed immediately, carefully breathing in and out.

Rosa's boss, Mr. Radcliffe, came into the room and sat down. He smiled benignly. Rosa introduced Megan, who opened her eyes and smiled, every ounce of her little being focused intently. And then the smile faded from her face. "He's mean," she announced. She looked at her mother. "He's not going to let you work here anymore." Rosa was utterly shocked. Before she could say a word, Megan added, "He's angry." Looking into her mother's face, the child slid lower in her chair. "You're angry too," she whispered.

Rosa turned to look at Mr. Radcliffe, momentarily bewildered, reflecting her own discomfiture. But he recovered quickly, his brow sinking, his mouth a steely grim line. He informed Rosa Byrne and her creepy little child that the housekeeper was indeed out of a job, accusing her – falsely – of stealing from a hotel guest.

When they were back at home, Megan ran upstairs to her room, crying. Rosa Byrne sat down at the kitchen table, staring numbly at the scarred wood table top. Finally, she got up and fetched a bottle from the cupboard, and poured herself a glass of dark amber liquor. She drank for the rest of the day, sitting in the kitchen, even after the crying stopped and the house was silent.

Megan Byrne had the dreams as long as she could remember.

Even as a little girl, all skinned knees and pigtails, bologna sandwiches and huge brown eyes, she'd dreamed of other lives, other places, other times. In her dreams, she was an adult woman with different faces, adult thoughts. Adult passions.

Her dreams didn't feel like dreams. They weren't strange concoctions of images and actions, following a dream logic which only made sense to the dreamer. Nor did they fade when she awoke. Instead, they felt absolutely real, more of a memory than a dream. And the memories of each dream stayed with her, never to be forgotten.

In her strange dream life, she was called by many names, but one always stood out from the others: *Rhiannon Elektra*. Her name. It echoed solid inside her, the name that felt like home. Like belonging. Rhiannon fit, resonated in her heart. The name that somehow had always been hers, had always been her. If souls could have names, hers would be Rhiannon.

In some cultures, the name is a thing of great power, closely guarded. Some believe that knowing a true name gives one power over another. Only those most trusted, beloved, are allowed to know a person's secret, innermost name, the name that connects to the deepest self, to the soul.

As a small child, she had never heard of such things. But instinct whispered truth. She never told her mother about her name. Never told anyone. It was secret, a precious thing that was hers and hers alone. She cherished her name, let it warm her, sustain her, when nothing else would. At night in her room, in the dark, she'd silently rock back and forth in her bed, reminding herself inside of who she really was. Rhiannon. No one could touch that single shining truth, more real than anything else, ineffably lovely and *hers*.

She dreamed of a palace, a ball. She'd never seen anything like it, not even on television, but somehow she knew exactly what it was, precisely where she was. The names, forms, function of things popped into her mind, an immediate understanding and appreciation of a reality she'd never known, a life she'd never lived – but a life that nonetheless felt intimately her own.

A vast room crowded with people: men in severe white or black, relieved only by sedately striped and colored cravats; women dotting the room like multi-hued flowers, scarlet, raspberry, shimmering blue satin, icy green and pink silk. The noise was constant: the hum of 200 conversations; a woman's peal of laughter; the clink of glasses and silver. And in the corner, an orchestra played sweetly: violins, flutes, and piano merging into a soaring, delicate music that begged dancing.

The ballroom itself was white, crystal, and ornate gold, with gilt baby angels playing trumpets above the high-arched windows. Cherubs. She marveled that some part of herself knew the proper name for baby angels. Even the ceiling was painted with rosy-cheeked cherubs, flowers, and columns that made it seem the room went on forever into a blue sky.

Lamps everywhere bore a thousand candles, filling the enormous room with twinkling lights, heightened and reflected in the gold-framed mirrors all around. Footmen in white uniforms with gold braid stood by the lamps, ready to trim smoking wicks. Other liveried servants moved through the crowd, bearing shining trays of glasses, sweetmeats, sliced apples and grapes.

Single men stood in groups, smoking cheroots, sipping brandy, older men pontificating, younger men eyeing the heaving crowd of dancers and ladies. Young women stood with their mothers and sisters, fidgeting with fans and gloves, trying to appear grown-up, eyes glittering with excitement.

And she was there, in the midst of it. She was laughing, drinking sparkling gold from a slender glass, smiling at a handsome man with dark hair and eyes the color of new leaves. A man who glowed, the air around his body gold and shining.

"Rhiannon," he whispered her name – her name! – his voice a deliciously deep, husky breath in her ear. "Dance with me." He pulled back to look into her eyes, favoring her with a dazzling smile.

She came into his arms, and they danced. They danced a kind of flowing celebration, his hand warm on her waist, her fingers curved over his shoulder. Looking into those impossibly green eyes and smiling, smiling, as though the bubbles in the champagne had contrived to fill her inside, incandescent, effervescent. Floating.

She looked again at her hand, resting on his white jacket. She glowed as he did, her skin suffused with a gentle radiance.

They danced over the intricate parquet floor, exquisite light and dark woods combining to create the illusion of three-dimensional blocks, flowers, diamonds. Her silk gown flowed fluid and weightless around her when she moved, skimming noiseless over the floor.

He smiled at her again, that wicked smile. "Ti takaya vaskhititel'naya." *You are so delightful.* She realized they'd been speaking another language all along.

"Zhulik," she responded, laughing. *Rogue.*

Megan's world was home, the vacant lot next to the neighbor's house, the community center, and Della Lamb Elementary School.

Adults look back at their school days through the warm lens of time, remembering playing in the grass and on swings, building snowmen, special teachers, drums, bells, and plastic recorders, wearing huge smocks, painting stars. Most forget that school can be a brutal social experiment.

Her dark hair, olive skin, and brown eyes earned her taunts of "beaner" and "spic" at school. The inaccuracy of the hateful language didn't matter. Rosa Byrne was from Columbia, and these insults filled Megan with rage. She'd clench her fists, tears burning her eyes, glaring fury but never saying a word. She wouldn't give them that.

Later, the teasing and taunts would grow even uglier, cruel. Children stepping back to avoid touching her, calling her "strange," "freak," "weird." The way they said it, "weird" meant something disgusting, ugly, frightening. "Weird" was a kind of wrongness that could never be fixed, a condition permanent and horribly innate, something she couldn't help and could never hope to change. A simple word became an epithet with the power to make Megan cringe. She ached inside. Cried. She just wanted to belong, to feel loved, to be wanted and special. Like everyone else.

She didn't want to be different. She tried to look like everyone else, act like the other children, but it never quite worked. She knew things, understood things. Had dreams and thoughts and memories which made perfect sense to her, but seemed disturbing somehow to others – not just children, but teachers, other adults. Her mother.

Megan retreated into herself, spent much of her time playing alone in her room. There, she watched the sun set over the ocean, danced in a Russian ballroom, and watched men build the Eiffel Tower.

Adults look backward over decades, remembering childhood, taking events and experiences and framing them in an adult context.

Imagination is an adult notion. In a child's world, flights of fancy, beliefs, dreams, ideas, creativity, make-believe – these things are genuinely magic.

Some children, like Megan Byrne, face hardships, adversity, traumas. It's easy for adults to see the horror of these experiences, to imagine that a difficult childhood is constantly fraught with pain and suffering. But they forget that in the spaces between the misfortunes and little tragedies, the secret agonies of youth, there is joy, delight, laughter, curiosity. Love.

Ever gregarious, Megan found friends who didn't care that she was strange, spent afternoons building fairy houses or snowmen in the vacant lot, climbing trees, reading books, roller skating and riding her bicycle. She had birthday parties and blew out candles. She went on field trips at school, made clumsy clay pots for Rosa, cut out paper snowflakes and taped them to the refrigerator. Furtively kissed boys – and once, a neighbor girl – in the old, tin garden shed behind the house.

She felt better when she could see or touch the world. Just being in nature, even in a backyard or vacant lot, felt soothing and electric all at once. Outdoors, Megan felt a swell of possibility, something just out of her reach, something huge and magnificent, waiting for her to take it.

She spent hours lying in the grass on her back, staring into an endless blue summer sky, ephemeral clouds sliding through the heavens, until she felt as if the earth were moving and the clouds were holding still. She loved the cool summer grass against her bare feet, and touching the rough bark of the oaks and cottonwoods. In the fall, she collected gold and scarlet leaves, pressing them to her cheek as if to take in their leathery dry texture. In the silence of winter, when the earth slept, Megan watched the sunset through an intricate black lacy network of bare tree branches, so beautiful she ached with it. She delighted in the first vibrant green crocus spearing through the cold earth, knowing tulips and cherry blossoms would follow.

She was insatiably curious about the world, always asking questions, wanting to know more, to understand, to make sense of

30

everything. Even if she had trouble with her fellow students, Megan's teachers at school loved her, though she could be exasperating, outrageous, too loud. A perfectly normal child most of the time, but also strangely adult at odd, unpredictable moments.

Adults define a child's world from a grown-up point of view, no longer able to see the magic, unable to put suffering in perspective. But in Megan's case, some magic was real. And some suffering was horrific.

When Megan was 10, Rosa Byrne married Oswald Geise. They'd met at the factory where Rosa was working at the time, and for weeks Geise had been coming to dinner at the house, complementing Rosa's cooking, making suggestions about shoring up the porch, and befriending Megan. He was a tall man, thickly built, with greasy brown hair and yellowing teeth. He always wore baseball caps, and told Megan he had a collection of 104 such caps, which hung on the wall in his house. He invited her to come see them, but Rosa said that she'd see them soon enough, blushing and giggling as though she were Megan's age.

Before Geise came over to the house, Rosa warned Megan to behave. By then, Megan knew exactly what "behave" meant. No looking hard at anyone's face, especially Mr. Geise. No feeling anyone. No finding that still place in herself, then opening herself outward. No being weird. The warning was the same, every time. Behave.

So Megan behaved. And Geise was so kind and friendly to her, it was easy. He always brought her Snickers bars, and once a Barbie doll, the one in the wedding dress – which made Rosa smile.

They were married at the County Clerk's office in November, and the following day Oswald Geise and two of his friends from the factory moved all of his things into Rosa and Megan's house in Columbus Park. There was a big bed for him and Rosa, an old stereo, two ragged cardboard boxes of clothes, and, of course, the 104 baseball caps.

He wasn't her father. Megan still talked to her father, her imagination building a parent who loved her alone, who didn't think she was weird, who actually encouraged her to look hard at people's faces.

31

Yet Geise seemed nice enough, and Rosa was happy – which meant she was happier with Megan, and the whole world. It was almost like a regular family.

But it wasn't. Not at all.

She dreamed she was in a dense forest, tall pines arching overhead, rough-barked trunks spreading out in all directions. She was wearing nothing more than a tattered, filthy homespun tunic, her feet bare. She and a young man – Jozef – were crouched by the side of a small river, water cascading over stones, the air clean and sharp. Both were panting for breath, as if they'd been running. Like her, he glowed, two thin rings of light like a halo around his body. His eyes were wide and darted back and forth, his breathing labored. He was terrified.

And so was she. She was shaking inside, fear and panic welling up, tightening her chest, closing her throat. Suffocating. And yet she pretended calm. They would survive. They would be all right. They had to. "Drink some water," she hissed, looking around. "We may not get another chance."

He shook his head. "We're not going to make it. They'll find us. I know it. They'll find us." He was babbling, shaking, looking everywhere at once. Like her, he wore a rough, torn tunic, plus a pair of homespun pants held up with a bit of crude rope.

Rhiannon took a deep breath. "Family is waiting for us in Regensburg. We just have to cross the mountains."

"And how are we going to do that?" he cried. "The forest goes on forever! We'll be eaten by beasts, or fall into a bog, or they'll catch us and drag us back to the caravan. We haven't a chance!" He was shouting now, shaking, and she was holding up her hands, trying to shush him, looking back into the trees.

"Pokoj!" she hissed. *Quiet!*

But it was too late. A shout came from the forest behind them.

Panic flared, exploding in her chest. "Run!" she cried, jumping to her feet. "Beh teraz!" *Run now!*

Jozef sprinted into the trees, Rhiannon close behind. There was a hiss of sound, and an arrow shaft seemed to sprout from Jozef's thigh. He fell, rolling to the ground, clutching his leg and screaming. Crimson blood soaked into the soft moss beneath him.

Tears burning her eyes, Rhiannon kept running. She could hear crashing in the underbrush behind her, grunting, yelling. Twigs pulled at her tunic, tore as she ripped free, ran on.

But then she, too, was falling, a heavy weight on her back, her face sliding into the moss and soil, her chin burning. She almost cried out then. Despair, grief, and loss blossomed dark in her heart. But she wouldn't cry. She wouldn't scream or beg. She wouldn't give them that.

The weight shifted, and she was rolled onto her back. A man's body covered her, huge and rough. He leered down at her, his broad, dark features coarse, his beard thick, matted. "Thought you'd run from us, slave whore?" He sneered. He pulled back one massive arm, then drove his fist into her cheek. She felt her cheekbone shatter in an explosion of pain, her vision swimming red. Somewhere, she could still hear Jozef screaming. Her captor laughed, hitting her again, and again, and again.

Megan lay in her little pink bed beneath the window, the blankets pulled up to her chin, curled in a ball. She was wide awake. Listening. Listening so hard it felt like her whole body was aware, listening so hard she ached with it.

There was a creak from the hardwood floor in the hall.

She squeezed her eyes shut, tried not to breathe, but her breath sounded so loud in her own ears, inside her head and chest, surely everyone could hear. *I'm not here. I'm a tiny ball of nothing. No one can see me. No one can hear me. I'm not here*

It had snowed the night before. The silence was complete, undiminished both outside the house and within. Only the sound of her breathing seemed to fill the space, and the pounding in her chest. She lay frozen, willing herself soundless, invisible.

Her door opened almost noiselessly, the hinge offering only the softest telltale moan.

The floor creaked beneath his feet as he crossed to her bed, the springs sighing as he sat down next to her, huddled motionless beneath the blankets. "Are you awake, angel?" He whispered. His voice was roughened, husky, raw, and she felt his hands shaking as he touched her shoulder through the fabric of the blanket.

She held still, so still. *I'm not here, I'm asleep, I'm a ghost, I'm dead, I'm not here*

He would just touch her, run his hands down her body the way he had before, stopping to fondle and stroke her bottom, her chest, the place between her legs, but never doing more than that. Just touching. Just touching that made her cry, ache with fear. Hide.

She kept her eyes closed, pretending sleep, shaking inside, quivering with the force of her fear, horror, revulsion. She felt him pulling back her blankets, exposing her little 10-year-old body curled in a ball, swathed in a blue flannel nightgown.

"Wake up, pretty angel," he whispered, shaking her shoulder. She kept her eyes squeezed shut, knowing that once she opened them, she was lost.

"I said, wake up," he hissed. He shook her a little harder now. He caught the hem of her nightgown and roughly pulled it up, over her hips, smiling at the gleam of her naked flesh in the dim light of the window. "I'll make this nice for you, I promise, Megan." She heard him fumbling with his belt, felt him shift on the bed, pushing his jeans down, the belt thunking on the hardwood floor.

I'm not Megan, she thought. *My name is Rhiannon.* And she opened her eyes.

When he reached for her leg, she sat up and grabbed his wrist, sinking her teeth into his arm, hard and deep. As hard as she could. He cried out and jumped back off the bed, standing in the light of the window with his pants down, his legs pale and thick. "Fuck! You bit me!" He clutched his arm, and she could see he was bleeding. His blood was on her face, and when she licked her lip she could taste the metallic salty tang of it.

And then she was inside him.

At first she couldn't make sense of it. She was looking down at herself, her body small and fragile, her nightgown pushed up, her

34

private parts shadowed. The strange glow around her body had flared bright and strong. She could feel a terrible pain in her arm, looked down to see *his* arm, two bloody half-moons livid on his forearm. But then she could *feel* him, feel his thoughts, his feelings, his hunger. He was looking at her with such rage, but a kind of sick delight, his lust hard and bright, his desire to punish her with his hands, his mouth, his cock. She would hurt for this, she would beg him to stop, and he would keep fucking the little bitch until she begged for more, until she liked it. Such a pretty little thing. He would be her first, she'd never have another man as good as he was.

God, she was sickened by it. It was so horrifying, to be there inside of him, to see her the way he did, to feel what he felt. It was like falling into the screaming black heart of madness itself. It had to stop. She had to make it stop. She couldn't stand another second, feeling this, being him.

From somewhere within her came a tremendous strength. In that huge dark space within him, she could feel all the parts of him, dragging them to her, pulling them into where she was. And when she had gathered it all, sinuous and fluid, all that was him, she pushed. Pushed with all her might. Pushed everything that was him out, out of that body, away from her. She pushed it beyond the edges of all that was him, pushed him out until he was all gone, and there was nothing left. Until his body was utterly empty.

And then she was back in her own self, her small 10-year-old body, crying helplessly. Rosa came then, throwing on the light, yellow and harsh. She stopped just inside the doorway, her mouth open, eyes wide, uncomprehending.

Megan was shivering and crying, curled in a fetal ball in her little bed beneath the window, her flannel nightgown pushed up over her hips. Oswald Geise lay on the floor, pants around his ankles, jaw slack, his eyes dead and unseeing through the veil of his greasy hair. Rosa started screaming.

Dr. Pope settled into her rocking chair, her pad and a file folder on her lap. It was a cozy office, with bright yellow wallpaper, large blue overstuffed chairs, and a variety of toys and dolls in the corner. Two miniature versions of the blue chairs flanked a small table. Megan Byrne, age 10, sat in one of the small soft chairs. Dr. Pope studied her, offering a genuinely sympathetic smile. The child looked remarkably calm, given her recent experience. The doctor carefully placed Megan's social services file on the desk next to her rocking chair.

"How are you today, Megan?"

The child didn't look at Dr. Pope. She was looking at the dolls.

"You can play with the dolls if you want to," the doctor said.

Megan looked up at her briefly, then back to the dolls. "Can I look at you?" she asked, finally. "I mean, *look* at you?"

"Of course you can look at me," Dr. Pope said kindly.

And then the child took a deep breath, and looked full into the doctor's eyes. She seemed to be searching for something. Finally she exhaled, relaxed in her chair for the first time. "You're nice."

"Thank you," Dr. Pope laughed. "You're nice too."

"Are you going to have them put me in jail?" Megan queried, utterly calm.

"No one is going to put you in jail." Dr. Pope made a note on her pad. "Why do you think anyone would put you in jail?"

"Because I killed my stepfather."

Later, the doctor would remember the way Megan Byrne had said those words. She'd said she had killed her stepfather as though it was an undeniable fact, like gravity, or roses, or hunger.

And while the doctor had reassured Megan that Oswald Geise had in fact suffered a heart attack, and further that it was normal for her to want him dead, under the horrific circumstances, she felt as though nothing she'd said to the child really got through.

From that point in her life onward, Rhiannon no longer thought of herself as Megan Byrne. "Megan" became a name others called her, the name she was born with. But inside she was Rhiannon, the name that was hers, had always been hers.

36

She dreamed and went to school, played outside in the wonderful world, went to psychologists and doctors, and dreamed some more. Rhiannon grew wild, intractable, outrageous and friendly, wicked and kind. At school, she helped smaller children when they fell down and skinned their elbows; she terrified bullies, speaking aloud their innermost thoughts and fears.

At home she fought with her mother, riddled with mistrust, tired of Rosa's fears and halting affection, her guilt. Tired of trying to make Rosa love her. Rhiannon had her own guilt and anger, stuffed down deep and locked away in the darkest jagged crevice of her soul. Full of rage one moment, brilliant and generous the next, she was delightful, impossible.

Rhiannon wanted to become the woman in her dreams, strong and confident, capable, brazen. Courageous. Loved.

But on some level she knew she was a *monstruo*, as Rosa snarled once in the midst of an argument. Monster, freak. Rhiannon wondered what happened to freaks when they grew up. Surprisingly, she wouldn't have long to wait.

CHREE

She dreamed of belonging, of love. There was a marvelous picnic beside a lake. Beneath the shadow of a spreading tree, several quilts were laid out on the manicured grass, soft and inviting, with silver and purple embroidered pillows and bolsters designed for lounging in comfort.

Rhiannon lay on her back, her head pillowed in another woman's lap. Maddie. She looked up into Maddie's face and smiled, receiving a brilliant grin in return. Maddie's thick auburn hair was piled neatly on top of her head, and in the sunlight it looked like glowing copper, with a streak of pure silver. Around her body were endless rings of light, a glow as vibrant as Rhiannon's own.

Rhiannon closed her eyes, breathing deeply. The country air was invigorating. It smelled of water and sunwarmed grasses, rich soil, roses from the estate's garden. Mmm, and a hint of Maddie's lavender and jasmine toilet-water.

With her eyes closed, the world somehow seemed filled with a cacophony of sound – the stream trickling into the lake, the sound of crickets, frogs, the hum of insects from the lawn and gardens.

Somewhere, the men were off riding, and the ladies had the delicious afternoon all to themselves.

"Hallooo!"

Rhiannon opened her eyes and sat up, turning in the direction of the house. Emma was crossing the lawn wearing a mint-green gown, her blonde hair shining in the sunlight. She was accompanied by Mrs. Hurst, the housekeeper, and a girl about 5 years old, dressed prettily in petticoats and a summer white dress. In her arms, Emma carried a baby. Mrs. Hurst was toting a huge wicker picnic hamper.

When they were around 20 yards away, the air around Rhiannon and Maddie seemed to shimmer, to stretch and expand. A tingling kind of energy filled Rhiannon, as though her entire body crackled with electricity. The energy felt utterly physical, seeming to flow outward. She could feel everything acutely, Maddie's body beside her, Emma's further away, the trees, the earth, the water, the sky – it was as though everything was connected, all things translated into power, flowing through her, through Maddie, through Emma.

Rhiannon looked at Maddie, and then Emma. They were looking at her, too, and each other. Smiling, secret joyful smiles.

The little party arrived at the tree. Everyone seemed to have the golden glow. Emma had dense rings of light around her, much like Rhiannon and Maddie. Even the little girl and the baby glowed.

Mrs. Hurst, who had two thin shining bands around her body, smiled broadly. "We've a lovely picnic with all the fixings," she said in her thick Welsh accent, looking pleased. "I have cold turkey, sweetbreads, pâté, tomatoes, cold baked asparagus, fingerling potatoes, fresh bread and orange marmalade from our orangery. For dessert, miniature apple dumplings, and chocolate truffles from France." She beamed. "Oh, and cherries, too."

"Oooh, cherries," Maddie sighed. She glanced sideways at Rhiannon, offering a wicked smile. "Have I shown you what I can do with a cherry stem?"

"Dangerous things, I imagine," Emma said demurely, seating herself and settling the baby against her shoulder. "That tongue of yours should be licensed by Scotland Yard."

Mrs. Hurst blushed. "Well, if there's nothing else, Cook and I are putting up the washing."

"Thank you for the wonderful luncheon, Mrs. Hurst," Maddie said. "We'll bring the hamper to the house later."

Mrs. Hurst bobbed a curtsey and set off across the lawn.

"You mustn't say such wicked things in front of Mrs. Hurst," Rhiannon reproved Emma. "She's new, you know."

Maddie started digging in the hamper. "Oh, she has to learn sometime." Her eyes widened. "Here, what's this?" She pulled a crystal decanter of brownish liquid from the hamper. "Oooh, an anti-fogmatic. Now who would put brandy in our hamper? Not Mrs. Hurst, I'll warrant."

Emma laughed. "We'd be lucky to get sherry from her." She looked over at the young girl. "Tessa, would you like to go wading in the water?" The child nodded and ran off to the water's edge, plopping down in the grass, enthusiastically pulling off her shoes and stockings.

Still holding the decanter, Maddie looked at Rhiannon. "Tell me who put this in the hamper."

Rhiannon sat up, settling her skirts over her ankles. "Oh, all right." She closed her eyes, breathing deeply, in through the nose, out through the mouth. Only one or two seconds passed, but to her, time stretched, slowed. A sense of total calm infused her, until she could feel and think of nothing but her breath. Her vision turned inward. It was as though the entire universe was within her body, an endless warm darkness sparked with shimmering scarlet, gold, blue. A thousand colors, and no color, vibrant with life. With Maddie and Emma, everything felt a hundred times stronger, more powerful, beautiful.

She began calling forth energy, inviting it to flow into her limbs, shimmering streaks of silver, gold, white that gathered in sinuous flows, fusing into cloud-like formations of glowing power. Rhiannon spun the energy now, pulling it through her legs and arms, into her chest. There, the light expanded, throbbed, finally sliding down her left arm and into her hand.

Rhiannon opened her eyes and smiled at Maddie. She raised her hand, which radiated seething gold energy like a glowing star. Reaching out, she touched the decanter of brandy.

41

Mrs. Hurst in the other room, have to be quick, wicked, glee, delight, such good brandy, Maddie will be pleased, happy, love, Maddie, love, Emma, love, Rhiannon, love, slip it in the basket, hurry, don't see me, ladies need brandy once in a while, good for their constitutions, fun, laughter, riding with Z, we'll stop by the lake after such fun, naughty, love.

Rhiannon gasped at the intensity of the vision and emotion, releasing the decanter and the energy in one sharp wave of her hand. She took a deep breath, two. And laughed. "It was Grayling. He wanted to give us a treat," she informed her companions. "And he and Z are planning on coming here after their ride."

Maddie sniffed. "Well, much as I hate contributing to Grayling's wicked plots, I see no reason to waste the opportunity for a good drink with luncheon."

They devoured the food, sharing with Tessa, who arrived at the blankets soaking wet to the waist, grinning unrepentantly. Emma nursed Albert, a beautiful baby boy who glowed with seven rings of light around his tiny body. The ladies started in on the brandy, pouring the ruby brown liquid into crystal glasses. After a time, Emma sent Tessa to the house, carefully carrying Albert over her little shoulder.

When the three friends were alone, they had another drink, a rather sloppy toast to one another. Then another toast. And another.

Emma flopped back onto the pillows on the quilt, her head buzzing pleasantly, looking up through the tree branches. "I hate when I'm not pregnant. I have to wear these wretched clothes. This corset is damned uncomfortable."

Rhiannon laughed. "I'll allow my corset is profoundly uncomfortable as well."

"We should take them off," Maddie said earnestly. "I don't think they're healthful, despite what the doctors say."

"That's good enough for me," Emma stood, weaving slightly, and began unbuttoning her gown.

Rhiannon did the same. "I trust your judgment far more than any doctor," she informed Maddie gravely, reaching down to pull the older woman to her feet. Maddie busied herself with her own buttons.

In short order, the three women were clad in only their thin lawn chemises, laughing uproariously, dancing barefoot beneath the shade tree. They danced and giggled and kissed, kisses evolving into yearning, heat, touching and caressing one another, feeling the water, the air, the earth itself hum with their desire and joy.

Utterly distracted with the pleasures of soft flesh and their own magic, they were completely unaware of the horses riding up to their tree.

"What have we here, Z?" Grayling swung down from his horse, laughing. "Three likely ladies, in most improper circumstances."

"Improper? I beg your pardon." Emma sniffed, looking toward the lake.

"I see nothing improper about our circumstances, behavior, or persons," Rhiannon added, pretending offense, but unable to suppress a tipsy smile for Grayling.

"I beg to differ," Z said. "It would appear you ladies are cavorting in broad daylight in your underwear."

"And practically fondling your way out of it," Grayling added.

"It's of no circumstance," Emma declared.

"Nor does it signify," Maddie waved her fingers in a shoo-ing motion, taking another sip of brandy. "Be on your way, Grayling, Z."

"Now, Maddie," Grayling stepped close, brushed a kiss on her cheek, trailing down to press another to her neck. His arm slipped around her waist. "Surely there's room for two more at this picnic?"

As she approached puberty, Rhiannon's dreams grew in frequency and intensity. Her night visions became a wonderful escape. She traveled to other places, times, worlds peopled with friends she'd never met, intriguing, fascinating people who seemed to know her, care for her, in a way that no one did in her waking life.

Through her dreams, she learned to do wondrous things. The Dream Rhiannon could touch objects and discover the thoughts and feelings of the person who held them last; the waking Rhiannon mimicked her dream-self and found she had this miraculous ability as well. She kept this gift secret, knowing from painful experience how Rosa – or anyone – might react.

Much as she loved the escape, the Dream Rhiannon's wild and imaginative life, invariably there were nightmares, too. Nightmares about people who sought to hurt her; nightmares about those who actually did so. Being lost, cold, hungry, afraid. Living in filth, privation. Losing people she didn't know, but loved nonetheless. Seeing people crippled, maimed, killed. And over and over, a suicide in a chipped white bathtub, her blood turning the water murky and dark.

Some dreams were almost worse than nightmares, and Rhiannon was ill-equipped to cope with them. Most of the time, she was an adult woman in her dreams, with a mature body and mind that craved decidedly grown-up pleasures. The adult Dream Rhiannon had many lovers, men and women, and in two particularly disturbing nocturnal adventures, enthusiastically savored orgiastic sensual delights with several men and women at once.

After such erotic dreams, the 12-year-old Rhiannon would awake in her little bed beneath the window, mortified, flushed with shame, her entire body aroused, aching. While her body might have been physically virginal, Rhiannon could close her eyes and easily imagine a man's weight on her belly, sliding hard within her, or a soft breast in her hand, the puckered bud of a nipple on her tongue, hear the sighs and heady moans of lovemaking.

Despite nightmares or strangely exciting sexual pleasures, Rhiannon loved her dream life. Loved having a fantastic secret all her own. She began to believe there was a reason for these dreams, as though God wanted to send her a message, to show her she was special, that she could be different. And perhaps there *was* something to believe in, to hope for, to trust. Her dreams gave Rhiannon permission to accept herself, when it didn't feel like anyone else would. She desperately wanted to believe there was more to her life than just her little world, Columbus Park, going to school, Rosa.

Holding that magic, that hope, her own specialness in her heart, gave Rhiannon joy and strength, but caused her sorrow as well. She could see and feel something beautiful no one else could. She couldn't share her vision or understanding of the world with anyone.

They wouldn't understand. They'd think her mad.

Once, when Rhiannon was 4, she'd been playing at the kitchen table. She had a piece of tinfoil, a nice long sheet of it, which she'd carefully wadded up into a loose ball. She became enchanted with the beauty of the thing. Hundreds of silver facets large and small caught the kitchen light, and the mundane tinfoil was transformed. Glittering and shining, it was utterly lovely, magical. The foil was a chunk of raw silver, a heap of pirate treasure, a meteorite, a diamond, an angel's song made tangible.

"Look, Mama!" she'd called to Rosa, who was chopping vegetables at the counter. Rosa turned and looked, but didn't see. "That's very nice, Meg," she said, her tone placating and weary. She went back to her chore without another glance.

Rhiannon felt like she had when she was little, looking at that prosaic tinfoil ball, or the first time she saw an optical illusion on paper, when her eyes shifted, crossed, and a flat image suddenly appeared, breathtaking with depth and dimension. She could see and feel something extraordinary, and even though it was right there for everyone else to see, they simply couldn't. Or wouldn't.

It was frustrating and lonely. But her belief persisted. Rosa told her God didn't make mistakes. Her dreams were not an accident. She'd been chosen. She was special. And while others might not see it, she could, and she held an even deeper, secret wish that one day someone else would too.

At 13, Rhiannon started seventh grade at Northeast High School. She walked almost three miles from Columbus Park to school every morning. There were two sisters from the neighborhood, Cassie and Marie Ledbetter, who also walked to Northeast. Rosa had a talk with their mother, and after that Rhiannon walked with Cassie and Marie. While they weren't exactly friends, the girls weren't overtly mean to her, and Rhiannon accepted the arrangement without objection.

Rhiannon liked the walk. It was the best part of starting at the new school, in her opinion. She loved the trees along Independence

Avenue, and up Van Brunt to the school. There was always lots of traffic and people, and it was fun to imagine where folks were going, what they did when they went there.

"His name is Edward Buttons," Rhiannon said to Cassie, pointing at a man in a delivery truck. "He has a wife named Sharon, and 14 children, and they all live in a teeny one-bedroom apartment with three cats."

"Really?" Cassie asked, looking curiously at the truck as it drove off. "How do you know?"

Rhiannon shrugged, grinning. "I don't. I just made it up."

Cassie scowled, and Marie said, "Don't be weird, Megan."

Socially, Northeast High School was even worse than Della Lamb Elementary. Children between the ages of 13 and 15 have the capacity for a level of cruelty so breathtakingly savage, most adults choose to block the memory, or ignore it when they see it. One did not go to teachers for rescue from bullies; it only made the bullies meaner, more vicious – and the realization adults were powerless to help engendered a hideous, agonizing sense of solitude.

The high school was an enormous old, four-story brick structure, vast and intimidating. Still, Rhiannon liked the big columns in front of the building. They reminded her of a dream she'd had about the Parthenon.

Her dreams were coming all the time now, not just once or twice a month, but every night. She approached bedtime with trepidation, wondering whether she would have an exhilarating, tantalizing adventure, or awake shaking, terrified. Or worse, aroused.

It had started to feel out of control, somehow. As if her dreams were beginning to take over her life. Her body was doing strange things, too. Rosa had taken her to get her first bra, a situation which greatly embarrassed them both. She'd also bought Rhiannon a box of maxi-pads – pre-emptively – but refused to discuss what they were for, or how to use them. Rhiannon already knew, thanks to her adult Dream Rhiannon, plus a detailed discussion on menstruation with Cassie and Marie, who were older and found Rhiannon impossibly childish. Both girls complained mightily about their monthly flux, but left Rhiannon with the impression that having one's period was a rite of passage, required if one wished to be more grown-up.

Growing up would be far different for Rhiannon, and come a great deal sooner than she could imagine.

The first vision struck Rhiannon in her second period English class. She was sitting quietly, doodling in the margins of her essay, when suddenly she was overwhelmed. She was in a forest, thick pine trees all around, the ground soft and damp beneath her feet. Morning light filtered weakly through heavy grey clouds and overarching tree branches. She smelled a peat fire, heard rough voices arguing quietly in the still air.

And just like that, she was back in English class, clinging to her desk white-knuckled, panting, terrified. A horrible tingling, creepy sensation slid over her scalp. She looked around. Everyone was staring. Some of the older boys were nudging each other, grinning. At the front of the class, the teacher glowered. "Megan, maybe you need to go see the nurse."

Rhiannon nodded mutely. It was as if her whole body was terrified, while her head didn't know why. Her hands shook, palms sweating, a choking tightness rising in her chest. She slid out of her seat, ignoring the snickers and giggles as she left the room.

The nurse called Rosa at work, then sent Rhiannon home.

Rhiannon was truly afraid. She couldn't tell anyone what had really happened, that she'd had a tiny dream while she was awake, in the middle of the day. The word "daydream" suddenly, unimaginably, had a foreboding connotation.

Her dreams were taking over. It was a betrayal. This thing which made her special was somehow changing, evolving in ways she couldn't imagine. Lying in bed that night, she prayed God would help her. Prayed that it wouldn't happen again.

But it did.

Over the next week, Rhiannon was overcome with visions, most thankfully brief, but two extensive and detailed, like her regular nocturnal dreams. It happened four times at school, and eight times over the course of the following weekend. She was suddenly gripped with visions, dreams so profound and intense she was completely removed from reality, wherever she happened to be.

She found herself at a depression-era circus sideshow, staring at a scantily-clad, tattooed bearded woman, somehow feeling a sense of connection, a secret understanding with the laughing hirsute beauty. In another vision, she was running up a very steep hill through a massive city, her breath strong and regular, filled with a sense of strength, contentment. In another, she was wearing a blue wool uniform, firing a gun at a firing range. One of the longer daydreams featured a sleeping car on a train, where she helped to deliver a baby, calling encouragement to the panting mother. Yet another found her in formal dress at a party, with a wizened old man lying on a bed in the center of the room.

At night, her usual dreams were longer, the intensity heightened, vivid, ghastly, exquisite. Rhiannon woke exhausted, drenched in sweat, often shaking with the aftershocks of pleasure so luscious she wanted to die with the shame of it.

It was madness. It felt like her life was falling apart, and she was helpless to stop it. During these visions, her eyes would close, her body shaking. She seemed insensible to everything around her. Teachers continued sending her to the nurse, who finally suggested perhaps Rhiannon was epileptic. Rosa made appointments for tests. The children at school either teased or treated her like a pariah. She wanted to hide, to run away from everyone and everything, but she knew it wouldn't matter. Her dreams would follow wherever she went.

On Monday, after that last terrible weekend, Rhiannon begged to stay home from school, but Rosa wouldn't hear of it, pointing out that tests were scheduled with the doctor the following day, and since she didn't have a fever, she still had to go to school.

Rhiannon walked silently behind Cassie and Marie, feeling strange, out of sorts. Her body ached inside. *Everything is going to be fine today.* She repeated the phrase over and over inside her head, a mantra, a prayer, a plea.

And it seemed as if the universe listened.

The day passed as if sliding on glass, smooth, uneventful, inevitable. Even the bullies found other victims to torment.

Late in the day, during math class, she felt a sudden urgency and asked for a hall pass to use the restroom. Rhiannon ran to the bathroom and locked herself in the last stall, pulling down her jeans. Her white cotton panties were stained red with blood. She felt a purely female swell of satisfaction, at this sign of her elevation to the rarified echelon of mature women.

After buying one of the outdated thick cottony maxi-pads from the machine in the bathroom, Rhiannon returned to the stall, locking the door. She put the pad in her panties and was in the act of pulling up her jeans when the next vision hit her. She was sitting at a table in a strange kitchen, the ceiling festooned with drying herbs and flowers. Three women were also at the table, playing cards laid out on the flowered tablecloth. "It's your turn, Rhiannon," said one.

And then she was back in the cramped bathroom stall, panting heavily, her jeans around her knees. *Not again*, she thought.

Before she'd caught her breath, before she had time to think, another vision overwhelmed her senses. For a few seconds, she was on a New York ferry, laughing with a blond man and pointing to the Statue of Liberty.

Abruptly aware of the bathroom stall again, she leapt to her feet, yanking up her jeans. She reached for the stall door handle, and was suddenly gripped by another vision. And then another. And then another. And still another.

When she came to her senses again, she was kneeling on the dingy blue tiles of the girl's bathroom floor, shaking and weeping. Rhiannon pulled herself to her feet. Gripped by an unadulterated panic, she ran from the bathroom. Ran down the hall. An eighth-grader serving as Hall Monitor tried to step officiously in her path, but she shoved him aside and kept running, senseless to his offended shout.

She ran for home. Five times on the three-mile journey, her progress was halted by more visions, coming in waves now of two, three, four in a row. Finding herself lying on the sidewalk, Rhiannon pushed to her feet, and ran again. Her terror, her panic, was so complete she was almost numb to it, like a distance runner in the last leg of his journey. She was no longer thinking, just moving. Going home.

No one along Independence Avenue stopped to help her. When she fell to the sidewalk again, one or two people stared at the young girl, bathed in sweat, her face a mask of terror and madness. Most

49

looked away. Those who did look were relieved to see her rise again, to take off running, away from that place, that moment, away from fragile questions of conscience.

Over and over she fell, clinging to the sidewalk as though the world might slip away, shaking with the force of the visions. But then she would raise her head, look forward, toward Forest Avenue and home. Rise and run again.

Every instinct screamed she must get home, to safety. She must get to a safe place. A murmur had begun in her head, a soft repetitive sound she couldn't make out, as though coming from far away, buried deep. The soft repetitions were almost a hum, urging her on, driving her home.

It was the middle of the afternoon. Rosa was at work, and the house was empty. Rhiannon threw open the front door, consumed with a sense of relief, but also driven by an incomprehensible urgency. Slamming the door behind her, she pounded up the stairs to her room, shutting the door and running to her oak dresser, scarred and scratched by time and many owners. With a strength she didn't know she possessed, she pushed the dresser across the room to block the door, leaving ugly gouges in the hardwood. Tears streamed down her sweaty cheeks, leaving wet trails on her skin.

Rhiannon sank down in the center of the room, on her round scarlet rug, once an island, a castle, a fairy ring. Another wave of visions gripped her then, three in quick succession, and she came to awareness kneeling on the rug, her muscles aching with the constant shaking and stress of her marathon run.

The repetitive murmur in her head had grown to a chant now, the low sound gradually crystalizing into something like words, still too low for her to make out or understand, like straining to hear a distant conversation. The sound flowed through her mind without ceasing, halted only by more visions, longer, powerfully intense. She was dancing under a full moon. A woman screamed on a flaming pyre. A man caressed her naked body, leaving a trail of gooseflesh.

Then her cheek was pressed against the stiff scarlet rug, her hands trembling. The chant in her head was louder now. It pounded in her mind, over and over, unceasing, undeniable. She could hear it at last. She wept with relief and gratitude. Rhiannon didn't understand the words, but it didn't matter. Rational thought was gone; every thought, every action, was primal, reflexive.

Instinct sang within Rhiannon's mind, her blood, her soul.

She threw back her head, arms wide, a supplicant to the universe. *I'm ready.* The incessant chant in her head swelled, its power absolute, and she began to intone the words aloud, following the undeniable rhythm in her mind. *"Amin'via, amin'ma."* She repeated the words hoarsely, over and over. *"Amin'via, amin'ma."* It was a prayer, an exultation, a celebration. An invitation.

And as she chanted, the glowing haze around her body brightened. Ring upon ring of shimmering light expanded, flowing outward, until the little bedroom was filled with shining light, and Rhiannon was a dazzling golden star.

"Amin'via, amin'ma." Remember. The words grew with the light, filling her, growing within until she didn't know where the words ended and she began. Her body and soul stretched and strained, reaching, aching, calling. *"Amin'via,"* Remember life. *"Amin'ma."* Remember me. Remember *me*. Remember who I am.

Her golden glow filled the room, and her body shone incandescent, lit from within, lustrous. *Remember.*

Then, with tremendous force, the universe slammed into her mind. It poured into her little body through the top of her head, a flood, a deluge, a tidal wave of memories that threatened to consume her. It was as though her body was an open vessel, a fragile container for the sheer force of a lifetime, the universe itself, screaming into her in a cascading torrent.

Winter sunset over the Golden Gate Bridge ... cat pee in the kitchen again, hate that smell ... hookah bar in the Haight, sitting with Cheryl, smoking peach tobacco ... making love with Mike ... my first bicycle, playing cards clipped to the spokes ... after-hours club, my red shoes, smell of alcohol and sweat ... rain ... no, I have to go, please understand ... riding on the Greyhound, cheek cool against the window ... doll from my 10th birthday, with the little pink shoes ... feeling lost, my first day of school ... my lumpy mattress in Brooklyn ... I can run, I can run faster than anyone, I am strong ... identifying trees in college Biology ... Grandma ... the Feeling ... I am Katania Ann Weiss ... he's after me ... he killed that woman ...

It went on and on. Rhiannon's body jerked with the onslaught. Every synapse in her brain danced, her mind pure, glowing energy as a lifetime's worth of experiences, dreams, feelings, smells, sounds, loves, and agonies were forced into her in a colossal rush. The light from her body was blinding. Arms outstretched, she spasmed and twitched, as though electrocuted from within.

And then it was over. Rhiannon sagged to the floor, still blazing with light, her eyes glowing like twin suns. She lay on the scarlet rug for hours, the shining strata around her body gradually dimming, returning to its customary ephemeral shine. She felt utterly exhausted, drained to the point of insensibility, unable to move.

It was a long while before she could even think, begin to examine what happened to her. Rhiannon had lived another life. It would be some time before she'd be able to fully integrate those experiences with her own.

Her mind was full of another time, living as Kat Weiss, a young woman in San Francisco. A woman who watched a dark-haired man kill a lovely blonde on California Street with only a touch, her skin pasty ashes, her eyes staring blindly to the heavens. And Kat Weiss had run home to her little apartment, slitting her wrists in the bathtub. *"You can't hurt me now,"* she'd whispered, as the water turned opaque with blood. *"You can't hurt me now."*

Rhiannon felt strangely incomplete. Almost none of Kat's life corresponded to Rhiannon's dreams. In those dreams, she *was* that Dream Rhiannon, felt what she felt, lived her experiences. Remembered them afterward. But, in some ways, she was an observer, a thief who lived inside the Dream Rhiannon, stealing little pieces of her life. The lives existing beyond those dreams were not hers. Whatever happened before or after those dream events, Rhiannon couldn't say.

But Kat's life was hers. A past life. A whole existence that was now part of who Rhiannon was. And yet, somehow, she felt that she was the Dream Rhiannon, too. She shared her name, a name she knew instinctively to be her own.

Rhiannon didn't know what exactly had happened to her, but she was utterly and completely different. An adult woman, living in a 13-year-old's body.

She had experienced the process aeternans call *Memora Magia*, the Remembering. The essence which defines Those Who Do Not Forget.

She had grown up.

Eternal Tales: The Sword of the Gods

Once upon a time, the people lived from one Season to the next in harmony. Many of the people had been given gifts from the Gods. With these miraculous gifts, they could make crops grow, rain fall, talk to the beasts, the sky, and the land. The wealth of the world overflowed, the fertile earth teeming with all manner of life. Prosperity filled the world.

But one day, a child was born with a demon inside him, instead of a soul. He killed his mother and family, and with each death he grew stronger, euphoric with corrupt pleasure. He grew to manhood in only three days, and began traveling the world. He brought death with him wherever he went. The people, the beasts, and even the land died, and the sky burned.

Those few who escaped death cried out to the Gods, asking the Universe for help. The Gods spoke, saying that for the good people, there would always be a sword to conquer evil.

"Where is this magic sword you have promised us?" the people asked.

The Gods directed the people to the land at the edge of the sea, thence to a small house on the cliff. There, they found a fair young man called Spava. "Do you have the sword the Gods have promised?" The people asked. Spava, a quiet fisherman, knew nothing of any sword.

The people were angry, and thought the Gods had tricked them. "The demon ravages our land. You promised us a sword."

"Send Spava," the Gods replied.

Strong and valorous, Spava agreed to try to fight the demon. The people armed him with spears, deep-forged knives, and luminous armor to defend against the demon's malignant power.

First, Spava went to the home of his beloved, Varenya, to receive her blessing before battle. But there he found the demon, who had already stolen Varenya's life. She lay dead at his feet.

Crying out in grief and fury, Spava charged the demon, but his spears and knives glanced off the evil one's flesh.

The demon reached out to embrace Spava, to end his life. But Spava did not die. Surprised and desperate, Spava looked within and found magic inside himself, glowing and strong. He thrust out a hand, shining with power, and stole the demon's magic for himself. He used the power to kill the demon, and then released the magic, harmless, back into the Universe.

The Gods rewarded Spava by giving the beloved Varenya life again, that they would always be joined from one Season to another.

And they lived ever after.

FOUR

Growing up is hard. Dying is harder.

One moment she was a child, precocious, odd, all charming and pigtails, crayon masterpieces and make-believe – and then suddenly she was an adult, a full-grown woman condensed into a puberty-wretched body, riddled with hormones and angst.

But the dying, that was the hardest part. The fundamental trauma. Physical wounds may leave scars, but mental wounds fester, suppurating lacerations that rarely recover, at best leaving irrevocable stains. Remembering the pain is ferocious, excruciating – physical pain, yes, but emotional anguish too, grief, regret, sorrow. Shame. The way it feels when your soul is ripped from your body.

As with any loss, time and distance can't dim the agony. Time only allows the torment to be set aside a little longer each time, tucked into a shadow box in the back of the mind. But unexpectedly, it's there, all over again, immediate. The scent of soap, honeysuckle. A blue door. Eyes just his color, laughing, easy. Little things that don't matter at all, suddenly ripping the scab from the wound, blooding the gash anew.

Rhiannon stood in the bathroom at the Topeka U-Rest Motel, staring at the chipped bathtub. She closed her eyes, feeling the sharp sting of water on torn flesh, swamped with appalling, pervasive despair.

"Hey, you gonna be in there all day?"

She opened her eyes at the sound of Greg's voice from the other room. Taking a shaky breath, she opened the bathroom door. "Sorry," she said, pretending a calm she didn't feel, offering a falsely cheerful smile.

Greg wasn't fooled. But his bladder wouldn't allow further discussion, and besides, he knew she wouldn't tell him what was going on, anyhow. Megan and her secrets. He ducked into the bathroom.

The U-Rest Motel was not one of the finer establishments Rhiannon had ever visited. The building had to be at least 50 years old, and it smelled of humidity, fried liver and onions, cheap perfume, cigarettes, industrial pine cleaner, and the lingering odors of thousands of occupants over the decades.

The small room was carpeted with ancient brown shag, the beds draped with garish nylon bedspreads. A horrific still-life oil painting defiled the wall above the bed. A similar work in an immoderately ornate gold frame hung across the room, over the television. Each was a testament to the artist's complete lack of appreciation for color, composition, perspective, decency, and almost all natural laws. They were so breathtakingly awful that Rhiannon decided she quite liked them.

Next to the door was a decent-sized window overlooking the parking lot. The curtains were polyeurathane-coated olive and brown plaid, a thick yellowing blackout liner on the other side.

The overall effect was atrocious, even to the woman raised in a dilapidated house on Forest Avenue, filled with second-hand treasures. Still, the room was clean, and the price fit her meager budget. Rhiannon reminded herself she'd had sex in worse places. She laughed out loud at the thought. It felt nice to laugh, if somewhat surreal, given her current circumstances.

"What's so funny?" Greg emerged from the bathroom, wiping his hands with a hand towel.

Rhiannon smiled. "I was just admiring the decor."

Greg snorted. "You've had sex in worse."

Rhiannon laughed again. Greg couldn't help but smile. It was good to hear her laugh. "Yeah, I have," she said.

She went to the bed, pawing through the contents of the purple duffle bag he'd brought from the truck."Oh good, you brought my jeans."

Greg leaned against the bathroom door frame, absently holding the hand towel, watching her. She moved smoothly, sure of herself, her body lean and softly muscled. He watched her extract clothes from the bag, examine each item, fold it neatly. Leaning over the bag, a section of her long black hair fell in thick shining curls, obscuring part of her face, and she tossed it impatiently over her shoulder.

She looked up and caught him staring, smiled knowingly, and returned to her task.

Nine years he'd watched her. For all he tried to deny it to himself, he'd loved her the first moment he saw her, 15 years old and sneaking out of her house in the middle of the night.

He'd moved next door, waiting three patient days for a glimpse of her. On the fourth day, he'd wandered outside at 2 in the morning, unable to sleep. He lit a cigarette and stared at the stars, marveling over the summer air, his Russian bones feeling pleasantly warm.

A sound from the yard next door, barely a rustle, brought him instantly alert. He didn't move, just stood still and waited, watchful.

A dark-haired, slender young woman slipped from behind the neighboring house. Sneaking out of her mother's home in the middle of the night. She moved with stealth borne of long practice, a soundless shadow against the side of the house.

She turned, facing the yard, but before she could sprint away through the grass, he said aloud, "Nice escape."

He didn't know what had come over him. His job was to observe, not engage. He was breaking inviolable rules, and he'd only been watching her for three minutes.

At the sound of his voice, she froze, half-hidden by shadow. He could feel her senses extending into the darkness, assessing, considering a possible response. Finally, she replied confidently, "I'm good at escapes." Her voice tightened. "You're not going to hurt me, are you? I'll scream like bloody murder."

He walked into the light, let her see him. "I won't hurt you. Just out for a smoke. I'm your neighbor."

She hadn't moved. She gazed at him for long moments, considering, then walked toward him, looking once over her shoulder at the darkened house. "Okay, neighbor. Give me a cigarette, will you?" She smiled beguilingly, raising her brows. She extended one slender hand.

Her hand, her body, was beautiful in the moonlight, surrounded by layers of light, her *fainna*, the glowing aura faintly gold. He wished he could tell her how lovely it was. He wasn't supposed to be able to see auras, a pleasure not only forbidden, but dangerous. Yet he was captivated, lost in the wonder of it. It was like seeing the wake butterflies leave in the air, or an angel's afterimage, the shining echo of perfection.

She accepted a cigarette and lit it expertly, cocking back her head and exhaling smoke at the moon. "What's your name?"

"Greg."

"I'm Megan. I live next door with my mom. Are you Russian? You have that accent."

"Yes, I'm Russian." He solemnly shook her hand, then grinned at her. He couldn't help it.

She grinned back. "Greg, what do you think happens when you die?"

His eyes widened slightly, but he suppressed any further reaction. Oh God, what was he to say to that? She was deliberately trying to confound him. Minx.

Stalling, he said casually, "Well, what do *you* think happens when we die?"

She took a drag off the cigarette and pinned him with a serious, dark-eyed stare. "I don't just think. I *know*." She glanced away. "But I can't tell anyone. You'll think I'm crazy."

"I would never think you were crazy."

"Yeah, well, whatever. Maybe I am." She laughed. "Anyhow, what do you think happens when we die?"

"I don't know." He didn't meet her eyes.

"Liar. Everyone has a theory. Heaven or something. Or just rotting to dust, nothing but electrical impulses and credit cards." She smiled at him, and it was breathtaking.

He pursed his lips, pretending to think. Finally, he faced her. "I think when we die, we're reincarnated into a new body, a new life."

Her smile seemed frozen. "You think so? Why, do you remember your past lives? Were you a wizard in Atlantis or something? Are you a Wiccan? Hindu? Buddhist? Do you know much about past lives?"

He laughed. "No, I'm not a Wiccan or Hindu or anything." He took a drag from his cigarette, exhaled slowly, buying a little time. "And, no, I don't know much about past lives," he lied. "As far as I know, I wasn't a wizard in Atlantis. I can't remember any past lives, either."

She frowned. "Then how can you believe in past lives if you don't remember having any?"

He shrugged. "I like the theory. It makes sense. I had a friend's mother who had an experience when she was young, which seemed to prove it to me."

"What kind of experience?" she demanded. She inhaled deeply from the cigarette, then dropped it, grinding it out on his patio. He raised a brow.

"Sorry," she grumbled, picking up the cigarette butt gingerly. "Where do you want me to put this?"

He handed her a rusty coffee can, then returned it to its customary place by the back door.

"What kind of experience?"

He considered briefly, his jaw working. He really needed to shut up. This was crazy. He'd been training for this all his life, and yet here, now, in her presence, he'd lost all sense of what was right. What was sacred.

"I can't talk about this anymore," he said, turning to go into the house.

"Don't go," she said. "I won't ask any more questions."

He turned back to look at her, nodding in the direction of her home. "Surely you had plans this evening?"

She looked toward the dark house. "Yeah, I was supposed to meet some friends."

He opened the back door. "I'll see you around, then."

"Wait!" She ran to the door, touched his arm. Her fingers were warm, and the glow around them seemed to melt soft against his skin. A fancy, of course. But it felt very good. He looked down at her, questioning.

"Can you tell me about that experience your friend's mother had on another night? Please?" She smiled, hopeful.

Between the smile and her fingers on his arm, Greg was utterly lost. "Okay. Tomorrow."

The brilliance of her smile increased, if that was possible. "'K! Tomorrow. You promised." Laughing, she backed away from him, across the wet dark of the lawn, her shapely legs moving sure and strong, even backward. "You can't go back on a promise," her voice, though soft, carried to him in the warm night.

"I won't." He wanted to say that he never went back on promises, but after that night, it would be a lie.

Now, nine years later, watching her organize her duffle bag in the sparse motel room, he knew he wouldn't see her again. The thought was unbearably painful. She made his life deeper, richer. Maddening. Wondrous.

If anyone had asked Greg, he could have told them she ate leftover rice with milk and artificial sweetener in the blue packets, never the pink ones. She loved going out in rainstorms, the bigger, the better; she seemed only mildly concerned about being struck by lightning. She liked to make things with clay, little sculptures, bowls, pots. She hated mornings. She took whole milk in her coffee, three sugars. She talked to Benny, the drunk who hung out at the 7-Eleven, gave him cigarettes and smoked with him while he told her about his cousin, Louise, who is almost through with that medical transcription course, this time for sure. When she was upset or happy, she liked to go barefoot in the grass. She knew everything there was to know about music, and she couldn't cook worth a damn.

It was true that her moral code was beyond loose, in comparison with most people. She was utterly honest and caring, respectful and kind, and took her personal honor very seriously. But when it came to sex, she was practical. Sex was for love. Sex was for like. Sex was for fun, comfort, entertainment, kindness, payment, communication, and just a nice way to say *hello*. She had a voracious sexual appetite – but then they all did, he'd been told. She was a forest nymph, a cat, a fox, innocently pursuing the satisfaction of instinctive hungers without trifling moral deterrents. Not that Greg knew from personal experience. He'd already broken enough vows.

She was smart and funny. She'd spent too much time trying to win her mother's love, too much time crying when she failed. Yet she'd mourned deeply when Rosa died of breast cancer, just days before Megan's 20th birthday. She rarely spoke of Rosa now, both grieving and furious. She hated injustice and defended anyone who would let her. She believed she killed her stepfather when she was 10, though everyone knew he'd had a heart attack. In her darker moments, she became swamped with self-loathing, believing she was a freak, weird, a monster. She could "nudge" people's emotions with a touch, a trick she swore she learned from a dream. And she loved getting to know new people, despite secretly being afraid someone was hunting her, out to kill her.

Now it seemed she was right.

Tormented by conflicted loyalties, the real, tangible danger made it somehow easier to continue his long deception. His vows. His calling. He was never supposed to become her friend, or anything else. She'd never trust him again if she knew. She'd hate him. Maybe that was for the best. He knew what was right, and being close to her wasn't it.

"Where will you go?" He felt like he was dying inside.

She looked away. "I've always wanted to see San Francisco." To see where she lived, so many years ago. To see Kat Weiss' grave. Her grave.

"I can't go with you." It was a statement, not a question.

She shook her head. When he didn't say more, she stepped close, reaching up and touching his cheek. "I watched him kill a woman, right in front of me. She died just so he could make me watch." She held his gaze. Her eyes seemed enormous, glittering with unshed tears. "He'd kill you just because you're my friend, and I couldn't watch that. I couldn't."

He didn't say anything for several moments. Finally, he bowed his shaggy blond head. "You must call me when you're safe, little *ved'ma*. Promise me."

She promised.

She ate dinner alone in a hole-in-the-wall Mexican restaurant a few blocks from the U-Rest Motel. Rhiannon loved tiny Mexican restaurants, hidden away in low-rent strip malls. Her theory was the more obscure the location, the more authentic the Mexican food. Intensive field research had yet to disprove her hypothesis.

Still, despite the quality of the smoky green chile and *carnitas*, Rhiannon picked at her food, staring out the window at the parking lot, not really seeing.

She felt strange, completely alone for the first time in memory. Kansas City was only 63 miles away, but it felt like a thousand miles, 10,000 years. Everything was different now. In one day, just like that, her whole world was upside down. She struggled with a disquieting juxtaposition of emotions, at once frightened and timid, but also breathlessly free, exhilarated, wild.

Rhiannon reminded herself that whoever *He* was, he couldn't know where she was now. She'd even given Greg her cell phone, asking him to get rid of it. The police could find someone using Global Positioning satellites and a cell phone; it was reasonable to think He might too. He could be a cop, or in the CIA or something. She had to laugh at herself then. She was starting to think like one of those paranoid people on the Internet, spouting dire warnings about government conspiracies. As if some secret government organization would watch Megan Byrne.

No, for the moment, no one on Earth knew exactly where she was. Well, Greg did. But that didn't count. And soon, even Greg wouldn't be sure.

She was completely free. No responsibilities, other than a Greyhound with her name on it, come the morning. A bus going to San Francisco, with stops at any and all points in between. She could be anyone, become anyone she'd ever wanted to be. Or finally be herself, Rhiannon, confident, outrageous, self-aware. Unafraid. She didn't have to please others — not Rosa, not Greg, no one. Just herself.

It was like standing on the edge of a cliff, a precipice so high even shifting clouds filled the space below. And she knew she could fly, just knew it. But having never tried, the leap was daunting, her faith theoretical.

The shadows were growing longer as Rhiannon left the restaurant. She was in no particular hurry to return to the dubious comforts of the U-Rest, deciding instead to wander past the shops in the strip mall. Next to the Mexican restaurant was a dry cleaner, its neon "open" sign ashen, plastic-wrapped shirts hanging closely in the darkened window. A gaudy digital clock glared overbright behind the glass, flashing the time in endless dizzying configurations.

Beyond the dry cleaner was a New Age bookstore called Magick Circle Books and Gifts. To Rhiannon's disappointment, the store was closed for the day. She loved these places, filled with the scent of incense and books, essential oils and fantasy. Display cases carried glittering offerings: quartz pendants and wands, silver pentagrams, earrings, crystal balls, black scrying mirrors. Shelves were loaded with mysterious tomes, esoteric studies of life, philosophy, magic. There were books of shadows, instructional manuals sharing the secrets of spellcraft, how to read palms, cast an astrological chart, grow and use herbs for healing and magical purposes, see auras, meditate, direct spiritual energy.

Rhiannon first discovered such places when she was a teenager, and enthusiastically delved into a variety of arcane and metaphysical studies. She'd kept most of her explorations secret from Rosa, but her mother discovered her Rider-Waite tarot card deck during a rare cleaning foray into Rhiannon's room. An apocalyptic argument ensued, Rosa screaming about Hell and, ironically, the overall fragility of Megan's immortal soul.

Rhiannon had already grown tired of the tarot cards, along with all forms of cartomancy, realizing quickly she had no gift for divination. It would seem obvious that Rhiannon's main interest in the metaphysical was the study of theories surrounding reincarnation, and auras. Eventually, psychometry and empathic sensitivity were added to her investigations.

While Rosa sent her to psychologists (including another hospitalization when she was 17), Rhiannon continued her clandestine research. Bucking her Western conservative, Christian upbringing, Rhiannon studied spiritual philosophies and belief systems, including aspects of Goddess worship, Hinduism, Buddhism, Taoist principles, the Kabbalah, Shamanism, and more.

She had an insatiable need to make sense of her world and experience. The universe was a puzzle, woven through with elegant conflicting threads, songs whispered within the heart of potentiality. No single belief system or philosophy seemed to have all the answers, or account for her first-hand knowledge and understanding. While the lack was infuriating, it only forced her to read further, study harder, learn more.

She spent hours next door, smoking cigarettes in the moonlight, talking with Greg about all she was learning, sharing ideas, concepts. Everything but her own truth, Kat's life. Something stilled her tongue, despite Greg's willingness to listen.

Rhiannon explored endless metaphysical and occult bookstores, shops, fairs, events. She read books, watched films, talked to hundreds of so-called psychics, readers, teachers, faith healers. She met many people who claimed to see or read auras, but only a handful could accurately describe her own multi-layered glow – and these were startled, claiming a single band of light was the norm. She met many more people who claimed to be able to feel another's emotions, yet were unable to read hers.

While Rhiannon could not dispute or disprove the experiences of those who claimed to remember past lives – and they were legion – she was also unable to find another who could remember a past life with the level of detail that haunted her, a thousand trivial moments that made up Kat Weiss' life. Additionally, many of the highly romanticized stories of incarnations seemed dubious, though Rhiannon kept her opinions to herself. Regardless, they were very nice people, for the most part.

Like most seekers, Rhiannon's spiritual beliefs were in constant flux. But she had developed a superstitious conviction that there were no coincidences.

Standing in front of Magick Circle Books and Gifts, admiring a rose quartz candle holder in the display window, Rhiannon noticed several colorful flyers taped to the window. The first advertised a psychic fair the store was hosting the following Saturday, featuring tarot readings and energetic healing sessions.

Just below that notice was a goldenrod sheet, promoting a lecture on the history of reincarnation doctrine throughout worldwide religions. The speaker was Zerik Denali, author of several books on the subject. The seminar was set for that very evening at 7 p.m., at the Ramada Convention Center in Topeka — not two blocks from the tiny shoppette where Rhiannon stood.

Rhiannon looked at the obnoxious digital clock in the dry cleaner's window. She had nothing else to do. She was a new person. Free. She could do anything. There were no coincidences. It was 6:50 p.m.

Rhiannon entered the Parlor, the meeting room at the Ramada, at two minutes before 7. The room was comfortably old-fashioned, decorated with original wood from the old Topeka Governor's Mansion. Several copies of Zerik Denali's latest book were stacked on a table. Around 20 people were seated in folding chairs before a raised dais, many quietly talking and laughing amongst themselves. The metaphysical community was small in any town; exceptionally so in Topeka, based on the size of the crowd. Rhiannon didn't know anyone, of course. She took a chair at the back of the room, near the doors to a small patio.

The other attendees were much as she expected; simply normal, average folks. A few of the men wore greying hair in ponytails. Several women wore crystal and amethyst jewelry, silver stars, colorful silk dresses. A warm summer breeze wafted in from the open patio doors.

When Zerik Denali entered the room, the audience clapped appreciatively. He smiled broadly, stepping onto the dais.

His skin was a smooth, warm brown, reminding Rhiannon of fresh earth, trees, rich coffee with cream, buttery-soft dark-oiled leather. His dark hair was woven into hundreds of tiny braids and hung between his shoulder blades, collected at the back of his neck with a strip of brown leather. He had a closely trimmed goatee, the dark beard and moustache emphasizing his smooth skin.

His attire was upscale, relaxed. He wore an ivory raw-silk shirt, unbuttoned at the throat. A gold pendant glittered there, warm against his dark skin. A pair of jeans and cordovan, well-made boots completed the ensemble.

Zerik Denali carried himself with confidence, a smiling, untroubled ease. It was obvious he was a man who was comfortable with himself and who he was. The effect was devastating. He exuded power and sensuality.

And around his body, he had a shimmering, rich luminous glow, a radiant aura composed of bands of golden light – almost as dense as Rhiannon's own. His light was warm and shining, not like the black aura of the man who hunted her.

Rhiannon sat frozen at the back of the room, hardly daring to breathe. No. She wouldn't be afraid. Not this time. She was the New Rhiannon, and she had nothing to lose anymore. She would talk to him, ask him if his golden glow was real, if he could see hers, too.

Would he be afraid of her, like the little man in the hospital with his shadowed aura? Would he ignore her, like the others she'd seen? What on earth would she say? "Hi. Do you really glow?" Or, "You look good enough to eat." Right. That would be great.

But the lecture was about to begin; she couldn't approach Zerik Denali in front of all these people. With no small sense of relief, she acknowledged that she'd have to wait until the talk was over.

Denali's gaze swept over the crowd, smiling, waiting for the applause to die down. And then he looked to the back of the room, saw Rhiannon. He stilled. His smile grew deeper, joyful. Suddenly it was as if there was no one else in the room but the two of them. He looked full into her eyes, and his deep, brown gaze seemed to go on forever, truly a window to his soul – full of promise, secrets, knowledge, passion. Then he nodded to her, gravely, solemnly. Respectfully.

He turned back to his audience, and the moment was over. He began his lecture, his voice deep, resonating.

Rhiannon was shaken to her toes. Outwardly quiescent, she listened to him talk, while nervousness and excitement fluttered, tangled within her chest. Part of her was already running back to the U-Rest Motel, hiding under the garish bedspread, pretending none of this ever happened. No. She would stay. Face this, face him. Find out the truth.

She'd spent so long searching for a way to explain her existence. Reading books was safe, easy. Here was someone real, solid, who might have the missing pieces to the puzzle she'd been trying to solve, without knowing what she was really looking for, the shape or scope of the thing. No. She would stay.

Zerik Denali was a wonderful speaker, inflective and passionate, vivid. He described how the concept of reincarnation appeared in many cultures simultaneously in the 6th century B.C. He talked of Indian religious traditions, including Hinduism and Sikhism, Buddhists, some Greek philosophical traditions, the Druids, the Cathars, Norse mythology, and more. He shared the literal definition of the word "reincarnation" ("entering the flesh again"), and the Greek "metempsychosis," or "transmigration of the soul."

Rhiannon had already read much of the history Denali shared, but he had a gift for taking complex concepts and breaking them down into easily understood ideas. When he finished his talk, the audience applauded enthusiastically.

Rhiannon sat quietly and waited. Some people filed out through the side door, others went past her, through the patio doors. Several more bought books, crowding the dais for autographs and the chance to talk to Denali. One blonde, heavy-set woman seemed intent on telling him all about her many past lives in great detail, which he listened to with smiling, endless patience.

Finally, the last guest left, leaving Rhiannon alone in the room with Zerik Denali.

He looked up at her from across the room, saying nothing, not moving. The silence, the moment, stretched. He seemed to be waiting for something. Waiting for her?

Gathering her courage, Rhiannon stood and took a step toward him.

He smiled, a brilliant heart-stopping casual grin. Then he did the strangest thing. He cupped his left hand, palm up, resting the side of his hand against his stomach. Then he cupped his right hand, covering the left, fingertips to the heels of his palms, his arms relaxed against his body. The cupped hands formed a space, as if to hold something. He nodded to her again, formally, and said, *"Zanav tu."* It was clearly a greeting, a salutation. Like the anjali mudra, or perhaps a formal Japanese bow.

Rhiannon halted. *I am anyone I want to be. I am Rhiannon*, she thought. Resolved, she took a breath. "I have no idea what that means. But I'm hoping you can help me."

Brows raised, he looked genuinely surprised. "Of course I will help you." He said it with unquestionable conviction. She believed him.

"I have this glow. An aura. And it seems like you do, too." She looked at him from across the room, pleading. "Do you see it too? Is it real? What does it mean?"

His face reflected an unmistakable confusion. "Of course it's real." He crossed the room to stand in front of her. Taking her hand, his dark brown skin felt warm against the olive brown of hers. Their mutual glow seemed to fuse, brighten, expand, golden light radiating from where they touched. "How can you not know these things?"

Rhiannon blinked back tears, frustration, relief, excitement, fear, and something more she couldn't identify skating across her nerves. She laughed shakily. "I don't know anything."

The pad of his thumb caressed her hand. "You are like me; you have died before. You remember a hundred incarnations, more. You are Family."

Rhiannon shook her head, then looked up into his impossible brown eyes. "I died once. I remember dying once." She looked away shyly. "Is that what this glow means? What auras mean? Remembering a past life?"

"You only remember one death, one life?"

She nodded. The warmth of his hand was soothing. Rhiannon looked down at where he touched her, the way his golden glow blended with her own. It felt hauntingly intimate, precious.

"That's not possible," Zerik shook his head. "Your *fainna* – you've lived many lives. Many times many."

Rhiannon was bewildered, a cold fear flickering to life within. *Danger*, something whispered. She might have left then, but that would have meant breaking away from his touch, the heat of him, so close. And she couldn't bear that, somehow.

Whatever the nameless danger was, it didn't come from this man, personally. "I don't know what you're talking about. I don't know what any of this means. Please explain it to me." Her gaze was beseeching, desperate.

Zerik looked down at her, unable to make sense of what she was saying. Her touch was inexplicably familiar. Her Form was beautiful, with a mane of curly black hair, a lithe build – a lush, exquisite Latina with a stunning aura which bespoke great gifts.

He closed his eyes and extended his senses toward her, feeling, *feeling* – and staggered, overcome with the sheer force of the power she carried. His eyes flew open, and he gripped her shoulders. "Who are you?"

FIVE

She was having the nightmare again.

This time Rhiannon was at a salon in a Parisian drawing room, amongst several people making genial conversation. Her tightly-laced corset made it difficult to take deep breaths, and her embroidered velvet gown was hot in the confining room. Fanning herself, she tried to pay attention to the Comtesse, expounding on the virtues of a new artist she'd discovered.

Her back began to hurt, a dull ache below her shoulder blades. Cold fear accompanied the pain, and her palms began to sweat inside her gloves. Something was coming. Something wrong.

The Comtesse's manservant announced a new guest, but Rhiannon couldn't make out the name. Time and sound slowed to baritone rumbles, as though underwater. Then He was there, his aura a black and glimmering grey mass.

He looked at Rhiannon and smiled. The pain in her back intensified unbearably, as though something was pushing hard into her flesh, a bar across her back. Her terror was absolute. She couldn't move, think, breathe.

"You want this," he said. The pressure on her back turned agonizing, panic gripping her throat. Her vision narrowed until she could see nothing but his face, his gruesome black smile and eyes. "You need this," he said. She started screaming then, but no one could hear.

Rhiannon stood holding the railing of the stone balcony, looking out over the city lights. She was at the pinnacle of the tallest building, and it felt like she was halfway to the moon. The city was spread out before her, a hundred thousand points of light defining space in three dimensions — lights at angles formed the shape of buildings, their height fixed where the night began. Overhead, the canopy of stars arched and stretched into forever, their very distance rendering them flat and infinitely vast.

Below, the sound of traffic was a low hum, the city drowsing, rumbling to itself in the Midwest night air.

A summer wind brought the humid scent of plants, fields of corn and wheat, the acrid odor of gasoline, oil, garbage, the spicy smell of night and magic and promise. She shivered, the chill engendered within.

The nightmare had left her terrified, sweating. Rhiannon felt as though her entire body were in conflict, not simply her emotions. It was 3 in the morning, and she was having the longest, most amazing, frightening, strange, wonderful day of her life.

Staring at the city, she tried to make sense of what she was feeling, define it, shape it. She was free for the first time in her life, yet hunted. Terror lurked behind every action, every thought, an undercurrent of fear like a dark thread running beneath her existence. The nightmare brought that fear to the forefront, and Rhiannon breathed deeply of the stars, trying to shove it back down.

She'd made a choice, to leap into the unknown. To understand who she was. What she was. And despite the fear, frustration, and confusion, the conflicting agony and elation, the world felt huge now, open as the sky, waiting for her to come take it. Her bones were weightless, her marrow helium; inside she was light, joyful, exhilarated. Only the fear and nightmares tethered her to the ground, prevented her from floating out into the lights and stars until she was one of them, a glowing point defining space.

She had thought her whole life changed, turned upside down, but it had only been a weak reflection of the vivid existence before her now, a tapestry of infinite threads in bright gold, scarlet, blue, unrolling endlessly outward in every direction.

And yet, how easy it was to accept nightmares, and so difficult to believe in dreams made real.

Rhiannon thought of those first moments with Zerik Denali in the meeting room at the Ramada Inn, the silence and the smell of old wood, new carpet, and the night coming in through the patio doors.

He'd frightened her, excited her, left her confused and conflicted, aching for answers and unsure if she could believe the explanations, even if she knew them. Something had happened; he'd closed his eyes for a moment, jerked back as if shocked, startled. He'd gripped her shoulders, asking who she was, as if she had some vital answer he too sought.

But she didn't have significant answers, only questions. And she wasn't ready to give anyone her name, her *name*, the name that felt real and whole and *her*.

So she offered the answer she gave everyone, the official truth that never felt true. "M-Megan. I'm Megan Byrne." She shook beneath his hands, trembled inside.

As if coming to awareness, his grip relaxed. "I'm sorry, I didn't mean to upset you." He stroked her shoulders, as if to undo his earlier, hasty touch. He seemed to gather himself. "You're afraid. I see that. Please know I would never do anything to harm you."

She nodded cautiously, trying to martial her calm, the floor feeling dangerously sideways, the world uneven, shifting.

His brown eyes looked into hers, steady, fathomless. "You're unique, Megan. I've never met an aeternan like you, nor heard of one. You have the aura of an Eldest – someone who has lived many, many lifetimes. But here's the thing," Zerik shook his head, obviously confounded. "You don't remember many lifetimes, just one. You are neonate – new to the Family."

"Who is the Family?" her voice sounded hollow, faint.

"We are. I am. You are. The mensaeterna, Those Who Do Not Forget. The race of people who remember past lives, who carry *e'drai*."

Rhiannon didn't know what to say. It was overwhelming, too much to take in. A *race* of people? That implied – a hundred things, a thousand. All of them enormous and unreal. Things that would, of necessity, turn the universe inside out, a perspective unimaginable. Unthinkable.

But despite her fears, the hunger to understand flared brighter in that moment, grew from a spark to a small but steady light.

"Let me try to explain," Zerik smiled then, warm, kind, reassuring. "I think you …"

He was interrupted as one of the main doors opened, and a woman wearing a red hotel uniform entered the meeting room. Zerik turned, moving immediately to step in front of Rhiannon, as if to shield her. An odd thing to do, somehow important.

"Oh, Mr. Denali," the woman said. "You're still here. Will you be needing the room much longer?" She looked embarrassed. "It's just we've got a wedding tomorrow, and we're trying to get the rooms set up."

Zerik smiled. "I'll be out of here in a few minutes. My apologies for the delay." He sounded wholly calm, adopting the façade of casual self-assurance he seemed to wear so easily.

"Thank you, we do appreciate it." The woman left the room, glancing curiously over her shoulder as she went. She left the main doors open to the hallway beyond.

Zerik turned back to Rhiannon, rooted to the floor, looking up at him, altogether lost, yet fostering the spark of her resolve. He took her hand again, his touch bringing a curious sense of relief.

"Megan, we need to go somewhere private. We can't talk here, where we might be overheard." He smiled encouragingly. "I can take you back to the *Maisonsur*. It's a Safehouse, a place for visiting Family, or a sanctuary for aeternans in trouble. It's also home to members of the Dao Yin, while they work."

76

She must have looked thoroughly confused, because Zerik laughed, squeezing her hand. "Okay, let me try again. It's a nice place to go where we won't be disturbed, and it's where I happen to be staying." He sobered. "I assure you, you can trust me. I will treat you with honor."

She studied his face, thinking about what he'd said, his oddly formal language. "Can I look at you?"

Now it was his turn to look confused. "Look at me? Aren't you doing that now?"

"No, I mean *look* at you."

His face registered surprise for a moment, but then an understanding dawned in his eyes. His brow cleared, and his face grew calm. "Look at me, then."

She took a breath, found her stillness, and looked into his eyes. A wave of feeling flooded her senses — genuine concern, kindness, intense curiosity, confidence, care. Protectiveness. And underneath all of that, the heat of sexual attraction, a desire he was trying hard to suppress, flowing out of a deep sense of duty, honor.

She blushed, dropped her gaze.

Zerik swallowed. "That was well done," he whispered.

Unable to meet his eyes, Rhiannon squeezed his hand. "I'll go with you."

He had a car waiting outside, a hulking, black SUV. Zerik helped her into the car with elegant, almost courtly manners.

They drove in silence, Rhiannon staring through the window at the city streets, twisting her hands in her lap, questioning the wisdom of accompanying this man — oh, she knew he was safe and wouldn't hurt her, but was she truly ready to hear the answers to her questions? But what was the alternative? Drift alone in the world, hiding from someone who stalked, hunted her? Or at best, a lifetime of depressing years trying, — and failing — to pretend she was like everyone else?

What harm in entertaining the wild fancy of a better life, not being alone, finally knowing her place in the order of the world?

As they inched through downtown traffic and endless red lights,

Zerik glanced at her periodically, before silently looking back to the road. Waiting for her again.

Finally, they pulled up in front of a bank, of all things. The Dynasty Bank, while only 20 stories, was a true skyscraper in the sleepy Midwest city. Rhiannon stepped down to the sidewalk, looking up at the building, a harmonious blend of classical and contemporary architecture, glass, steel, and stone.

Zerik came around the car, grinning and shaking his head. "Modern women," he sighed. "If you would only wait, some old fashioned bastard might actually open a door for you."

She had to laugh at that, and when he took her hand, once again, the immediate sense of peace she felt almost – but not quite – dispelled her agitation.

The bank was closed, but as they approached the wide glass doors, a guard appeared from the depths of the lobby, smiling and waving to Zerik from behind the glass. He fumbled with his keys, and unlocked the doors. As they entered, Zerik handed the guard the keys to the SUV with a quiet word of thanks. He ushered Rhiannon inside, his hand warm on the small of her back.

The lobby was marble and dark wood, with an elaborate chandelier overhead, dimmed for the evening. The entrance to the bank itself was on the left, two heavy, polished wood doors closed for the night. The security guard's desk sat to the right; beyond it was a row of elevators. Their footsteps echoed in the silence.

Zerik led Rhiannon to the last elevator, which had a keypad instead of a button. His fingers danced on the numeric keys, as he entered an elaborate sequence. When he finished, the elevator doors opened almost immediately.

The roomy elevator cab was paneled in rich cherry wood and glass, with its own understated little chandelier in the ceiling. Near the doors was a small, etched-crystal vase in a curving, silver bracket. The vase held a miniature bouquet of fresh flowers, iris and delicate lavender roses. Rhiannon giggled; she couldn't help it. Zerik turned, one brow raised in question.

"I'm sorry," she said, embarrassed. She felt out of place in her old black T-shirt and jeans. "I've just never seen such a fancy elevator in my entire life." She giggled again, nervousness getting the better of her.

He laughed. "I know. But it is rather pretty, isn't it? The *Kir* in charge of this Safehouse is a man who believes even the utilitarian should be beautiful."

Rhiannon smiled. "I guess all elevators should be beautiful." She stopped. "A man did this?"

"Yes," Zerik replied, examining the button panel in the elevator. "I think he said he was a female decorator in his last incarnation."

This offhand remark left Rhiannon stunned into silence. She watched as Zerik began pressing buttons on the alphanumeric keypad.

Finally she found her voice again. "Your Safehouse is in an office building?"

Still keying in numbers and letters, he answered, "We own the penthouse." With a flourish, he pressed the last number, and the elevator ascended.

Rhiannon felt half dizzy with shifting emotions, from nervousness to excitement to curiosity to flat-out panic and back again. Her palms felt damp, and she wiped her hands on her jeans. "That's a lot of security, with all of those codes and stuff."

He smiled a little sadly. "We always have to be careful."

Rhiannon could relate to that. Unbidden, an image filled her mind: black eyes consuming hers, a dark aura draining light. She shuddered.

The penthouse was spectacular, with a vaulted ceiling and a bank of gracefully arched windows, reminding Rhiannon of a dream she'd once had, a ballroom in another time, another place. The city lights glittered all around, and a wide balcony beckoned, inviting closer views.

The penthouse was a curious mix of old-fashioned and modern, classical, comfortable.

The space was open and airy, paneled in pale wood, with hardwood floors softened by a profusion of lusciously thick carpets in bright jewel tones. Overstuffed chairs and a burgundy leather sofa formed a seating area in the center of the spacious main room. A chaise longue was tucked in a corner, next to a reading lamp and a low table carelessly strewn with books. Across the room was a darkened kitchen, stone counters gleaming dully in the dim light.

Lavish vases of roses, lilies, and iris filled the air with the scent of summer, combining pleasantly with the smell of lemon oil and polished wood.

Several paintings hung on the warm oak walls, each carefully lit and displayed. Rhiannon walked closer to one, which depicted a colorful riot of flowers by a stream. She'd taken art classes in high school in Kansas City, remembering another life in New York, when Kat Weiss' grandmother would take her to the Met. Her grandmother had loved art, particularly Impressionist works, and shared her passion with Rhiannon.

Rhiannon always loved those trips to the museum, where paintings were displayed with such care, like the charming landscape before her now. This painting was clearly a master-level work. She was awed by the brushstrokes in the oil, the luminous quality of the color, the effortless play of light and shadow.

Rhiannon turned to find Zerik watching her thoughtfully. "It's beautiful," she said.

"Yes," he agreed softly, without looking at the painting. Before she could say more, he straightened, looked toward the kitchen. "Let's have something to drink and talk for awhile – then I can take you home – or wherever you like." He offered a casual grin.

A little embarrassed, Rhiannon shrugged, affecting nonchalance. "Everything I own is in a duffle bag at the Topeka U-Rest Motel." At his quizzical stare, she added hastily, "I was planning on catching a bus to San Francisco tomorrow morning."

"Why San Francisco?"

She laughed, blushing. "Well, until I met you, I wanted to prove to myself that all of this was real. That I really remembered being another person. At least, that was part of it." She looked at her feet. "Her name was Kat Weiss. I wanted to see her grave. My grave." Rhiannon giggled nervously. "That sounds so weird, doesn't it?"

He laughed, a warm, full-throated sound. "Actually, it doesn't sound weird to me, but I know it's hard to get used to when you're new to it." He headed toward the kitchen. "What will you have to drink?"

"Something non-alcoholic," she rubbed her forehead. "I'm having a hard enough time figuring all of this out sober."

He chuckled. "Lemonade it is."

Rhiannon settled on the big sofa, looking at the paintings on the walls, the lights outside the windows, and trying very hard not to think beyond that. Her eyes were drawn back to Zerik, watching him as he fetched glasses in the kitchen.

He was a big man, muscular, strong, but he moved with smooth grace. He looked so normal, a handsome black man in blue jeans and a silk shirt, with all those little braids and his goatee. He could be anyone she might meet at the grocery store, a nightclub, a workshop somewhere. Yet he was undeniably different, with his glowing aura, shimmering gold bands of light creating a shining haze around his body.

After a few minutes, Zerik came and sat next to her, offered her lemonade and his dazzling smile.

"Thank you." She reached for the glass, took a sip. The lemonade was good, perfectly tart. As she placed the glass on the coffee table, a tremor in her hand betrayed her.

"This must be difficult for you," he said. "I can hardly remember what it was like, being new to all of this, but I work to help people through it." His smile was sympathetic. "You must feel overwhelmed – and probably have more questions than you can even think to ask."

She laughed shakily. "That's true enough."

"Well then, let me tell you what I already know." He reached out without thought, touching her hair, his fingers gentle. "You've spent your whole life – even your last life – feeling different, like no one understood you. Feeling alone."

Tears pricked her eyes. "Yes."

He smiled sadly. "I know. It's hard to see the way you do, being able to do the things you can do."

Rhiannon shook her head. "It's been horrible. I've tried to understand, to figure things out – that's why I came to your lecture tonight. I go to lectures, seminars, workshops, classes ... no one seems to have answers."

He touched her knee, his face kind, earnest. "That's why I do

81

the lectures. To try to find others, people like you." He leaned forward, took a deep breath. "How would you feel if I told you that you're *not* alone. The world is full of people like you, like me. Millions of us. We are Family. You are like us – Those Who Do Not Forget."

She looked up at him in surprise. "Millions?" she echoed faintly.

"We make up about five-hundredths of one percent of the world population. A few million, worldwide." He laughed at her wide-eyed expression. "It's really not a lot. There's between 150-200 thousand living in the U.S." Zerik was animated as he talked, unconsciously using his hands to emphasize, illustrate. "We're spread out all over the world, in every country – because we're born in every country."

She sat back, trying to absorb that. "So there's millions of people in the world who glow – who have auras, like you and me. And that means they remember having a past life."

"Yes. Well, not quite like you and me." He put a hand on her knee. "Everyone has an aura. You've probably seen that."

"I've seen a thin strip of light around everyone. Once in awhile I've seen someone with more, like me." She shook her head. "But every time I've seen someone like that, I've been afraid to talk to them. And they never talk to me."

He laughed. "I'm not surprised. Let me explain." He pointed to his forearm, his shining aura. "Every aura has rings or bands of light, called *fainna*." His hand moved outward, encompassing the full scope of his radiance. "Each ring in an aura represents one lifetime, one incarnation on this planet. Kind of like the rings on a tree." He smiled, leaning forward. "So a neonate – someone new to the Family, who only remembers one past life – they'll have two bands of light. One for their last life, one for this one."

She frowned. "That doesn't make sense. I only remember one life, and I have lots and lots of rings."

"Well," he raised an eyebrow, "that's what makes you quite the conundrum." He took her hand. "I'm going to help you figure out why, if you'll let me."

Her spark of resolve flared brighter still. "Thank you."

He picked up his glass, took a drink. "As to why the other aeternans wouldn't talk to you – you know, when you saw the glowing people – that's because it wasn't polite."

She laughed. "What?"

"We have a culture, traditions going back more than 3,000 years. Part of that is some pretty strict protocol, manners, rules for polite behavior." He smiled. "We've learned the hard way that good manners are a kind of social lubricant, making dealing with one another easier, even pleasant." He leaned back against the couch. "You accomplish a lot more that way."

She stared at him. "So you're saying it was bad manners for those people to talk to me."

Now he laughed. "Well, in a way, yes. You see, in our culture, those who have lived longest command the most respect. They are Eldest. One does not approach an Eldest; one waits for the Eldest to approach you." He nodded to her with exaggerated formality, the gesture belied by a wide grin.

Her eyes widened. "You mean, they were waiting for me to talk to them first?" Suddenly she remembered speaking to Zerik, at the Ramada Inn. The way he'd waited for her to make the first move. His strange response when she did. "You waited for me, too," she said. "And what was that bow thing you did?"

"It's a formal bow, showing respect for other aeternans, particularly Eldest." He repeated the gesture, cupping his hands fingertips to heels, against his belly. "It's called the *anam'sal*."

Rhiannon shook her head. "It's like a whole different universe."

"It is, that." Zerik nodded.

"So auras tell how long someone has lived, how many lifetimes." She grimaced. "Except for me."

"Yes, except for you," he laughed. "But auras convey other information, too – generally, you can see when someone is sick, has a disease. Anything from cancer to gonorrhea." He swept his hand up his body, indicating his glimmering gold aura. "Illness shows up as shades of brown, usually. Aeternans with healing gifts can distinguish disease in detail, just by looking. And some can see pregnancy and other benign things."

"What do you mean, gifts?"

He held her gaze. "Remembering past lives is only part of being Family. As we remember, through centuries, we develop *e'drai*. Gifts." He grinned, brilliant, disarming. "Like the way you *looked* at me, the way you can look at others."

Rhiannon was stunned. "You mean, the things I can do – that's part of the glowing thing, the aura, too?"

"Yes."

"Then you can do it, too."

He took her hand again, and she tried to ignore her now-familiar reaction. "I can't do what you can do, no. I have my own *e'drai*."

"What's your gift?"

"I'm Eldest, so I have several. I can sense the scope of others' *e'drai*, the magnitude of their gifts. Which also means I can feel when gifts are being used, particularly when directed at me, and always in my proximity." He didn't mention his sexual *e'drai*, his ability to sense lies and truth when in intimate, sensual contact with another. He wouldn't tempt her, or pressure her. Or frighten her. He looked into her eyes, his thumb rubbing lazy circles across the back of her hand. "I could feel you *look* at me, as you call it. I could feel what you were doing, and what you were feeling from me."

She blushed, remembering what she felt, his kindness, protectiveness, the heat of his desire. She was glad he couldn't feel what she felt too – fear, a desperate need to find some kind of balance. Her own attraction to him.

Rhiannon was a highly sexual creature and had entertained many lovers, many sexual encounters that began with only the briefest of acquaintances, ending almost as quickly. And while, for the most part, they'd been a great deal of fun, they lacked the intensity of interest she'd inexplicably developed for this man.

Perhaps it was insecurity, her need for something solid in a world turned quicksand. Perhaps she was simply desperate to feel safe, to belong. Sex, the barnyard dance between potential mates, had always been easy, natural, a source of solace. An escape. Insecure, safe, belonging, escape – maybe she should proceed with caution.

84

But it felt deeper, somehow. And she was damned tired of caution.

Zerik was watching her face, as though searching for something there. "You are very strong in *drai'sentia*, the Feeling gift. The way you 'look' at someone. But it doesn't account for a tenth of your power, the magnitude of your *e'drai*."

"What did you call my 'looking'?"

He smiled. "*Drai'sentia*. Feeling. There's more to it than that, but that's the root *e'drai*."

Rhiannon suppressed a nervous giggle. Lord. "I told you I go to all these classes, New Age bookstores, read this stuff. I always thought I was an empath."

"That's a modern word for it, I suppose, though not very accurate." He reached for his glass of lemonade, and she sipped hers as well, watching his face, his long fingers holding his glass.

Sighing, she leaned back against the soft leather of the couch. "The whole empath thing is kind of embarrassing, actually."

He laughed, watching her face. "Why would you say that?"

"Because empaths are so cheesy in movies, on TV. I mean, I don't just feel people's emotions all the time, every second of the day – "

"Which is a good thing," he interrupted, "Otherwise I think you'd go insane. I've heard of cases."

She blanched. "Insane? Oh, great." Then she laughed. "Really, it's amazing I'm *not* insane. No one should have to remember *two* humiliating trips through seventh grade."

His answering laugh was deep. "Try three. Junior high was a terrible invention."

She shook her head. "Well, anyhow, I don't feel it all the time. Just when I focus, concentrate. But then, when I do, it's not just emotions I feel. I feel the person, who they are." She touched his hand. "Not so much *what* they think, but the *way* they think."

"Hmm," he studied her face, thinking. "Sounds like a mix between Feeling and Knowing. *Drai'sentia'sien'dao*."

She giggled again. When was the last time she'd *giggled*, before this crazy night? "Please tell me there won't be a quiz."

He leaned forward, suddenly serious, his eyes warm, kind. "I think you'll remember."

They talked for hours, long after midnight. Zerik explained to Rhiannon about the Order of the Dao Yin, aeternans traveling the globe seeking Family, helping neonates, and rescuing those in need, providing Safehouses in every major city worldwide.

Grimly, he told her about the 14th century Dynasty War, a brief conflict by aeternan standards – three generations of killing one another, over and over, and over again. Without ever knowing why, tens of thousands of oblivi died for the aeternan cause, the Family's hunger for power and control. Once there were more than 100 *dinachs*, mensaeternan dynasties. Only 21 of the great Houses remained.

"It sounds horrible," Rhiannon said quietly. "So many people lost."

Zerik knew his pain showed in his eyes; he saw it reflected in her face, before he carefully blanked his expression. He stood, crossing to the window, staring blindly into the humid midwest night. "In the end, despite the cost, it was the best thing for the Family. We built the Family bank, and instituted the Caistras, a kind of world-wide system of governance – all managed equally by the 21 dynasties."

Rhiannon looked up suddenly. "Your Safehouse. This is the Dynasty Bank."

"Yes." Zerik turned from the window. "We own the bank. Many branches of the Dynasty Bank offer Safehouses."

"But why do you need Safehouses?" He could see she was frightened, afraid of something that had nothing to do with him, or this night. Something else disturbed Megan Byrne, and while she wasn't ready to talk about it – any more than he was ready to share his own darkest fears – he knew it was something horrific. He felt a wave of protectiveness, a rage deeply constrained beneath his artfully calm veneer, second nature now.

Zerik clenched his jaw, looking back at the lights of Topeka. "There are people who hunt aeternans, believe we're too powerful. So we've had to protect ourselves. It's always been this way, for thousands of years – great power attracts powerful enemies." He sighed, looking back to her. "And we have always had to fight. In the Dynasty War, we fought each other. But aeternans have been part of every war, in every century, the world over."

He was relaxed, casual, as he stared back at the window, but his reflection was dark, murky, hands clenched to quell the shaking. He couldn't tell her how many centuries he'd served as a soldier for House Spava, the endless bloody wars, conflicts, battles, skirmishes. His *e'drai* allowed him to move with preternatural speed. He'd killed men with swords of all sorts, his prized throwing knives, spears, crude clubs, crossbows, elegant longbows, war scythes, morning stars, even Zulu knobkerries, their blunt weight good at close range. Zerik had mastered the slashing triple-bladed Indian katar; the heavy clawed iron hand of the Chinese zhua. And guns, of course. Thousands of guns, the metal cold and black in his hand, his eye keen, unwavering, death immediate.

Zerik remembered them all, every man or woman he'd looked in the eye, before stealing their lives with his blood-slicked weapons, even his bare hands. He remembered, too, ghastly visions of death forged by others, monsters with black souls. Just closing his eyes, he could see scrubby ditches strewn with filthy bodies spattered with blood, eyes staring, lips wide in never-ending silent screams. Zerik's nightmares were consumed with images of burning villages, screaming, howling women and the lifeless bodies of children tossed like rag dolls, half-trampled into the mud beneath soldiers boots.

Centuries of killing and death. Some aeternans couldn't endure it, becoming bitter, fanatic killing machines, marinating in vivid adrenalin and trusting only in the camaraderie of their fellows – and often, not even that. But Zerik had managed to keep to the light, blessed with women who offered him succor, peace, and a gentle return to sanity, when he staggered back from yet another battle.

Looking past his own muted reflection in the window, he saw Megan Byrne's image in the darkened glass, sitting in a pool of golden light from the table lamp. She reminded him of a woman who once touched his scarred spirit, tender, strong, powerful in her own right.

He didn't know Megan, not enough to strip his soul bare, to share the darkness like a sliver of black fog beneath his skin. But he wanted to tell her, and that alone was disconcerting, this deep sense of connection with this petite woman. Part of him craved her, with a need so ferocious it was unsettling, almost disturbing.

With natural, fierce skill, Zerik rediscovered his inner light and peace. Suppressing rough emotion and inexplicable desire, he sat on the sofa beside Megan, wearing his easy grin. He couldn't tell her of the pain he carried — not yet. But he could tell her of his choice, almost a century before, the decision to stop soldiering and work with the Dao Yin, finding new Family, or rescuing Family from harsh circumstances.

Megan listened, intent, fascinated, as he told her how in the Second Great War, he'd helped Jews, Rom, and others escape Germany and Austria. During subsequent wars, he'd smuggled both oblivi and aeternan families to safer locales. To protect these people, he'd had to kill once more, but somehow those deaths didn't weigh as heavily on his heart.

Zerik explained to Megan how now, on behalf of the Dao Yin, he gave reincarnation lectures throughout the country. He loved reaching out to neonate aeternans, their two golden *fainna* shining from the audience, their eyes filled with hope and a kind of desperation, yearning to understand. It felt good to offer welcome and acceptance to those who felt lost, alone. People like Megan, with her neonate mind, and her ancient, ancient soul.

She'd smiled shyly, looking up into his eyes, gratitude and something else, something hotter, simmering in her gaze. "I'm glad you found me."

It was close to 2am when Zerik went to the kitchen, refilling the lemonade glasses. He could feel Megan Byrne's eyes on him.

He felt distinctly uncomfortable, a novel sensation after so many lifetimes. She reminded him of someone he loved — not physically, necessarily, but the way she spoke, her aura.

She was neonate, new, always a very emotional process. The way Megan vacillated from fearful, to curious, to relaxed, mature woman – and back again – made her vulnerability obvious. Zerik was not the sort of man who got personally involved with vulnerable women.

But as he returned to her side, handing her a glass of lemonade, he had to admit that somehow this situation felt different. *She* was different. And while it was uncomfortable to acknowledge it, *he* was different, when he was with her. It was definitely a strange night.

She sipped her lemonade, looking at him over the rim of the glass. "Tell me more about your *e'drai*."

Zerik hesitated. She was so small, sitting on the big leather couch, all enormous brown eyes and petite curves, half-hidden by an overwashed black T-shirt and jeans. And radiating the beautiful aura of an Eldest who had walked the earth long before he had.

"Your gifts," she prompted. "What else can you do?"

He couldn't help himself. Leaning forward, he brushed a kiss across her forehead, a featherlight touch, her skin warm against his lips. As he did so, he sent a whisper of thought directly into her mind. *"I can do this."*

Rhiannon gasped, the combination of his voice inside her head and his mouth on her skin wholly unexpected. He pulled away, and she stared at him mutely.

"My apologies," he said, abruptly formal, distant. "I don't wish to offend you, or take advantage of – "

Unable to bear his changed demeanor, she reached out, touched his chest. He caught his breath. And just like that, suddenly it seemed the most natural thing in the world to be here, in this moment. Her fears and confusion fled, leaving behind a confidence, a kind of knowing. A rightness.

She smiled into his eyes. "It's okay. You can't 'take advantage' of me – I'm a big girl and make my own decisions." She laughed a little, almost breathless, not quite steady. "And more than once, I've decided to enjoy some friendly nice-to-meet-you sex." She looked at her hand, still pressed against his chest, feeling the heat of him through his silk shirt. "But you're different, and I don't know why. It's like I already know you, like I've known you a long time."

He regarded her seriously, his dark eyes searching hers. He didn't return her smile. "I feel that way too." He cupped her cheek, pulled her mouth to his in a kiss that started indescribably gentle, but quickly evolved into something needy, grasping, ravenous.

For long minutes they clung to one another, as though drowning, gasping kisses oxygen. Finally, he simply scooped her up off the couch, carrying her wordlessly to his bedroom.

He turned on the bedside lamp, so he could see her. She kept her eyes closed, conceiving sensation. He feasted on her mouth, her throat, the soft curves of her flesh. When he entered her, she inhaled sharply, breathing in the spicy, musky scent of his skin, pulling him deeper into her, as though she could take his essence inside herself.

But then she opened her eyes — tensed, froze. He was glowing like a star. His skin had grown incandescent, as though lit faintly from within. She looked in wonder at her hand, clutching his shoulder, amazed at her own shining golden skin. Their mutual auras had combined, fused into one blazing halo, brilliant, exquisite.

"This is how it is when we're together," he whispered in her mind. "Please don't be afraid." Holding still within her, the heat of her body was fierce, transcendent. He pressed his damp forehead to her throat, gritting his teeth, ready to stop if she asked, praying she wouldn't.

"I'm not afraid," she thought, lost in the feel of him, their mutual light, resplendent. And somehow he heard her, groaning, sobbing exultation, and moving again.

SIX

Zerik woke from a dream like a memory. He reached out, touching the cool sheets, the empty bed beside him. Sitting up, he looked toward the windows, his eyes drawn inexorably to the balcony outside the bedroom, and the slender woman swathed in his oversized grey silk robe, the night breeze sifting through her hair.

He didn't bother to dress, but prowled naked to the balcony, coming to stand behind her, wrapping his arms around her, pressing his lips to the side of her neck. She shivered, whether from his touch or something else, he couldn't tell. "Are you okay?" he whispered.

"I had a nightmare," she said.

"Do you want to talk about it?" His voice was sleep-roughened, his concern genuine.

Rhiannon shook her head. "No. Not right now." Her hands trembled slightly, evincing her tension. "I want to talk about it, but I can't."

"*Come back to bed, divya varenya.*" His voice sounded in her mind, as his lips explored the delicate flesh behind her ear. He caressed her cheek with the back of one finger. In her mind, she heard him add, "*Some things are easier to talk about in bed.*"

The breath of a smile flickered on her lips then, as though kissed by the wind, and she turned away from the night.

They lay in Zerik's wide bed, talking the way lovers do, limbs twined, cheek to heartbeat, fingers caressing, discovering, questing. In the small hours after midnight, the sheet-tangled conversations of lovers are far-ranging, questions breeding excited answers, interruptions, laughter. Each yearns for touch, physical and intellectual – to offer something of themselves, heartfelt truths, long-held beliefs, confessions, dreams. Commonalities are lauded, differences effortlessly dismissed, a deeper bond paramount. Words are silenced by kisses, teasing turns heated, only to dissolve into laughter and play again, and then again.

He told her about his need to paint, that the charming landscape in the main room she'd so admired was one of his works. He talked about an essential demand for creative expression, the euphoria in articulating a thought by tactile, visual means. The warm pleasure of color, vibrant and wet. The path of a brush through the oil.

She told him about going to the museum with her grandmother, when she was another woman, in another place, another time. She talked about art classes in high school in Kansas City, and her love of sculpting. The way wet clay slid in her hands, bringing form into existence from thought. Her connection with earth, her need to touch the grass, the trees, the soil.

They talked about politics, people, sunsets and fall leaves, the way children play when they're in public and no one is watching. They debated the merits of various movies, funeral rites, religion versus spiritual thought, and hot dogs – she preferred ketchup and relish only, while he insisted on having it all, from onions to chili.

Eventually, the conversation drifted to really important matters, like music, babies, and marigolds.

While they talked, her fingers strayed upward, to the gold pendant he wore, shining warm against his coffee skin. She pushed herself up on one elbow to look closely. It was a small spiral, resting above a larger gold ring. An elongated figure eight ran from top to bottom, bisecting the circle. She traced its contours with her fingertip. "What's this?"

"The *anam pratik*, a symbol of our people." He ran a fingertip over the spiral. "This is a very old symbol, representing the cycle of life – birth, death, and rebirth." His fingers slid down to hold the edges of the circle below. "The open circle has several meanings. As a circle, it represents the unending nature of our souls, our minds. It also denotes *e'drai*, the open mind, and some say the open third eye – if you go in for Eastern thought." He smiled. "I rather do, myself."

Rhiannon touched the figure eight in the center of the ring. "What about this?"

He dropped the pendant to his chest, began caressing the hair back from her face. "It's an infinity symbol, on its side. Again, representing the eternal nature of aeternans. It's also an empty hourglass – an hourglass whose sands can never run out." He smiled. "I've also seen the hourglass completely filled, incapable of running out. And some Eldest still use the older symbols, a phoenix, or the ouroboros – a snake devouring its own tail." He shrugged. "They all mean the same thing."

Rhiannon touched the pendant. "It's beautiful." She looked up into his eyes, smiling. "It's a whole culture, like Egyptians or something. But it's like discovering ancient Egyptians for the first time, and it turns out they're still around after thousands of years." She laughed. "Secret Egyptians."

He grinned. "I know a man who was an Egyptian pharaoh, his incarnations went back that far. He has a passion for sand. Beaches, you know."

She laughed. They began discussing tropical destinations then, and the conversation spun out from there, covering vast oceans, the Aloha Spirit, whether kindness and generosity were natural to the human species, or learned behaviors. They smiled until their faces ached with it, and almost, but not quite, discovered a heretofore unknown method of kissing.

When they got to the subject of language, she asked about the aeternan tongue, the words, their origins.

"We don't have a specific language," he replied, his hand tracing lazy circles on her back. "Instead, we have shared words to describe things unique to our culture." He chuckled. "And those words are bastardizations, an illegitimate mish-mash of words from languages and cultures all over the world."

She lay curled against his body, her head on his chest, the warmth of him somehow safe, necessary. Her fingers traced the dark whorls of hair on his chest. "What do you mean, unique to your culture?"

"Our culture," he whispered, and even without looking at his face, she could tell he was smiling.

"Okay," she laughed, "Our culture."

"Well, we have our own ideas about things, about what's important. Some of that derives from the reality of our existence — words like *e'drai*, for example — but some of it is just things you learn after a couple thousand years on the planet. And, I guess, some things are a little of both."

She ran her fingertips across his chest, tracing circles around his flat nipples, looking up into his face. "Like what?"

He grinned. "We have 48 names for different types of lovemaking."

Her eyes widened, then she laughed. "Like Eskimos have all those words for snow."

"That's a myth. Eskimos have no more words for snow than those who speak English." He stroked her hair, smiling. "But I spent an incarnation as a Northern Sami, in Norway. Now, the Sami people, they actually do have hundreds of words for snow."

"You lived in Norway."

"Yes. Beautiful place, in a desolate way. Huge. I helped my father herd reindeer, until the Remembering. Then I sought out my true Family." He shrugged. "But that was more than a thousand years ago."

She caught her breath, swallowed hard. "You've lived that long?"

"Yes." He kissed her forehead. "But let's get back to *era*, lovemaking. Much nicer than reindeer."

She tilted her face up for a proper kiss, savoring the taste and feel of him. Then she pulled back, looking into his eyes, beguiling, seductive. "Can you show me these 48 kinds of lovemaking?"

His smile was slow, lazy, steeped in sin. "There are many I could show you, though probably not all of them tonight."

"Only many?"

He shook his head. "I don't want to show you *era'dr'noch*, which is lovemaking to say good-bye for a long time. And logistically, we can't make *era'tau'kai* work, which is lovemaking in front of a large audience."

She blushed furiously at her swift, instinctive reaction to the latter idea.

He slid down to kiss her collarbones, his lips drifting southward. *"For tonight,"* his words sounded in her mind, his lips exalting the swell of her breast, *"We'll practice the art of era'cahres, lovemaking with a loved one, a friend."* Even in her mind, she could hear his lascivious purr. *"And perhaps era'nour ... I have some chocolate sauce and raspberries in the kitchen. These —"* he flicked his tongue across her nipples, *"would look wonderful in raspberries."*

But *era* would wait. Raspberries and chocolate evolved into a late night banquet, both suddenly famished as they pawed through the refrigerator, exclaiming with pleasure over the seemingly miraculous discovery of cheeses and meats, grapes, crusty fresh bread. She helped him carry their treasure back to the bed, along with a bottle of cold, crisp wine. A previously discarded blanket became a naked picnic ground, and they laughed, talked with their mouths full too often, toasted and teased, while the night air stirred the open curtains.

Rhiannon felt like she was living in one of her dreams, root nourishment for her lonely soul, leaving her breathless, bursting with joy when she woke — while Zerik simply felt like he'd come back to something he didn't know had been missing, the lack made stark only in the presence of fulfillment.

Leaving the bed and their impromptu picnic, she wandered to the open balcony doors, the sheer curtains fluttering, framing her as she stood nude against the night sky. Zerik sat amidst the wreckage of their meal, watching her. Her olive brown skin was smooth, unblemished, her petite curves soft over a layer of gentle muscle. She'd grown quiet, thoughtful. He studied her profile, as she stared out over the city. He'd known many beautiful women. She was especially lovely, her face almost elfin, with those huge brown eyes.

She was spared perfection by a slightly crooked nose, as though it had been broken once. The idea of her being hurt was deeply disquieting.

"What are you thinking?" he asked.

She turned and smiled, seraphic, a tawny Venus in the dim light. "I was thinking that I don't want to go to sleep, because I don't want to wake up."

His answering smile was gentle. "I won't let you wake up then."

She laughed and returned to the bed. Retrieving the wine and glasses, he gathered up the remainder of their feast, setting the food on the floor next to the bed, tossing the blanket in a heap on the carpet. Grinning, he pulled her down onto the mattress, holding her close against the length of his body, savoring the feel of her warm skin against his. He buried his face in the fragrant cloud of her hair, pressing his lips to the top of her head. *"You feel so good,"* he sighed, sending the words to her as thought.

"So do you," she thought, in response. After a few moments, when he failed to reply, she looked up into his face, questioning. Aloud, she asked, "Can't you hear my thoughts, the way I can hear yours?"

He pulled back, propping himself in the pillows on one arm, looking down at her. "No, I can't."

Her forehead wrinkled, confused. "But you're a telepath."

Zerik laughed. "That's a modern word. My *e'drai* is a Speaking-Sharing gift – *loqui'su'dar'itae.*" He stroked her cheek, her arm, her hip. "But it's not like in the movies or on TV. I can send messages, but I can't receive. Not very handy, much of the time. Being Eldest, I have strength, so I can send messages to those in my immediate vicinity with relative ease. But when I go for distance, it takes a lot of my energy. It can be really exhausting. But it has saved lives, on more than one occasion."

A chill slithered up her spine. "Why would you need to save lives?"

"Because there are those who hunt us. Who have hunted us since the beginning. For many reasons." He shook his head. "So many reasons." He sounded suddenly weary, old.

She snuggled closer, wanting to tell him about the man who hunted her, afraid to give voice to it. "Speak the name of the devil, and he'll appear," Rosa used to say. Words had the power to conjure so many hurts into being.

Instead, she said, "I thought you could hear my thoughts too."

His fingertips traced the curve of her hip, looking into her eyes. "Why did you think that?"

She blushed, looked down at his chest. "When we — I mean, when we were making love, you spoke to me, and ..."

Understanding dawned. "Yes, you responded. You told me you weren't afraid, and I heard you then." He tipped up her chin with his forefinger, smiling into her eyes. Her hair was softly curled dark silk, framing her sylphine face, those huge expressive eyes. His eyes wandered lower, her nipples and aureola rosy brown, mouthwatering. Distracting. He met her gaze again. "During *era*, you saw how our auras joined. Our *e'drai* join similarly."

Rhiannon sat up, staring at him. "I don't understand."

Zerik laughed, he couldn't help himself. "It only works if one actually wields the *e'drai* – you can't share a latent gift. So when we join in *era*, I can't use your gifts – only the *e'drai* you choose to share during that moment."

"Oh," she said. She looked relieved somehow. Zerik studied her face, appraising. Megan Byrne was an enigma, offering herself openly in so many ways, and yet her hidden roots went far deeper than the persona she allowed.

Watching her eyes, he said, "Usually, Eldest have very strong *e'drai*." He rubbed his chin thoughtfully. "As I said, one of my *e'drai* is the ability to sense the scope of others' gifts. And from what I can feel, you are very, very powerful."

She looked down, snuggled against his body again, as though clinging to his warmth.

"And the *e'drai* you've mastered just doesn't reflect the sheer intensity of your power. Either you haven't told me about all of your gifts, or you have yet to recognize all of your *e'drai*." He shook his head. "I'm not sure I understand it. But I'd like to."

Fighting an inexplicable panic, she stroked his chest, pressed a kiss to his chin. "Can't we talk about something else? I don't know why I'm the way I am."

But he wouldn't let it go. "I don't know why you're afraid to talk about this, but you know you're safe with me, don't you?" She nodded without speaking. "I know you have other *e'drai*, gifts. What else can you do?"

She looked away. "Um... I can nudge people. But it's wrong to do it."

"Nudge?"

"I can touch someone, find a feeling or thought, something they already have, and nudge them in that direction." She looked defensive. "It only works if they were already thinking that way to begin with — I can't make people do things they weren't already thinking of doing." She shrugged. "I just help them make up their minds."

"Show me."

She looked at him in surprise. "What do you mean? You want me to nudge *you*?"

"Yes." He gazed at her steadily, serious, calm.

She looked at him doubtfully. "Okay, if you want me to."

He closed his eyes, waiting.

"You don't have to close your eyes," she said. "I can do it with you watching."

Eyes still closed, he smiled. "I want to be able to focus. My *e'drai* allows me to feel what you're doing, to sense the power you're using."

"Oh." She took a deep breath and reached out with her left hand, laid her fingers on his wrist.

Outwardly, her face went blank, as she pulled information, a flood of emotion, feeling. Golden yellow curiosity, deep blue weariness, concern and kindness in swirling shades of rose and white. With a flash, she felt a wave of shifting gold and red, his lust, passion, desire. Wickedly, she took those feelings and pushed, expanded them, nudged them over into fullness.

In a surge of electrifying power, he was suddenly consumed with desperate need, hunger, his body straining and aching.

"Oh my God," he breathed. He opened his eyes and looked into hers, his smile feral. "Do that again."

Sometime later, he moved over her body, tasting, his quick fingers everywhere at once, their bodies a sheen of sweat and radiant light, as their mutual auras coalesced into an effulgent nimbus. He rolled into a sitting position, pulling her onto his lap, her full breasts pressed against his chest, holding himself just outside the sodden fever of her body. They paused then, breathing heavily, and he looked into her eyes. *"Nudge me now,* varenya," he whispered in her mind. *"Do it again."*

"Yes," she thought, staring back at him, her chest heaving. Her slick skin against his, their mutual light so intimately fused, she could sense him instantly, his feelings now so close to hers. Gasping, trembling with her own hunger, she grabbed the gold and red, so large now it almost blocked out everything else. She took his euphoria, his lust, his joy, and thrust it wide, amplified it.

Clutching her hips, he pushed inside her at that moment, as her *e'drai* joined with his. Her own desire blossomed, doubling, trebling, her body overflowing with heat. She was swamped with the electric tingling rush of her own power, flooding back to her through him.

She threw back her head and cried out with the intensity of it, while he roared his approval, within her mind and without.

The bus to San Francisco left the station in Topeka at 8:45 in the morning. Stops were planned across the country, everywhere from Rock Springs, Wyoming, to Winnemucca, Nevada. By the time passengers traveling to San Francisco arrived at their final destination, they would spend a grueling 37 hours on the bus, hellish by any definition, regardless of the free Wi-Fi access. Thirty-seven hours staring through the tinted windows, watching fields, rugged mountains, the Utah salt flats, all passing at a tedious pace – while trying to ignore the vague scent of the chemical toilet, the cacophony of unruly children, snoring old men.

But while the San Francisco passengers were already enjoying a scant 20 minute rest-stop in Salina, Kansas, trying to find time to use the restroom, buy a soggy ham and cheese sandwich from the concession stand, and still walk around, futilely stretching muscles destined to be re-kinked, Rhiannon was blissfully sleeping in an extravagant penthouse bedroom, sprawled inelegantly on her belly, snoring.

Something woke her; she didn't know what, exactly. Her first thought was that she hadn't dreamed, had slept deep and true. She opened her eyes, coming to focus on her old purple duffle bag, sitting on a chair. For a moment, there was a cruel stab of disappointment, a bleak millisecond of belief that she was back at the Topeka U-Rest Motel, and perhaps she'd dreamed after all.

"I said I wouldn't let you wake up," came a thought in her mind. *"It's the only promise I will ever break."*

She rolled over to see Zerik lounging in bed next to her, smiling lazily. He'd been watching her sleep for over an hour. Awash with relief and effervescent happiness, she kissed him, morning breath be damned. "Naked man in my bed. My favorite way to start the day."

If Rhiannon was a Greyhound bus leaving Topeka, Kansas, at 55 miles per hour, and Zerik was a high-speed train leaving San Francisco at 98 miles per hour, their instantaneous collision would call into question almost all laws of time and space, but perhaps have profound quantum significance.

They breakfasted on the wide, sun-drenched balcony, she wrapped in his silk robe, he in loose-fitting black pajama pants, bare-chested. The table had been prepared ahead of time, spread with crisp white linen, set with sparkling china and silver, and a crystal vase bearing a small bouquet of scarlet roses. Lifting silver covers, they found buttery, hot omelets with spinach and brie, thick slices of maple-cured bacon, sausages, toast, and raspberry crepes, plus fresh melon, bananas, oranges, and grapes, wonderfully strong coffee, several kinds of tea, and fresh-squeezed orange juice.

"Where did all of this come from?" she asked. "It's like I've died and gone to Lady Astor's."

His laugh was deep, hearty. "She was such a bitch."

She stopped short, stared. "We can talk about your personal relationship with a dead rich woman another time." She shook her head. "Seriously, did you do all of this?"

He grinned unrepentantly. "No, Charles did. He's the *Kir* here at the *Maisonsur*, the Safehouse."

She thought about that for a moment, something tugging at her memory. "You mean the one who decorated the fancy elevator."

"Yes."

"Who used to be a woman."

"Yes." Zerik's smile was large enough to put a bus into.

Rhiannon sighed, pouring herself a cup of coffee. "I've woken up, but I'm still dreaming."

He laughed again, and she couldn't hide her answering smile.

The invisible Charles had apparently thought of everything. In addition to the splendid breakfast, their messy bedroom picnic from the night before had vanished from the floor, the blanket washed and folded neatly. Further, he had arranged for Rhiannon's duffle bag to be rescued from the U-Rest, and when she opened the bag later, all of her clothes had been freshly laundered and pressed. "I just have to meet this Charles guy," she muttered, while Zerik laughed.

They bathed in a decadent car-wash style shower, featuring six water heads spaced evenly around the roomy, slate-tiled enclosure, and in which Zerik expertly demonstrated the many delights of *era't'stom*. For hours afterward she was unable to look at his mouth without blushing, to his great amusement.

But as Rhiannon was dressing, pulling on her old jeans and a faded blue T-shirt, the whispers of reality that had been skittering around in the back of her mind coalesced into something solid, tangible. Perhaps it was the feel of her clothes, the fabrics which covered who she had always been, the woman reflected in the mirror someone who had nothing but fear to wear.

Coming down to Earth is sometimes a violent crash, but more often a slow sinking descent, with every reminder of the past, every misgiving about the future, every self-criticism and agonizing doubt weighting the soul as it falls.

Rhiannon looked at herself — outwardly the same person she'd always been, too curly hair and a crooked nose, a weird half-Irish, half-Columbian girl who talked too much, saw too much. A mental patient with a golden luminescence radiating from her skin, a glow no one else could see. A woman who, underneath all of that, believed in the impossible anyhow, believed in love and magic, believed there was something more to who she was, in the face of continuing evidence to the contrary. A woman who clung to hope, because without it, life was desolate, unbearable.

And yet deeper still, hiding in the tenebrous depths within, a scared little girl knew with wounded, cynical certainty that her heart was tilting at windmills, choosing to believe solely because the alternative was simply to die.

Her reflection stared back at her, lost. While, on some level, her heart was still soaring, the child within wasn't ready to accept that it was all real after all. One night of lovemaking and fairy tales did not instantly manifest some utopian future. What would she do now? Where would she go? She knew what her heart wanted, to stay with Zerik and learn more about his people – her people – to pretend she was wealthy as an empress and luxuriate in *era* all day long.

But bitterness and doubt whispered, mocking and derisive, sibilant questions about men and women, one-night-stands, and foolish women who put significance on such brief connections. Serotonin- and dopamine-fueled, rose-colored perception rarely had any bearing on reality.

And the fear was waiting, a black pool floating beneath her consciousness, icy waters defying breath. Whoever *He* was, he was still out there, still looking for her, undoubtedly taking sickening gratification in the pursuit.

Standing before the full-length mirror, Rhiannon could only gaze at her slight frame, her faded second-hand clothes, her bare feet small and dark in the creamy plush carpet, could only try to remember how to breathe.

Zerik appeared in the mirror behind her, strong and capable, unflappable and kind. "You're upset," he said, putting an arm around her.

She turned into his embrace, burying her face in his chest. "I missed my bus."

He chuckled a little, stroked her hair. "You don't know what to do now. Feel all at sea, I expect."

"I thought you couldn't read my mind." Her answer was muffled, her face still pressed against his body. She sniffled. Lord, she was crying. How embarrassing.

"I can't. But your face was pretty legible." He seemed content to just hold her there, warm, safe.

"I'm sorry," she croaked, wiping her eyes with the back of her hand. "I'm getting your shirt all wet."

"I'm sure Charles can find me a new one."

Rhiannon laughed at that, still sniffling. "Good old Charles." She pulled back to look up at him. "I'm sorry," she repeated. "I just don't know what to do with myself. Everything has changed so fast, and part of me feels like I'm still back where I started. But the rest of me is different." She shook her head. "And I don't know where I stand with you, with the world." She was babbling, she couldn't stop, her fears like a river swollen with snowmelt, thoughts tumbling one over another in an uncontrollable rush. "What am I going to do with myself? Now that I know these things, I want to learn more. I thought if I found out the truth about myself, everything would make sense. But I feel more lost than ever. Where do I belong? Where do I fit in? I never fit in the real world, but where do I fit in this one? I want to feel safe. I want to know more. I want to feel the way I do with you all the time."

To her mortification, she started crying anew, and she pressed her face to his chest again.

His arms squeezed a little tighter for a moment. He slowly stroked her hair, from her scalp to her shoulders, and back again. "Megan, this situation is different for me, too. You're not the typical neonate. Normally we invite new Family to stay at the *Maisonsur* for a time, to get acclimated, to learn to use their *e'drai*, if any, to find their place." He rubbed her shoulders, pulled her away from his chest, so he could look into her eyes. "This is your incarnation, your life, and you get to make your own decisions. You're a big girl, as I believe you explained to me." He smiled.

She wiped her eyes furiously. "How can I make a decision when I don't even know what my choices are?"

"True," he said calmly. He tipped her chin up, lowered his lips to hers in a fleeting, gentle kiss, before meeting her eyes again. "As I said, this situation is different for me, too. There is an undeniable connection between us, which is a little strange for me, but I'm not running away from it, either."

She offered a tremulous smile. "Oh, good, I'm glad it's not just me."

He laughed. "No. Hardly. But aside from the personal connection, you are unusual in other ways – your intense *e'drai*, your Eldest aura. And I told you I'd like to help you find the truth about yourself, and I mean that." He took a deep breath. "So if you want me to take you to the bus station, I'll do that. But what I'd really like to do is invite you to my home, my *dzina*, my own personal family within the Family. The *Kir* of my *dzina* is a very powerful woman, and I think she might be able to help you, or at least help you figure out what to do next."

She stared at him incredulously. "Let me get this straight. You want to take me home to meet your parents?"

He laughed. "No. I want to take you home to meet my wives. And my husband."

Rhiannon stared at him openmouthed for a long moment, then began stripping off her clothing.

"What are you doing?"

She looked at him sharply. "As you pointed out earlier, some things are easier to talk about in bed."

Eternal Tales: The King's Child

Once, in the time before memory, the King of the Faeries was walking through the wild wood. He came upon a crystal-clear pool in a clearing. A mortal woman called Alessa was bathing in the pool. The King of the Faeries was transfixed by her beauty, and watched her from the darkness of the wood.

Every day for seven days, Alessa came to bathe in the forest pool, and every day for seven days, the Faerie King secretly watched her.

Finally, on the seventh day, the Faerie King could keep hidden no more. He approached Alessa as she stepped from the pool, declaring his eternal love for her, singing praises of her golden hair, her skin like first snowfall, her cornflower-blue eyes, her cheeks as the first blush of dawn.

Alessa was terrified of the Faerie King, part man, part beast, part forest tree. She made to run from him, but he captured her with a Word whispered on the wind, and carried her off into the wild wood.

For seven months, Alessa's mother and father searched for her. Finally, they stopped looking, thinking her dead, drowned in the forest pool. Yet they never stopped grieving her loss.

Seven years to the day after she vanished, a man appeared on her parents' doorstep. He was wrapped in a dark brown cloak of winter branches, wood, and earth, revealing only a face of frighteningly pure beauty, and eyes the color of new leaves.

A child peeked from behind the stranger's cloak, with Alessa's golden hair and rosy cheeks, but green eyes the color of new leaves. The stranger said the boy was the child of the Faerie King and the lost Alessa, who had died birthing him.

His words were like wind and rough bark, dust and sunset. "The Faeries have given Alessa's child the Word. The dryads of the forests will always listen to him. To mortals, his speech will be clear as the forest pool. As the son of the Faerie King, he is immortal, but as the son of a mortal woman, he must follow human footsteps on this Earth."

The stranger melted as mist into the wood, leaving the boy with his grandparents. They named him for his mother, and raised him in the Light.

It is said that he still walks the Earth today, and speaks the Word to all.

And they lived ever after.

SEVEN

There is a vast necropolis, a City of the Silent, a city of the dead. Its hills and valleys are populated with angels, weeping and triumphant. And beneath the angels, beneath carved stones and careful pathways, below the hushed chapels, tumuli, and columbariums, almost 2 million fragile husks lie deep, once splendid houses for souls long flown.

Massive old tombs feature intricate bronze doors, multihued stained-glass windows, marble enclosures for whole families with bronze handles, black with time and the damp air. Modern grave markers lie flat against the earth, granite incised by machine sandblasting, finished by hand. Small marble and granite stones, carved with lambs and cherubs, mark the graves of children. One place is reserved for circus folk; sedate, traditional stones carved with names like Edward "Blinky" Davis.

Death, relentless, is an equal-opportunity unemployer.

Chinese, Japanese, Italian, Irish, German, Greek, Serbian, Catholic, Jew, Protestant, and more – even furry friends, pets – are represented and welcome in the 16 cemeteries that comprise almost

75 percent of the land in the necropolis, Colma, California. The scant half-mile of land remaining offers an automobile dealership, a pizza chain, a locksmith, a podiatrist, and a Pier 1 Imports. Life goes on, and it needs wicker papasan chairs and cobalt blue wineglasses from Mexico.

It is remarkably easy to drive past the Colma exit, to spend a lifetime traveling to somewhere and from someplace else, never aware of the millions of sleepers lying in the hills beyond. In a place as overpopulated as California, in an area where land is more precious than gold, the cemeteries are often silent, the only movement a breath of warm wind in the tree branches, the only sound the nearby freeway, as the world streams urgently by.

Colma, once called Lawndale, is situated less than 10 miles south of downtown San Francisco. In 1902, the City by the Bay passed an ordinance outlawing the construction of cemeteries in the city, due primarily to increased property values – though no doubt encouraged by San Francisco's severely limited land mass, hemmed in on three sides by water. The city grew up and around cemeteries originally built on the edges of town, graveyards in which embalming was not yet standard practice, body theft for surgeons common, and the stench of decay strong. In another ordinance in 1912, San Francisco evicted all existing cemeteries from the city limits. Colma was born, a city of cemeteries.

San Francisco's ordinances coincided with a change taking place in the United States, a change in the way people understood death. Embalming began to be commonplace, and this allowed mourners greater time to plan funerals, to arrange suitable tributes for their loved ones, to take time to grieve. Victorians approached death as a kind of emotional art form. Elaborate rituals and rules for funerals and mourning were created, covering every detail, including what sort of black fabric a widow must wear and for how many years, to endless romantic poetry connecting death with beauty, souls to heaven.

Cemetery gardens were created, sophisticated graveyards landscaped with trees and grass, flowers, fountains, reflecting pools, and sculpture. Angels took frozen flight in the hills. Families were encouraged to walk amongst the gravestones and statues, to pause and reflect, to recognize the peace and beauty that death brought, to remember the achievements of man. Colma was one such place, a peaceful spot of beauty and remembrance.

A train brought the deceased and mourners from San Francisco to Colma, with a special comfortable car for widows and family.

Death was immediate for Victorians, personal. Modern death takes place in hospitals and nursing homes, hospices. The dead are taken away, unseen and sanitized, cremated, gone. But for Victorians, death most often occurred at home, sometimes after long illness. The family, themselves, washed and dressed the body, laid it out for viewing, made arrangements.

Children died with horrifying frequency. Marriages rarely lasted many years, regularly ending with the death of a spouse. Death was common, a constant occurrence. It happened all the time, often without warning. Victorians were close to death, and they sought to make sense of it. They took sepia photos of themselves with their dead, *memento mori*. They tried to create an afterlife that made sense, to codify the grieving process in order to gain some control over it. They embraced death, rather than running from it. Or driving beyond it.

And while the modern world speeds past the silent, bucolic Victorian pleasure gardens of Colma, the angels wait with arms outstretched, turning blind eyes to heaven, a mute bequest reminding that even now, for some, death is astonishing and sudden.

Zerik helped Rhiannon out of the rented car. She'd been surprised; after leaving the San Francisco airport, it had only been a 15 minute drive to Colma. She was glad Zerik knew where he was going. It would have been easy to miss the exit, to never see the necropolis, just drive past.

They turned to survey the hillside, densely crowded with headstones and tombs, recessed walkways between rows of monuments, sarcophagi, catafalques, broken columns, pillars, obelisks, sculpted draped urns, curved exedra benches adorned with stone flowers and leaves. The bright summer sunshine seemed merrily inappropriate.

"Oh my God," Rhiannon pivoted on the spot, looking at the seemingly endless rows of headstones all around. "We'll never find my grave."

Zerik put a hand on her shoulder. "We'll find it."

The Hills of Eternity Memorial Park in Colma was one of several Jewish cemeteries in town, and while a records search indicated that Katania Ann Weiss was indeed buried here, the exact location of the grave was not available.

Rhiannon looked at the map they'd picked up at the Colma City Hall, which offered directions to the graves of most of Colma's more famous inhabitants, including William Randolph Hearst, Levi Strauss, and members of the Hell's Angels, among a great many others. "I guess this isn't going to do us much good," she grimaced.

They had the entire cemetery to themselves, for the most part. A few rows up the hill, they could see a woman wearing a pink baseball cap, moving slowly, reading the headstones, clearly looking for a specific grave, as they were. At that moment, she looked up and saw Rhiannon and Zerik standing next to their black SUV. She smiled and waved, walking toward them.

"Hi!" she called. "I'm not interrupting your grief or anything am I?" She grinned.

"*If we were in mourning,*" Zerik whispered in Rhiannon's mind, "*It would already be too late.*"

Rhiannon tried to keep a straight face. "Don't make me laugh," she hissed under her breath. To the approaching woman, she replied, "No, we're just looking for an old family member's grave."

The woman stopped in front of Rhiannon, smiling brightly, an odd contrast to the somber atmosphere. She had short greying hair and bright blue eyes, wore jeans and a T-shirt that read, "I went to Alcatraz and all I got was this lousy T-shirt," in addition to the breast-cancer research pink baseball cap. She gave Zerik a friendly glance, then looked back to Rhiannon, sticking out her hand. "Hi, I'm Nancy Holliday. From Arizona."

Rhiannon shook her hand. "I'm Megan."

"Where did you get that?" Nancy nodded toward the cemetery map Rhiannon held.

Rhiannon looked down at the map, then back to Nancy Holliday's friendly, rapt face. "Oh, they give these out at City Hall." She shrugged. "Honestly, it's not much help finding graves, unless you're looking for someone famous."

Nancy Holliday's face brightened, if that was possible. "I am! I'm looking for Wyatt Earp's grave. He's supposed to be buried here."

Zerik looked dubious. "This is a Jewish cemetery."

"Yeah!" Nancy enthused. "His wife Josie was Jewish. He's buried with her." She planted one hand on her ample hip, waving the other expressively. "Most people don't know that. My great-aunt was a cousin of Doc Holliday, and she actually saw the real gunfight at the OK Corral." She dug into the pocket of her jeans, pulled out an old bullet casing. "Look at this! This is from that gunfight. I brought it to put on Wyatt Earp's grave." She grinned. "Is that cool, or what?"

Rhiannon couldn't help but smile. "That's very cool." She held out the map. "Here, you take this. I bet Wyatt Earp is on there somewhere. We can't use it anyhow."

Nancy Holliday accepted the map wide-eyed, almost reverently. "You sure you don't need it?"

Zerik laughed. "No, seriously. Take it."

The woman favored him with another winsome smile. "Thank you guys so much." She shook Rhiannon's hand again. "Good luck finding the grave you want." She turned away, studying the map, her forehead creased in concentration.

"You're welcome," Rhiannon called after her. Nancy waved, walking up the hill, toward the right. Rhiannon turned to Zerik. "Well, at least someone will find what they're looking for."

He put his arm around her shoulders, kissed her forehead. "We'll find it. I promise. We'll stay here until we do. My family's nest is only a few hours from here. We have plenty of time."

She tilted up her face, pressed a kiss to his lips. "Thank you."

Zerik scanned the area around them, the sheer number of memorials daunting. Everywhere they looked were headstones adorned with menorahs, Stars of David, yahrtzeit lamps, ewers,

Cohanim hands, curtains, doors, gates, stone books, horses, lions and doves, even small photographs of the deceased sealed behind glass. "Let's split up." He waved a hand up the hill. "You take that side, and I'll take this one."

Sighing, Rhiannon nodded, and began walking up the hill.

Nancy Holliday stood in front of Wyatt Earp's final resting place, a black granite stone with Western-style lettering. Unconsciously, her lips moved as she silently read the epitaph: "...That nothing's so sacred as honor, and nothing so loyal as love!" Nancy smiled. "That's real nice," she said aloud.

She fished in her pocket for the bullet casing, brought with such care from Arizona. Maybe it wasn't really from the OK Corral, but maybe it was. It was the thought that counted, right? Stooping, she placed it on the headstone's base, next to a candle and a few coins left by other visitors.

She straightened, red-faced and a little winded, and almost screamed. Standing behind the tombstone was a man. Where had he come from? "Hey, you startled me," Nancy said, smiling at him. She looked a little more closely. He was a weird one. Tall, bald as an egg, wearing a hooded sweatshirt beneath an old, brown leather jacket. He was pale, so pale it looked as though he never saw the sun at all. Even more peculiar, he had a tattoo on his forehead, a black triangle about an inch high, just above his nose. His piercing eyes were black, utterly cold, his face like carved marble.

"Only in San Francisco," Nancy thought nervously. Outwardly, she offered her cheerful grin. "I'm Nancy Holliday." She stuck out her chubby hand. "You come to see Wyatt Earp's grave, too? My great aunt was a cousin of Doc Holliday, and — "

The man moved around the headstone, fast, too fast. People shouldn't move like that. Nancy Holliday was suddenly afraid. Every nerve sang with fear, electric and icy, slithering through her veins. She looked up at the man, now standing a scant 10 inches from her. His face, his eyes, hadn't changed, hadn't moved. He stared down at her, his bleak gaze devoid of any feeling.

Nancy took a step backward, risked a look over her shoulder, glanced around the cemetery, the elegant Victorian gardens, hoping to see that nice couple with the map. But she seemed completely alone, in the bright sun amidst the stones and the dead.

Taking another step backward, she felt her skin tingling, sensing his proximity, and looked back at the tattooed man – who had followed her with each step, now still inches away, watching her with his face like frigid stone.

Nancy Holliday began to shake. "Please," she whispered. "I don't know what you want, but as God is my witness – "

The man reached out with unnatural speed, grasping Nancy Holliday's head with long, pale fingers, and snapped her neck. Her body dropped to the grass, lifeless, twisted unnaturally in the sunshine.

"My witness," the man echoed, his rasping susurration both reverent and grimly content.

Rhiannon was meandering through her fifth row of graves, reading each headstone, stopping to admire a granite stone shaped like a grand piano, complete with etched keys and a bar of music, and a picture of a smiling older woman, her name and epitaph in Hebrew.

"I think I found it," came Zerik's thought in her mind. *"I'm on the other side, seventh row, sort of in the middle."*

Walking quickly, Rhiannon crossed the narrow road running up the center of the cemetery, counting rows, until she spotted Zerik half-hidden by an obelisk some way ahead. She waved. He smiled, returning the gesture.

She was a little out of breath when she caught up to him. Zerik was standing in front of a headstone, his blue silk shirt vivid against the red granite. Engraved into the stone was the name – her name. Katania Ann Weiss. Rhiannon caught her breath. There was an oval photo, encased in glass, the image of a young woman with dark hair. "That's me," Rhiannon breathed, stunned. While Kat Weiss looked nothing like the way Rhiannon looked now, in this lifetime, it was nonetheless a painfully familiar face, one she'd seen every day in the mirror. A happy face.

Zerik didn't say anything, just put his arm around her, gazing at the photo.

"It was real." Rhiannon laughed. "I mean, after meeting you, I knew that, but I guess it's just something else to see it. Physical evidence. Undeniable."

"I understand," Zerik said. He pointed to the flat surface on top of the headstone. Three round stones were sitting there, including one larger rock that looked like quartz. "You've had visitors."

Rhiannon's eyes widened. Following Jewish tradition, someone – three someones – had placed a stone on her grave, sending the silent message: "I was here."

She looked at Zerik, a little embarrassed. "I haven't told you about this yet, but now's as good a time as any."

"Told me what?" Zerik looked at her curiously.

Wiping her damp palms on her jeans, Rhiannon closed her eyes, took a deep breath, found her focus. Time slowed, a second becoming a minute, longer. She dove into the deep warm darkness within herself, seeking the threads of white, silver, gold, pulling them together into a tapestry of glowing energy. She drew the energy up through the velvet darkness, through her arms and legs, into her chest, holding it there, allowing it to grow, expand, throb with power. Dimly, she heard Zerik's sudden intake of breath as he felt her *e'drai*, but held her focus on the power.

Finally she released the energy to slide down her arm, into her left hand, and she opened her eyes. Her hand was radiating gold light and energy, shimmering vivid and bright in the sunlight.

She reached out to Kat Weiss' tombstone, laying her luminous, shining fingers on the large quartz stone.

Weeping, weeping, one year today, a headstone for my kindella, child of my heart, your mother wanted you buried in Brooklyn I told her no California you had to run, that Dybbuk didn't get my girl, oh I miss you so, one year, I will never stop missing my girl, a stone for your grave, a stone from your Bubby, I love you

Rhiannon released the stone with a gasp, tears trickling down her cheeks. "My grandmother." Her grandmother had always believed her, believed an evil soul, a Dybbuk, was hunting Kat. She flicked her hand into the air, releasing the energy without thought. She searched the ground, picking up a small tawny rock, little more than a pebble of softly rounded sandstone. Carefully, she placed it on the headstone next to the quartz rock from Kat Weiss' grandmother, left so many years before.

When Rhiannon turned, she found Zerik waiting. He held her then, his arms safe and strong, warm through her thin T-shirt. He didn't say anything about her *e'drai*, though she knew he'd felt it, through the power of his own gift, felt what she was doing.

Instead, he said, "It's okay to mourn the you that was. Kat couldn't remember; she wasn't you."

"No, she couldn't remember. But she could see auras. My aura."

"What?" He stilled.

"She could see her own aura – this –" she held out her arm, the glowing *fainna* radiating from her skin. "She could see it in others too, didn't know what it meant." She looked away. "And she was afraid."

Zerik didn't say anything, just held her tighter. And thought. Something important nagged at the back of his consciousness, but dissipated when he tried to grasp it, cobweb and vapor.

They stayed there for long minutes, Rhiannon content to just rest her cheek against his chest, crying a little for her long-dead grandmother, listening to the wind in the cypress trees, smelling the sun-warmed grass and flowers adorning graves. In the distance, the hum of the freeway was lulling, gentle. Zerik kissed the top of her head and stroked her back gently.

Finally, she pulled away slightly, enough to see his face, still safe in the circle of his arms. That was when she saw him. Behind Zerik, not ten feet away, a man stood watching them. He was short, dark-skinned, wearing a brown leather jacket. His head was shaved, and he had the strangest tattoo, a black triangle in the middle of his forehead, just above his eyes. His eyes were most startling, black, glacial. Almost dead. Frightening. Rhiannon didn't need to *look* at him to know there was something very wrong about the man.

She met Zerik's eye. "There's a man behind you," she whispered urgently.

In one fast, graceful motion, Zerik spun around, pushing Rhiannon behind him at the same time. Protecting her. But there was no one there, just the still stones and the sky.

Rhiannon peeked from behind Zerik's solid body, clinging to his shirt. "He was there a second ago, really!" She flushed with embarrassment. "There was something about him. Something scary."

Zerik turned back to her, holding her shoulders, gazing steadily into her eyes. "What did he look like?"

Rhiannon ran a hand through her hair, exasperated. "Weird. He was dark, kind of short – he was bald and had a tattoo on his face."

Zerik felt his blood turn to ice. "What kind of tattoo? Where?"

She shook her head. "I didn't see it in detail, but it looked like a black triangle. On his forehead."

Zerik fought to remain calm. Panicking wouldn't do either of them any good. "I need you to listen to me very carefully. We have to get out of here. I'm going to see if I can find him – he must have headed up the hill."

She felt a wave of alarm, dismay. "You're leaving me?"

Zerik nodded. "I have to find him, if I can. I need you to go down to the SUV and stay there. Lock the doors."

"Who is he? What's going on?" she demanded, clutching his sleeve.

"I can't explain right now. But we aren't safe." He clutched her hand, and she could feel his tension, fear. He pressed the keyless remote for the SUV into her hand. "Just go down to the car. Hurry. I'll be with you soon." Without waiting for additional discussion, he turned and sprinted up the hill.

Rhiannon needed no further urging. She ran to the end of the row, terror high and tight in her chest. She couldn't imagine what would frighten Zerik, always so relaxed, a thousand years of experience rendering him imperturbable in any situation. At the thought, her fear redoubled, and she nearly fell headlong as she ran down the hill toward the waiting SUV.

Breathing hard, Zerik ducked behind a tomb, pressing his back to the heavy stone. Despite his choices in the past 100 years, he'd fought for endless centuries before that. On some level, he knew, he would always be a soldier. He was triggered now, every sense heightened, electric, a cold tension filling his bones, his very cells. He closed his eyes, extending his *e'drai* to sense other minds. Almost immediately, he felt himself weakening slightly, using his gift this way, like a slow drain on a battery. He wouldn't be able to do it for long, or he wouldn't have the strength to fight if he needed to. Worse, his quarry would try to block just such an intrusion, if he had the ability. Or the training. Grimly, Zerik forced himself to breathe, to stay calm, focus.

He stood against the heavy marble tomb for nearly a minute, silent, immobile, sweating in the sun. There – a breath of thought, off to the right. Close.

When he wanted to, Zerik could move like they did, silent, fast. He slipped noiselessly between tombs, obelisks, like the flicker of a shadow. As he moved, his mind raced. What could he be after? Why would he be here?

He slid soundlessly behind a domed granite tomb, sensing the man crouched on the other side, like an earthbound gargoyle, leering, watching, waiting. Zerik took a moment to slow his breath. He had to get close enough to touch the man, without being seen. Unfortunately, his target didn't have such restrictions – if he could see Zerik, he could take him.

Zerik would have to move fast, as fast as his prey, faster. He edged silently around the tomb, barely breathing, every ounce of energy focused, deadly calm. As he rounded the west side, he tightened the gathered energy, springing forward with preternatural speed.

With sudden awareness, the dark-skinned bald man looked up, a chilling smile creasing his face. But it was too late, and Zerik's hands closed around his throat.

Within seconds, the little man with the tattoo on his forehead lay on the grass in the shadow of the domed tomb, his black eyes open, vacant, staring heavenward. His chest rose and fell with gentle regularity.

117

Zerik clenched his fists until his nails dug into his palms, looking down at his victim. He was shaking with rage, and in that moment wanted – more than anything – to kill him. But killing him would only unleash him on the world in a couple of decades, with more power and a new Form, a new face.

No, he'd done all he could, and it would have to be enough. He couldn't risk binding the man; he'd surely kill the innocent who found him. They never left witnesses. He and Megan would have to hurry now; they had maybe 30 minutes before the monk came to his senses. Zerik searched the man's leather jacket, found the expected pistol. And something else. Two plane ticket stubs, from Kansas City to San Francisco. Two. A *dha*.

All at once everything made a horrible kind of sense. "Oh my God," Zerik whispered. "Megan." He started running.

About 50 yards from the SUV, Rhiannon slowed, stopped. The vehicle sat at the side of the road where they'd left it. No one seemed anywhere around. She turned and looked back up the hill, hoping for a glimpse of Zerik, afraid she'd see the dark little man. All was silent, peaceful. Even the wind seemed to have stopped, and the cemetery lay basking in the bright sunlight. The quiet was unnerving. She was breathing hard, the adrenalin causing her hands to shake uncontrollably.

She looked to her right, down one of the rows of headstones and tombs. Something was lying on the ground near the end of the row, a splash of bright pink against the grass. "Don't go look," she whispered to herself. *It's like a horror movie*, she thought. *Don't look.* But she found herself moving down the path anyhow, slowly, as though the air was water. She glanced back up the hill, and again at the SUV, but stillness reigned.

Rhiannon didn't have to go far before the suspected truth became apparent. Even 20 feet away, she could see Nancy Holliday's frozen stare, her neck twisted at a grotesque angle.

Rhiannon spun to look behind her, expecting to see the dark bald man, ready to kill her too, the predictable horror movie reveal.

118

Instead, there was nothing but the unremitting silence, the columns of pale marble and dark granite in serene repose, like those in the earth beneath.

Casting a last panicked, pitying glance on poor Nancy Holliday, Rhiannon ran back to the end of the row, looking up the road for Zerik. She couldn't call out to him; whoever the man was, he'd hear. What if Zerik was dead, too? A horrible, dizzying foreboding paralyzed her. She fought it. No, he would be fine. He was immortal, right? He was probably a ninja or some damned thing in a past life. He'd be fine. She steeled herself. Zerik had told her to go to the SUV, lock herself in.

She wheeled and ran down the road to the waiting vehicle. She stood in the grass next to the door, fumbling in her pocket for the keyless remote, her breathing unnaturally loud in the stillness. Without warning, a hot, prickling sensation started at the back of her neck, gooseflesh breaking out all over her arms. With sick dread, she raised her eyes to the man standing next to the SUV, not four feet from where she stood.

He was smiling. A horrible, funereal smile, black and yet frighteningly elated. This was another man, bald and tattooed like the other, but tall, thin, disturbingly pale. His eyes were the same black, endless pools, like hell itself was bound in his gaze.

"Rhiannon," he whispered, a sibilant croak, ecstatic.

He knew her *name*.

She couldn't move, could only stare at him, unable to look away. She heard, rather than felt, herself taking great gulps of air, panic driving her heart so hard she thought it might come out of her chest. Her terror was absolute, dizzying.

And then she noticed – he didn't glow. A single, thin strip of light surrounded his body, not the shining *fainna* of an aeternan, but the aura of a normal, mortal man. An oblivi, Zerik called them. Those Who Forget.

Somehow, that knowledge calmed her. He knew her name, but he was just a man. Someone who could be hurt. Someone who could die. Watching him, unmoving, she pulled strength from the thought. Found steel inside herself. And with it came a wash of anger, red and strong. She was tired of being afraid. Tired of being hunted.

Slowly, looking into his pitiless black gaze, she smiled at him, an evil smile all her own. For a breath, she thought she saw fear register in his dark eyes. "Come close to me, and I'll bite you," she said. *Until you bleed.*

He laughed, a dreadful, hollow sound that almost suffocated her resolve. "No, dear. Not a chance." He pulled a large pistol from his leather jacket, a huge mass of dark metal nearly a foot long. He pointed it at her head.

She held her breath, waiting for the explosion of light, the inevitable darkness to follow. The man's smile deepened, and his finger curled around the trigger.

And then he was screaming, clutching his wrist, a knife embedded in his flesh, the metallic scent of wet blood sharp in the air. The pistol dropped to the ground. Rhiannon whirled to see Zerik running toward them at unbelievable speed, throwing another knife into the man's leg.

Still screaming with pain and transcendent fury, the thin man strained forward, reaching for the pistol with his left hand, but then Zerik was there, tackling him, rolling him to the ground. His long, pale fingers clutched at Zerik's shirt, and as they moved, Rhiannon caught a horrified glimpse of the man's face. He looked truly frightened. Zerik rolled on top of him, gripping the man's head between his hands. "*Mirsyati,*" Zerik snarled. The man spasmed, shook beneath Zerik's hands, and Zerik himself swayed, nearly fell away.

The man stilled, staring up at Zerik unseeing, his mouth slack.

"He's dead," Rhiannon was sobbing, quaking with the physical aftermath of her fear.

Zerik crawled off the body, rolled over to lie in the grass. "He's not dead," he gasped. "He's forgotten."

Rhiannon looked at the pale man then, saw his chest moving with slow, even breathing. She looked back to Zerik. He was shaking, and his face had an unhealthy pallor. His blue silk shirt and jeans were stained dark with the man's blood. She ran to him, knelt at his side, touched his cheek, his chest. "Are you okay?" Even his aura seemed dimmed. Panic rose in the back of her throat, choking.

Zerik's smile was gentle, weary. "I'm okay. I'm just very, very tired. And we don't have much time – the effects of my *e'drai* only last about a half hour." He reached up and caressed her cheek with faltering fingers. "You're going to have to drive. We have to get to Family."

She helped him stand, guided him to the SUV. He leaned heavily against her as she hurriedly activated the keyless remote. Zerik was a big man. It took almost all of her strength to help him into the passenger seat. "Get my knives and the pistol," he whispered. "And anything else he's got in his jacket." She nodded.

Rhiannon turned, approaching the still form with trepidation. He looked like a corpse, with his waxy pale skin and empty eyes. She steeled herself. Now was not the time to be squeamish. With some satisfaction, she roughly pulled the knives free of his wrist and thigh, wiping them clean with decisive strokes on his brown leather jacket. Curling her lip, she ran her hands through the pockets of the jacket, inside and out. She found a package of strange darts with green fletches, and a disposable cell phone. There was no wallet, no identification.

She left him there, lying in the Victorian pleasure garden, staring mindlessly into the unending summer sky.

Out of breath, Rhiannon climbed into the SUV, dumping her finds on the passenger side floorboard. Zerik was conscious, but barely. "Was there a phone?" he asked.

She nodded. "Yes. One of the cheap throw-away kind."

"We have to get out of here. There was a lake in front of one of the other cemeteries," he said, closing his eyes. "Throw the phone into the lake. So it can't be tracked."

Rhiannon started the engine, turned the vehicle around. "Are you going to be okay, Zerik?" She was trying very hard not to cry. He opened his eyes again, smiled at her, that warm brilliant smile which curled her toes. "Brave girl. I'll be fine. Just need a good nap. Running silent, wielding strong *e'drai* is draining. Get us up the coast. Head for Fort Bragg." He reached out and touched her hand. "Don't be afraid, Megan."

She almost told him her name then. As if the sound of the syllables on his lips could undo the dark echo in her head. But he was already asleep.

121

EIGHT

Rhiannon drove for hours that felt endless, moments running together in a haze of desperation, panic. She raced like a madwoman on the 101, going far too fast in their big black Cadillac SUV, changing lanes erratically, her eyes dancing between the road and the rearview mirror, terrified of pursuit. Those men had known her name. They were looking for her. The thought sat heavy inside her gut, congealing black and hard.

It felt strange, but she knew where she was going. Megan Byrne had never been anywhere as exotic as California, but Kat Weiss had lived here. It was her decades-old memories that guided Rhiannon now, and she navigated the highway with breathless, grim confidence.

Rhiannon felt as though she was everywhere at once. The world felt sharp, immediate. It was like going within herself and focusing, except that now her consciousness was centered beyond her body, outside – as though her aura, her senses, were radiating outward in bright, jagged shards of awareness.

Sharp details, fragments assailed her. A battered Toyota Corolla, shimmering ocean blue in the sunlight, a dented bumper bearing a faded sticker from long-ago political campaign. The surface of the highway baked grey in the sun, ridges in the concrete hard and physical beneath the tires, jangling rough through her skin. The way her hands curled hard on the steering wheel, until her knuckles were white, her flesh pinched, trying to stop the shaking. The smell of drying blood.

Each moment stretched, painfully slow, and yet later it all felt like a blur of terror and roads, yellow lines spinning outward into the distance, red taillights, boxy-pale houses nestled into green hillsides, the bristling masts of clustered sailboats, automobile dealerships and shopping plazas, houseboats impossible and ludicrous hovering over the water, golden hills shining in the afternoon sun, cathedrals of redwoods.

At one point early on, stuck in traffic in San Francisco, trying to get to the Golden Gate Bridge, she became aware of a black sedan in the rearview mirror, tinted windows and dust on the paint, like something from a movie, carrying visiting dignitaries – or nightmares with guns, spies, killers. There was no way to escape in the gridlock. She could only look in the mirror, again and again, flicking her eyes from the traffic ahead, back to the mirror once more. When the sedan finally turned right onto Lincoln, just before she entered Golden Gate Park, Rhiannon felt dizzy with relief. Only to notice another car behind her, and then another.

Every car on the highway looked like it might hold bald, tattooed psychopaths. The unrelenting vigilance was exhausting.

Worst of all, she kept glancing at Zerik, the big, muscular man sprawled unconscious in the passenger seat, his head slumped forward on his chest, his aura pale and faint. Rhiannon kept reaching out with her right hand, touching his chest through his bloodstained shirt, assuring herself he was still breathing.

She'd never felt so frightened and alone in her life.

Each passing minute racheted the tension, her nerves ragged, biting. Trying to keep track of so many vehicles was sending Rhiannon into an uncontrollable panic, and after an hour, she decided to get off the highway at San Rafael. She thought she'd head over to the coast highway. Only two lanes of traffic seemed easier to manage. It would greatly delay their arrival in Fort Bragg – if indeed that was their final destination – but it felt safer somehow. Following her instinct did nothing to abate the strain, but she regained at least some sense of control.

About 20 minutes northwest of the little town of Fairfax, the pressure on her bladder grew overwhelming. She'd been driving for nearly two hours by then. She pulled off into a turnout by the side of the road in the forest and cut the engine. The sudden silence felt discordant. Expectant. She watched the rearview mirror for several minutes, but no one seemed to be following or stopping.

"Everything's gonna be fine," she mumbled under her breath, determined, unconvinced. She looked at Zerik. He hadn't moved. Despite his deep, even breath, his sleep seemed unnatural, almost comatose, a twilight sleep. Rhiannon reached down to the floor at Zerik's feet, scooping up one of his ebony-handled throwing knives. She tested the weight of it in her hand, noting the balance. It was wickedly sharp. She'd never used a knife before, but somehow it felt comfortable in her hand, natural. Gingerly, she slid the knife in the back pocket of her jeans.

Climbing out of the SUV, she circled around to the passenger side, watching the two-lane highway all the while. A few cars drove past, but none slowed. She opened Zerik's door carefully. Strapped into his seat belt, the big man didn't stir. She wanted to be able to see him clearly.

Rhiannon looked over her shoulder. There was an embankment at the far edge of the turnout, leading down to a small stream. She backed down the embankment, her sneakers digging into the soft, damp earth, her eyes never leaving Zerik. Powerful and strong though he was, in his current state, he seemed disturbingly vulnerable. He couldn't defend himself, and she would keep him safe.

She hurriedly unbuttoned her jeans, obeying her body's dictates, and was already half-way back up the embankment as she pulled up her jeans. Zerik hadn't moved.

She stood there in the stillness by the side of the road, swamped with a sense of helpless fear.

A thought struck her, and Rhiannon reached down and pulled off her sneakers and socks. Just feeling the cool, wet grass and earth beneath her feet imparted an immediate sense of calm, as it always had. She took a deep breath, wiggled her toes in the rough grass. It would be okay. Everything would be okay.

Barefoot, she walked over to the SUV, standing close to Zerik, watching his steady breath. She wanted to help him so badly. She'd come to care for him a great deal. From the moment they'd met, she felt like she knew him already. Now, that feeling was even stronger, the connection to him more profound. She needed him. She was lost in a dangerous new world, utterly at sea, and he was her lodestar.

Her feet were cold, standing there in the wet grass. She pressed her right hand to his chest, against his bloodstained blue silk shirt. The feeling of his breath against her fingers was calming, gave her focus. His face was peaceful. Some of his slender braids had come free of the tie at the back of his neck, and a few strands were hanging over his forehead, partially obscuring his eyes. She brushed the braids back with her left hand, gently tucking them behind his ears.

She wanted him to be okay. More than anything, she wanted him to be well, the laughing, vibrant man with whom she'd spent the last night. She closed her eyes, feeling the living heat of his body under her hand. Breathing deeply, she intuitively found the warm shimmering darkness within herself.

Suddenly, her feet weren't cold anymore. She opened her eyes and looked down at her bare toes, surprised. The cold damp grass and earth were now pleasantly warm, as though she'd dipped her feet in a hot bath. Following instinct, she closed her eyes again, dove into the soft darkness within. *Please,* she thought. *Please help Zerik be okay again.*

She felt a tingling in the balls of her feet, her arches, the pads of her toes. Down within the warm darkness inside herself, she found pale tendrils of green energy, a vibrant mist. She knew what to do then, as if she were going to touch something and listen to it, feel it, like the stone on her grave.

Rhiannon pulled the green light higher into herself, wisps of celedon and spruce, yellow-green, moss, ivy, malachite. Gauzy threads coalesced into translucent clouds, a dense vapor of vibrant energy. She pulled it up through the darkness, through her feet and legs, into her chest, where she allowed it to grow and throb. The power coiled in her chest, until she released it to surge giddily down her arm, into her right hand.

Rhiannon opened her eyes. Her hand resting against Zerik's chest was shining, not with the gold effulgence she was used to, but a dazzling emerald brilliance. The energy wasn't born inside herself, but coming from someplace else. Even now, she could feel the power continuing to flow up from her feet, through her body, and into her hand. Rather than a generator, she had become a kind of conduit.

Instinct whispered. Taking a deep breath, she felt her connection to the glowing green, felt it touching her, filling her, dancing electric on the surface of her skin – and then with all her strength, she pushed, pushed it out, forcing it through her body, through her hand, and into Zerik.

There was a powerful physical shock as she released the energy, and Zerik's body jerked, while Rhiannon stumbled backward, releasing him from her touch. For a heartbeat, Zerik's aura brightened like a verdant star, his skin incandescent, glowing from within. Then it was as if he absorbed the light, the shining viridescence soaking into his flesh. When the green faded, his aura had returned to its customary, healthy, lustrous bright gold.

Zerik took a deep breath and opened his eyes, sitting up straighter in the seat. He appeared as he had the night before, prior to the horrific encounter in the cemetery. He turned his head and looked at Rhiannon, standing three feet away, barefoot in the coarse grass, breathing hard, staring. He smiled, that fine, big smile that went all the way up to his eyes. "I had the strangest dream, *varenya.*"

That morning, Lady Madeline Sofia, *Kir* of the Ciatri *dzina*, awoke from a dream, a vision. Zerik was coming home. The joy of the knowledge was tempered by a sense of tension, danger, a flicker of black flame simmering beneath the dream. Still, there was a sense of relief as well. She hoped the dream heralded an end to the symbolic pattern that had haunted her for days.

She'd been seeing circles. Everywhere. Circles in the tea leaves at the bottom of her cup, orbs in oil, floating on water, gelatinous spheres in broken egg yolks. A halo in her black scrying mirror, a fairy ring in a rock crystal ball. Roundels when she threw the bones, threw sticks. Circles in coffee grounds, cheese curds, wine sediment. Parabolas in the clouds. And of course, circles in her fires, in the spiraling smoke, in salt thrown on the flames; the burned fig leaves, straw, leaves, twigs of mistletoe, holly, oak. Wreaths and crowns in the cold ashes. Every divination method Madeline used resulted in the same thing.

She was desperate for clarification – the universe had always provided it, offering new symbols, ways to interpret the initial symbol. But this was like being blind. She didn't know what was happening anymore, anywhere. Circles were all she was given, and circles could mean a thousand things, a hundred thousand. Yet, so many circles must mean something in and of itself, something undoubtedly important. Very important. Now that the pattern was broken by her precognitive dream, she could begin to break it down, understand the message she'd been given.

Madeline sipped the last of her morning tea, thinking of Zerik, glad to have him home at last. Then she looked into her empty cup, and sighed. The tea leaves had settled at the bottom of the cup, forming a perfect circle.

Zerik watched the highway carefully, but it seemed they had avoided pursuit thus far. If they could make it to Point Arena, they'd be safe. The monks probably knew where they were headed, but he reasoned they wouldn't dare come that close to the Caistra, the Family Seat. Zerik allowed the tension in his shoulders to loosen, but only a fraction. He could relax when they were among Family again.

He glanced at Megan, curled barefoot in the passenger seat, her head resting on the window, watching the countryside slip by.

Something had happened while he was asleep. It should have taken at least four hours of sleep for him to recover enough to even function – and another 12 hours of solid sleep beyond that, to return to his usual condition. But now, not two hours after using his most debilitating *e'drai* – twice! – he felt better than he had in weeks. He felt good enough to do it all again, climb a mountain or six, and follow it with a few rounds of *era* for good measure.

He'd had a dream. There was someone there, and he was overcome with unbelievable power, *e'drai* that came from somewhere long vanished, ancient, irretrievable. The dream left him with a feeling of tremendous joy, and yet an aching sadness, loss.

But when he opened his eyes, there was only Megan Byrne, her brown eyes wide, reflecting shock, surprise. For a scant moment, Zerik thought maybe she had done something, caused his miraculous recovery – there was much about her *e'drai* he didn't understand yet – but anyone using that much power would be utterly drained, weary and weak to the point of incapacity. As he had been.

And Megan seemed fine.

He'd tried tentatively asking her about the incident, but she seemed afraid to discuss the matter. When he prodded gently, she changed the subject, but not before making it clear she was as clueless as he was.

Yet she had to have done something. There was no other explanation.

"Zerik?"

He looked over at her, then back to the road. "What is it, *varenya*?"

Rhiannon twisted her hands together in her lap, miserable, torn between fear and guilt. "I - I'm sorry. For getting you into all of this." She looked away. "It's my fault you were hurt."

Zerik kept his eyes on the road, winding sinuously through the redwoods. "You don't owe me an apology. For anything." The road smoothed out briefly, and he glanced at her, his gaze warm, sincere. "I wasn't hurt. I just used my *e'drai* to protect us both."

She winced. "I think those men were after me. They knew my name." She didn't specify further.

He reached out, resting his hand on her thigh. His touch was gentle, comforting. "I know. I think they were after you, too."

Surprised, she turned to look at him. "Why do you think that?"

"Because I found plane tickets on the darker one. They came from Kansas City. You're from Kansas City, aren't you?"

She nodded, unable to speak. How had they known where to find her? If they came from Kansas City they hadn't followed her to Topeka. No one knew where she was going, except — "Oh my God," she whispered, horrified. "They must have found Greg." She clutched Zerik's arm, panic flaring. "I have to call Greg." A sudden vision of Nancy Holliday's grotesque broken neck and empty, staring eyes filled her mind. "Oh God, they probably killed him."

Zerik spared her an appraising glance before returning his attention to the demanding, serpentine highway. "We need to make it to Point Arena before we can make any calls, provided we can even get cell service out here." He sighed. "Is Greg the only one who knew where you were thinking of going?"

Rhiannon was biting her lip, trying not to cry. "Yes."

Zerik experienced an uncomfortable sinking feeling. "How long have you known Greg?"

"Since I was a teenager. He was my next-door neighbor. He's always been a good friend."

The forest opened out into a sunny valley, golden-brown grassy hills, scrubby trees huddled in the creases of earth. The road straightened for a while, and Zerik was able to look at her fully. "All right, we'll call as soon as we can. Try not to worry."

He didn't know how to explain to her that there were only two possibilities, both bad. Either her friend had never been her friend to begin with, or he was dead.

Zerik touched her thigh again briefly. "Do you know why they would be after you? Have you seen men like that before?"

Rhiannon shook her head. "No. Never. Who were they? Why were they trying to kill us? Why did they look like that, with those tattoos?"

His grip tightened on the steering wheel, as he stared stonily through the windshield. "Those were the *Monaco Morto*, the Dead

Monks. They're part of a society called The Guard. They watch aeternans."

"They were doing a lot more than watching."

"The monks are the worst of The Guard. They are able to see auras. They use their ability to find aeternans, to mark them for further observation. Or worse."

Rhiannon rubbed her forehead, staring unseeing through the window. She thought of the tall, pale monk, a single, thin band of light around his body, and looked back at Zerik. "Wait. They can see auras, but they're not Family?"

"Yes. Oblivi, mortals, can sometimes see auras. It generally means that in their next incarnation, they will begin to remember, to become aeternan. Not always, but much of the time." He turned into another sharp curve, maneuvering the big SUV expertly. "The Guard have been watching aeternans for centuries. They fear us. And fear breeds anger, and hate. They believe that because we have great power, we are a danger to humankind. They believe we can take over the world. There are some who think we already have." His jaw clenched. "They don't understand that the vast majority of aeternans just want to be left alone, to live our lives, just like they do."

Rhiannon shook her head wryly. "Taking over the world – it sounds like a bad movie."

He glanced away from the road, his eyes serious. "I guess we could, if we wanted to." He gripped the steering wheel a little tighter. "It's a bad movie plot because it's not really possible – for mortals, anyhow. For us, I imagine it is." He sounded tired, suddenly. "There are aeternans who are dangerous, Megan. We are human beings, after all. Everyone has light and shadow in their souls."

Rhiannon looked away. She knew about shadows.

Zerik shifted in his seat, straightened. "Anyhow, because The Guard reviles who and what we are, the worst thing they can possibly imagine is to become one of us. The monks can see auras – they are destined to become Family with their next incarnation. To them, it's like going to hell." He grimaced. "And frankly, we don't want them in our Family, either."

"But there's no way to stop that. Everyone has to die eventually."

131

They were passing back into the forest again, mossy, impossibly huge redwood trees lining the roadway on either side, the shadowy canopy of branches far overhead. Zerik slowed for a pothole, the rutted road layered with previous asphalt repairs in various states of disarray. His voice was low, brittle. "In the past few hundred years, The Guard think they've figured out a way to kill the soul, to burn it from the body. The victim is *mortaetun*, dead forever, never to be reincarnated."

"Oh my God," Rhiannon sat open-mouthed, appalled.

Zerik shook his head, frowning. "The monks choose to be *mortaetun*, rather than become one of us. They are the walking dead, knowing that at any time The Guard will destroy them, to protect their secrets. Every mission they undertake could be the one that ends their existence forever. It is an honor death for them."

"Why do they look like that? The tattoos, shaved heads."

"They wear the mark of their impending doom with pride, even arrogance. They don't hide from death, or from us. They mark themselves. The triangle represents the monk's cowl; the tattoo covers their third eye, the symbolic rejection of becoming aeternan, of developing *e'drai*. The monks are the eyes of The Guard. Most of the time, they simply track us, mark our locations, report back." His expression grew grim. "But they are also dangerously skilled hunters."

He didn't voice the thought that the monks had come looking for her alone, not knowing he'd be there. One monk was more than sufficient to trap even most Eldest. But for the most powerful aeternans, Family with *e'drai* like hers, they'd send a *dha*, a team. They were hunting big game.

Rhiannon stared at him bleakly. "Why do they want to kill us?"

"They don't. They wanted to take us alive." He nodded toward the back seat, where he'd thrown the pistols and the green-fletched darts. "Those are tranquilizer guns." He met her gaze fleetingly, his eyes pained. "An eternally powerful mind is pretty much helpless when unconscious."

She blanched, remembering Zerik's abnormal sleep. "What do they do with you once they take you?"

Eyes on the convoluted highway, his profile looked carved from dark stone. "They keep us alive as long as possible, prisoners. They study us. Experiment on us, like animals. They use drugs to suppress our *e'drai*, or they break the will, force us to use our *e'drai* for their ends. They torture us. For prisoners of The Guard, death is a blessing, an escape, and we are reborn in another body, another time, another place. But by then it's often too late, as their methods create madness, or *aura'kur*, a shadowed aura. We become *anam'liath*, shadow souls."

Rhiannon looked blindly out the window, overcome with revulsion, dread, and the familiar cold fear she'd lived with for so long. She remembered the little man in the hospital in Kansas City with the shadowed soul, darkness smeared into the gold. And she thought of the man who stalked her through two lifetimes, absorbing light into his dark aura. "Death is an escape," she whispered. *For a while.*

Zerik put a hand on her arm, rubbing lightly. "I'm sorry to have to tell you all of this. But you should know."

"I know," she answered, afraid to look at him. Finally, she managed, "Are some souls not just shadowed, but black?"

He jerked to look at her, swerving slightly on the narrow highway, immediately regaining control. "Black auras? A black aura is *erim*. Evil." He took a breath. "Why would you ask me that?"

Rhiannon suddenly felt ineffably weary. "Zerik, I have to tell you about how I died. And why."

His eyes following the crooked pass, he nodded. "Death is often traumatic, but it's *always* very personal. You don't have to tell me about it if you don't want to."

She shook her head. "No, I think I have to. There's someone after me. Someone who was after me in my last life, and is still after me in this one." She swallowed. "Someone with an aura that's black."

The highway finally met with the coast road, and despite her concerns, Rhiannon was thrilled to finally see the Pacific Ocean. She rolled down her window to inhale the salt air blowing on her face, to soak in the beauty of the water stretching endlessly into the horizon.

For no reason at all, it felt like home. A kind of fragile peace settled in her heart, and she squeezed Zerik's hand.

After another hour or so, they arrived in the tiny town of Point Arena. The village featured charming, slightly dilapidated Victorian two-story buildings and cottages, time and the salt air conspiring to erode wood and paint. Trees, brush, and flowering thorny bushes overflowed fences and stone walls. Nature was trying to reclaim the sleepy town for its own.

Zerik finally allowed himself to breathe a little easier. After more than four hours on the road, they were both ready for a rest. He glanced at Megan. She'd tried to call her friend Greg using Zerik's throw-away cell phone, but was unable to reach him. Her face was drawn, her shoulders hunched as she looked numbly out the window. She was afraid. He was afraid for her. But all they could do now was press on, get to Family. After so many lifetimes, he knew that allowing himself to become lost in fear never solved anything, only made for a miserable existence.

Just before the highway curved toward the sea, Zerik pulled over next to a peeling picket fence. At her questioning look, he nodded toward the neat little cottage beside the road. "I thought we could clean up a little. It wouldn't be polite to show up at home covered in monk blood. It would upset the *Kir*, who might mistake it for mine. I don't want her to worry that I might have been hurt. Besides, she'd have my head." He smiled. "And I'm sure we could both use a bathroom, stretch our legs a little."

"Is it safe to stop? What if they're following us?"

He rubbed his beard thoughtfully. "I think if we were being followed, we'd know by now. And I really do think we're safe at this point. We're within 100 miles of the Caistra — and I don't believe a monk would get that close."

"The Caistra?"

"The Family Seat. The palace, government, and home to almost 20,000 aeternans in this country."

Rhiannon's eyes widened. "Wow, 20,000?" The number seemed more comprehensible, easier to grasp, than the "millions" of aeternans worldwide he'd mentioned before. It felt huge.

She shook her head, looked at the cottage with its worn, peach-colored paint, the windows dark. "I am feeling pretty grubby," Rhiannon admitted. She felt jittery, nervous. "Who lives here?"

Zerik unbuckled his seat belt. "An old friend of mine, Peter Letsha. I don't think he's in the country right now, actually. But I know where he hides his key."

Zerik took his black overnight bag from the back of the Cadillac, and after feeling around under a mottled rock by the back door, produced the key to the cottage. It was small, a studio with a queen-size bed in the main room, a diminutive kitchen, and a bathroom. Everything was neat, if a bit dusty, an air of disuse about the place.

Rhiannon went to the kitchen window, which had a small peek at the sea between the trees. She sighed, somehow feeling better at the sight of that little strip of grey blue on the horizon. She rubbed her forehead, fighting a headache, trying to let go of her fears and tension.

"*I know what you need.*" Zerik came up behind her, wrapping his arms around her, his lips brushing behind her ear, trailing down her neck. "*Hell, I need it too.*"

She shivered, his touch raising gooseflesh on her arms. Rhiannon closed her eyes, suddenly feeling warm and languorous. "We don't have time," she whispered, already surrendering.

She could hear his laugh in her mind, erotic, deep. "*We have time for* era'e'soku. *That's what oblivi call a 'quickie.'*"

A scant 45 minutes later, they were in the SUV again, driving up the coast toward Mendocino. In addition to rumpling the faded quilt on the bed, they'd taken showers, and changed clothes. Rhiannon was glowing, well-pleasured and beautiful in sandals and a new sleeveless dress the color of warm earth, intricately embroidered along the deep neckline with green vines and leaves.

"Where did this come from?" she had asked him, fingering the soft fabric wonderingly.

Zerik laughed. "I think when Charles was laundering your clothes, he took the liberty of doing a little shopping. There's more in my bag."

Rhiannon had vowed to return to the *Maisonsur* in Topeka one day, and make an honest man of Charles. They'd laughed, imagining the undoubtedly perfect, elaborate wedding. It felt good to laugh.

Zerik left a note for his friend Peter, thanking him for the hospitality, and they were off again. The brief respite had improved Rhiannon's outlook, and Zerik was feeling substantially better as well. Still, he was anxious to be home, where he knew they'd truly be safe.

Highway 1 hugged the coastline, snaking its way north. The drive was breathtaking, vast waves crashing against jagged rocks and cliffs, the wild spray subsiding into patterns of white foam on the surface of the water. The sunlight created a dazzling, sparkling path on the sea, and Rhiannon imagined walking on its blinding steps, disappearing into the sun, where the sky began.

"We should be at the nest in about an hour," Zerik said, laying a warm hand on her knee. He smiled broadly. "We'll be home in time for dinner. I haven't been home in months – I'm sure there'll be a celebration. Madeline is always looking for an excuse to celebrate something."

Rhiannon looked at him quizzically. "She doesn't know you're coming, though, does she?"

Zerik laughed. "Oh, yes, she does." He glanced at Rhiannon, grinning. "She knows almost everything. It's her *e'drai.* I guess you could say she's a witch, by some definitions."

Rhiannon laughed nervously. "A witch. Who's lived a thousand years."

"Longer."

Rhiannon felt a hint of cold tension seeping back into her bones. She swallowed. "Zerik, I have to admit – I'm kind of nervous about meeting your family. Your husband. Your wives. What if they don't like me? They're going to know I slept with you, and – "

"Of course they will. And they will decide you must be someone special, for me to have done so." He glanced her way, touched her cheek with light fingers. "Aeternan marriages are a bit different than oblivi marriages."

Her laugh was short. "Yeah, well, that part I figured out already."

"Megan." His fingertips brushed her hand. "We don't deal in petty jealousies and sexual insecurities. It's a waste of time and energy." He offered her a gentle smile. "We understand that love isn't something you have to contain, or save for just one person. My attraction for you doesn't diminish my love for anyone else – it enhances it."

Arms crossed over her chest, Rhiannon eyed him cautiously, but didn't speak.

Zerik laughed. "Sweetheart, love, caring, intimacy, and friendship are big, open things. Jealousy is about fear, and that's a small, closed thing. And who needs that?"

She took a deep breath, squaring her shoulders. She liked Zerik. She wanted to like his family, wanted them to like her, too. "Okay. I don't know if I totally get it, but I'll try."

He picked up her hand, pressed her fingers to his lips. "Trust me, *varenya*."

When they reached the outskirts of Fort Bragg, Zerik was close enough to his *dzina's* home to make mental contact with Madeline. He glanced at Megan, looking out the window, watching the town unfold around her, big corporate drugstores and coffee shops, funky local businesses with colorful window displays of clothes, jewelry, and toys.

As he guided the SUV through the early evening traffic, he sent part of himself outward, his mind seeking. Within a minute, he felt the warm presence of his wife, her mind dear and welcome, wonderfully familiar.

"*Navtu, socia varenya.*" Hello, beloved spouse. Zerik's thought came to Madeline as if on the wind.

She returned his thought, her harmonious *e'drai* effortless. "*Zerik, love! Welcome home!*"

"*We should be there in just a few minutes.*"

"*We?*"

Zerik frowned, confused. "*Yes, I brought someone with me. You didn't know?*" His thought held a note of laughter. "*I can't believe it. I've finally surprised you.*"

"*No, I didn't know,*" The tone of Madeline's thought was clipped, frustrated.. "*I had a dream you were coming home, but other than*

137

that, I've been stuck in a pattern for days. I've never experienced anything like it. Circles, over and over."

"My poor love. Listen, I must tell you about this woman, before you see her." Zerik looked back to Megan, still watching the boulevard, oblivious to the mental conversation.

"Oh, a woman? Trust you, Zerik. I hope you plan on sharing."

"Enough, wife. She's very unusual, and I'm hoping you can help. She glows like an Eldest, with incredibly powerful e'drai. But she's neonate."

"That's not possible."

"Apparently it is. She only remembers one incarnation. I'm hoping you can help her figure things out."

"You care for her." It was not a question.

Zerik hesitated. "It's only been a short time – but ... yes, I care for her. Deeply."

Madeline's response was immediate. "Then I will adore her, too."

"There's more. We ran into The Guard. Monks. A dha."

"Oh my God, Zerik, are you all right?"

"Yes. We weren't followed. But I don't think they were after me. I think they were after her. I had to use engi'ka'mirsyat'al. Twice. I was horribly weakened; it should have taken at least a full day of sleep to recover. But I think she healed me. Or something. All I know is that two hours after making two monks forget, I was back to my usual self. Better." He paused. "And she showed no ill effects at all."

"I must meet this woman."

"We'll be at the gates shortly. Until then, Love."

Zerik glanced back at Megan, and she looked up at him with those huge brown eyes, smiling. He took her hand, murmured softly. "Are you ready to leave the world behind?"

NINE

Grigori Valentin Sokolov was afraid.

He'd always been careful, lest he be exposed. He had managed to arrange his life to minimize risks, to live up to expectations, without calling undue attention to himself. Fear had always shadowed him, close, intimate. Though on reflection, he'd grown complacent over the years. Almost comfortable. It had been easy, with her.

But now he was not just fearful. He was truly, deeply frightened.

They'd beaten him badly. His whole body hurt, the pain excruciating when he tried to roll over. He had at least three broken ribs, by his reckoning. Every breath was agony. The scorched wounds on his face and palms still burned, where they'd seared his skin with cigarettes. He lay on the bathroom tiles in a pool of his own blood, one eye swollen shut, his wrists and ankles bound behind him, hogtied.

Sitting on the edge of the bathtub was an hourglass. A goddamned hourglass. The bastard had a sick sense of humor.

He'd been given an hour. To make a choice.

Greg closed his eyes, trying to shut out the pain, taking shuddering, shallow breaths. When, he wondered, had he ever really had a choice?

He'd grown up in St. Petersburg, and had always hated the cold.

From the moment he first drew breath, his destiny had already been chiseled in granite, irrevocable.

Greg's father, Vladimir, was a *Capitano*, a Bishop in The Guard in the influential St. Petersburg Column. He and his twin brother, Valentin, had taken their vows together when they were 12 years old, the recommended age. Greg's grandfather had also been a member of The Guard, and his father before him, and his father before that — going back six generations. Valentin had been killed just days before Greg was born, some said at the hands of a witch. He'd grown up listening to stories of his uncle's bravery and devotion to the cause, his ultimate sacrifice.

It was simply natural that Greg would accept the honor offered by The Guard and his family. Vladimir had been training his son since the child was old enough to walk, old enough to fire a gun, hold a knife. He instilled in Greg the meaning of duty, honor, sacrifice. His instruction included stories passed down through centuries, of the glowing creatures that walked among humankind, monsters with the visage of angels, demons with inhuman powers to destroy, kill, to bend mortal men to their corrupt designs.

Most men and women lived idyllically unaware of the imminent horror all around them. The majority would never believe the supernatural forces working against their survival, easily dismissing glaring evidence, obvious proofs. They couldn't be blamed. They needed to cling to their ignorance. Only the strongest souls could face the truth, and only the bravest of these were chosen by God to lead the fight.

Vladimir explained to his son that *La Guardia*, must, of necessity, be secret. The identities of its members would always be protected. Because an innocent in this lifetime could turn demon in the next. The potential for total absorption of the human race was chillingly real.

Since The Guard's inception in Florence in the 15th century, the society had operated in guerilla-style, self-contained Columns throughout the world. Leaders had minimal contact with the *soldatos*, no one man knowing the identity of more than a handful of other righteous soldiers.

In his father's lore, those warriors who were not worthy could become infected, defiled, impure. Only they could see the mark of the beast, the glowing light that showed these beings for what they truly were. Those who could see the monsters had been judged by God and found wanting, their destruction assured. The demons would seek to make them their own.

These polluted souls must take the ultimate vow, become *Monaco Morto*, the Dead Monks, give their lives and their souls to The Guard, that they might have any hope of being saved.

Greg listened to his father's stories every night before dinner, in front of the fire, where he always sat too close, trying to warm the chill in his bones that never seemed to go away.

He'd never told anyone he could see auras.

Greg saw his first aeternan when he was 9 years old. It had taken the shape of an older woman with flowing silver hair, walking bold as you please down Nevsky Prospekt. He'd been told they could make themselves appear attractive, but he hadn't been prepared for the beauty of its aura, the shimmering gold rings of light, a luminous strata. She — it — had an expression of peace, contentment. The demon really did look like an angel.

Greg had run all the way home, arriving breathless and terrified. His mother, Taisiya, had tried fruitlessly to console him, to discover the source of his panic. But he knew what it meant, that he could see the creature, its aura. He was flawed, impure. They would turn him into a demon, too. He couldn't confess it; the shame was unspeakable.

One night when Greg was 10, a man came to their house with a message from the *Generale*, the Cardinal, for Greg's father. He wore a dark brown, wool coat, and his head was shaved. A triangle was marked on his forehead, between his eyes. He was a monk, a defiled soul who had chosen what little honor remained to him. He was gaunt, his expression dour. When he turned and caught sight of Greg, standing next to his mother, he smiled. Greg didn't know until then that a smile could be dark, utterly cold, like bleak hell itself.

Taisiya had cast a fearful, disapproving look at both her husband and the man, before hurriedly ushering Greg from the room. He'd had nightmares for weeks afterward, reliving that moment, that smile, in tortured dreams.

Despite his father's stories, he wanted to believe that he could somehow undo the damage, his unquestionable taint. He wasn't trying hard enough, daydreaming during his lessons, drawing when he should have been practicing with his knives. He vowed to work harder, study more, so that when he took his vows, he would be the best *soldato* in The Guard, keeping on the side of righteousness, a worthy man. A man who could keep his soul.

On his 12th birthday, draped in the initiate's blood-red robes, Greg stood next to his father and made his vows to *La Guardia*. The ceremony took place in a hidden basement chamber, strangely beneath one of the most respected banks in St. Petersburg. The room was exactly as Greg had imagined, like something from a gothic novel – shadowy, the only illumination racks of votive candles like they had at church, and dim sconces set into the stone walls. Vladimir had told Greg that he and his brother had taken their vows in that very room.

The Cardinal himself presided, representing the *Arcivescovo*, the Archbishop in Italy. Six other boys and young men proudly made their vows as well, new *soldatos*, priests, in the clandestine fight for the salvation of humankind.

Greg had kneeled on the embroidered hassock to receive his blessing, the Cardinal using a shining ceremonial blade to mark him with a tiny cut on his forehead, mingling his blood with the others' present. Back at home, after a late celebratory dinner, Greg's father proudly presented his son with his brother Valentin's knives. Greg's solitary, private disgrace was all-encompassing.

His studies continued, along with a strangely alien, dual life at the local school, a place in which children played and laughed and did their homework, oblivious to the secret worlds around them – worlds of demons and those who watched them. Almost instinctively, the other children avoided Greg. He had a reputation for being shy, a big boy with sandy blond hair who stumbled when he tried to speak. Sometimes he wished he could be like everyone else, only to be crushed with guilt for even allowing the thought.

The weight of the responsibility, and his own secrets, was suffocating. It only grew worse.

When he was 13, in his spare time after dinner, he started woodcarving. It always gave him peace. Mostly, he carved little animals – deer, rabbits, bears. He took pleasure in choosing fragrant, fine-grained woods, watching his hands move, a flash of light on the blade of his knife, the fresh-scented wood chips falling to his work table. He loved the way the delicate creatures were gradually revealed within the thick wood. It was like opening a present that took hours to unwrap, each careful move revealing more of the gift within. He savored these evenings, the quiet outside his window, the dog drowsing warm against his feet.

"Your Uncle Valentin used to waste his time playing with wood, too," his father had said, when he found out. "You should be studying, practicing."

"*Vovochka*," his mother said, laying a hand on his father's arm. "Valentin did honor to the family. His little animals didn't hurt anyone."

His father had grumbled under his breath, but said nothing more about Greg's woodcarving. Then, or ever.

As a young man, Greg was sent to a Guard training camp for two years. Their methods were harsh, even brutal. Priests in *La Guardia* were guerilla soldiers for God, for humanity. Their targets were intelligent, dangerous, and supernaturally powerful; all caution must be taken. Members of The Guard must not only be accomplished killers and hunters, but highly superior stealth operatives, capable of perfect, invisible surveillance and intelligence. Greg was trained in the use of all manner of weaponry, plus cryptography, digital steganography, recruiting techniques, effective disguise and surveillance skills, lockpicking, evasive techniques, sabotage, counterintelligence, clandestine communications, and more.

Even minor failures during training were severely punished. Greg learned to go along with whatever they asked of him, and was accorded honors for his service.

He was promoted, and in the course of his new duties, was required to assist in the forceful examination of a captured aeternan. It was a young man, maybe only 20, not much younger than Greg. Its aura was thin, only two glowing rings. The priests in charge of the interrogation had the man beaten, branded, forced the creature to undergo simulated drowning, kept it awake for days on end, starving, living in its own waste.

Every day, Greg watched the pathetic beast deteriorate, grow painfully thin, shaking uncontrollably, filthy and stinking. Greg couldn't bear it. Its eyes were the worst, bruised pools of blue agony, every day heavier with grief and madness. He knew the demon wasn't human. He knew these things were a terrible danger. But this creature seemed only young and frightened, desperate. It didn't have information that would be useful to anyone. He was just a child.

One night, Greg slipped the young man a piece of greasy broiled chicken from his own dinner tray. The next morning, he was called into the Bishop's office. Greg's only friend, a fellow priest called Leonid, had reported the matter.

The resulting uproar was nothing short of a scandal, given the prominence of Greg's family in The Guard. Vladimir was unqualifiedly shamed, and refused to speak to Greg. He would die four years later, without ever saying another word to his son.

Greg was reassigned to a Column in the United States, in the Midwest, a poor, backwater posting. But secretly, he was overjoyed to escape St. Petersburg, to bask in the humid Missouri summer sun. Eventually, through diligence and dogged focus, he would redeem himself enough to land an assignment as a Watcher. His job would be to observe a specific aeternan target, report behavior patterns, known associates, connections with other demons.

File a report once a week. He could otherwise live a relatively normal life, mowing the lawn, drinking Coors at the neighborhood bar, watching cable news shows. Carving little wooden animals. Hiding his secrets and shame. It sounded almost unbelievably ideal.

So Greg had moved into a rundown little house on Forest Avenue, in the Columbus Park neighborhood of Kansas City. And waited three days for his first glimpse of Megan Byrne.

His target was a bit unusual, and it was a mark of his improved status that he'd been given the assignment. She had apparently been of interest to The Guard for some time. No less than four monks had verified that she glowed like an Eldest, but a Bishop had done a thorough investigation and determined that she was neonate, that she clearly remembered only one incarnation. Further, there was no evidence of any active *e'drai*.

Neonates were no threat to The Guard, though they were regularly used and studied. However, the Eldest were always watched carefully. Cautious, but convinced of the sincerity of her behavior, the Bishop assigned a low-level *soldato* priest, Greg, to continue surveillance of the anomalous target and make weekly reports in case anything changed.

Nothing had changed for nine years. The Bishop in his Column continued to accept Greg's reports, but never commented, and paid him almost no attention at all. Which suited Greg just fine. Because while Megan's status hadn't changed in nine years, Greg himself had.

He'd hidden himself away all these years. He should have been a monk, at some point, should have confessed his tainted soul. Given himself up to the honor death, to have his soul burned from his body. He dishonored his father, his family, and The Guard with his very presence, from the day he was born.

And then he fell in love with her, and was irrevocably lost. He often thought that he should just give in, let *La Guardia* destroy him. And sometimes, he thought they already had.

Choices. It seemed like he was always making them, but looking back, they seemed predestined, his eventual actions foregone conclusions.

After he'd left Megan in Topeka, he'd made a choice. Whoever was after her was clearly aeternan; doing his job could pose no further risk to her. So he did what he'd been doing every week, 52 times a year, for nine years. He filed his weekly report, edited, sanitized, omissions defining the substance. His target was on the move, and he could not follow and maintain cover. She was possibly headed to San Francisco, to find the grave of Katania Weiss, her previous incarnation. He had hopes that he would have further intelligence as to her location soon. End report.

Within a day, a *dha* had come for him. Dragged him from his work bench with a filthy blanket over his head, kicked him savagely over and over, as he lay gasping on the floor. They'd interrogated him endlessly about Megan, and an Eldest found in her company, a dark-skinned demon with powerful *e'drai*.

Greg babbled his ignorance, pleading. Begging. He repeated himself again and again. The truth was the only story he had to tell. While they beat him, his eye filling with blood, he could only see Megan's face, her enormous, brown eyes, sitting small and alone in the Topeka U-Rest Motel.

Not long after they'd burned his hands, a man had come into the room, standing in front of Greg. The monks fell back, bowing, hissing, obsequious.

Bound, kneeling at his feet, every fingerspan of flesh aching, drooling blood, Greg stared at the man's shoes, obviously expensive, glossy black leather. He raised his shaggy head, squinting up through his right eye, the left pummeled and swollen.

The man was perhaps in his early 50s, his features so pure as to be beautiful, streaks of silver bright against his dark hair. Through Greg's forbidden vision, he saw an Eldest of horrifying power, his aura a black, twisted mass of glimmering darkness, roiling sulfur, lead, and ocher, shifting to reveal streaks of crimson, like raw meat.

He leaned down, smiling almost pleasantly, and lifted Greg's chin with one finger. His eyes, glittering black, were pitiless. Soulless. There was a momentary frisson of energy skittering across Greg's skin, quickly suppressed.

The man released him, straightened. "He's lying. About something." His voice was smooth, dark. Delighted.

Greg had never known fear like that, breathless, utterly bleak, lost without hope of redemption. He closed his eyes to shut it out, the beautiful, angelic face of the abyss.

And now, lying hogtied on a bathroom floor, soaked in his own blood, he watched the last grains of sand trickle out of the hourglass. Any illusion of choice had always been made for him. The thought was comforting, somehow. Greg prayed for forgiveness then, even though God had never answered.

TEN

"This is wrong."

Zerik turned to look at her, smiling. "Really? Why do you say that?"

Rhiannon thought about it. "I don't know." She shook her head. "But I'm telling you, this isn't the right driveway. You've made a mistake. We have to go back to the highway."

They were sitting in the SUV, the engine idling, on a rutted track in the forest. A few short miles north of Fort Bragg, Zerik had made a left turn into the poorly-tended driveway, which had immediately curved behind the dense trees, out of sight of the main road. After only a few more yards, they'd come upon an old gate, rusted heavy steel set into a stone wall on either side of the track, with formidable hinges and bolts. Beyond that, the forest seemed impenetrable, the mossy undergrowth wild.

Rhiannon glanced at Zerik. He appeared nonchalant as usual, handsome and relaxed in a cream-colored silk shirt, buttery soft against his dark skin. Her eyes were drawn back to the gate, and the nagging sense of wrongness intensified. She was utterly certain they'd made a mistake somewhere. This simply couldn't be right.

Grinning, Zerik took pity on her. "It feels wrong to me, too."

She looked up at him, relieved. "Good. Let's go back to the highway."

He laughed. "Nope. The wrongness is how you know we're in the right place."

Rhiannon stared at him, uncomprehending.

"It takes very old, powerful *e'drai* to leave an indelible mark, to effect permanent change," Zerik explained. "Our outer gate is infused with the echo of a thought, a deep conviction the traveler has made a mistake, found a wrong turning, and must immediately return to the main road." He smiled broadly. "The longer we sit here, the worse it gets."

"So the gate is making us think we're in the wrong place." She couldn't quite believe it. They *were* in the wrong place, after all.

"Well, in this case, the 'gate' is the driveway, the forest, the wall, and the gate itself, but yes. It's causing a strong feeling of wrongness. *Drai'sentia'pro'kan'relin'e'kai* – Feeling, Pushing, Leaving." He touched her hand. "I promise, we're in the right place. But the feeling is just going to heighten, amplify, until you open the gate."

Startled, she turned to him. "You want *me* to open the gate?" The very idea redoubled her sense they were making a mistake, and she struggled to accept his words intellectually, even as her senses rebelled.

"You haven't been here before. The gate has to accept you. I'll show you." Leaving the engine running, he unbuckled his belt and opened his door, came around to her side of the vehicle. For a wild, inexplicable moment, she was tempted to lock the door against him. Instead, she took a deep breath and opened the door, took his proffered hand and stepped down onto the dirt road.

Holding her hand, Zerik led her around the front of the SUV to the gate. The sense of wrongness was overwhelming, but she swallowed, trusting Zerik. He released her fingers and stepped back. "Touch it," he said, nodding toward the rusty steel.

Rhiannon reached out and laid a shaking hand on the cold metal. Instantly, her aura flared brighter, and the gate glowed red and gold beneath her fingers. With a sudden creaking of the hinges, the gate opened into the forest beyond, the irregular dirt road curving away out of sight. The feeling of wrongness evaporated.

Zerik watched, surprised. New visitors to the Ciatri *dzina* often had to spend several minutes convincing the gate of their sincerity, having their aura and *e'drai* examined thoroughly as they touched the Fae-forged metal. He stroked his beard thoughtfully, shaking his head. He supposed he should be surprised only when Megan failed to surprise him.

Standing in wonder before the open gate, Rhiannon was delighted. She spun to look at Zerik, her eyes bright. "Okay, *that* was cool."

Zerik laughed, enjoying her spontaneous enthusiasm. "It surely is."

He helped her back into the big Cadillac, and they passed between the stone walls. The metal gate swung shut behind them. Rhiannon looked at Zerik questioningly, "Now what?"

He sent her a smiling glance before returning his gaze to the dirt road ahead. "There are three gates, three rings of protection for the house." He nodded toward the road. "You can see the second ring coming up ahead."

Rhiannon looked. Amidst the tangled anarchy of the forest, a pattern of order began to emerge. Not far ahead, a neat, close line of trees curved away on either side of the road, as though enclosing something beyond. As they approached, she could see a tall, imposing gate spanning the width of the road, supported by huge columns of rough-hewn stone. Between the trees, Rhiannon could see only the unrelieved forest, endless, old-growth trees, an impassible snarl of bushes and undergrowth.

Zerik pulled up in front of the gate and put the Cadillac in park, once again leaving the engine running. He leaned back, contemplating the gate before them. Watching the quiet pleasure on his face, Rhiannon couldn't help but smile. He seemed so genuinely happy to be there, as though all was right in the world. His world. She felt like she was having some kind of magical adventure, as if she'd found herself living one of her best dreams.

She looked more closely at this second gate. It was easily 12-feet high, made of what looked like iron and a heavy, warm coppery wood that gleamed in the early evening light. The wood was intricately carved, the iron twisting and winding through the wood like veins or bones, a web of black metal swirling around the carved panels. Rhiannon frowned, trying to imagine how the wood and metal could be fused so seamlessly, the metal curving and twining intimately with the minutely-detailed reliefs. It looked impossible, as though the two substances simply grew together that way, organic.

The wood carving was masterful, elegantly done. The gate seemed overgrown with flawlessly textured vines, veined leaves, branches, gnarled roots, arching and twisting into circular shapes. In fact, she realized, the whole gate was a mass of spirals, rings, whorls, and circles. In the center was a round panel of golden-colored wood, surrounded by an ornate crown of iron three-feet across, the delicate filigree edges flush with the wood. The circular panel depicted six sinuous human figures, hands clasped, dancing in a circle around a vast tree, its branches swirling outward, as if to enfold the dancers.

"Wow," Rhiannon breathed, awestruck. She looked at Zerik, only to find him already watching her. "How do we get through it?"

He smiled apologetically. "This might be a little startling. Trust me, alright?"

Wary, she nodded. "Okay."

He threw the SUV into drive and stepped hard on the gas pedal.

Rhiannon only had time to draw a breath to scream, before they drove straight through the gate – right through it, like it wasn't even there, an illusion, a trick of the light. Gasping, she twisted in her seat, looking behind them. The gate appeared solid and real enough from behind.

She turned back, staring straight ahead, catching her breath.

Zerik put a sympathetic hand on her thigh. "Sorry about that. But on the plus side, we're still on the driveway."

She eyed him dubiously. "Was there any doubt?"

He laughed. "Well, if we weren't supposed to go through it, we would have found ourselves back on the highway, two miles south, completely unable to remember how or why we got there." His smile held a touch of pride. "I helped make this gate. I did the *mirsyati*, the forgetting part."

Rhiannon didn't know what to say. This was an experience completely beyond anything she'd ever imagined.

The row of trees had curved inward to line the road on either side, their massive trunks towering over the uneven track. Far overhead, the branches joined, interlaced, forming a natural gothic cathedral. Splashes of evening sunlight filtered through the trunks and branches, vibrant gold, red, and orange vivid against the shadowed wood. It was beautiful, primal. Ancient. It was as though the furrowed road was a living thing, like the trees themselves, all of it growing together for a thousand years.

"It's like something from a fairy tale," Rhiannon said.

Zerik glanced at her. "You like fairy tales?"

She nodded. "As a kid, I loved Grimm's, the Eternal Tales, Oz books, Harry Potter, all that stuff." She blushed. "I guess I still like them. The Eternal Tales were always my favorites. Grimm's was good, but they were ... y'know, grim." She laughed. "The Eternal Tales could be dark, but they always seemed hopeful, too."

"Hmm. Hope is always good," Zerik said, his face inscrutable.

The road continued for a little more than a mile, winding through the dense forest, the trees a constant on either side of the track, the overarching branches forming a tunnel of light and shadow. As they drove, sunlight flashed and illuminated the heavy bark, gnarled branches like arms and eerie fingers holding the road clasped in a somber embrace. Finally, the murky light eased, the promise of sunlight around the next bend.

As they rounded the curve, Rhiannon could see light ahead, the end of the sylvan cavern. They broke out into the evening sunlight, the trees curving away to the left and right, stretching out of sight, encircling the land beyond.

Straight ahead was the third and final gate, much taller than the last, set into a forbidding stone wall, several feet thick. The gate looked like something from a European siege castle, utterly daunting, composed of colossal heavy wood timbers, medieval iron hinges and supports.

Rhiannon stared up at the gate, dismayed. "What do we have to do to open that?" She looked over at Zerik. "Get an army of knights and a battering ram?"

He laughed. "Actually, this gate is both the easiest and most difficult to open. Only a member of our *dzina* can open it. If you were visiting without me, you'd have to wait until someone inside opened it for you." He offered her a conspirational smile. "All we need is the key."

Zerik closed his eyes and held out his hand, palm up. His aura brightened. A silvery glow appeared in the air a few inches above his palm, the light shimmering. As Rhiannon watched, the shadowy shape of a large, old-fashioned metal key began to form in the midst of the radiant light, growing darker, solidifying, from translucent to opaque. The silvery light sparkled and danced on Zerik's skin. Just watching, Rhiannon could almost imagine a tingling in her own hand. Finally, the key seemed real, solid, heavy, floating impossible in the shining glow above Zerik's palm.

Zerik opened his eyes, winked at Rhiannon, and grasped the shining key. He pushed it in front of him, as though sliding it into a lock, and turned the key to the right. For a moment, nothing happened. Then, with a loud groaning of wood and creaking metal hinges, the enormous gate before them slowly began to move.

"Wow," Rhiannon breathed, watching as the gate majestically swung open. Smiling, Zerik released the key, and it evaporated into nothingness, the shimmering silver light fading last.

Rhiannon looked at Zerik. "It's all like magic. Magic isn't real."

Zerik laughed. "Neither are psychic abilities, and remembering past lives."

She had to smile at that.

"It's all *e'drai*. Different types of gifts, being combined and used in different ways." He shrugged. "Fire was magic to a caveman. I'm sure the first time some people saw an automobile, they thought it was magic. Particle physics is magic." He took her hand. "Magic is a matter of perspective."

Rhiannon looked down at their clasped hands, her tan skin against the darker-warm brown of his, the now-familiar feeling of comfort suffusing her. She looked up into his eyes, smiling. "Okay. Show me your perspective."

They drove forward between the massive stone walls. The driveway, now neat, well-tended gravel, curved off to the left.

The Ciatri home was situated on a headland, an immense promontory overlooking the rugged Pacific. The property was surrounded by the perfectly ordered ring of trees, everything from redwoods to eucalyptus, apple trees, elder, oak, hawthorn. The line of trees was broken only by the sheer cliffs overlooking the sea. Brutal and achingly beautiful, the icy cold and tumultuous ocean was an effective, nearly impenetrable defense.

The road curved out onto the headland, ending in a circular drive in front of the house. Zerik stopped the SUV, turning off the engine. "Welcome to my home," he said.

Rhiannon simply stared, unable to say a word.

Such a house had never existed. Such a house perhaps couldn't exist. But it sat there anyhow, enormous and shining, defying reality.

The Ciatri home was a fantastical thing, at once part castle, part Victorian mansion, part ancient tree, a wild yet harmonious mix of architectural styles and natural forms. Fanciful stone turrets and huge, curving towers seemed to grow upward from thick, sculpted, stone roots, sprouting rounded, compressed minarets and gothic arches set with sparkling glass. Mullioned windows and stained glass glittered in the summer evening light, set like jewels into walls of stone and richly carved wood. Brightly painted ornate balconies and cupolas blossomed from polished redwood walls, the rounded sides of crenellated granite towers.

A turret in the back appeared to be an observatory, moon phases in relief ringing a shining gold retractable dome. Another tower at the front of the house looked as though a mammoth tree had somehow grown into the side of the structure, a tree constructed of stone chiseled to look like tree bark, and wood carved to look like stone blocks. Recessed, arched windows gleamed at regular intervals around the Brobdingnagian trunk. A grand roofed cupola sat at the top, four stories above the ground, like a treehouse, its balustrade constructed of sinuously interlaced stone branches, the vaulted roof shingled in delicately-rendered wooden leaves.

On the left, closest to the edge of the cliff, one whole side of the house was taken up by a splendid conservatory, three stories high, the glass shimmering, reflecting the last light of the day. The entire

155

structure was glass, the roof bulging outward slightly before curving in again, a spire at the peak. Later, Rhiannon would discover the conservatory curled around the back of the house like a glittering snail.

Looking back at one of the crenellated towers, she began to notice the faces. Leering gargoyles, grotesques and hunkypunks supported balconies, guarded walls and spires. Peeping from beneath ledges, hiding around corners, almost everywhere Rhiannon looked were lions, monkeys, mermaids, eagles, and griffins, fairies and sprites, both lovely and wicked, carved from wood and stone, painted on balustrades, doorframes, windowsills. Beneath one window, a sharp-featured sly wooden elf was in the act of chiseling a stone leaf. A carved granite wood-nymph emerged frozen and silent from a casement, looking over her shoulder to pull her gown from the stone. Near the conservatory, a tiny marble water sprite was eternally diving into a rippling marble pool. Everywhere, painted faces stuck out their tongues, laughed, affected shock and surprise.

The house was surrounded by a colorful profusion of wild bushes and flowers, all barely held in check. The salt air intertwined with the perfume of roses, vivid pink azaleas, gardenias, lilacs, rhododendrons, and pale blush camellias, while the incessant roar of the ocean beyond the cliffs was a lulling counterpoint to the hum of bees and rasping frogs. Vines of ivy, wisteria, clematis, and honeysuckle climbed the towers and walls, and surrounding the front door was a lush cascade of fuchsia and purple-blue hydrangeas.

Wide, worn stone steps led up to the massive arched front door, crafted of superbly carved wood, with curling iron hinges and hardware. The door was recessed into a stone wall, the big blocks etched with waves, licking flames, clouds, trees. Above the door was chiseled the symbol Zerik wore around his neck – a small spiral, with a larger circle below, enclosing an elongated figure eight. Above the aeternan symbol was a crude, grinning stone sheela-na-gig.

Rhiannon was dazzled by the eccentric structure, straight out of a fairy tale. She felt Zerik take her hand, but was unable to look away from the house. Every time she looked, she saw something new, a detail she'd missed.

Just then, the front door opened, and a man came out. He was perhaps 5 feet, 5 inches tall, slightly pudgy, with fine coppery hair. He wore khakis, a white polo shirt, well-worn deck shoes, wire-rimmed glasses, and a garish pink, rose-printed women's kitchen apron. Three thin *fainna* defined his gold aura. He stood on the front stoop for a moment, looking at their big SUV. Finally, he cupped his hands, offering a brief *anam'sal*, the formal bow. Then he waved at them impatiently. "Are you going to sit in the car all day, or are you coming in?"

Zerik laughed, opening his car door.

Standing on the stoop, Zerik had introduced Rhiannon to Lyds, the bespectacled man in the pink apron. Looking at Rhiannon, Lyds had flushed and bowed again. He explained proudly that he and his *socia*, spouse, had been serving the Ciatri *dzina* for two lifetimes. Turning a disapproving eye on Zerik, he'd informed them the *Kir* was waiting — none too patiently, if Lyds' fidgeting was anything to go by.

The little man led them into the house, past a circular entry hall with an imposing curving staircase, a cavernous room fraught with shadows, through a long hallway, and finally to a back door leading outside again. Rhiannon wasn't able to get a very good look at the inside of the house — night was falling, and most of the interior lighting hadn't been turned on yet. She only had an impression of vast spaces, tall ceilings, sparkling glass, shadows, and soft, rich carpets beneath her feet.

The darkened hallway had been lined with framed portraits of all sizes, and she had the uncomfortable feeling the eyes were following her as she moved. She put it down to fancy – the outside of the house had clearly stimulated her imagination. *This isn't a mystery movie, for God's sake,* she chided herself inwardly.

The sun was just beginning its descent into the sea as they stepped outside. There was still more than enough light; Rhiannon looked around curiously. A manicured grassy area behind the house was about the size of a soccer field, with the cliff beyond. On the left was a large pavilion with a ruby, cream, and gold striped canopy supported by polished brass rods. Jewel-toned silk divans and wide couches were deployed around the space, and in the center a table was set for five, with china and sparkling glassware, candles, and fresh flowers.

Some distance behind the pavilion were two round slate pools, a larger pool on the left, a much smaller hot plunge on the right, a breath of steam hovering over the water. The pools were connected by an open, swirling slate aqueduct.

"This way," Lyds announced, waving them toward the right. This side of the grounds had been allowed to grow wild, the natural grasses trimmed, but with no formal planting or garden. Another ring of trees encircled the area closest to the cliff edge, the trees spaced about 10 feet apart, defining a circle some 50 feet in diameter. When they reached the trees, Lyds halted. "I expect you can find your way from here," he said, smiling. "I have to get dinner on." Offering another bow, he left them, walking back toward the house.

Zerik took Rhiannon's hand, and she was grateful for the comfort and warmth. He led her between the trees, and they stepped into the Circle.

Madeline was standing in front of her firepit, near another, smaller pavilion at the far end of the Circle, on the ocean side. She turned as they approached. Her aura was unmistakably that of an Eldest, radiant gold rings of light surrounding her body. She was of average height, with a mane of silver-laced auburn hair that fell halfway down her back. Madeline was voluptuous, her curves softly rounded, her skin creamy and freckled. Her generous bosom was exposed liberally by the deep neckline of her ankle-length black dress. She was barefoot, and her nose was smudged with what appeared to be soot. Her smile lit her entire face. "Zerik!" she called, coming forward.

When she stopped before them, her glowing smile was all for Rhiannon. Zerik didn't release Rhiannon's hand. He looked down at her, his smile reassuring, then up to Madeline. "Madeline Sofia, may I present Megan Byrne."

Rhiannon dropped Zerik's hand, ignoring his almost immediately controlled surprise. Her eyes on Madeline, she carefully cupped her hands, fingertips to the heels of her palms, resting her hands against her belly. She nodded gravely.

To her astonishment, Madeline returned the gesture, performing a formally respectful *anam'sal*. Madeline held the pose for a moment, then held out her arms. "Welcome to our nest." She enfolded Rhiannon in a warm embrace. Her mouth brushed against Rhiannon's lightly, her lips soft and pliable, moist, sweet. It was a warm, friendly kiss, lasting a second longer than might be proper, suggesting a hint of promise.

Slipping her arm around Rhiannon's waist, Madeline looked up at Zerik. "About time you made it home, Husband."

He kissed her then, thoroughly, his passion restrained but evident. Rhiannon watched, expecting to feel jealous, or uncomfortable, or out of place. Instead she felt joy, genuine pleasure and happiness, and unexpectedly, a flush of arousal, heat singing through her veins.

Sighing, Zerik pulled back from the kiss, his smile lighting his dark eyes. "It's good to be home." He gently wiped the smudge of soot from Madeline's nose. She laughed.

Madeline took Rhiannon's hand. "Come, sit down. You've had some adventures, I hear." She led them to the pavilion, and a wide, silk-embroidered couch. A small, inlaid-wood side-table held a tea tray. She looked at Zerik. "The rest of the family should be home any time. Thicket sent them to Ukiah for something or other." She looked at Rhiannon. "Would you like some tea, Megan?"

Rhiannon nodded, sitting down next to Madeline. Zerik chose to remain standing, pleading long hours behind the wheel.

Rhiannon smiled shyly at Madeline. The older woman looked as though she were in her early 40s, vibrant, with laugh lines around her eyes, testifying to a life well-lived. Madeline pulled a thick cotton cozy from a silver teapot. The teapot was battered and dented, even crudely made, but it shone with loving polish. Steam wafted from the top of the pot. She smiled at Rhiannon. "I've had this teapot since 1460. It was a Saturnalia gift from one of my wives. I'm rather fond of it."

Wide-eyed, Rhiannon tried to absorb that information, failed. Madeline smiled wryly. "I know, Saturnalia is a bit old-fashioned. But it's far more fun than Christmas, or Chanukah or something." She nodded toward the house. "Lyds and Robbie just love it. We serve them dinner."

Abjectly confused, Rhiannon just nodded politely. Zerik put a sympathetic hand on her shoulder. "Madeline, Megan is neonate. This is all very new for her."

The *Kir* blushed, genuinely embarrassed, offering Rhiannon an apologetic smile. "I don't want to make you feel uncomfortable. You look like an Eldest. I suppose you know that. I'm sorry to prattle on." Her eyes were earnest, warm. "I really do want you to feel at home here."

Megan touched Madeline's hand. "It's okay. I just have a lot to learn." She smiled into the older woman's eyes. "And believe me, I already feel more comfortable here than anywhere I've been in a long time."

Impulsively, Madeline leaned forward and pressed a kiss to Rhiannon's cheek. "Thank you, sweet."

She sat back, smiling, and poured a stream of dark tea into a bone china cup, loose tea leaves swirling. She offered the cup to Rhiannon, who took it gratefully. Something about sitting down for a hot cup of tea had always been soothing. It had been a long day. She took a cautious sip, sighed.

A sense of peace pervaded her bones, and she listened to the roar of the waves beyond the cliff, the crackling of the fire. She really did feel safe here, in this fairy tale place by the sea, so far removed from her life in Kansas City, her fears, new dangers and old.

Madeline poured herself a cup. "I suppose you'd like something a bit stronger, Zerik," she commented.

He turned to look at her, smiling. "I'm fine for now. Just glad to be out of that car."

"Me, too," Rhiannon agreed fervently. She blushed, feeling unexpectedly shy.

As if reading her mind, Madeline touched her hand. "I know you've had a hard time of it. Let's have some tea, and after the rest of the family arrives, we'll have dinner – and then you can get some rest. Robbie – that's Lyds' wife – has a room ready for you, and, of course, you're welcome to company or not, your choice." Her smile was

160

genuine, kind. "We can talk tomorrow about all the excitement you've had today. And I'd love to hear how you found Zerik."

Zerik was studying the open firepit, flames dancing into the darkling sky. "What witchery are you up to tonight, Wife?"

Madeline looked up briefly at the fire, then back to her battered teapot. She sighed. "I'm still stuck on circles. Honestly, dear, I've never seen anything like it. The same symbol, repeated over and over, for days. Circles. It's maddening."

Rhiannon took another sip of the strong tea. "Your gate has circles all over it too."

Madeline's hands stilled, and Zerik turned from the fire to look at Rhiannon. "What do you mean?"

Rhiannon poured milk into her teacup from a china jug, blithely unaware of their scrutiny. "The second gate we came to – " she glanced up at Zerik. "You know, the one we drove right through? With all the iron and wood carvings. That was beautiful. All circles and spirals, made of leaves and stuff. And the dancers in the middle. How long did it take the artist to create that? It's really amazing." She laughed a little. "I guess that's an understatement."

Madeline glanced up at Zerik, then put a gentle hand on Rhiannon's knee. "That gate is special. It looks different to different people." She smiled kindly, her blue eyes bright. "You say you saw circles?"

Rhiannon put her cup down, embarrassed. "Well, yes. Circles made of branches, and leaves, and roots. The whole thing was big and little circles, all sizes. And in the middle, I saw six people, dancing in a ring around a big tree."

Zerik came and sat next to Rhiannon, taking her hand, looking at Madeline. "Six."

Madeline nodded, her eyes meeting Zerik's. *"Who the hell is this girl?"* her thought whispered in his mind. *"You say her name's Megan – is that her* Praenom, *her primary name?"*

Zerik felt the blood rush to his face, realizing he'd never asked Megan her name. Just "Megan Byrne" when they'd met. At the time, he'd thought her to be Eldest, and simply assumed she'd offered him her true name. Later, he'd been too busy wallowing in *era* to think clearly. Sheepishly, he met Madeline's eyes. *"I don't know."*

Lips pursed, she cast him a knowing glance, then offered Rhiannon an encouraging smile. "I need to ask you about your name," she said.

Rhiannon looked uncertainly at Zerik, then back to Madeline. She'd protected herself for so long. But she yearned to feel secure here, accepted. To belong.

"Halloooo!"

The glad cry came from the direction of the house. From beyond the trees marking the Circle's boundary, they could see a man and woman approaching, hands clasped. The man was tall and lean, with long, silver hair, in jeans and a close-fitting long-sleeved T-shirt. The woman had short, blonde, tousled curls, and was wearing a pale, green dress that glowed in the twilight. Both had the luminous, shining auras of the Eldest.

Zerik stood, grinning broadly, and Madeline waved. "Oh good, the whole family's home." Madeline looked over at Zerik. "Z, did Lyds say if he'd started dinner or not?"

Rhiannon had been watching the blonde woman walking toward them across the grass, but turned suddenly to look at Madeline, then Zerik. "What did you call him?"

Madeline's brow creased in confusion. "Z. A nickname."

And then Rhiannon remembered a dream, and then another. So many dreams throughout this life and the last, dreams in different times, different places. Dreams of dancing in ballrooms or barefoot around forest bonfires, wild lovemaking under the stars, a woman giving birth on a train, a glorious Victorian picnic by a lake.

The man with the silver hair and the blonde woman were almost to the Circle, about 20 yards away.

All at once, Rhiannon was overcome with an intense sensation, an electric tingling feeling that started in her scalp and flared throughout her body, traversing her skin like sparks. She recognized this feeling, the reality as vivid as the remembered dreams. The air itself shimmered, amplified, expanded. The prickling energy flowed outward from her body, and Rhiannon was acutely aware of Madeline's body, the blonde woman by the trees, the earth and the snapping fire, the gloaming sky, the crashing ocean beyond the cliffs.

She was intensely connected with everything, aware of the potent force animating and joining all things, through her, through the other two women.

The magnitude of the energy could be felt by the men as well, a wave of power that caused both to stagger, momentarily unsteady. Abruptly, Zerik threw his head back, laughing.

At the edge of the trees, the blonde woman dropped her companion's hand and started running toward them, crying out her name — not "Megan," but her name, incontrovertible, the name which had always been hers, the name that felt real and true and right. *Rhiannon, Rhiannon.*

Maddie looked up at Zerik with tears in her eyes. "Trust you, Zerik. You pick up a strange woman, and she turns out to be your own wife."

Eternal Tales:
The Traveler and the Queen

Once upon a time, there lived a Traveler. He could Travel between the many worlds, from the world of men to the Fae realms, to the Dark Places, to the stars and beyond. Even the Spirit World offered a path he could safely walk.

One Midsummer night, the Traveler was walking his paths, his spirit far from his body. He absorbed the light of the stars and moon, talked to Forest and Sky Beings.

On that night, the Faerie Queen thought to dance at a festival, in the guise of a mortal woman. During her transformation, she was weak and vulnerable to the wiles of demons and men.

The Queen assigned a Fae Guardian to watch over her and keep her safe. This he did, and she became human. She danced and laughed under the full moon.

Before dawn, the Faerie Queen wished to return to her own Form. But her Fae Guardian had grown tired of waiting, and unbeknownst to the Queen, had deserted his post.

As she began the metamorphosis from human woman to Fae, she was caught in one of the Dark Places, held fast by an evil creature who craved her beauty and power. She struggled, but was unable to escape.

The Traveler came upon the Faerie Queen in that Dark Place, and fought the creature who held her there. He was strong and managed to free the Faerie Queen. She returned to her own Form.

The Faerie Queen found her faithless Guardian in the wild wood. Realizing he had almost lost his Queen with his actions, the Fae sentinel begged for forgiveness. But the Queen was enraged and would not listen to his pleas.

The Traveler, who had saved the Queen, was gravely wounded in the Dark Place. His spirit was damaged beyond repair, and he would soon die.

In the moonlit wild wood, The Faerie Queen knitted the Fae Guardian's spirit to the Traveler's, intertwining the two until they were one, making the Traveler whole once more. The powerful Fae's spirit changed the Traveler's hair from dark to shining silver, his brown eyes to grey.

Thus, the inconstant Fae Guardian was punished, to cleave forever to the spirit of a man, and the Traveler was rewarded, to always be joined with the Fae.

And they lived ever after.

ELEVEN

The best lies are woven with a golden thread of truth. The best fairy tales are lies once real, facts embellished with dreams, adorned with fantasy. Perhaps the best stories of all are utterly true, but their honesty so magnificent and wild as to be fabricated, imagined – even as we yearn to believe.

The mensaeterna, Those Who Do Not Forget, have been telling stories for thousands of years. At first, their histories were told around campfires and sung before kings – oral traditions, spoken word and songs. The narratives of the first aeternans, their lives, their loves, their fights and triumphs, and most importantly, their deaths and resurrections, were passed from one person to another, memorized, set to music, whispered. And with each retelling, as stories are wont to do, they grew, expanded, details added, others forgotten.

By the time aeternans began to commit their histories and experiences to parchment and papyrus, painting words with inks of burnt bone, plant dyes, and crushed minerals, the first stories had already transformed. The histories of the mensaeterna had evolved into fairy tales, folklore, myths, legends.

Replete with Fae magic, demons, spirits, talking animals, ageless queens and kings, people who are continually reborn, their lives like seasons, the stories lay bare a secret world, expose it for anyone to know, yet utterly conceal it in the guise of fiction and fancy.

Today, aeternan and oblivi parents alike read the stories to their children, only the former knowing the shining thread of truth at the heart of the magic.

Stories speak to us on a deeper, subconscious level. Different cultures around the world tell similar stories, communicating a profound shared experience. The story of Cinderella is retold thousands of ways, from the ancient Greek Rhodopis, to the Vietnamese Tam Cám. The concept of unjust persecution and victorious reward resonates throughout human understanding.

We need to hear the same stories, over and over, finding comfort and understanding in familiar themes and satisfyingly expected endings. Like rules of behavior for children, religious constraints, or natural and scientific laws, the familiar boundaries of stories are a touchstone for existence, reminding us of our place in the order of the universe. Stories help us make sense of who we are.

On occasion, it's not the stories themselves, but elements of a story which are continually retold. These tropes become cliché, trite, so often used and repeated they become unreal, unbelievable. And yet they persist in popular culture. Because, like the best lies, clichés are predicated on a truth which echoes in the heart of experience.

"Amnesia? You can't be serious."

Zerik sent his husband a withering glance. "I said *mirsyatun*. Amnesia is an oblivi word for an oblivi problem."

Grayling snorted. "Call it what you like, it's still fiction. *King Lear*. Dalayrac's *Nina*. Hell, bad TV shows, soap operas."

Zerik and Emma were sitting on the wide couch in the pavilion within the Sisters' Circle, Madeline's fire snapping and crackling, sending sparks flying upward into the darkness. Grayling stood outside the shelter of the canopy, brooding, staring into the flames. His face was that of a man in his early 30s, his silver hair a startling contrast to his unlined features. Beyond the circle of light, the night waited breathless, while the sea crashed against the cliffs.

Emma looked up at her second husband, her blue eyes earnest. "Amnesia is real, Gray. There's lots of different kinds of amnesia. The one in the movies or on TV is the fugue state. And, it's true, it's overused, but it does exist. It's just very rare." She sniffed. "Besides, I don't think Rhiannon's in a fugue state anyhow."

Grayling turned from the fire, casting a sideways glance at Emma, suspicious. "Since when are you an expert on amnesia?"

Emma folded her hands in her lap primly. "Maybe I haven't been a medical doctor for a couple of incarnations, Grayling, but I keep up with the latest journals." She looked away, embarrassed. "Besides, I do write romance novels. It's a classic plot device."

Grayling threw up his hands, sat down hard on the divan next to Zerik. "Okay, fine. So tell me about amnesia."

Emma looked at Zerik. "Are you relaying this conversation to Maddie?"

Zerik nodded. "She's got Rhiannon in the kitchen right now, helping her calm down, relax. Maddie's better at that sort of thing than the rest of us, you know."

"Always has been," Grayling nodded.

Zerik got a faraway look in his eyes for a moment, then looked back at his spouses. "Maddie says Lyds is getting her a fresh cup of tea, and she does seem better. With all of us fussing over her, I think we overwhelmed her."

"You did, dear." Maddie's thought resonated in the minds of all present.

Zerik winced. "I feel so stupid. I should have known who she was. In retrospect, all the signs were there." He shook his head. "Especially after she used Earth *e'drai*, restoring me like that. I didn't even recognize it for what it was."

Emma patted his knee sympathetically. "Well, from what you describe, I'm not even sure she knew she could do it. Anyhow, you brought her home to us, and that's what's important." She looked at

Grayling. "And I think Zerik is right — it makes more sense to call this *mirsyatun* – forgotten – than to call it amnesia."

Grayling ran a hand through his hair, frustrated. "What would be the difference?"

Emma laughed. "We aren't oblivi. We don't store permanent memory in the hippocampus or neocortex in the brain. We don't even know how we store memory at all. I mean, it must somehow become part of our souls, because it carries from one incarnation to the next."

Zerik nodded thoughtfully. "I've always thought aeternan souls must be like computer hard drives, storing our personalities and memories, downloading that information into our new brains when we go through *Memora Magia*, and Remember who we are."

"That makes sense," Emma agreed, enthusiastic. "Surely scientists at one of the Caistras have studied this sort of thing. I've really been remiss on paying attention to the most recent theories."

"Humph," Grayling grumbled. "Family scientists are just guessing. Going on faith. They don't know anything more about why we're here and where we're going than anyone else. May as well be Lutherans or Muslims or something."

Emma frowned at him. "Gray, plenty of aeternans are Lutherans or Muslims. Just because you don't agree with their philosophy doesn't mean they don't have — "

"Emma, my love," Grayling interrupted. "I'm sure you're right. And I apologize for my part in distracting my infinitely distractable wife. But if you don't return to the subject at hand, I'll be forced to kiss you senseless."

Wide-eyed, Emma started to respond, thought the better of it, and closed her mouth.

Zerik frowned. "Grayling, our wife has just returned to us after nearly 100 years, and has no idea who we are, or really who she is."

"Yes," Grayling agreed gravely.

"Do you honestly think this is the appropriate time to be flirting with Emma, carrying on as if nothing has happened?"

"Yes," Grayling repeated. He gave Zerik a serious, sideways glance. "I'm open to sharing."

"Grayling!" Emma was scandalized, blushing despite herself.

Grayling shrugged, a fluid, natural movement. "I see your point, but I've got a Fae soul. Well, a piece of one. It's hard to take anything seriously, to be honest." His expression, characteristically stoic, belied his words. "And while she's been gone a while, it hasn't been so long that I've forgotten how to love her, or indeed any of my wives." His grin was rare, sinful.

Emma stamped a foot petulantly. "Grayling, you are a wicked thing. Flirt later. I just want to see her, to touch her again after so long."

"And there's still that matter of *mirsyatun*," Zerik put in. "She may be back, but she is far from okay. Something serious is wrong with her. A terrible thing happened, to make her forget us, forget everything."

Glaring at Grayling, Emma tossed her blonde curls, her nose in the air. "Well, amnesia in the movies, the fugue state, is when a person doesn't remember their past at all, or who they are. Basically, it's like they have a whole new personality."

"Well, that can't be right then," Zerik said. "I'd have to say she's definitely herself, though perhaps more insecure, and a little more timid at times." He frowned. "For good reason."

"Maybe it's repressed memory. Dissociative," Emma said thoughtfully, tapping her lower lip with her index finger. She frowned. "Something happened to her, back then. During the war. We never did find out what."

"At this rate, we may never know," Grayling said. He looked over at Zerik. "She doesn't remember anything except her last incarnation, right?"

Zerik shook his head. "Well, yes and no. I think she remembers *something*, something more." He shrugged helplessly. "But I think she's afraid to talk about it."

"What is she afraid of?" Grayling stilled, tense.

Madeline's voice sounded within their minds, clear, soothing. *"We're coming back outside, dears. Maybe we should meet in the dining pavilion? Lyds is fretting about dinner being overcooked."*

While the thought had been broadcast to all, only Zerik had the requisite *e'drai* to respond. *"We'll meet you there,"* he told Maddie. He held out a solicitous hand to Emma, who took it and rose gracefully from the couch.

As the three walked across the grass toward the house, Zerik slowed, falling into step a few feet behind Emma. At his meaningful glance, Grayling slowed as well. "She's got someone after her." Zerik kept his voice low, his eyes on Emma's back. "Someone *erim*. And we were attacked by The Guard – a *dha*."

Grayling stopped abruptly, staring at Zerik in shock. "Are you serious? Jesu." His features hardened, grew forbidding, cold. "Memory or not, she's ours. They'd best leave her alone." He looked Zerik in the eye. A silent exchange took place, a communication that didn't require *e'drai*. Zerik nodded grimly.

"C'mon, husbands," Emma called over her shoulder. "Let's keep walking. I'm hungry. And I'd like to see my wife."

The men lengthened their strides, catching up to Emma. No one said anything further as they walked toward the house, which glowed like a fairy palace in the darkness.

They reached the large pavilion. The ruby, cream, and gold-striped silk canopy shimmered in the light of the candles on the circular dining table, and the garden torches burned in the grass beyond. Before they had a chance to seat themselves, the air abruptly rippled and expanded, a powerful energy skating through all three, Emma especially. She smiled. "They're here."

Maddie and Rhiannon appeared in the doorway at the back of the house. They walked toward the group waiting by the table.

Rhiannon looked from one to another, smiling shyly. "I'm sorry, I kind of freaked out a little." She held tight to Maddie's hand.

Emma came forward and kissed her, her lips tender. "It's okay. We'll help you in any way we can. I'm sorry if we overwhelmed you." She blinked back tears. "We've just missed you. It's been a long time."

Rhiannon nodded, looking uncertainly at Emma, and then Maddie. "Can you tell me – what is that feeling? It's like sparks all over my body. My skin. And the air moves with it, like energy." She blushed. "I can feel you. It happens when I'm with both of you. I've had dreams when it happened, too."

Maddie laughed. "That's me. And you. And Emma. It's the *e'drai* of the Sisters."

Emma took Rhiannon's hand, her blue eyes earnest. "When we're together, in close proximity, we are very powerful." She smiled wryly. "Well, even more powerful."

Maddie motioned toward Emma, then herself, finally indicating Rhiannon with a wave of her manicured hand. "We're a *nahyin*, a Circle. Aeternans who have great gifts, powerful *e'drai*, when we work together." She stopped, her eyes widening. Unexpectedly, she began to laugh. "The Circle! Of course. That's why I've been seeing circles in all my divinations. The Circle is complete. The Sisters are finally reunited." Her face was suffused with joy.

At Rhiannon's baffled expression, she laughed again. "I can see we're going to have to do a lot of explaining. Let's have some dinner and talk." She nodded toward the beautifully laid table.

Zerik and Grayling pulled out three chairs, bowing before the women, Zerik with his customary grin, Grayling sober, his eyes warm, intent. Rhiannon suppressed a nervous giggle. She still wasn't used to men who offered such boldly gallant behavior, old-fashioned. Maddie and Emma seated themselves without comment, nodding thanks to the men, and Rhiannon did the same, unconsciously copying Maddie, pretending a composure she didn't feel.

Zerik and Grayling seated themselves at the round table, across from the three women. "So we can keep an eye on you," Zerik teased.

Lyds and his wife, Robbie, appeared, pushing a cart laden with covered silver dishes. Rhiannon hadn't yet met Lyds' wife. She was stocky and busty, with a broad nose and mouth, her dark, greying hair pulled back into a severe bun. She wore blue jeans, a grey T-shirt, and a blue apron that was as simple and plain as Lyds' floral apron was garish. Like her husband, three thin glowing *fainna* defined her aura.

Robbie turned to Rhiannon, offering a brief *anam'sal*. "*Navtu*. It's a pleasure to finally meet you," she said. "I've heard so much about you." She placed a dish before Rhiannon, removing the cover with a flourish, revealing a perfectly grilled steak, an artful swirl of béarnaise sauce, and lightly steamed mushrooms and asparagus. Rhiannon's stomach growled, loud enough to be heard, and she flushed with embarrassment.

Zerik winked at her. "Always good to bring an appetite to the table." She smiled back into his brown eyes.

173

" 'Hunger is the best sauce,' " Maddie quoted, patting Rhiannon's knee with a reassuring smile.

Rhiannon looked back at Robbie. "Thank you very much."

The woman favored her with a gap-toothed smile. "Not at all, dear."

While the couple bustled around the table, delivering various dishes, ensuring water glasses were filled, Rhiannon looked around her. A few feet from the dinner table was a U-shaped seating area, comprised of three wide backless couches, upholstered in vivid jewel-toned silk, centered around a Moroccan table inlaid with gleaming mother-of-pearl. Shimmering, iridescent, cutwork candle lanterns with thick, creamy candles cast dazzling patterns on the surface of the table and the canopy above. Beyond the pavilion, torches burned in dark metal sconces on stakes, seemingly without fuel. The smell and sound of the ocean came in from the darkness, soothing, yet invigorating, energizing. It was as though the world around, the air itself, held promise, a sense of anticipation.

Rhiannon looked at her companions. She'd had dreams about these people. And when she'd awoken, those dreams had felt as solid and real as memories, as if while she'd slept, she had remembered a genuine experience. But whatever their intensity, she'd always believed they were nothing more than dreams. They were magic, soothing her soul as a child, giving her hope and a belief in love. She'd never dared to believe they might actually be more than dreams. She'd never even hoped to meet these people, the fantasy companions and lovers of a desperately lonely little girl.

And yet here they were, her imaginary friends, real and solid and breathing. But if those dreams were real, did that mean all of the others were real as well? That every nocturnal memory had really happened? She abruptly found herself remembering the excruciating torture of flames licking her flesh, or being savagely beaten in a dark forest, or ... her back suddenly began to ache, and she shook herself inwardly. She wouldn't think of these things. Not here. Not now, not with these people. Why was it so easy to believe pain and fear was real, and not love and kindness?

She looked up across the table to find Zerik's brown eyes watching her. *"It's alright,* varenya," he whispered in her mind. She smiled at him, feeling awkward, and looked away.

Surreptitiously, she studied the others – her family, apparently. A family of her own. People who loved her, all of her, who thought she was special, not weird or different or wrong. The thought filled her with a rush of pleasure, even as the wounded child in her heart clung to doubt.

Grayling looked much as he had in her dreams. But how was that possible, if people had different incarnations, different lives, different bodies? She herself looked nothing like Kat Weiss. But Grayling's appearance was startlingly similar to the man in her dreams. He had a hawkish nose, a serious demeanor. His face was different, but his eyes were the same pale grey, his hair utterly straight, flowing silver falling midway down his back. Even his basic body structure seemed the same, lean, and muscular.

Emma looked like a different person, but was still somehow the woman she'd seen in dreams. Rhiannon felt as though she would always know Emma, no matter what she looked like. Her hair was cropped into short, blonde curls. Her pale green dress set off her creamy skin, the soft blush of her cheeks, her bright blue eyes. Her face was classical, with a little upturned nose and a generous mouth. Rhiannon imagined kissing those full lips and blushed. Emma seemed unflaggingly cheerful, her laugh merry, free. For Rhiannon, who could only remember two lives, both marked by grief, Emma was summer rain on parched ground.

Maddie and Zerik chatted while Lyds and Robbie served them. Rhiannon wasn't jealous, exactly. Envious, maybe. Maddie was so beautiful, with that cascading red hair, and so confident, comfortable with herself and everything around her. She could see the love Zerik had for her, when he looked at her. It shone in his eyes.

As if sensing her regard, Zerik turned to look at Rhiannon. She was startled to see the same love in his brown eyes, this time for her. She smiled shyly. *"You look beautiful tonight,* varenya," his thought sounded in her mind. *"That brown dress suits you, our little Earth goddess."* He smiled, and she could feel the warmth of it as something physical, tangible.

175

Robbie set a plate in front of Emma, smiling her gap-toothed grin. "I'm feeding the children in the nursery tonight, so you all can have some peace."

Emma touched Robbie's hand. "Thank you so much. Let them know one of us will be up for a goodnight kiss and a story later."

Robbie laughed, deep, from her belly. "I think Miss Eva has decided she's in charge of stories and kisses. But I'll tell them."

Maddie rolled her eyes. "That child will be the death of me."

"You're only saying that because she's just like you," Emma said, trying not to smile, failing.

"You have children?" Rhiannon asked Maddie. If she was truly married to these people, how did that work with children? She'd long ago given up on the idea of ever being a mother. The very thought opened an empty ache in her chest.

Maddie laughed. "Do we have children? Do we ever. I birthed Eva, Emma managed the other six on her own." She winked. "Emma's a baby factory. Of course, it doesn't matter who birthed them, they're all ours. Though I think you're quite overwhelmed enough for one night — you can meet the little horde tomorrow."

Rhiannon sat back in her chair, trying to absorb it all. "I can't have children," she blurted out, surprising herself that she'd said it aloud. "Doctors couldn't figure out —"

Maddie laid a hand over Rhiannon's, her pale blue eyes soft, kind. "Sweetheart, you've *never* been able to have children. For thousands of years." She touched Rhiannon's cheek, as if to gentle the stunned expression she found there. "We've never known why. But it's always been true."

"You get to share my babies," Emma said earnestly. "I have plenty for all of us."

Rhiannon nodded, unable to speak. Her throat felt tight. Revisiting the loss of something she'd never had left her feeling hollow, lonely. And yet suddenly there were seven unseen children she was being invited to share, as if she had as much right to the parenting of them as the women who'd brought them life. Every moment since she'd left the hospital in Kansas City had just grown exponentially more outrageous, breathlessly hopeful, more difficult to take in, to believe.

176

She thought of the monster who stalked her, but somehow here, in this place, she felt safe, secure. This home was an escape, a haven he could not reach.

Lyds approached Zerik. "I took the liberty – that is, I – " he waved at a standing ice bucket, where a bottle of champagne chilled.

"Good choice, Lyds. Tonight is definitely a celebration." Zerik smiled at Robbie. "I think we'd all like you both to join us in a toast."

Robbie flushed, clearly pleased. Lyds handed glasses around, and Zerik popped the cork. "Veuve Clicquot, 1897. I've been saving this bottle for something special." He grinned at Rhiannon. "After nearly a hundred year absence, this is definitely special."

Following a toast to a blushing, discomfited Rhiannon, Lyds and Robbie withdrew to the house, leaving the Ciatri *dzina* alone. Before an awkward silence could develop, Maddie draped her napkin across her lap with a flourish. "I'm starving." She smiled at Zerik. "Pass the salt, beloved."

"Of course." He handed it over. He smiled at Rhiannon. "I'm sure you have a lot of questions for us – and we have a few for you, as well."

Emma leaned forward eagerly. "I think we should take turns, asking and answering." She tossed Rhiannon a radiant smile. "And don't let us overwhelm you."

Maddie nodded agreement. "First one to overwhelm Rhiannon gets a spanking."

Emma blushed to the roots of her hair. "Maddie, that's not a threat."

The older redhead grinned. "Not for you, maybe, but Gray hates spankings."

"Correction," Grayling said quietly. "I hate receiving spankings."

Rhiannon cleared her throat nervously, looking from one to the other.

Zerik rolled his eyes. He reached out, patting Rhiannon's hand. "My apologies – we tend to be a flirtatious lot. Having you home feels like everything's finally back to normal. You don't remember – but aeternans are highly sensual creatures. *Era* is one of the few things that make any life not just bearable, but delightful." He shrugged.

"After thousands of years, we suffer so much. So we enjoy *era*, and each other, whenever possible."

"*Era* is highly portable," Grayling commented, as he cut his steak. "Goes anywhere."

Rhiannon offered a nervous laugh, thinking of her many sexual adventures and encounters throughout her life – up to, and including, sleeping with Zerik. "I guess I've always been like that, too."

Maddie cleared her throat, straightening her shoulders. She smiled at Rhiannon encouragingly. "Don't mind the teasing. Ask us anything."

Rhiannon returned the older woman's smile. "Maybe I should just tell you all about me. There so much I want to understand." She looked down into her lap. "There's a lot I've kept secret. A lot I've never told anybody." She twisted her napkin between her fingers. "I have to admit, I'm not sure I can talk about some of it. But I'll try."

"Just do your best, *varenya*," Zerik nodded encouragingly.

She looked at Maddie, and then at Zerik. "I've had dreams about all of you. Dreams like memories. I always thought they weren't real, but you're here and you're real. And I guess that's why I feel like I know you – but I don't know you – but I ..." she faltered, took a breath. "I care about you, and I don't know you." A shaky laugh escaped her. "Which is weird, but there it is."

"It's not weird," Grayling said. "We've been married for centuries." His expression was characteristically serious, but his eyes were warm with emotion. "We love you."

Zerik reached across the table, touched her hand. "The weird part is that you don't remember. But I told you that I would help you, and I will. We will. We'll figure this out, I promise."

Rhiannon looked down, hesitating, forced to give voice to her fear. "What if I'm not who you think I am?"

Maddie laughed. "Only one woman in the world could complete the Circle, become part of that powerful energy reaction you feel when Emma and I are near you." She took Rhiannon's hand. "And you know it. You feel the connection with us, and with Zerik and Gray. Even if you can't explain it." She stroked the back of Rhiannon's hand, her blue eyes gentle. "We divide *e'drai* between us. Take turns carrying the soul *e'drai*."

"And there's your name," Zerik said quietly.

Rhiannon looked up into his eyes, hopeful, afraid. "My name?"

"You never told me your real name, your *Praenom*, your primary name. Rhiannon. Yet we knew it." His eyes were earnest. "Our names are part of who we are, carried from one lifetime to the next. Everyone has two – the *Praenom*, and the *Secunom*, the secondary name. The names we are born with in each incarnation mark that particular lifetime. You have yet to tell us your *Secunom*." He reached across the table, took her hand. "Shall I tell you that name as well?"

Rhiannon flushed, looked away, then up at Maddie. Her name – the name that was hers, and hers alone, the name that had always been a source of strength and a place to retreat – that name echoed in her mind.

Maddie smiled, her eyes sparkling with tears. "Rhiannon Elektra. My wife. My Sister."

Rhiannon nodded, looking down in her lap. "I've never told anyone my name." She felt swamped by feeling, confusion warring with hope, mixed with fear and an inexplicable sense of affection for these people she didn't really know. Or maybe she did. She thought about that immediate attraction and connection she had for Zerik. She realized she felt that closeness with all of them.

Emma leaned forward, her smile sunny, reassuring. "You said you've had dreams about us. Dreams like memories."

"Yes. They feel real, not like dreams at all, but like actual memories."

"Do you retain them afterward?" Grayling asked. "You don't forget them, like a dream?"

Rhiannon shook her head. "No, I remember them afterward. Every detail. It was a little awkward when I was a kid." She blushed. "I remembered some pretty adult things."

Zerik sat back in his chair. "Hmm. So as a child, you have these dreams like memories – but then, when you went through the Remembering, you didn't remember any more of these experiences?"

"What's the Remembering?"

Maddie laid a hand on her thigh. "When you were a teenager, didn't you have an experience where you suddenly remembered your

179

last life? Almost all at once, in a rush? You said you could remember your previous incarnation."

Rhiannon nodded, wide-eyed. "Oh, hell yes. That was – I don't even know how to describe that."

Emma laughed merrily. "Remembering – *Memora Magia* – is a little uncomfortable."

"Yeah, like childbirth was uncomfortable," Grayling grumbled.

Rhiannon stared at him. "You were a woman in another life? You've had a baby?"

Grayling nodded. "Once. Before Emma Chose me. Since then, I've always been male."

"Me too," Zerik added. "I was female in two incarnations, before I married the Sisters. I've been male since."

Maddie smiled approvingly. "The Universe seeks balance. The Sisters are always female, therefore, our Consorts must be male."

Rhiannon took a sip of her water, feeling as though she were trying to find her equilibrium, a sense of balance. It was as though she'd fallen into a deep pool, and couldn't figure out which way was up.

"Oh, damn," Maddie said, putting down her fork. "It seems I'm the one who's overwhelmed her." She patted Rhiannon's hand. "I'm sorry, dear."

"You'll have to have a spanking," Grayling said quietly.

Maddie shot him a look.

"You'll enjoy it." Grayling's eyes were intent, serious.

"Spankings later," Emma announced. "I believe we're supposed to be staying on the subject at hand." She sent Grayling a hard look, then turned to Rhiannon. "So let me understand. You've had dreams that are memories – of us, and I guess other things too – but you didn't remember them fully when you went through *Memora Magia*?"

"Most of us have flashes of memory throughout our early lives, which grow more intense as *Memora Magia* approaches," Maddie explained. "Once we go through the Remembering, all of those pieces fall into place, and we remember everything in detail."

"No, I only remembered my last life. My name was Kat Weiss." Rhiannon's hand shook as she lifted her water glass again. "In my last life, and in this one, I've always had these dreams. I still have them. And they feel real, like memories. But I don't remember anything else."

"What do you mean?" Zerik asked.

"Well, okay, like I had a dream where Emma and Maddie and I had a picnic by a lake near a huge mansion. I think it was in England, but I don't know for sure. We were wearing these tight corsets, and drinking – we weren't supposed to; Grayling put brandy in the picnic basket – I felt it, that's how I learned how to touch things – and, we were kind of drunk, and – "

"Oh, that was a fun day!" Emma interjected enthusiastically. "Mmm, *era'famil* under the tree by the lake. Zerik got me pregnant."

Zerik sighed, smiling. "I remember that day."

Rhiannon looked from one to another. They were all smiling. "Yes, but I remember only the dream. I knew your names, but I never knew exactly where we were, what day it was, what we were all doing there, nothing."

Zerik stroked his beard thoughtfully. "You remember the moment, but not the context." At Rhiannon's questioning look, he added, "You remember pieces of your life, but without any frame of reference, any way to make sense of it."

Rhiannon frowned. "I guess so. But sometimes it feels like I'm remembering someone else's life, someone else's feelings." She rubbed her forehead. "Someone with my name."

Grayling ran his hand through his hair, thinking. "Let me see if I understand it. These dreams *are* memories, but in vignettes. You can't remember the situations leading up to or after these memories, or the extent of the relationships with others in the dream – only what you feel about those people, when you interact with them in the memory."

Rhiannon sat up straighter. "Yes, that's it. I remember having fun on that day, I remember all of you. I remember that I – " she stopped, blushing.

Zerik reached out and took Rhiannon's hand, and that familiar warmth suffused her. His eyes were kind. "In your dreams, these memories, you cared for us. Knew that we cared for you."

"Yes," Rhiannon whispered. She looked down, twisting her napkin in her lap. "In my dreams, I care for you. All of you. It's real. A fact. But I don't know who you are. I just love you." She scrubbed a tear from her cheek. "Growing up, the dream of that love meant everything to me."

Maddie leaned over and pressed her lips to Rhiannon's cheek. "We love you, too," she whispered brokenly. "We always have. And we always will. No matter what you remember or not."

After dinner – they'd let the steaks go cold – they'd left the table, retiring to the wide divans at the other end of the pavilion. Maddie waved a careless hand at the table as she walked away, and the candles extinguished at once. She glanced at the torches burning in the grass beyond the silk pavilion, and the flames lowered as if by one accord, leaving a flickering blue and gold light. She left the candles burning on the smaller inlaid table. The space with the couches was rendered romantic, a soft place of light and dancing shadow, rich color and texture.

Rhiannon sat on a dark purple and red embroidered lounge. Emma promptly sat down beside her, offering her a sunny smile and taking her hand. Maddie sat on the wide divan to their left, and Zerik and Grayling joined her there, sitting on either side of the voluptuous redhead. Lyds brought another bottle of chilled champagne, then retired for the night.

After everyone had filled their glasses and settled in, Zerik looked encouragingly at Rhiannon. "You said your dreams lacked context," he said, taking a sip from his glass. "What if we could give you some context? Maybe that would help."

"Yes, we could help you try to remember," Emma agreed enthusiastically.

"And even if you don't remember, we can at least help you to understand more about your life, and us." Maddie smiled. She looked around at her family. "Let's tell stories."

Grayling nodded. "Stories. An excellent idea." He looked at Rhiannon, his grey eyes soft, a feeling there that warmed her all over.

"Our people have always told stories. Even today, the *S'lai* – our Historians – tell our histories in the form of stories."

"And some of the oldest stories have become fairy tales," Emma said.

A sudden realization gripped Rhiannon. "The Eternal Tales – the story of the Three Sisters – that's not –"

Emma glanced at Maddie, and they both smiled at Rhiannon.

Rhiannon could only stare, open-mouthed.

"Give her some more champagne," advised Grayling.

Zerik topped off her glass. "Drink this, *varenya*, and tell us one of your dreams. Tell us a dream, and we'll tell you a story."

TWELVE

Rhiannon dreamed of a medieval castle near a dark waterfall coursing cold over stone. She was filled with a sense of love and joy. There was to be a wedding. The Great Hall had been scrubbed until the stones glowed, fresh rushes and dried heather strewn on the floor. The Hall bustled with activity. Maids hung garlands of flowers from the walls and carved balustrade of the gallery. The air was redolent with the scent of flowers and greenery, roasting meat and bread.

Tonight she would have a new husband to love, to protect. To give her the same.

Rhiannon stood before a precious looking-glass in the solar. Her black hair was braided into an intricate coiffure, and a dark green kirtle hugged her figure, a girdle of hammered gold links shining against her hips. Emma came up from behind her, her shimmering blue gown just matching her eyes. "You look beautiful," she said, her smile incandescent.

"So do you." Rhiannon smiled, turning into Emma's arms, kissing her cheek, savoring Emma's body warm and soft against hers. "Te a'behs, varenya." I love you, beloved. "You have made a good choice."

Emma pressed her lips to Rhiannon's, heat flaring between them. "Te a'behs, Rhiannon. My Sister."

England
1083 AD

His horse's hooves were muffled on the damp trail, which wound through enormous primeval trees arching overhead, the leaves and branches a cool, emerald canopy. He didn't think it possible, but he'd almost forgotten the magic of this place, the ancient power flowing through the vast trees and gnarled roots, the mossy stones, the earth itself. This was a place occupying two spaces at once, one world, and another.

It's good to be home.

Grayling hadn't been back to the Forest of Dean since ... when? It had to be close to 700 years now. Early in the fifth century. When everything had changed.

Has it been that long?

He'd been riding hard for nearly a sennight now. He'd been sorely tempted to stop at the stew in Lydney, enjoy a rest, a meal, perhaps a woman or two, but he was so close to Whitemead Abbey now, he knew he had to press on.

Six days before, Grayling had been summoned by Edward Angelis, newly crowned *Kir'da* at the decades-young Caistra in Ellington. The Family Seat in England was a manor house, well-appointed, with room for the *Kir'da*, the Chorus of 21 Senators, and perhaps a hundred guests. Edward himself was helping to fund it, born into a powerful oblivi house, and supported financially by the Spava *Dinach*. They were actively working to raise funds to create more Caistras throughout the world. Another had recently been started in France, and a third in Italy.

"One day," Edward had announced at his coronation, "we will have a Caistra in every country in the world." The assembled guests had applauded enthusiastically. Edward was a visionary.

While the House of Spava sought to create a worldwide Caistra system, Edward had grander plans – a centralized aeternan government to protect its people, provide health care, education, training, plus the furtherance of knowledge and understanding, studies both practical and esoteric. Some thought him a genius; others thought him mad. Privately, Grayling believed both to be true.

The powerful Order of the Dao Yin, the Thamas *Dinach*, and many other aeternan dynasties had thrown their support behind the Caistra system, and the need for formal government within the Family. Too many aeternans were suffering, unable to find or return to their loved ones with each incarnation, or escape untenable circumstances. Some kind of organization seemed natural. Still, the mensaeterna were deeply divided over issues of governance. There were many factions with widely varying ideas as to how to go about it, anarchists who were utterly opposed, and still others who supported the idea but didn't wish to pay for it.

It was a difficult time for the Family, but as a senior member of the Dao Yin, Grayling believed they were on the right course. The Dao Yin was founded to protect those born female, and other Family facing difficulty at the hands of the oblivi – slaves, orphans, physically or mentally disabled, those born into families of the wrong skin color, religious, or political beliefs. Anyone could be reborn into a physical body in peril; today's king could be tomorrow's female slave. Creating a governmental system that would help protect those in need seemed a natural aid to their work.

Abbeys, monasteries, and nunneries had been put into place a couple hundred years back, as the aeternans effortlessly adopted the guise of the growing and expanding Catholic church. These institutions – run by the Thamas, primarily – helped greatly in the effort to assist aeternans in dangerous positions in oblivi society. The centrally located Caistras would enhance their work.

Edward had shown Grayling a missive from Whitemead Abbey in Dean. The simple parchment contained no text, only a symbol: the ouroboros , a serpent devouring its own tail – a symbol for the mensaeterna, Those Who Do Not Forget, Those Who Are Reborn. The Family had long since stopped any kind of overt written communication, for fear of interception by oblivi – many had been stoned, or burned as demons or witches when such communications had been discovered. Instead, aeternans communicated through symbols, *e'drai*, stories and songs, or carefully, innocuously worded messages.

The sign of the ouroboros made it clear that some sort of help was needed at Whitemead Abbey, one of the institutions run by the Thamas.

"This is exactly what the Caistra system is for," Edward had told Grayling. "One group can communicate to us; we can then send assistance." He smiled. "In this case, you. I believe this falls under the milieu of the Dao Yin."

Grayling nodded.

"This is an early test of our new system, Gray. Whatever the issue is, you must handle it. I want some of the more dubious members of the Chorus to broaden their minds, to see the possibilities." He grew serious. "Your failure will not reflect well on me. You understand that, yes?"

"Aye, *gestu*." I understand.

He'd covered more than 40 leagues in six days, traveling from Ellington to the Great Forest. Grayling traveled light, carrying only the precious missive, his pipes and rebec, some barley bannocks, and a skin of apple beer. His ebony-handled throwing knives were sheathed in his boots, his hazelwood bow slung over the quilted gambeson across his back.

Unsurprisingly, he failed to encounter thieves or brigands on the journey. Grayling had the look of a man to be reckoned with – tall, all lean, hard muscle, with grey eyes the color of storm, and a visage like cold stone. He wore his prematurely silver hair unfashionably long, in a thick braid down his back.

Since the fifth century, in every new incarnation, he always had grey eyes and silver hair. It was the mark of his gift, and his curse.

Weary though he was after his long journey, now, so close to the Abbey, the forest itself was somehow charged, energy suffusing the very air, and Grayling felt exhilarated, anticipation singing in his blood.

There are women in the trees.

What?

There are women in the trees. Watching. They blend with the bark and leaves, almost like Fae.

The last thought held a note of admiration.

Somewhere, a bell rang. Once, twice, three times.

One rings the bell with her mind. We are expected.

After only a few more yards, the dense forest opened up abruptly to reveal a large meadow, a stream meandering through the grasses and wildflowers. In the center of the clearing sat the lofty stone walls and tower of Whitemead Abbey.

Grayling had heard a great deal about the place from Edward. Whitemead was an old Benedictine Abbey. The Thamas had purchased it from the dissolute monks who had lost their way, teased, tempted, and tormented by the deeper forces at work in the ancient Forest of Dean. The Church had been glad of the coin. Wielding their unique *e'drai*, the Thamas – at Whitemead, calling themselves the Petites Soeurs de Sainte Marie-Madeleine, or the Little Sisters of Mary Magdalene – found the Forest infinitely more hospitable than their predecessors.

Grayling rode up to the main gate on the north wall and dismounted. He rang the bell, waited. A woman's head appeared over the top of the wall. She was wearing a nun's habit, and had a glowing aura with three shimmering *fainna*.

"Zanav tu," Grayling called. He offered the *anam'ta*, bowing his head briefly.

The nun – if that's what she was – returned his nod, but looked suspicious. "Pass the gates if you can," she said, and disappeared behind the wall.

Grayling sighed. The Thamas were always damnably careful. A good trait, but inconvenient. He approached the gate, and placed his hand on the metal.

Fae-forged.

He passed through a succession of three gates – traditional, with aeternans – each stronger than the last, each reading him, tasting him, draining his energy. The third gate held him immobile for nearly five minutes, rendering him weak as a mewling babe.

Finally, the last gate swung open to reveal the Cloister and the interior of the Abbey. Grayling stumbled through the opening, falling to his hands and knees, utterly exhausted and frightened, knowing that in his current condition he was incapable of defending himself.

A woman approached, dressed not in a nun's habit, but in a shimmering green kirtle. She carried a plain goblet of some dull, humble metal. "Drink this." She held the cup to his lips, and he drank, suddenly desperately thirsty. It was a cold, sweet wine, and with every gulp, he felt his strength returning. By the time he finished the goblet, he felt better than he had since he began his journey a sennight before.

"Thank you," he said, wiping his mouth. He looked up at the woman. She had a cascade of blonde hair, a generous mouth, endlessly blue eyes. She was smiling, and it was like the sun and the sky were smiling with her.

Mate.

Must you immediately think of mating?

Be not deaf, clotheared ass.

Grayling pulled himself to his feet. He tried not to stare at the petite woman. Her Form was perhaps only 18 years, but her aura was that of the Eldest. She shone. He offered her the *anam'sal*, waited.

She laughed merrily. "Oh heavens, such formality. You're almost as old as I am." She dropped a careless curtsey. "I'm Emma Nayeli."

He couldn't help but return her smile. "Grayling Sonam."

"Well, welcome to Whitemead, Grayling Sonam. I suppose I should take you along to the Abbess."

Just then, a pack of children appeared as if from nowhere, boys and girls a variety of ages, from 3 up to about 12 or so. "Emma, Emma!" They clamored about her, pulling at her skirts, each one demanding attention. "We want to play hide and seek!" "I want a story!" "No, a song, we want a song!"

Emma looked up at him apologetically. "I am sorry. Sister Caroline must have released the children after you made it through the third gate. We try to keep them out of sight, in case of trouble."

The children were all glowing, each one carrying the shining aura of the aeternans. One or two were medius, with several *fainna*, but most had only a few rings. They'd quieted down and

190

were watching him warily, one little girl in particular hiding behind Emma's skirts, peeking up at him with enormous dark eyes.

"All orphans?" Grayling asked, surprised.

Emma shook her head. "Oh, no. We have a couple orphans, but almost all of these children have Thamas mothers." She patted a curly-headed boy, about 9 years old. "This one belongs to the Abbess. Of course, everyone here shares in the parenting of them." It made sense – all of the children were mensaeterna. While oblivi could bring aeternans into the world, the reverse wasn't true. Aeternans always birthed Family.

Looking down at the children, she favored them with a cheery smile. "I have to take this gentleman to the Abbess right now, but when I come back, we'll have a song. Now, go have Cook give you some treacle candy. Tell her I said you could have it." She shooed them off. They ran in a noisy group across the cloister, disappearing into the shadows of the refectory.

Emma called out to a hard-faced old nun, who led Grayling's black Friesian horse toward the Abbey's stables.

"This way," Emma announced, leading him past a fountain at the center of the cloister, and into the church. The church was empty and silent. Behind the altar was the Abbess' office and a tiny antechamber, where Emma bade Grayling be seated. "I'm quite sure the Abbess knows you're here. Perhaps I'll see you again." She nodded, and made as if to leave.

"It was good to meet you, Emma Nayeli." He felt awkward somehow, flustered, which was irritating. He'd seen thousands of pretty women in his lives.

She touched his hand, gifting him with her merry smile. "Likewise, Grayling. Perhaps you can introduce me to your friend one day." And with that, she was gone.

What the hell had she meant by that?

Clay-brained ass.

The Abbess turned out to be a woman Grayling knew from his

previous incarnation, a renowned courtesan called Naia. Well into her 60s, she was still beautiful. They'd talked for more than two hours, catching up, exchanging information, gossiping about mutual acquaintances, before Grayling finally had pulled the ouroboros parchment from his bag, mentioning Edward Angelis and the Caistra.

Naia explained that a young woman had come to Whitemead escaping an oblivi uncle, who intended to marry her off to a mortal associate. "Being female is trying for so many," Naia had murmured. "She needs to be returned to her true Family. You met her – Emma Nayeli."

Grayling had raised a brow. "Emma?"

Naia regarded him shrewdly. "Oh, I see how it is with you. She is fetching, isn't she?"

Grayling frowned. "Her Form is lovely, but that's not – "

"Hmm," Naia smiled wickedly. "Don't waste breath in denial. I know men. Just be careful, dear. A little friendly *era* is fine, but this is a special task. Emma is one of the Sisters *nahyin*. You'll be returning her to her family, reuniting the Sisters."

Grayling sat back in his chair. The Sisters were legendary. Separately, they were gifted, but together, they were said to be nearly invincible. Their *nahyin*, or circle, was the first ever recorded in the Family. In truth, they were as close to royalty as aeternans could conceive.

Naia had taken Grayling to the Abbey's guest chambers near the gate, fed him well, and arranged for two Thamas trainees to see to his every need throughout the night. Naia had flashed that wicked smile as she left. "You and Emma can plan your journey in the morning. Perhaps a night of rest and *era* will help you manage her with a clear head."

But despite exhausting the sensual talents of the Thamas women, Grayling had lain awake much of the night, his mind filled with visions of blue eyes and shining gold hair, a glowing aura, and a smile born from the heart of joy itself.

In the morning, he found Emma in the cloister, singing with the children. Her voice was melodic, almost ethereal. The children sang with her, swaying, and Grayling realized she was using *e'drai* in her song. Just listening to her, he wanted to sit down in the grassy cloister, and sing with the children. He fought the urge.

She looked up and saw him, her face lighting in a genuine smile. She stopped singing and sent the children to play, then crossed the cloister to stand before him. Today she wore blue, a watery shade that paled next to her eyes.

"I'm here to take you home, or at least help you find your home," Grayling said, feeling awkward and strange. She was this powerful Eldest, and yet he found himself feeling ...

Now who's thinking of mating?

Stop it.

"Oh, yes! You're from the Caistra! You got my note!" She was so delighted, positively effervescent. She laughed. "I should have known that when you came."

He nodded. "How can I help you find your *dzina*?"

She thought for a moment, one slender finger tapping her chin. "Well, I have a husband and two wives. I hope they'll be together. My wives are Madeline Sofia and Rhiannon Elektra – we're the Sisters, you know – "

She said it so casually, as if it were a matter of no import.

"And my husband is Zerik. I imagine he'll be easier to find, what with men running the world and all." She wrinkled her nose, then laughed.

Grayling was startled. "Zerik? Surely not Zerik Nicolau?"

She nodded, her eyes alight.

"I actually know where he is. In this incarnation, he's a chieftan, of all things, living in some drafty keep at Drochaid an Easain Duibh, near Inverness in the Highlands of Scotland. It's a long journey from here, more than 150 leagues. It may take well over a month."

"Is the keep so very drafty?"

The corners of his mouth lifted slightly. "I shouldn't tease. No, I'm told it's a rather nice castle. He calls it Dark Falls."

She looked down, smoothed a non-existent wrinkle in her blue kirtle. "And how do you know this?"

Grayling regarded her seriously. "He's been in touch with Edward Angelis, supporting the Caistra system. And I know Zerik personally. We first fought together at Chalons sur Marne, against Atilla. Zerik fought like a God, wielding sword, knives, and *e'drai* with deadly result."

"You know my husband well, then?"

Grayling offered her a rare, slow grin. "We are friends. We fought side by side, shared meals, confidences, women, and on occasion, each other."

She laughed. "I think he's mentioned you – a silver-haired, silver-tongued devil." She looked up at him through her lashes. "Though you don't seem terribly talkative. Perhaps you can show me what he meant by the latter."

He didn't smile, just regarded her steadily with those grey eyes. "Gladly, milady."

"Though, I should warn you, I impregnate easily."

He blinked. "What?"

Her smile was saucy. "I get pregnant. A lot. This body is presently virginal, but I assure you, if you bed me, I'll be with child." She held up a hand. "I don't subscribe to oblivi ways – I'm aeternan. A baby is a baby, physical fatherhood be damned. My husband and wives and I will raise it." She smiled. "I only warn you, as some men seem to harbor these mortal ideas about fatherhood and marriage. If you're that sort, please keep out from under my skirts."

He thought about that. "But what if I wish to marry you, child notwithstanding?" Now what had made him say that?

Mate.

She laughed. "I am one of the three Sisters *nahyin*. It is said that each of us may choose a Consort. Maddie chose Zerik. Rhiannon and I have yet to make our choices. If you're applying for the position, you'll have to please not only me, but my Sister wives as well." She smiled. "We'll assume that Zerik already likes you."

She turned to leave, glancing back at him assessingly over her shoulder. "However, that doesn't preclude babies. Your Form is pleasing; you seem to be of good stock. I like healthy babies to house Family souls."

It would be weeks before his need for her became so great that he didn't care anymore whether he was playing stud to her brood mare.

They traveled for more than a month. The gelding he'd purchased for her in Lydney kept up with his huge Friesian admirably. They made good time.

She drove him half-mad with her incessant cheerful chatter. His typical stone-faced silence only made her want to talk more, tease him further, force a response. The more irritated he became, the more jovial she was, laughing, delighted. Everything pleased her, from the sunlight shining through the dark veins on a leaf, to the crackling of their campfire, which she said reminded her of her Sister wife. Even plodding through dismal rain, Emma was enchanted with drops of water magnifying the suede of her boot, the green scent of damp emanating from the ground, the sound of rain dancing on the trees.

"When will you introduce me to him?" She asked one night, as they sat before their fire.

"Who?" He stared into the flames, avoiding looking at her face, the way the firelight played on her cheekbones, her full lips.

"I carry *Anam Fhios*," she'd answered. "It is a Soul *e'drai* I share with my Sisters. I can see your soul, Grayling Sonam." Her smile was gentle, and she reached out, touched his hand. "You look just alike, you know. Only his eyes are green, and yours are silver."

Mate.

Enough.

Grayling looked up at her, and he saw the truth in her eyes. And he was lost. "My soul is forever joined with that of a Fae."

Her eyes widened. "Oh, that explains a lot."

"His name is Thicket. Thicket Curdletree." Grayling looked away. "It is his punishment. It is my gift." He would never insult the Fae. "Gifts come with a price."

Her fingertips were soft on his skin, her aura blending with his. "You're both beautiful to me."

And you are suffering's reward, queen of my soul.

Grayling looked into her eyes then, and suddenly everything was different. The world was different. Better.

195

They truly made beautiful music together. Her *e'drai* allowed her to sing feeling, emotion, into being. When he made music, whether he hummed, played his pipes, or strummed the strings of his rebec, his *e'drai* and Fae soul allowed him to create or change what was. Together they harmonized, physically and supernaturally.

A month and a fortnight since they'd left Whitemead Abbey, they arrived at Dark Falls in the Highlands. By the time they reached the castle, he'd gravely asked for her hand, and permission to court her wives and husband. Glowing with happiness, Emma had given her consent. She was carrying their child.

The day Grayling married into the Ciatri *dzina* was perfect. The Great Hall had been scrubbed until the stones glowed, fresh rushes and dried heather strewn on the floor. Garlands of flowers draped from the balustrade of the gallery and the walls. The air was redolent with the scent of flowers and greenery, roasting meat and bread.

Musicians played sweetly in the gallery. Rhiannon wore a deep green kirtle with a girdle of hammered gold links. Maddie was dressed in a flowing red gown, with a gold shift underneath. Emma wore blue, the exact color of her eyes. Both grooms wore black; Zerik's tunic was trimmed in gold, Grayling's in silver. As the new edition to the Ciatri family, Grayling was nervous, but glad, ready. *Family. Mates.*

Maddie cast a circle in the center of the room, and the five joined hands and said their vows before the joyful assembled crowd. A gala feast followed, with friends, servants, and even the Fae celebrating.

When night fell, the happy brides and grooms retired to their chamber. The *era'famil* lasted a full night and day.

" 'And they lived ever after,' " Maddie laughed. She leaned back against Grayling's chest. "That was a wonderful day, love."

"Aye." He brushed a kiss against her forehead.

Rhiannon looked away, into the darkness beyond the pavilion. The story of the wedding to Grayling had left behind a sense of hazy, disconnected emotions, thoughts that melted out of reach when she tried to focus on them. She felt uneasy, strange. Part of her ached to remember, to connect with these people – her family – her feelings, herself, but another part was fearful, afraid of what remembering might mean.

The ocean breeze teased the silk canopy, the fabric rippling overhead. In the darkness outside the torchlight, she could hear the roar of the sea, the waves crashing against the cliffs, but she could only see the unending night.

"More champagne," Zerik announced. He popped the cork on another bottle, refilled glasses.

Emma rested her head on Rhiannon's shoulder. Her curly blonde hair smelled of strawberries and baby powder, and summer. And wishes on stars. "Give us another dream, Sister."

"Yes," Maddie leaned forward, her generous bosom nearly spilling from her black dress. She took a sip from her slender champagne flute. "Give us another dream, Rhiannon. And we'll give you another story."

Rhiannon dreamed she was in a sleeping car on a train, helping deliver a baby. The mother – Emma? – was panting, her face red, her brown hair damp with sweat. Her shimmering aura flared bright, the light growing.

"You're doing wonderfully," Rhiannon called out, watching as the baby's head, covered in slick dark hair, began to crown.

"Make it stop, Rhia," the mother cried out. "Make it stop!"

"You're almost there," Rhiannon urged. "Push for me now. One big push, sweetheart."

The mother bore down, her eyes squinched shut, her face contorted in effort and pain, and she screamed ...

United States of America
1895 AD

Maddie loved traveling by rail. The scenery was excellent and most diverting, and the luxuries of the *Overland Limited* were superior. The three Sisters had reserved a Drawing Room in a Pullman car, very spacious, with three beds, including the upper-berth fold-down bed. Not that they really needed three beds, but still. The car was equipped with gas lighting, and an air-pressure water supply for the washrooms. It was definitely plush, with mahogany carving and ornamentation, lush burgundy carpets, and embroidered upholstery. Maddie enjoyed her luxuries.

They were on their way to San Francisco, on the Overland Route. Maddie was ready for a change from England, a home of her own. Zerik and Grayling had gone ahead some months before, building a dream house for their brides. They'd sent a cable two weeks before, letting the Sisters know their latest home was ready, near the new American Caistra in the north.

In their hotel in New York, Rhiannon and Maddie had argued about the trip. Emma was near her time, and Maddie felt they should wait until Emma's baby was born; Rhiannon argued the child wasn't due for a month, and it would be better for the baby to be born amongst Family. In the end, Emma herself had insisted they make the trip, wanting to be near her husbands when she gave birth. Maddie had conceded. Cheerful though she may be, Emma had a backbone of iron. One didn't argue with Emma once she'd made up her mind.

The train was not only comfortable, but the service was excellent. Further, the scenery was spectacular. As they passed into Utah, the earth and stones were almost otherworldly. They'd just passed Devil's Slide, the three women enjoying a lovely dinner of roast beef and new potatoes in the dining car, when Emma suddenly dropped her fork, her eyes wide. "I think my water just broke."

Maddie glared at Rhiannon. "I knew it."

"Argue later," Emma whispered, taking deep breaths and looking around at the other diners. "I'm having a baby." She gasped. "Now."

Maddie and Rhiannon helped Emma to their car. Their Drawing Room suddenly seemed very small and heated. All three began shucking off excess clothing. Maddie opened a window. Emma pulled off the heavy, fringed-satin jacket she wore, and her skirts.

Rhiannon unbuttoned her mutton-sleeved jacket, loosening her corset. She pushed the cushions together on the bench seats closest to the window, forming a bed. Emma lay down, panting, groaning.

"We need hot water. Towels. Blankets." Rhiannon looked up at Maddie.

"I'll handle it. You stay with Emma."

Fanning herself, Maddie stepped into the vestibule, waving at the porter. The dark-skinned young man approached, smiling. "May I help you, ma'am?"

"What is your name?"

"Everyone calls me George, ma'am," the porter responded.

Maddie shook her head. She had no patience for these oblivi practices toward darker-skinned peoples. Naming all porters after the owner of the company – ridiculous. She smiled at the man. "Mr. Pullman is not waiting on me. What is *your* name, young man?"

The porter blinked, surprised. "My name is Howard, ma'am."

"Excellent," Maddie smiled at him. "Howard, my Sister is having a baby." His eyes widened. She continued. "We need a basin of hot water, towels, and blankets." She touched his arm, and he looked down at her hand, surprised at the touch. "I'll tip you the cost of my passage if you can make it quick."

Howard straightened. "Yes, ma'am!" He ran off.

Maddie returned to the suite. Rhiannon was sitting in her chemise on the floor, facing Emma. Emma's legs were spread, and she was panting hard, her face glistening with a sheen of sweat. Her aura had brightened, extending outward. "Ahh!" she cried out. The baby was coming unbelievably fast.

Maddie came forward, took Emma's hand. "Squeeze my hand, honey. You can't hurt me. Squeeze."

"Breathe for me now, Emma," Rhiannon said, calm, focused. "Take a deep breath, let it go."

Emma closed her eyes and breathed. For the next half-hour, her pains increased, allowing only a minute to rest between contractions. The incessant sound of the train, the rocking motion as it moved over the rails, seemed somehow soothing. Finally Emma cried out. "I have to push."

"Here we go," Maddie said, clutching Emma's hand. "You know what to do, Emma. Hold on."

"Why do I always do this?" Emma panted, anguished. "Why do I think I can do this?" She moaned, bearing down, pushing.

"You're doing wonderfully," Rhiannon called out, watching as the baby's head, covered in slick dark hair, began to crown. "I can see the head, Emma."

"Make it stop, Rhia," Emma cried out. "Make it stop! It burns!"

"You're almost there," Rhiannon urged. "Push for me now. One big push, sweetheart."

Emma bore down, her eyes squeezed shut, her face contorted in effort and pain, and she screamed.

There was a knock. Maddie hastened to the door. Howard's eyes were round as saucers. He held a basin of water, the towels and two blankets draped over his arm. "I also brought a knife, and a needle and thread," he said, blushing. "I used to help my ma."

"Well done, young man," Maddie said. "Thank you."

Emma screamed again then, and Maddie shut the door in Howard's startled face. "One more big push, Emma," Rhiannon coaxed.

With a terrible cry, Emma bore down, and the child's head pushed through. "Again, Emma!" Rhiannon commanded. Throwing back her head and gritting her teeth, Emma pushed, her aura shining, blinding bright. The baby slithered out from between her thighs, the umbilical cord still connected to his mother. Rhiannon used her finger to scrape the mucus from the baby's nose and mouth.

" 'The soul enters the body with the breath,' " Maddie whispered, her eyes on the child.

The baby opened his mouth and took his first gasping breath. As he did so, a flood of shining light coalesced, rushed into his tiny body, his aura suddenly flaring bright. Three shimmering *fainna* described his little form, and he began to cry lustily.

Grinning, Rhiannon looked up into Emma's exhausted face. "You have a son, Sister."

Maddie mopped Emma's brow, as Rhiannon cleaned up the child with the water in the basin, tied off and cut the umbilical cord. She wrapped the baby in a blanket and held him up to Emma's breast. The baby latched onto her nipple and suckled hungrily. Emma smiled wearily, looking down at the child, his shining aura melding with hers.

"Welcome to the world, my son," Emma whispered. "Welcome back to the Family."

" 'And we lived ever after,' " Emma smiled.

"I think we tipped that porter more than $100 in silver," Maddie mused.

"And we named the baby Howard," Rhiannon said, her voice low, almost inaudible. The baby's name echoed in her mind, even as the moment faded from her grasp. The ocean crashed against the cliffs, unseen, beyond the circle of light.

THIRTEEN

Rhiannon dreamed of naked corpses stacked like firewood on the street, the snarled rigor of arms and legs, grotesque, necrotic skin, blackened and rotted to pale ash. As she rode by on her horse, she was unable to look away from the body of a small child, his face a rictus of agony, milky eyes wide, unseeing.

"Don't look, sweetheart," Maddie urged her horse closer, riding next to Rhiannon's. "Keep your eyes forward."

But just ahead, a dark-haired woman came out of a house, dragging another body. Tears streaming down her face, she roughly jerked the linen sheet from the body, and ran back into the building, slamming the door behind her. They rode past the corpse, sprawled halfway into the street, an old woman with blackened hands and lips, huge swollen blisters on her neck and thighs. Her fingers were curled like claws.

Hands shaking, Rhiannon clutched her horse's mane and closed her eyes.

Byzantine Empire
Constantinople
541 AD

They'd been hiding in the house for almost a fortnight. Today, they would have to slaughter the last chicken; the only remaining food was a few dried figs. But Maddie assured Rhiannon they would be all right. She'd seen it, in the clouds, in the lots, in the stars. Everything pointed to their survival.

She didn't say that survival could still be painful and frightening. Surely, after almost a thousand years, Rhiannon could figure that out for herself. Maddie was determined to stay hopeful.

Two weeks before, she'd gone out to their grassy, well-shaded courtyard, and thrown her sortes into a bronze urn filled with rainwater. Maddie had made each sors herself, the small tiles carved from oak and olive wood, inscribed with symbols of her own devising, in addition to passages from Homer and Virgil ("Though really, Virgil could be such a pompous ass," she once commented.).

While Maddie stood frowning over the results of her divination, Rhiannon brought out some watered wine and honey cakes. "Well?" She asked, setting down the tray. "Where is he?"

Zerik had been gone nearly three months. A routine business trip to Thessalonika should never have taken so long, and with the terrible black sickness engulfing the city, Rhiannon and Maddie were hard-pressed to remain calm. It seemed they were surrounded by death. They couldn't leave the city without their husband, and further, Emma's latest incarnation wasn't known to them. Moving would make it harder for Emma to find their *dzina*.

Maddie turned to Rhiannon, ignoring the cup of wine the latter held out to her. She clutched one of her wood tiles with shaking fingers, overcome with a sense of dread. "He's alive. But something's wrong." Maddie took a deep breath, fortifying herself, resolved not to give way to her fears. "I'm consulting the Books."

Madeline had taken possession of the Books from an aeternan Greek hetaerae visiting Constantinople. The Thamas had closely guarded the Books for hundreds of years. Maddie helped write them, centuries earlier, as a renowned sybil in Delos, among other places. It had been a golden era – a time of Gods and men, when the line between aeternans and oblivi was blurred, when a woman could live for generations and be a prophetess, celebrated rather than feared.

What seemed like an otherworldly gift from the Gods was really nothing more than Maddie's powerful *e'drai*. Some aeternans were cursed with *drai'v'sio'natura*, looking directly into the burning heart of the universe itself, seeing the future through unbidden visions or touch, their minds seared, invariably driven to madness. But the universe had been kind to Maddie, allowing her to see the future, to read the Story, the truth of the world, through the filter of symbols, portents, omens, tokens, signs. Though spared insanity, she would spend her many lives striving to master accurate translation and clarification.

Any means of obtaining random symbols from the universe worked for Maddie's purpose, though the most effective methods were often traditional forms of divination – including, to her great embarrassment, those used by false prophets and town witches, tricksters, manipulators, those seeking power over the gullible, ignorant, and weak. What was merely a game to most offered genuine information to Maddie.

She used the Books for cleromancy, much like casting lots with her sortes. A scroll was opened at random, her finger falling naturally on the passage destined to provide her with information, or clarification of a previous symbol. The Books were priceless, filled with the prophecies of the sybils, many aeternan, most frenzied lunatics, for the Story scalded their minds. The three precious volumes were rescued from the hands of men in Rome in 83 B.C., stolen from the Temple of Jupiter hours before it burned to the ground. The sybils and hetaera had secretly guarded the Books ever since.

Maddie kept them in a trunk with her clean laundry.

She pulled out one of the vellum scrolls arbitrarily, chose a passage, and for good measure, asked Rhiannon to do the same. For long minutes, she studied the results, comparing with symbols obtained from her earlier divinations.

205

In the end, Maddie looked up at Rhiannon. "The future is in flux. If we're going to survive, we have to dismiss all the servants, avoid contact with others, and stay in this house. No matter what."

Rhiannon was appalled. "For how long?"

Maddie shook her head grimly. "I don't know. When it's time, I'll know more. Oh, and we're not to make bread. We can have food brought to us, but we're not to make bread, or go near the grain storage."

A horrified laugh escaped Rhiannon. "This is madness. Well, I didn't like baking anyhow."

The servants had been glad to return to their families. One young girl, Cloris, had volunteered to bring the women bread and food several times a week. Maddie had cautioned her not to make any bread herself, but to purchase it in the market. Cloris was good to her word, every other day handing a basket of bread and fruit through one of the windows, and giving Maddie and Rhiannon news of the terrible plague devouring Constantinople. It seemed that half the city was dead or dying.

Then one day, Cloris didn't come anymore.

Now, two weeks into their self-imposed isolation, Maddie went into the courtyard and slaughtered their last chicken, poking the viscera with a stick. "I better figure this out," she muttered. "I hate doing entrails for nothing. Disgusting." Rhiannon laughed for the first time in days.

They paced around the entrails, Rhiannon eyeing the mess with distaste, pulling the hem of her tunic out of the way. Maddie looked this way and that, using the tip of her stick to nudge a bit of intestine here, the liver there, then tilting her head to get another view, frowning with concentration.

Finally her brow cleared, and she met Rhiannon's eyes. "Help is coming. We need to pack. We won't be able to carry much, perhaps one extra tunic and stola, whatever we have left to eat. The Books. A couple cloaks, they'll double as blankets. We have to be ready."

"And Zerik?" Maddie could see Rhiannon straining to hold her composure.

"All I know is that he is not dead."

Rhiannon pulled Maddie into an embrace, burying her face in her wife's shoulder. Both women cried for a minute, but no longer. Then they resolutely wiped their eyes and went to pack.

That night, they fell asleep curled together, listening to the sound of a fire somewhere nearby, the scent of burning flesh on the wind.

Just after dawn, there was a knock on the front door. Hastening to the front hall, Rhiannon looked at Maddie, her dark eyes wide, then back to the massive barred door. She tried to keep the fear from her voice. "Who is it?"

Even muffled by the heavy wood, the man's voice was strong, deep. "I'm Family. I come from Zerik Nicolau."

Together they lifted the heavy bar and opened the door. With only a cursory glance, Maddie caught hold of the man's tunic and pulled him inside, as Rhiannon looked out to make sure he was alone. They hurriedly closed and barred the door again.

The stranger was a great hulk of a man, his clean-shaven face swarthy, with a hawkish nose and startling, unusual green eyes, the color of new leaves. He wore a half-moon shaped earring in his right ear, and a painted, highly-ornamented belt. His long dark hair, leather armor and mail, and the pale scars just visible on his chest and arms proclaimed him to be an Avar warrior.

But it wasn't his barbaric appearance that caused Maddie to gasp aloud. The big man not only had the shining, radiant aura of the Eldest, but he was also the oldest aeternan she'd ever seen. His glowing, uncountable *fainna* indicated unimaginable power.

Reflexively, she and Rhiannon cupped their hands together, fingertips to heels – hands symbolizing the body, cradling the empty space representing that which cannot be held, the soul. Holding their hands against their bodies, they nodded, completing the *anam'sal*, the formal aeternan bow of respect.

The man laughed aloud. "Ah, now I've got the Sisters bowing to me." Grinning broadly, he added, "Next I'll have Emperor Justinian himself pleading for my favors."

Rhiannon giggled. Maddie turned to look at her, brows raised. Rhiannon did not *giggle*. And given the current circumstances, laughter of any sort seemed impossible, or at least wildly inappropriate. Rhiannon sobered, her fingers against her mouth, as if to smother the scant smile that lingered there.

The devil hadn't stopped grinning.

"I'm Rhiannon, and this is my Sister-wife, Madeline," Rhiannon said, coming forward. The barbarian took her hand, slowly pressed his lips to her fingers. Though she hid it well, Maddie saw her wife jump slightly at his touch, no more than a twitch, quickly suppressed.

He dropped Rhiannon's hand and lifted Maddie's next, those incongruous eyes never leaving hers as he pressed the warmth of his mouth to her skin. The man was outrageous.

He straightened, grew almost solemn. "I'm Alexander Lazarus. Of *Dinach* Zel'mori." He fumbled in his satchel, pulling forth a small silk bundle. He held it out to Rhiannon. "Zerik told me to give this to you, that you would know what to do with it."

Startled, Rhiannon looked at her Sister-wife, then back to the stranger, Alexander. She took the object, carefully unwrapping the silk to reveal a small grey stone. "Yes, I do know what to do," she whispered.

Rhiannon closed her eyes and began breathing deeply. As Maddie and Alexander watched, her aura began to brighten, intensify, until the radiance seemed to flow into her left hand, glowing with celestial brilliance. She opened her eyes, which likewise shone in the dim hallway, and touched the grey stone nestled in the silk. After only a moment, she gasped and released the stone, snapping her wrist to discharge the seething energy. She turned to look at Maddie, her eyes dark, pained.

"Zerik is ill. He has the pestilence."

Maddie uttered a strangled cry and turned her back to them, pressing her fist to her belly. She was forever saying goodbye to those she loved, but a worse death she couldn't imagine.

"He will not suicide," Rhiannon continued, as though reading Maddie's next thought. "Some in Thessalonika have recovered. He wants to hang on, in hopes of being with us again, of finding Emma."

"Noble bastard," Maddie hissed through gritted teeth. "He should cut his own throat and see us in the next incarnation."

Rhiannon came up behind Maddie, resting a hand on her shoulder. "Well, he won't. And he's sent this man, Alexander, to bring us out of Constantinople. He trusts him, and wants us to trust him in his stead."

"Normally, I'm completely untrustworthy," Alexander interjected, wearing that damnable grin again.

Maddie spun on her heel to look at him. "Of that, I have no doubt," she snapped, her eyes glittering with unshed tears.

Alexander sobered, his green gaze soft. "But Zerik is a comrade in arms, a sworn blood brother. For his wives, I would lay down every life I have ever had, or ever will have." The big man touched Maddie's cheek with surprisingly gentle fingers, then raised his eyes to meet Rhiannon's. "And now that I have met you both, I would offer, too, the lives I will only dream of."

Blushing unaccountably, Rhiannon looked down at the intricate mosaic gracing the floor of the hall. "Where will we go?" she asked, her voice thready.

Alexander suggested they leave Thrace and cross the Danube, into the Avar Kingdom. "What of the Bulgars?" Maddie had asked.

Alexander waved a hand dismissively. "I helped them defeat Atilla. And I speak their language – I know the Word." Maddie's eyes widened at this, but she said nothing. He continued, "We will be safe, madam, I assure you. Zerik will meet us there." Neither woman wanted to confront his certainty on the latter point.

They left the house within an hour, delayed only by the need to acquire horses for the Sisters.

"Where did you find them?" Maddie asked in wonder, when Alexander returned leading two beautiful Arabians. "I nipped down to the Hippodrome and stole them," Alexander laughed, utterly unrepentant.

Rhiannon shook her head. "How can you laugh so easily, when death is all around?"

He sighed. "Death is always all around. It's just easier to see, this morning." For a moment, his dark features seemed to reflect every minute of the staggering number of years he'd lived. He turned to face the street. "Laughter is one of the few ways we remind ourselves that we're still alive, not lying in the gutter with the dead."

They rode in silence northwest, toward the Gate of Charisius, Maddie and Rhiannon following Alexander's black Turkoman horse. He rode easily, but held his bow strung, his naked sword across his lap.

It was not yet noon and the streets were relatively cool, but the stench of death and decay was overpowering. A man sat weeping in the middle of the street, rocking a dead infant. Alexander called out to him in a language Maddie didn't understand, but the man didn't seem to hear. They carefully rode around him, his sobs growing faint as they passed.

Everywhere, all around, were the bodies of the dead. Hundreds, thousands of them. There was nowhere left to bury them. They passed piles of corpses, nude, stacked like firewood on the street, necrotic skin blackened and ashy. Maddie looked over at Rhiannon, who was staring helplessly at the body of a child, his face frozen in an endless scream, open eyes milky and utterly dead.

"Don't look, sweetheart," Maddie urged her horse closer, riding next to Rhiannon's. "Keep your eyes forward."

But as she said it, just ahead, a dark-haired woman came out of a house, dragging another body. Tears streaming down her face, she roughly jerked a linen shroud from the body, then ran back into the building, slamming the door behind her. They rode past the corpse, sprawled halfway into the street – an old woman with blackened hands and lips, huge, swollen buboes on her neck and groin. Her fingers were curled like claws.

As they were climbing the Fifth Hill, a man ran out from an alleyway, screaming, frenzied, mad. He grasped Maddie's bridle, trying to shove her from her mount. Before she could even think to draw her knife, Alexander's horse wheeled effortlessly, and he shot an arrow into the young man's chest. The man dropped to the street, dead, and Maddie saw the large blister-like buboes on his neck. "A merciful death for him," Alexander murmured. He glanced up at Maddie, a question in his green eyes.

"I'm fine," she whispered. He nodded, turning his horse up the hill once more.

The horror of that long ride through the city left Maddie feeling hollow and numb. For days afterward, as they rode north through the countryside, she felt as though she were watching herself, observing her own behavior with a kind of empty detachment, disconnected from her own body, perhaps even her soul.

Despite brief acquaintance, shared nightmares breed profound bonds. Every night when they made camp, Alexander slept holding both women close against his big body, and they all took comfort in it. Later, all three would say it was the only time in their very long lives when they had no desire for *era* – just that precious closeness, the feel of warm, breathing flesh, holding back the darkness.

And Maddie would always remember how Alexander, through sheer determined wickedness, eventually reminded her what it felt like to laugh, when she never thought she would again.

There was a long silence when Maddie finished the story, everyone staring at the dancing patterns cast by the candle lanterns on the inlaid table and the canopy overhead, listening to the roaring sea. Maddie took a long gulp from her glass, then looked up at Rhiannon, something bleak lingering in her eyes, and offered her a weak smile. " 'And we lived ever after.' "

Rhiannon turned to Zerik, silently asking the question, already knowing the answer. He smiled wryly, dropped his gaze. "No, I didn't make it. Not that time."

"But that's what we do," Grayling said earnestly, stroking Maddie's hair as she leaned against his chest. "We die. But we're reborn. And we find each other again."

"And love each other some more," Emma said, clearly determined to regain her usual cheer. "Besides, it's easier now."

Maddie sat up, touched Rhiannon's hand, her skin warm, somehow comforting and sensual all at once. "She's right. It's easier now. Not just because people live longer – though that's awfully nice – but because the number of aeternans has grown over the centuries, and we've got a government, systems in place that help us find one another."

"And sooner, too," Emma said.

Zerik straightened, looked around, picked up the champagne bottle. "This is the last of it," he said, refilling glasses. "It's getting late."

"I don't want to stop telling stories on a sad note," Emma complained. "Can't we have one more, a happy story?"

Everyone looked at Rhiannon. She laughed nervously.

"Give us a happy dream, Sister," Maddie urged. "And we'll give you a story."

Rhiannon thought for a moment. "How about a dream that felt happy, when it didn't seem like it should?"

Rhiannon dreamed of an exotic night marketplace, guttering oil lamps and torches lighting a vast stone courtyard, overwhelming with vivid color and sound, the humid air filled with the conversations of sellers and buyers, the screeching, bleats, and trumpeting cries of camels, horses, elephants, sheep, peacocks.

The stalls and stands were a glittering, colorful chaos of leopard furs, sapphires and rubies, rare embroidered silks, bronze, iron, gold, ivory, jade, woven baskets of pomegranates and apples, astrolabes, leather, wine, peacock feathers, weapons, lacquerware, carved stone and ceramics, safflowers.

Rhiannon stood just inside one of the stone niches along the north wall, her wrists bound with a long strip of raw silk. She was a slave, waiting to be sold. And she was brimming with happiness.

She turned to look at the two women standing next to her, similarly bound. Like Rhiannon, they were dressed in the finest silk, vibrant shades of red, blue, and purple, their oiled fingernails reflecting the light. Their faces mirrored her exhilaration, excitement palpable.

Rhiannon smiled at Emma, her olive skin glowing in the light of the oil lamps, her long black hair falling in a thick braid to her waist. She was radiant. "Not much longer, now," she said. "Do you think we'll fetch a good price?"

Pataliputra, India
78 AD

"I'm so sorry I have to do this." The Dao Yin trader, Quon, looked genuinely embarrassed. He tied the silk around Emma's wrists as gently as possible, his glowing aura blending with hers where they touched.

"It's all right," Emma smiled at him. "It's necessary."

Maddie held out her arms, wrists together. "I'm next."

Rhiannon turned from the window, her eyes alight. "The market is already full of people."

Their small caravan had arrived at the caravanserai in Pataliputra early that afternoon. "I hope I never see another camel again," Maddie grumbled, as they made their way into the shaded interior of the inn.

Rhiannon laughed. "I like camels. You just have to know how to talk to them." She'd spent much of the journey perched on top of a camel, swaying easily with the animal's gait, her legs folded before her like the experienced caravan masters. Emma rode occasionally when her feet grew tired, but after the first hour on camelback, Maddie had elected to walk with the camel-pullers for the remainder of the long journey.

The aeternan House of Spava had offered the Sisters sanctuary in India, eager for an alliance with their powerful *nahyin*. It was an opportunity to live together in a private home of their own, leading autonomous lives in a world ruled by oblivi and men.

The Spava *Dinach* had been building a fortune traveling the Silk Road. Their agents were the Dao Yin traders, and in the process of buying and selling wares, their travels allowed them to find new aeternans, and help Family in need. While Maddie was generally leery of forming alliances with the budding dynasties, the Spava altruism was encouraging.

Three women traveling alone to India seemed impossible at first, but as Rhiannon had been born into slavery in Korea, the Sisters decided to retrieve their wife from the relative safety of a Thamas brothel, then continue on the Silk Road in the guise of slaves themselves, under the protection of the aeternan Dao Yin merchants.

Not that they needed much protection.

They tried to stay close to the caravan master, Quon, and the other aeternans, keeping to their line of camels and avoiding contact with others in the caravan. But one night, after they'd pitched their tents, a Syrian camel-puller from one of the other lines wandered into their camp, drinking wine from a skin. Boisterous and overloud, the stocky man tried joking with the wary Dao Yin cooks and camel-pullers, then spied the Sisters sitting by the fire with Quon, eating lamb stew and drinking tea.

He walked over to them, standing close to Emma, looking the Sisters over appraisingly. The women kept their eyes downcast, as would be expected in their station. Glancing at Quon, the man laughed. "You allow your slaves a great deal of freedom." He leered at Emma. "I have some coin. Perhaps you would not mind if I tasted your wares."

Before Quon could object, the man reached out and grasped Emma's breast roughly.

Maddie's head snapped up to look at him, her eyes flashing. The Syrian cried out and jumped back, clutching his wrist. "My hand is on fire! It burns!" The flesh on his fingers and palms was a livid, dark red.

"Perhaps the Gods punish those who touch what is not theirs," Maddie said.

Wide-eyed, the man backed away, still holding his wrist and injured hand.

Emma began humming quietly, a gentle, sweet sound. The stocky man looked down at his hand, then stretched it out before him in wonder. The redness had vanished. "It stopped," he said.

"Perhaps the Gods have mercy," Emma said.

Rhiannon smiled, slow and dark. The man froze. He looked down at his feet, clutched his thigh, then his knee, trying vainly to move his feet. Panting with fear, he struggled and fell to the ground, his feet still planted flat against the earth where he'd stood. He looked up at the women, his eyes wild, terrified.

"And perhaps not." Rhiannon said. Her terrible smile deepened. "It would be awful, to be trapped in this barren place, deserted by the caravans, like a camel that will not rise." She met the Syrian's gaze, her face like stone. "Don't come near us again."

The man suddenly found himself freed, and he scrambled backward in the dirt, rolled to his feet, and ran from the camp. His wine skin, forgotten, lay in the dust, purple-red wine flowing from the gaping neck, soaking into the sand.

The remaining two weeks of their journey passed without further incident. Now, in the caravanserai in Pataliputra, after naps and deliciously luxurious baths, they'd dressed in jewel-toned silk, and allowed Quon to bind their hands for their presentation in the market. Soon, they'd be home, wherever home was. It didn't matter – it would be a home of their own, together.

The three women stood together in the stone niche that was the Dao Yin's market stall. The night air was humid, filled with the scent of flowers and earth, roasting lamb, camel dung, spices, sweat, incense.

Emma thought she might burst with excitement. This was a wonderful adventure, and it was just beginning. Maddie had thrown the bones earlier, and prophesied great joy, and love. Emma looked at her sister-wife. Like her, Maddie had been born in Persia. Her Form was exquisite, with smooth, olive skin and raven hair. Rhiannon was petite, her Korean features exotic. All three were in good health. They were together again. Emma felt like singing.

Rhiannon glanced at her, smiling, and Emma grinned in return. "Not much longer, now. Do you think we'll fetch a good price?"

Rhiannon laughed.

Maddie watched the bustling marketplace, traders arguing and haggling over the profusion of furs, jewels, silk and cloth, fruit, jade. The Dao Yin stall bristled with weaponry, knives and swords in particular. But Madeline wasn't interested in the wealth of goods and wares. From the crowd of merchants and buyers, a man approached their stall, Persian by the look of him, tall, his bronze skin marred by a scar bisecting his cheek. His aura radiated rings of light, the *fainna* of the Eldest.

"That must be him," Emma whispered excitedly. A member of the Spava House was to meet the Dao Yin caravan, to "purchase" the Sisters, and take them to safety. To take them home.

"Make sure he's a good man, Maddie," whispered Rhiannon, her eyes on the stranger as he grew closer.

Emma nodded in agreement. "Ask his soul."

It was Maddie's turn to carry the Soul *e'drai,* in that incarnation. This time, it had taken the form of *Anam Labhartha,* the Speaking

Soul. Maddie closed her eyes and drew breath, focusing inward. She could feel the man as he came to stand a few feet away, feel his eyes on her, on her sister-wives. Silently, she asked his soul to speak to hers. And when it did, she staggered back a step, her eyes flying open, blood rushing to her cheeks.

Rhiannon took her arm, her brow creased in concern. "Are you all right?"

"Is he a good man?" Emma whispered.

Maddie felt as though a butterfly were trapped in her chest, fluttering light within her. "He's fine," she managed, trying to regain her equilibrium. "He's wonderful."

The man offered an elegant *anam'sal*, smiling at the three women, his dark gaze lingering on Maddie. And then he spoke, not aloud, but within their minds. *The House of Spava is honored to welcome the Sisters to Pataliputra. I'm called Zerik. Zerik Nicolau.*

Emma clapped her hands delightedly. "Now that was a happy story!"

Zerik leaned forward and kissed Maddie, as she lay back against Grayling's chest. When he pulled away, she regarded him with a smoky, heavy-lidded gaze, a wordless promise.

"I'd say they definitely lived ever after," Grayling said, the corners of his mouth lifting in the barest smile.

Blushing, Rhiannon looked at Emma. "We can do all those things without touching anyone? The *e'drai*, I mean. Like when Maddie burned that Syrian's hand."

"We can do a lot of things without physical touching, but especially when we're together, when we're strongest."

Rhiannon rubbed her forehead, suddenly weary. "I guess I can do a lot of things I don't even know I can do."

Maddie sat up, took the last sip from her champagne flute. "I imagine that's true. Tomorrow, after you've had a good rest, we'll go out to the Circle and see what you can do — and help you remember, if necessary."

"It's late," Grayling said quietly, watching Rhiannon's face.

Emma stood up, pulling Rhiannon with her. Maddie rose as well, taking her hand. "Let's get you to bed. We can tell more stories another time."

The two women led Rhiannon to a large circular room in one of the towers near the front of the house. The walls seemed to be made of intricate, interlaced grey-green roots, the windows like colossal, open, organic tree knots looking out into the night. A small lamp burned golden on the night stand, beside a vast bed with a shadowed canopy, blankets like thistledown, and crisp, clean sheets.

Rhiannon was so tired. Not only had the day itself been long and terrifying and fantastic all at once, but the strength of emotion, the dreams and stories, left her feeling almost lightheaded. She moved toward the bed. Everything felt soft and hazy, wonderful, almost like a dream state, unreal and warmly lovely.

She stopped at the foot of the wide bed, the enormity of all that she'd been through overwhelming her. And she didn't want to be alone.

She looked back at Maddie and Emma, standing by the door, and smiled shyly. "I don't suppose either of you wants to stay? I have plenty of room."

Emma bounced forward, her smile dazzling. "You do have a lot of room there."

Maddie approached and put her arm around Rhiannon, winking conspirationally at Emma. "I'd love to stay, but I have to keep Grayling and Zerik occupied, or they get up to mischief." She kissed Rhiannon on the cheek, and disappeared into the darkened hallway beyond the door.

Once they were alone, Emma seemed to melt into Rhiannon's arms. "I hope you don't mind, beloved. I wanted you all to myself." She pressed a kiss to Rhiannon's mouth, gentle at first, then her lips growing firm, gently demanding, passion stealing breath. Weariness evaporated.

Rhiannon found herself kissing Emma back, her mouth hot, delighting in the feel of Emma's softness against her own giving curves. Emma tasted good. She smelled yummy, too.

They used every inch of that enormous bed. At least once.
Finally they slept, tangled together like sleeping children.

In the small hours of the night, Rhiannon opened her eyes. The large windows invited moonlight, drenching the room with cool light, rendering the remaining shadows deeper, imminent. She could smell the ocean, and, unaccountably, the fresh scent of grass and earth. Something had woken her, but all was silent. Emma was curled warm and still at her back, her bare skin against Rhiannon's, her breath even as she slept.

Rhiannon's eyes were drawn to a shadowy corner of the room, a shimmer of faint luminescence. From the darkness, a man emerged, his hair glowing silver in the moonlight. Grayling. She thought then that she should have been startled, but she wasn't.

"I'm sorry to wake you," his voice was low, rough.

"It's okay," she whispered back.

He looked away, toward the windows. "I just had to see you, to look at you. You've been gone so long."

Rhiannon sat up, covering herself with the sheet carefully, so as not to wake Emma. "I wish I could remember." She sighed. "Zerik said I've been gone for almost a hundred years. Has it really been that long, since – since I –" she faltered.

His profile was like stone, limned silver in the moonlight. "Yes. Since the second World War. Not long, for aeternans, I suppose. But if felt like longer." He turned to look at her. "You really don't remember?"

"No, I really can't."

He moved closer to the bed. "The Fae half of my soul tells me you won't remember."

Rhiannon was horrified. "You mean I'll never remember?"

"No," he kept his voice low as he came to stand beside her, his face half in shadow. "Not that you *can't* remember, but that you *won't*. You hide your memories from yourself. And I wonder why, *anam cara*. Why you would choose to forget us. Forget me."

"Oh, God, I don't know," Rhiannon whispered, suddenly anguished. She looked down at her shaking hands, clenching the sheet against her chest. "I'm sorry."

She wanted to explain, find the words to tell him what she herself couldn't fully understand. How comfortable she was with him, with all of them – when reason suggested she shouldn't be. As though her heart, or some part of her, remembered what her mind could not. But the right words wouldn't come.

He reached down and touched her cheek then, his aura blending with hers, his fingers warm, gentle. "I don't offer recriminations. I offer aid. I want to help you, if I can. *Te a'behs*. I love you."

Rhiannon looked up into his pale grey eyes, saw the truth of his words reflected there, and deeper, a simmering heat. Just the thought of remembering her life inexplicably frightened her. But the thought of hurting him – or anyone in this family – was physically painful, left her aching, hollow, raw.

With conscious effort, she pushed her fears aside, looking back at him steadily. "I don't know how you can help me. I don't even know how to help myself." She offered a tremulous smile. "But I will take whatever you're willing to give."

His eyes held her, and she couldn't look away. "I'll give you everything I have," he whispered hoarsely.

Emma stirred fractionally, mumbling in her sleep as she drowsed against Rhiannon's side. Grayling took a deep, shuddering breath, taking a step backward, away from the bed. He looked back toward the windows and the moon. "Jesu, this is so hard. Fighting myself." He glanced her way again, his face expressionless, his strained voice betraying emotion. "I just want to touch you. To come to bed. To stay."

Rhiannon swallowed. "Why do you fight it, then?"

"Because you're not yourself. You're like neonate. I don't want to pressure you – "

"I had this same conversation with Zerik, I think," Rhiannon whispered. Holding the sheet to her chest with one hand, she reached out with the other, touching his hand. Somewhere within, she found words – maybe not the perfect words, or even the right words, but they were the best she had. "I don't know why, I guess I should be nervous or thinking of you all as strangers, but I don't. Or maybe you're strangers, but you're the most comfortable, wonderful strangers I've ever met."

Grayling didn't move, his face inscrutable. She traced the back of his hand with her fingertips, and he shivered. She felt an answering shiver dance across her skin.

"I may not remember, but apparently I'm your wife." Just saying it aloud was somehow grounding, liberating. The rightness of it resonated like deep song in her chest, her belly. She released her grip on the sheet, which slid down to pool around her waist, and held out her arms to him. "No one pressures me to do anything I don't want to."

He was already pulling off his clothes, sliding into bed next to her, his body lean and silvered in the moonlight. Then, groaning, his mouth was on hers, and she could feel Emma stirring behind her, Emma's lips on her shoulder, her hand sliding over Rhiannon's hip in a sultry caress. "Mmm," Emma mumbled sleepily. "I was wondering when you'd get here, Gray."

Eternal Tales: The Circle of Six

Once upon a time, the three Sisters traveled the world. They had a long journey and took turns carrying the Song of the Soul between them, for it was heavy and strong.

While together they had great magic, the Sisters were also isolated, and the world was out of balance, lost in chaos.

The first Sister spoke to the Water, asking for direction on their journey.

The second Sister sang to the Air, asking for counsel on their journey.

The third Sister called to the Earth, asking for guidance on their journey.

And then the first Sister whispered to the Fire, and the three Sisters danced in the light of the flames, asking for love on their journey.

The Gods heard the Sisters, and were pleased with their dance. The next morning, the Sisters woke to discover a golden child, shining like a star, floating weightless in the air before them.

The Gods spoke through the child, and told the Sisters each would be allowed to choose a Consort, a male whose gifts would harmonize with all three Sisters. The Consorts would help the Sisters on their journey through the world, and receive untold blessings in return.

But just one Sister could choose a mate at a time. Once every thousand years, while taking her turn carrying the burden of the Song of the Soul, only then could each Sister make her choice.

When the last Sister had chosen, the world would know balance. The three Sisters and Consorts would form a Circle, the Circle of Six. Then the shining child pointed to each Sister in turn:

The first Sister would choose the first Consort, at the rising of the Sun.

In a thousand years more, the second Sister would choose the second Consort, as mankind descended into darkness.

A thousand more years would pass, and the third Sister would choose the final Consort, at the beginning, when all things change.

The Sisters bowed in joy and gratitude. But before the golden child faded as if mist, it whispered that all gifts come with a price. The Circle of Six would be called upon to both embrace and defeat Darkness, to utterly lose itself before it began, to be wholly destroyed, to be reborn.

And they lived ever after.

FOURTEEN

"Are you ready to make some magic?"

Rhiannon looked up at Zerik. "Magic?"

He offered her his dazzling grin. "Well, all right, maybe not quite magic. But I think most aeternans would agree your *e'drai* is about as close to magic as you can get."

Holding her hand, they walked across the grassy meadow behind the house, toward the ring of trees marking the outer boundary of the Sisters' Circle. The afternoon was especially fine, a mild salt-scented breeze coming off the ocean beyond the cliffs.

Rhiannon sighed, trying to ignore her fears and worries, and infuse a sense of peace into her bones. Her first day at the Ciatri nest had already been wonderful, almost unbelievable. Even magic seemed possible.

She'd awoken late in the morning to find Emma and Grayling gone. Instead, Maddie sat on the edge of the rumpled bed, sipping tea, wearing only a pale green kimono and a smile. Her cloud of red hair glowed vivid in the sunlight coming through the wide windows. She handed Rhiannon a steaming mug of coffee. "Milk, not cream, and three sugars, my dear," the *Kir* said, sipping her tea with a knowing smile.

Rhiannon drank gratefully. It was exactly the way she liked it. She had the mug halfway to her lips again when she stopped, her eyes widening. She looked at Maddie. "How did you know how I take my coffee – I mean, I didn't mention – I didn't tell Zerik – " she fumbled to a halt.

Maddie patted her knee. "Rhiannon, you've never been good at waking up. Always needed a little while to adjust. And you've been starting your day with coffee – milk, three sugars – since sometime in the 17th century, I think." She laughed at Rhiannon's wide-eyed expression. "Honey, I know who you are, even if you don't."

After a second cup of coffee, Maddie told Rhiannon she had actually spent the night in her own room, where she'd lived with their *dzina* for nearly 50 years, until the early 1940s. Rhiannon ran a frustrated hand through her hair, wishing she could remember.

Her room was one of the circular tower rooms, large and airy, with a balcony she'd failed to notice the night before. As Rhiannon had already seen, the walls were tangled roots, as though the room was carved from the earth beneath an enormous tree, the effect somehow belied – and yet simultaneously enhanced – by the huge windows shaped like colossal knots in a tree trunk.

Beneath the sunny windows, following the curve of the wall, there was a circular patch of grass set into the floor, about seven feet across. Rhiannon marveled, recalling the inexplicable scent of growing things and damp earth from the night before. Maddie said the earth beneath the grass ran all the way down, against the side of the tower, into the ground beneath the foundation – like an outsized chimney, a column of earth enrobed in stone.

"Why is there grass in my room?" Rhiannon asked, even as she tried walking on it experimentally, savoring the feel of the cool grass on her bare feet.

"It's there so you can do exactly what you're doing," Maddie replied. "You don't know why you do that, do you?" Her tone seemed deliberately casual.

Rhiannon flexed her toes in the damp grass. "I've always done it. It just makes me feel better."

Rhiannon's room included an opulent private bathroom, and a walk-in closet crowded with racks of clothes that looked like something from a vintage clothing shop, festooned with dresses from the late '30s and early '40s. "Yours," Maddie murmured, at Rhiannon's raised brow, her silent question. Carefully covered in plastic was a dark blue skirt and jacket with dark blue plastic buttons. On closer inspection, it was a Navy WAVES uniform from World War II. Just the sight of it filled her with cold dread, and Rhiannon backed out of the room, closing the door hurriedly.

Maddie was watching her, her blue eyes bright as a bird's, sharp, missing nothing.

Zerik knocked at the open door, delivering some clothes for Rhiannon from his luggage, courtesy of Charles, the *Kir* at the Topeka Safehouse. Rhiannon dressed in jeans and a soft, fawn jersey scoopneck T-shirt. Zerik was equally casual, in jeans and a pale blue, sanded silk shirt.

"I'm taking you on a tour of the house," Zerik said. He kissed the side of Rhiannon's neck, sending a shiver of gooseflesh down her side. *"If you don't mind, of course,"* he whispered silently. Rhiannon shook her head, the barest smile hovering on her lips.

"I asked Zerik to come," Maddie's thought echoed in Rhiannon's head. "I'm sorry I have to leave," she added aloud. "I have to go see to the children. They haven't been watching enough television. I'll see you after lunch, I promise." She sailed through the door into the hallway beyond, her green kimono billowing behind her. *"Have fun, my loves,"* her parting thought a bright bell in Rhiannon's mind.

Rhiannon turned to Zerik. "Did she just say, not *enough* television?'"

Zerik laughed. "Well, yes. Basically, it's like this – aeternans can only birth other aeternans. So we're really only their parents until the children are 12 or 13, when they go through *Memora Magia*, and Remember who they really are."

Rhiannon thought about what it had been like, being a child, and then one day suddenly remembering being Kat Weiss, an adult, with an adult life, feelings, beliefs, freedoms, passions.

"Until they Remember," Zerik continued, "We have to make sure they're thoroughly enculturated into the current decade and language, so they'll be able to function in the modern world, once they remember their previous incarnations." He smiled wryly. "So these days, that means watching television, playing video games, surfing the Internet. Plus aeternan language and customs, *e'lain* – aeternan arts – and storytelling, among other things."

Rhiannon could only stare at him, dumbfounded. Growing up in the Ciatri home would make for a wondrous childhood. She felt a brief, absurd pang of envy.

His hand warm against the small of her back, Zerik ushered Rhiannon around much of the vast house, the interior as fantastic as the exterior.

Their first stop was Zerik's own room. It was more artist's studio than bedroom, a massive, open space, flooded with light from oversized windows, the groin-vaulted ceiling supported by regularly spaced classical Roman Ionic columns. Several draped canvasses stood on easels, the hardwood floor spattered in vivid dried paint – magenta, lapis, crimson. A chaise longue, swathed in a white sheet, rested on a raised platform against a back wall. In one corner was a bed large enough to easily accommodate the whole family, draped in the extravagant folds of a tent-style canopy of creamy sheer linen. Other than the bed, a couple of Louis XVI-style Baroque chairs upholstered in striped silk, and a heavy mahogany antique desk, the remainder of the room was taken up with Zerik's art.

"Do you like it?" Zerik came up behind her, his question a warm breath in her ear.

Rhiannon smiled, turning to him. "Very much."

"Will you pose for me sometime?" He caressed her cheek with gentle fingers. "In this light, your skin is drenched in gold. I'd love to paint you."

Rhiannon flushed, pleased. "Yes, of course." She looked around the roomy chamber, and a thought occurred. "Zerik, why do we all have our own rooms? I mean, don't married people usually share one room?"

He laughed, kissed her forehead, his beard pleasantly rough against her skin. "Everyone in the family has their own room, but we have shared 'family' rooms as well. Over the centuries, we've found it's very important for everyone to have a private place they can go to, for contemplation, to work, to create, get away from the rest of us, or whatever else they desire." He grinned. "I think more marriages would last longer if people understood that."

Zerik's room was adjacent to an enormous Roman bath, complete with rows of columns, marble floors inlaid with alabaster, and walls painted with detailed frescoes of trees, flowers, birds, and deer. The mammoth shallow bath was easily as large as an Olympic-size swimming pool. Shimmering under the clear, still water, Rhiannon could see an intricate mosaic depicting six mer-people with blue and green glass tails — three male, three female — swimming around a tree with tangled roots. The area also offered a cold-plunge, and a sauna, plus a circular, sunken lounging area filled with lavish embroidered pillows and silk cushions.

The house was filled with whimsical secret passages, connecting one bedroom to another, or to "family" playrooms. It boasted a small theater, complete with a heavy scarlet velvet curtain and a diminutive orchestra pit. In a fanciful ballroom, the *anam pratik*, the symbol of the aeternans, was inlaid in gold in the floor; the soaring domed ceiling painted like a summer sky, complete with ephemeral clouds that actually moved and drifted in an enchanted, summer-scented breeze. There were several sitting rooms of various sizes, from traditional to modern medieval — including stone walls and floors graced with furs — most with fireplaces and comfortable, welcoming couches and chairs. Rhiannon marveled at an indoor icy pond for skating, in the midst of an elaborate artificial winter forest. Zerik showed her a "family" playroom with a plush bed nearly 14 feet wide, on an ornate carved cherrywood dais, huge rosewood and mahogany framed mirrors on the walls, and a green glass-tiled hot tub easily 12 feet across sunk into the floor.

The conservatory was spectacular, three stories of glittering glass, curled around the end of the house. The space was filled with trees, flowers, and shrubs from all over the world, rich with the scent of growing things, the air warm and humid. Zerik said that Maddie was particularly proud of her extinct Cry Violet and St. Helena mountain bush. The conservatory had the most extensive herb garden Rhiannon had ever seen. "We use herbs for everything, from seasoning to healing," Zerik commented.

In the kitchen, they found Robbie and Lyds preparing lunch. Lyds, in his flamboyant pink apron, was kneading bread dough, a smear of flour on his nose. He smiled broadly when they came in. Robbie, who was dicing tomatoes, offered a friendly nod.

The kitchen was an amalgam of the contemporary and something out of a European fairy tale. The room was large, but small enough to have a sense of intimacy. At one end was a traditional kitchen with all of the modern conveniences, the appliances shining, the counters polished slate. A scarred, weighty oak table with seating for 12 stood before a bank of sunny mullioned windows overlooking the lawn. At the far end, two rocking chairs sat on flagstones in front of a huge, open fireplace, where a cast-iron cauldron hung on a hook, bubbling and steaming.

Following Rhiannon's gaze, Lyds waved a sticky hand toward the cauldron. "Madeline is making an unguent today. I think for sunburn." He sighed, shrugged helplessly. "She does everything the old-fashioned way."

They left the house through the back door, and Zerik led Rhiannon past the large striped pavilion where they'd had dinner the night before, across the manicured lawn, to the circular pools beyond. The pools were lined with granite, the largest quite deep, the water clear and cold. It was connected to a smaller hot pool by an aqueduct about three feet deep, allowing one to wade or float to the other pool without stepping out of the water.

They sat on the lawn by the pools, listening to the roar of the ocean, enjoying the sunshine. Rhiannon felt a sudden tingling sensation at the back of her neck and turned, startled to see Grayling standing beside them. She hadn't heard him approach – it was like he was just *there*.

Zerik looked up at Grayling. "Must you do that?" he asked mildly.

"Yes," Grayling answered solemnly, a glint in his grey eyes.

Zerik snorted, rolling his eyes.

Ignoring him, Grayling folded his legs with feline grace, sitting down in the grass next to Rhiannon.

"It's good to see you," Rhiannon said, smiling shyly at Grayling.

"It's good to see you in daylight," Grayling returned, the trace of a smile on his lips.

"We've been touring the house," Zerik said. "You'll have to show Rhiannon your room sometime soon."

Grayling caught Rhiannon's eyes, held them, his heated silver gaze stealing her breath. "At your earliest convenience, madam."

Jesting, Zerik swatted Grayling on the arm. "Enough, knave. *Era* can wait until later." Growing sober, he speared his husband with a frowning glare. "And just to be clear, you *will* be expected to share."

Rhiannon gave a half-hearted chuckle. So far, being married was fun – but it was hard to forget that she was being stalked by a black-souled monster, and the terrifying Dead Monks. And her friend Greg was missing, too. Still, she reminded herself, Zerik said the monks wouldn't come within 100 miles of the Caistra, and the Ciatri home was within 25 miles of the government center. Besides, there were the gates and *e'drai* protecting the house. She told herself she was safe here – truly, she felt more secure than she ever had, in either lifetime. She glanced at Zerik and Grayling. Here were two protectors, who would fight to the death for her, she knew. She took a shaky breath, forcing herself to release her fears.

They sat quietly for long minutes, soaking up the sun and the salty breeze, content simply to be together. For Rhiannon, so used to anxiety and disquiet, the sense of peace was almost physical, an ease in her skin. Reflecting on her tour of the house, Rhiannon thought about Lyds and Robbie. She glanced at Zerik, staring out to sea, his little braids cascading down his back. "Lyds said he'd been serving the Ciatri *dzina* for two incarnations."

Zerik looked at her, nodded. "They're *anu'giao*. Indentured servants, sworn to serve our family for three incarnations."

Rhiannon was appalled. "You mean they're slaves?"

Zerik laughed, laid a reassuring hand on her thigh. "No. Well, yes, but no." He explained that many neonate aeternans chose to indenture themselves to others, usually in order to study with those carrying similar *e'drai*, to improve their mastery of various techniques and skills – but they were also paid for their efforts, the funds deposited in a Family bank account at the end of each incarnation. "That way, they're able to amass capital over several lifetimes – a large financial stake for the future."

"And the contract can be broken by either party, especially in unlikely cases of abuse," Grayling put in.

"While *anu'giao* serve, they are also treated like family," Zerik said. "Lydia and Robert are very dear to us, and we are honored to have them help with our very large family."

Rhiannon sat back, the cool grass under her palms, absorbing what they'd said. Her eyes widened, and she turned to look at Zerik. "Did you say – "

Grayling couldn't help a rare chuckle. "I was wondering when we'd get to this."

"Lyds is Lydia – Robert is –" Rhiannon stared from one man to the other, her mouth hanging open.

Zerik grinned. "It's not too complicated. For his first two incarnations, Lyds was a woman. Family Names are based on the incarnation when we begin to Remember – so in his second lifetime, he was Lydia. Same with Robbie, actually. She was male in her first two incarnations. Both swapped genders in this lifetime. Robbie's adjusted rather well, less so Lyds."

"You get used to it, after enough incarnations," Grayling commented.

Rhiannon ran a hand through her hair. "I don't remember who I am – how many times have I been male?"

"Never, to my knowledge," Zerik said. "You're one of the Sisters. Female in every incarnation. I only know of one other – besides Emma and Maddie – who has always been female." When Rhiannon opened her mouth to ask another question, he held up his hand to forestall her. "I know what you want to know next – *why*. And honestly, I have no idea."

"Who can know the whole Story, the heart of the Universe?" Grayling said quietly.

Rhiannon looked at Grayling, his silver hair, the sunlight, and his aura combining to envelop him in a translucent, shimmering glow. "You said you'd been female before, didn't you? You had a baby."

Grayling nodded. "Aye. Just once – unusual."

"Most aeternans tend to trade genders on a fairly regular basis," Zerik interjected. "Though I myself have only been female twice."

Grayling frowned. "I can't know the Story, but having birthed a child does allow me to understand Emma more deeply." He looked into the waters of the pool. "I am grateful for that."

"Once we were honored to become Consorts to the Sisters, we have always been born male," Zerik said, leaning back on his elbows in the grass. "As Madeline says, the Universe seeks balance; thus if the Sisters are female, their Consorts must be male. Of course, other physical characteristics of my Form – skin tone, eye color, that kind of thing – have continued to vary from one incarnation to the next."

Grayling cast a sly, appraising glance at Zerik. "You've done well in this incarnation. I like that dark skin of yours, *socia*."

"And I, your silver tongue," Zerik returned lazily. He flashed his blinding grin. "Well, most of the time."

Blushing, Rhiannon looked out to the ocean beyond the cliffs, a shimmering ribbon of blue-grey against the sky. She tried very hard not to think about Zerik's skin, his warm brown flesh as he draped a long, bare leg over hers. She also tried not to think about Grayling's tongue, with which she'd had acutely intimate acquaintance the night before.

Zerik slapped Rhiannon's arm teasingly, as he had earlier with Grayling. She jumped, startled. Zerik grinned. "I said, *era* later."

Rhiannon laughed.

"Lunch now," Grayling announced, unfolding his legs and rising to his feet in one smooth, flexible motion. Looking down, he held out a hand to Rhiannon, his grey eyes never leaving hers. "Milady."

Lyds served salads, fresh bread, and a delicate lobster ravioli at the linen-draped table under the outdoor pavilion. Rhiannon poured herself a glass of iced tea from a cut-crystal pitcher. For a moment, she closed her eyes, delighting in the feel of the warm breeze, the sound and scent of the ocean. It had been a stupendous, unbelievable morning. She could almost pretend she was in one of her dreams, that dark, haunted world, someone else's life, someone else's nightmare. With a sigh, she opened her eyes, applying herself to finishing her meal.

Rhiannon looked at Zerik and Grayling, so relaxed and comfortable with each other. She supposed they must be, after being married for hundreds of years. "You said you were chosen as Consorts to the Sisters," she said to Zerik.

He nodded. "I was chosen first. According to legend, each Sister may choose a Consort, but only every thousand years."

"And Emma chose me a little over a thousand years ago," Grayling said quietly.

Rhiannon sat back, incredulous, as that information sank in. "So you're saying it's my turn?"

Zerik smiled. Grayling looked away, his face stony, unreadable.

"Oh, that's just great," Rhiannon laughed mirthlessly, tossing down her napkin. "As if I don't have enough to deal with."

Zerik laid a sympathetic hand over hers. "*Varenya*, you love who you love. When the time comes, it will be natural, real. Something you desire with all your heart and soul." He touched her cheek. "Besides, you may not even be able to choose the Third Consort in this incarnation. It depends on your *e'drai*. You'll have to ask Maddie about it." He poured her another glass of iced tea. "Don't worry. Finish your lunch. You don't want to hurt Lyds' feelings, right?" His brown eyes were kind, his smile coaxing.

Rhiannon shook her head helplessly, picked up her fork again. She was living in a fairy tale. It was as if the world had gone mad. Or she had.

"Where are Maddie and Emma, anyhow?" Grayling glanced at Zerik. Knowing the way Zerik and Maddie could communicate with their thoughts, Rhiannon had long since stopped wondering how the two seemed to know what the other was doing.

Zerik wiped his mouth with a linen napkin, looked over at his husband. "Apparently, Emma's with the children. Madeline is getting the Circle ready – after lunch, she's going to start helping Rhiannon explore her *e'drai*."

Rhiannon swallowed, overcome by a sudden sense of apprehension. With that familiar feeling came an unbidden image of Greg, and she remembered she'd been unable to reach him the day before. She was gripped with a dark urgency, foreboding – and guilt. While she'd been selfishly dallying with her new family, Greg could be

... she didn't want to think what. She clutched Zerik's hand. "I need to make a phone call."

"All right, sweetheart. Are you comfortable?" Maddie smiled encouragingly.

Standing barefoot in the damp grass in the Sisters' Circle, Rhiannon nodded. "I'm fine." Her insides felt like they were vibrating, her hands unsteady. She was worried about Greg. He hadn't answered the phone again. Zerik had promised to send two members of the Dao Yin to Greg's house for her, to check on him. She was terrified something truly horrible had happened to him. All because of her. But she felt a strength within, her resolve like unbending iron running the length of her soul. She wouldn't give up on him. He'd never given up on her.

"*Don't be nervous,* varenya," Zerik's thought was like a warm breath in her mind. He was watching from the silk chaise in the shade of the nearby pavilion.

Maddie came forward and touched Rhiannon's arm, a warm flood of reassurance in her fingers, her smile gentle, solicitous. "Try to focus. I know you've got a lot on your mind, my dear – anyone would." She stepped back a few feet. "But you can do this."

Rhiannon took a deep breath, looking out to sea, the constant scintillating dance of the sun-dappled water. Instinctively, she had a fear of allowing others to see the things she was capable of. But she trusted Maddie, her new family. She offered Maddie a tremulous smile.

"Good girl," Maddie said. She pointed at the turf at Rhiannon's feet. "There is a seashell before you. Just look, don't touch. Not yet."

Rhiannon looked down. A small abalone shell rested in the grass, the sunlight rendering the inner curve of the shell iridescent, vibrant with green, turquoise, brilliant carmine, purple.

"In a moment," Maddie continued, "I'll ask you to pick up the shell, to use your *e'drai* to tell me who has touched it last, and any other information you can gain. But I want you to think about what you're doing – the actual process you use to get that information."

233

"Okay," Rhiannon stilled herself, ready.

Maddie glanced back at Zerik, then nodded to Rhiannon. "All right, sweetheart, go ahead."

Rhiannon closed her eyes. From Madeline and Zerik's perspective, only one or two seconds passed, before they could see Rhiannon's aura flare, the light flowing down her arm, until her hand was illuminated with a bright, coruscating halo of light. Rhiannon opened her eyes; they, too, shone with a golden radiance.

"Ah," Zerik's sigh was involuntary, and he closed his eyes for a moment, as he felt the rush of power flowing from his wife. Maddie didn't move, watching closely.

Rhiannon bent down and picked up the shell, cradling it in her luminous hand. After only another second, perhaps two, she dropped the shell, shaking her hand with a snap, the energy vanishing.

Rhiannon looked up at Maddie. "Emma held this shell. She's helping you to explore my *e'drai*. She'll be here in a little while, to help me understand the power of the Sisters. Grayling is with the children." Rhiannon blushed, reliving Emma's thoughts, the feel of her. "And she's looking forward to something called *era'famil* tonight, which seems to involve the whole family." She looked down at her feet, a little embarrassed. "Her whole body felt warm when she thought about it."

"*My body feels warm thinking about it, too,*" Zerik thought, his dazzling grin shameless.

Rhiannon pursed her lips, frowning reprovingly. "'*Era* later,'" she quoted. Zerik laughed.

"That was excellent," Maddie said, nodding, the sunshine rendering her tumble of red hair into a glowing nimbus around her face. "Come sit in the shade, we'll have some tea, then try something else." Her blue eyes were bright, curious. "Can you describe exactly what you did, in order to retrieve the information held in the shell?"

Rhiannon followed her to the pavilion, sitting next to Zerik on the chaise, her thigh warm and close against his. She took a steadying breath. "Well, I close my eyes and go inside myself. It's like there's a giant dark place inside me – it feels endless. But it's safe, comforting. And in that place are these wisps of white or gold, kind of like clouds, or mist."

234

"That's your energy, the energy of your *e'drai*," Zerik said.

Next to the chaise was a small table draped in white linen, with a bone china teapot and cups, a book of matches, an unlit votive candle in a gold mercury glass cup, and a pitcher of water. Maddie poured tea. "Go on, then what?"

Rhiannon thought. "Well, I gather up all the little clouds. I ask them to come to me, and they just – do. It's hard to describe."

"You're doing fine," Maddie encouraged, handing her a cup of tea.

"Thank you," Rhiannon accepted the teacup, took a cautious taste of the steaming, strong brew. "Well, then I pull all of it up into my chest. Like my heart beats with it. And it gets stronger. Then I move it down my arm, into my hand."

"How long does that take, would you say?" Zerik asked, leaning back against the cushions, his expression curious.

"Oh, at least a couple of minutes." Rhiannon waved a hand expressively. "It takes time to pull it all through me."

Maddie picked up the matches next to the tea tray. "It actually only took one or two seconds, from our perspective," she said, as she struck a match. With steady fingers, she lit the small candle.

"Really?" Rhiannon was surprised. "It feels so much longer inside me." She shook her head. "Well, anyhow, once it's in my hand, I can open my eyes, and pick things up or touch them. And then, for a couple of minutes, it's like I'm inside whoever touched the thing – I can feel who they are, what they're feeling and thinking, everything about them." She sipped her tea. "It's too much to take for long, all that flooding into me. So I let go, and then shake the energy out of my hand."

"Again, for us, it was only a couple of seconds," Zerik said.

Rhiannon stared at him. "Wow, it feels so different."

"Where did you learn to do all of this?" Maddie asked, sipping her tea. "It's a rather intricate process."

Rhiannon gave a short laugh and looked away, her eyes haunted. "From a dream. I dreamed of being with you, and Emma. And in the dream, I could do this thing. So when I woke up – I was just a kid – I tried it. And it turned out I could do it, too."

Maddie laid a hand on her knee. "That ability is your oldest *e'drai*, aside from your connection with the Sisters. It is *drai'tacti'sien'dao*, Touching and Knowing. The way you touch things and can feel who has touched them last, what they were thinking and feeling."

Zerik sat up and took Rhiannon's hand, his golden-brown eyes kind, holding hers. "Also, I saw – and felt – that you've mastered a gift you've had for the last few centuries – *drai'sentia'sien'dao*, what you call "looking" at someone, feeling and knowing who they are."

Rhiannon nodded, bemused. "If you say so."

Maddie leaned forward, her face intent, excited. "But Zerik says you've picked up something new in this incarnation. You can 'nudge' people, as you've called it. From his description, it sounds like a variation of *drai'sentia'pro'kan*, Feeling, Pushing." Maddie paused, a wicked glint in her eye. "It sounds like a great deal of fun."

"*Oh, Gods, yes,*" Zerik's thought was half moan, half wistful sigh.

Rhiannon flushed, avoiding his eyes. She pretended to study the flickering candle flame. "It doesn't have to be sexual."

While Maddie's smile was demure, her bright eyes were decidedly devilish. "Certainly. But any *e'drai* that enhances *era* is always lovely. Promise you'll show me later."

Rhiannon nodded, her face still scarlet, imagining what Zerik must have said.

"But back to business," Maddie continued, suddenly brisk, cheerful. She reached over and poured water from the pitcher, but left the glass sitting untouched next to the flickering candle. "As aeternans evolve – that is to say, die and are reborn, again and again – we develop new *e'drai*. The new gifts remain with us in subsequent incarnations, gaining strength and power with each death and rebirth. So this 'nudging' ability will continue to grow with you, as you die."

Zerik squeezed Rhiannon's hand. "When we – any of us, you, me – when we use our *e'drai*, we pull that energy from within ourselves. The process is different for different people, and for different types of *e'drai*, but it's roughly similar. We find the energy inside."

"And while we're doing that," Maddie added, "Our perception of time can slow down. Especially with stronger, immense gifts."

"*As we grow more powerful with each incarnation,*" Zerik's words shimmered in her mind. "*Some types of* e'drai *become almost effortless ... like talking to you with my thoughts.*"

Maddie nodded agreement, clearly privy to Zerik's mental dialogue. "And some types of *e'drai* use so much energy, they can render you nearly helpless, exhausted and drained, sometimes for days." She drank her tea, watching Rhiannon over the edge of her cup. "But you are powerful enough now that this particular *e'drai* – touching objects, feeling who held them last – has little to no physical effect on you."

Rhiannon looked from Zerik to Maddie. "So when Zerik was sleeping like that, after the monks attacked us – "

"I used *engi'ka'mirsyat'al*," Zerik said. I made the monks forget us, for a time. Forget everything. And it weakens me terribly. I should have needed at least a full 24 hours to recover."

"But you did something to help him, didn't you?" Maddie asked gently. Her azure eyes held Rhiannon's.

Rhiannon shook her head helplessly. "I don't exactly know what I did."

"Well, I do," Maddie said, laying a hand on Rhiannon's arm. "That's what we're doing today. We're helping you remember your most powerful *e'drai* -- the thing that joins you to Emma and I." She held up her hand, and suddenly the flame from the votive candle soared higher, until it was a spear of light nearly two-feet high.

Rhiannon gasped.

Maddie's smile was placid, her expression gentle, intent, as she fluttered her fingertips. The water in the glass flowed impossible and smooth into the air, a glistening ribbon twining around the flame in a perfect, unbelievable spiral of water and golden light.

"*Mmm, lovely,*" Zerik whispered in their minds, and for a moment Rhiannon imagined she could feel the heat of Maddie's power flowing through him, his own receptive *e'drai*.

"Emma commands the energy of the air," Maddie said, smiling into Rhiannon's eyes. "I carry the *e'drai* of fire and water. And you, my dear, really are the original Earth goddess."

237

FIFTEEN

Once again, Rhiannon dreamed of dancing with the man with eyes the color of new leaves, this time in an elegant Regency ballroom in Brighton, an opulent winter Frost Festival, crowded with glowing aeternans.

"We always seem to find one another on the dance floor," she said.

"Of course," he murmured, his smile against her ear. "Because we met in tears, forever after we must dance to dry them."

She shivered, but not with cold. As they waltzed, she couldn't restrain her smile, a heady exhilaration, safe in the circle of his arms. Then she caught sight of a lean man with grey eyes, his pose casual as he slouched indolently against the far wall.

"My husband is watching us."

He laughed. "Let him watch, then."

And she was laughing too, because she couldn't help it, because he always made her laugh, always made her feel like she was filled with light and fireflies, champagne bubbles and the last petal on the daisy, he loves me not, he loves me.

Summer at the Ciatri nest felt altogether natural, as much a part of Rhiannon as her own skin. Her family had quickly become an intrinsic part of who she was, as if they'd always been hers. She had husbands and wives who loved her, who not only accepted her for who she was, but celebrated it. Here, she was not "weird," but special, cherished. She had seven children, and while not of her own flesh, they readily called her mommy, mama, mom.

Yet once in a while, something would remind Rhiannon of her life in Kansas City, of Rosa or Greg, or Kat's life in San Francisco beyond that. Perhaps a dream, or the way someone laughed, a breath of musk or chocolate, or the way the evening sunlight gilded a patch of grass – meaningless little things, suddenly startling, discordant, reminding her that the past few weeks were only recent, new, not something which had always defined her very essence.

She had continued to try to reach Greg by phone, though Zerik's Dao Yin friends had been unable to locate Greg. His house in Columbus Park was ravaged. Rhiannon didn't want to believe the worst, but the evidence seemed incontrovertible. Something terrible had happened to Greg, and it was her fault.

Swamped with guilt, she banished the old memories, whenever they appeared like unwelcome guests at her heart's doorstep. Instead, she threw herself into practicing her *e'drai*, learning more about aeternan life and manners, sculpting, delighting in the company of her wives and husbands both in bed and out, playing with her new brood of children.

She felt safe here, in this luxurious cocoon, and she thought that if she could stay here forever, she'd never have to face the dark *erim* man, or the terrible monks. So she pretended this was forever, knowing it was a lie, choosing to savor these moments with her new family.

That summer, Rhiannon spent endless days creating the perfect childhood, a loving mother for the children she'd given up hope of bearing, a salve for Rosa's wounded child who never grew up. She read bedtime stories, built lopsided sandcastles down at the small private beach below the cliffs, frowned over math problems, adjudicated disputes, made peanut butter and jelly sandwiches, felt little fingers curl trusting into her palm.

All seven of the Ciatri children were aeternan; "Family always births Family," Emma once declared. Each child was a unique, wondrous being, glowing with the shimmering *fainna* of the aeternans. Emma explained that some of the children were neonate, with five *fainna* or less; others were medius, carrying up to 19 rings of light in their auras; or even Eldest, such as the Sisters and their husbands, with 20 or more *fainna* – each representing a life lived.

Many of the children were old enough to perform halting, childlike experiments with their particular *e'drai*.

Melody, a 7-year-old neonate, had four *fainna*, curly blonde hair, plump cheeks, and a gift for healing. Her ability came to light one afternoon when her little brother, Joshua, fell and skinned his knee. At the time, the adults were seated under the pavilion in the shade, but before anyone had time to react, Melody knelt next to her brother, saying, "Let me kiss it, and make it better." As she pressed her lips to his blooded flesh, her aura brightened. She rocked back on her heels, satisfied. "It's almost all better."

Maddie came over and inspected Joshua's knee. The 5-year-old's fresh wound looked as though it had been healing for a week – scabbed over, with new, puckered pink flesh around the edges.

Maddie smiled at her daughter, much pleased. "Very good, Melody." She turned back to Emma. "We should have Melody help with the herb garden in the conservatory. She can learn to make unguents and salves." Melody beamed proudly, her brilliant smile all the more charming for her missing front baby teeth.

Eva, the oldest at 13, was a beautiful child with coffee-and-cream skin and shining black ringlets. She looked remarkably like Zerik, and could communicate with her mind just as he could. A medius with ten incarnations, her power wasn't particularly strong – to speak to someone's mind, she had to physically be within a few yards. But she could also hear mental responses, which made her gift unusual and potentially very powerful, as her *e'drai* would grow in strength with every new incarnation.

Powerful gifts aside, Eva was also a young teenager, a bossy tomboy who had decided she was in charge of the other children, by virtue of her obvious maturity. She used her *e'drai* with instinctive skill to order the younger ones about, the latter tolerating her leadership with varying degrees of grace.

Children with strong *e'drai* are able to get into all kinds of serious trouble that oblivi parents could never imagine. One night in his Travels, Grayling discovered their son Marcus, age eight, wandering on the paths between worlds. The ability to Travel outside the body was a rare gift, very powerful and extremely dangerous. Marcus, a medius with seven *fainna*, was ill-prepared for the Dark Places and Fae Worlds, among the many places a Traveler can go. Grayling sternly told the child that he mustn't Travel without him, under any circumstances. Sensing the gravity of the situation, Marcus nodded, his freckled face solemn. Then he looked up into Grayling's eyes, pleading, hopeful. "When we Travel, can I hold Thicket's hand?" The child could see the Fae half of Grayling's soul.

In bed that night, Grayling looked over at Maddie. "I think when Marcus Remembers, we'll find he's from House Zel'Mori."

"What's that?" Rhiannon wanted to know, sitting up to look at him.

"One of the great Family dynasties, the *Dinach* of the Fae," Grayling answered shortly. "I am of House Zel'Mori."

Lying next to Maddie, Emma laughed. "Oh, good! More fairies in the family."

Grayling scowled. "Humph."

The youngest child, Missy — short for Melissa — was born with a strangely deformed left arm and hand, almost like a featherless wing, with pale, leathery pebbled skin. Her left hand was almost twice the size of her right, long on one side and terminating in a wicked claw. She was also Eldest, with close to 30 *fainna*. Her *e'drai* had yet to show itself, but Zerik declared he could feel tremendous power in the child, centered particularly in her deformed arm. He said that part of her was stronger than all the rest, possessing an energy so pure and powerful as to be unbelievably beautiful, simple, immediate, violent.

Yet little Missy, at 3 years old, had a heart of pure joy and love.

"It has always been so," Zerik explained to Rhiannon, while they sat with the children as they played on the beach. "Great gifts come with a price. Those born with deformities, or mental illnesses, are always given the most power." He shook his head. "Sadly, though, many are unable to control their *e'drai*, or lack the capacity to judge how best to do so."

Zerik stroked Rhiannon's hair, watching little Missy digging deftly in the sand with her wing-like hand. "But Missy may grow up to be one of the Prodigies, those aeternans with physical disabilities who have perfect, elegant control over their powerful e'drai."

As if sensing Rhiannon's regard, Missy looked up. A spontaneous, radiant smile blossomed on her face. "*Te a'behs*, Mama Re'nannon."

Rhiannon felt something warm inside her chest burst outward from her center, like blowing dandelion seeds, melting everywhere they touched. She smiled back at the child. "*Te a'behs*, Missy. I love you, too."

One cloudless afternoon, Rhiannon stood in the grass with Grayling, watching the children play in their magnificent treehouse. The Fae-built structure was a perfect miniature grey stone castle, lodged incomprehensibly in the branches of an enormous cottonwood on the edge of the cliff. Their oldest child, Eva, swung out from the parapet on a rope swing, squealing with delight as she leapt into space, landing rolling on the greensward. Her brothers and sisters crowed approval from the crenellated walls amid the branches above.

Rhiannon looked up at Grayling. He was so sternly handsome, all lanky muscular elegance. Watching the children, and unaware of her scrutiny, contentment warmed his serious features, and a smile undefended graced his lips.

Following his gaze, she turned back to see Eva and 6-year-old Charlie preparing to storm the battlements. "They're like little magical fairies," Rhiannon said, laughing.

Grayling's smile faded, and she caught a brief glimpse of something bleak in his eyes. "No. Not fairies."

Human.

Rhiannon spent endless summer days making mud pies with 10-year-old Jacob; lying in the grass with Eva and Melody, finding dragons and ducks in the clouds; picking bouquets of daisies for Maddie; helping Robbie and Lyds make snickerdoodle cookies; pushing Joshua on the swings, laughing at his exhilarated squeals as he flew through the air; fingerpainting with Missy, giggling when Emma found them covered with vivid canary-yellow and violet paint; blowing glistening rainbow soap bubbles into the salt-scented wind; closing her eyes and stretching out her *e'drai*, feeling her grubby barefoot companions all around her, their light and energy flowing easy and effortless into the world; leading the way down the cliff trail to the private beach below, to splash in the ocean, laughing and smiling so hard her face ached with it, coming home at sunset, sunburned and sandy, exhausted and joyous.

And she spent every night with her husbands and wives, sharing her dreams, telling her stories, holding her close in the invulnerable darkness.

But the *erim* man with the black aura haunted her dreams with his terrible, deathly smile, and Rhiannon would wake shaking, cold, and afraid once more.

Remember, remember this.

Sitting alone on the circle of grass in her room, Rhiannon felt the Earth deep and endless beneath her, and could almost hear Maddie's voice, that first day at the Ciatri nest, in the Sisters' Circle by the sea. If she closed her eyes, Rhiannon could see Zerik sitting on the chaise in the shade, Maddie leading her to the center of the Circle, the hem of her pale, silk gown flowing like water around the *Kir*'s ankles.

"Close your eyes and just feel the earth beneath your feet," Maddie murmured, circling around Rhiannon as she stood barefoot in the Circle, the waves crashing against the cliffs, the warm salty breeze against her skin. "Breathe deep, in through the nose, out through the mouth. Be here, now. Be present in this moment. Nothing else matters but right here, right now."

Rhiannon breathed, feeling the heat of Maddie as she moved around her body, circling slowly, inexorable.

244

"Haven't you always felt somehow better or stronger when in touch with nature? You've always loved being barefoot in the grass or mud. Feel the earth beneath you. Feel it connecting to your feet, your body."

With an innate understanding, Rhiannon found herself delving into that endless, warm darkness within, as though the Universe, vast and eternal, was a part of herself, her body a gateway, a shell for the infinite.

"Find the green *e'drai*, the earth connecting to who you are." Maddie's voice seemed to come from a great distance, hushed and slow, the syllables drawn out, extended.

And then suddenly her feet were warm, awash with a gentle heat, and Rhiannon could see it, feel it -- the wispy haze of green energy coming up through the ground, through her feet, into the soft darkness within. Like that day with Zerik, by the side of the road. Her flesh was tingling, energy like sparks crackling against her feet, pulled up through the very earth.

"You don't take this energy from yourself," Maddie's voice came drifting from a thousand miles away, as though through water, muted, indistinct, distorted. "You are the channel for the earth itself, Rhiannon. You carry and direct the energy."

Instinctively, Rhiannon began gathering the energy, pulling the shimmering amorphous fog and wisps of green into herself, into her chest. She called to it, asked for it, needed it. An ease, a sense of calm, overcame her, and the shining veridian clouds began flowing freely into her body, into her heart and head, throbbing with power.

"Yes ... don't stop ..."

The energy flowed up through her body to the crown of her head, then back down, streaming down her spine, her legs, back into the earth. She had become a living circuit, holding and carrying the shining green power, before pouring it back into the Earth – only to receive more.

Roots of power spun from the soles of her feet, tendrils of light twining breathtaking into the ground, spinning outward. She touched the roots of the trees, the strong sentinels forming the boundary of the Sisters' Circle, feeling the tawny gold, brown, and emerald power flowing up from the roots, the shimmering trunks, dancing leaves quaking as she touched them with light.

Dimly now, she became aware of Emma walking across the grass from the house, her feet touching Rhiannon's skin lightly, traipsing on the surface of the ground. Emma, her aura like a glowing star, reaching outward.

"Emma!" Maddie's voice was stretched, expanded, deep, and slow. "Wait!"

But then Emma was there, stepping within the circle of power. As the Sisters united, a wave of electrifying power swept through the air, the earth beneath Rhiannon. With the three women connected, suddenly everything expanded, becoming amplified a hundred times over. The green energy flowing through Rhiannon swelled to a frenzied, endless torrent, pouring through her body, back into the earth.

The sheer enormity of the planet streamed into her awareness, and she was so small, so very small. But the earth was feeling *her* now, feeling her inside, embracing her essence.

She was brown, loamy soil, flinty stone, crusted sand. She could feel the earth solid beneath her, radiating out from her center, touching everyone, all things. She could feel the depths of the cliff, the beach below, the lick of water against her skin as the waves touched the beach. Grass tender nerve endings, clay and topsoil, her bones rock deep, feeling the earth spinning out in all directions.

She touched Emma standing within the trees, the golden brown and ivy power spiraling around her ankles, fusing glowing into Emma's aura. Rhiannon felt Maddie's feet against her body, against her ground, felt her *e'drai* spinning up Maddie's legs, joining with Maddie's blazing light. The earth flowed under the pavilion, and her shimmering malachite energy touched Zerik, felt him moan as her power touched him, here, now, everywhere. Brown and rust, black soil and rock, shimmering jade, tourmaline, moss, loden, citron. She could feel the poles of the pavilion piercing her back, the chaise legs resting against her flesh.

She couldn't hold it anymore, the earth so big, she, so small. The energy built and grew within, bottle-green threads of power coalescing into a throbbing force, until her eyes opened and she cried out, arms flung wide, throwing back her head, releasing it all in a colossal thrust, an explosion of intensity.

The Earth erupted, split wide, a concussion of force rocking the cliff. Maddie and Emma fell to their hands and knees, gasping, and Zerik cried out, "Stop, Rhiannon, pull it back!"

Rhiannon spun to look at him, her aura flaring radiant, eyes glowing an unearthly emerald. "I feel you," she whispered, and collapsed to the shuddering ground.

"Just what the hell were you thinking, Maddie?" Zerik paced in front of the pavilion, shouting, shaking with anger.

"She wasn't," Grayling snapped, glowering at his wife.

Maddie stood in the grass, staring stone-faced out to sea. Her attitude was one of total defiance, spine rigid, arms crossed, but her tears betrayed her, trickling down her cheeks unrestrained.

Emma sat at the foot of the chaise, where Rhiannon lay unconscious. Wide-eyed, Emma watched Zerik, trying to remember the last time she'd ever seen him so angry. Sometime in the 16th century, she thought. He was swearing in aeternan, and several other languages besides – Latin, Gaelic, Chinese.

"*Vahs'da!* This has to be the most irresponsible – *naire!*" *Shame!* Zerik gestured to the raw gash in the earth, stretching outward from the center of the Sisters' Circle, extending some 90 feet to the edge of the cliff. The fissure was more than eight feet wide, the shadowed depth extending fathomless into the belly of the Earth.

"Someone could have been killed! One of the children!"

"*Gestu!* You think I don't know that?" Maddie whirled to look at him, her face flushed, eyes glittering with tears and fury. She pointed at Zerik. "You were there, too. You knew what I was doing. You didn't seem to have a problem with it then."

"He should have," Grayling interjected, his mouth a forbidding line, eyes like ice.

Zerik turned to look at his husband, offering Grayling a sarcastic sneer. "Well, forgive me for assuming the Sisters knew what the *diu* they were doing. As if you would have done differently."

Emma couldn't stand to see them fight. She jumped to her feet, arms wide, entreating. "Please stop," she said tearfully.

"And you," Grayling rounded on Emma. "Couldn't you feel what Rhiannon was doing? How dangerous it would be for you to enter the Circle?"

Wounded by the sudden attack, Emma pulled herself up to her full, petite height, turning up her nose, her lower lip trembling. "Don't you lecture me, Grayling Sonam." She stomped her foot, like a petulant child. "No, I didn't know. And neither did Maddie. It was an accident."

Maddie stalked over to stand next to Emma. She speared Zerik with a withering glare. "You're just frightened. Both of you. It scared you, and it scared me, too. But when men get frightened they lose their tempers." She scowled. "Like little boys."

"*Woman, you have pushed me too far,*" Zerik's thought was like an explosion in their minds.

"No."

They turned to the chaise, where Rhiannon lay pale and wan against the striped cushions. Her eyes were open, pleading, tears streaming down her cheeks.

"Please, please don't fight. It was my fault. I'm so sorry." She broke down, covering her face with her hands. "I'm so sorry."

Maddie came and sat next to Rhiannon, taking her hand. The older woman was crying outright, now. "No, Sister, it was my fault. I thought I could help you remember. I thought I could help you control your *e'drai*. I was wrong." Madeline looked up at Zerik, her eyes shimmering with tears and regret, her face etched with grief. "I was wrong, husband."

Then Emma was bawling, clutching Rhiannon's arm, and the three women clung to one another and cried.

Zerik's shoulders sagged, his fury dissolving into weariness, and he dropped his head. "Oh Gods, Madeline."

Grayling stood unyielding, his own anger slower to fade, sinking into an uncomfortable tension. He hated when his wives cried. He looked over at Zerik, who seemed suspiciously moist-eyed as well. Grayling sighed, suddenly drained, spent. "Well, Z," he said sardonically, "I suppose you won't need to have a good fit of temper for a few more centuries." He shook his head, allowing a wry smile. "I must say, though, I didn't know you could swear in Croatian."

Zerik and Grayling stood in the shadows of the hall, just beyond the library doors. Eavesdropping.

"Are you sure he was the only one who knew she'd be in San Francisco?" Grayling whispered, looking back at Rhiannon, standing within the library, near the broad windows. She clutched the untraceable cell phone Maddie had given her, chewing her lip. Unconsciously, she shifted from one foot to the other.

"I'm sure." Zerik's face was grim.

Grayling turned to his husband. "Monks don't interrogate oblivi and then leave them alive. If he's not dead – "

"Then we'll have to kill him ourselves." Zerik closed his eyes, his face pained. She cared for this man. "He must be with The Guard."

Grayling held up a hand for silence, glancing back into the library. Rhiannon had begun speaking again.

"Oh, Greg, I'm just so glad you're okay. I've been trying to reach you for days." Her hands were trembling, her voice choked with emotion. After a short pause, she said, "No, I can't tell you where I am. It's not safe, I just –" She stopped, listening. Finally, she spoke again. "Yes, I'm fine. I swear. I *swear*. Okay, look, I'm near Mendocino. In California. That's really all I can say." She turned to stare blindly through the library windows. "Are you *sure* you're all right?"

"Dammit," Zerik hissed, turning on his heel and stalking down the hall.

"I would think after a couple thousand years, people would get bored with living," Rhiannon said.

The three Sisters were floating nude in the big stone pool at the cliff's edge, the water glistening in the light of the full moon.

"It's getting chilly," Emma complained.

Maddie's aura flared brighter, and a wash of warmth spread through the water. "Better, dear?" Maddie inquired.

"Mmm, much. Thank you, love." Floating on her back, Emma sighed happily, fluttering her fingers languidly back and forth in the water.

Maddie paddled closer to Rhiannon, who was likewise floating on her back, gazing at the night sky. "It is true that some grow tired of living. It's also true that some become *anamcaillte* – they grow mad after too many incarnations."

Rhiannon shuddered. "The idea of losing your mind – it seems more horrible than death."

"But it doesn't happen often," Emma said.

"No, it doesn't," Maddie agreed. She swam in lazy circles around the other women. "Many believe *anam*, the soul, stays young when we have some kind of spiritual life – trying to read the Story, understand the Universe. Following The Way. But," she added, "I think it's also important to celebrate our physical existence. We are ever reborn into these physical bodies. An exploration and passion for *era* is one part of that understanding."

"Creativity, too," Emma said. She paddled over to Rhiannon, the gentle swell of her breasts floating pale on the water. "Using any kind of creative gift makes your soul young. And since creativity is a gift from the Universe, using that gift honors the Universe." A merry smile blossomed on her features. "And when you give back to the Universe ..."

"You make magic," Maddie finished. She glided over to the side of the pool, to look out at the ocean, the moonlight creating a sparkling path on the endlessly shifting water, into the horizon. She looked over her shoulder at Rhiannon. "I like to do work with textiles, particularly batik, and weaving. Though I also quite enjoy a bit of glassblowing, when I'm in the mood. Zerik draws and paints; Grayling makes music, plays any instrument you put in his hand." She smiled fondly. "And you sculpt, of course."

"I sing," Emma said. "A lot of the time with Grayling. We harmonize." She grimaced. "And, heaven help me, I write."

Rhiannon allowed her legs to sink, treading water with lazy fingers. "You don't sound happy about it."

Emma shook her head, her damp blonde curls bouncing. "I've been writing for hundreds of years. The writing only improves slightly, but the misery is a constant. I think it's the cross I bear for getting to make babies."

"Oh, you say that," Maddie said, laughing, swimming over to Emma. "But you seem awfully pleased with yourself when your books are published."

Emma sniffed. "I'm not proud of the books – I'm proud of getting them published. Believe me, the latter is far more painful than the writing." She glared at Maddie. "Have you ever had an editor?"

Rhiannon shared Maddie's grin. "Can't say that I have."

A splash fight broke out then, leaving all three dripping and laughing, arms entwined around one another's shoulders, graceful and loose.

They played and splashed until they were tired, until the water was work to move through. They floated quietly for a while, taking turns pointing out constellations, drifting lazy, like pale clouds on the surface of the water.

By then, the moon was low, and the women didn't speak for some time, simply enjoying the feel of the water, and each other.

Finally, Emma broke the silence.

"I'm going to have another baby," she said, looking into the endless stars.

"God's wounds. That was incredible," Zerik gasped, his chest heaving. The combined light of their auras still shone brilliant. Grayling lay with his head on Zerik's chest, Emma draped languorously over his thigh and belly. Maddie and Rhiannon were curled opposite, hands on Zerik's chest, legs, face.

"Mmm, it was," Rhiannon mumbled, feeling as though every part of her body was suffused with soft warmth, even now joined and connected to her husbands and wives. "I don't think I've ever had an orgasm like that."

"Oblivi have orgasms," Maddie sighed, eyes closed, still luxuriating in sensation. "That was *vosha'ni*. The ecstasy shared through the aura and *e'drai*."

They lay together for long minutes, drinking in the delicious afterglow of *era'famil*, lovemaking only spouses could share. As their auras gradually faded to their customary luminescence, Maddie extracted herself from the pile of warm limbs, padding barefoot to the sideboard for water and hot towels.

"Thank you, wife," Grayling said, as he accepted a hot cloth from her hands. He began wiping Emma down from neck to toes, using long, slow strokes. Eyes closed, she sighed contentedly and submitted to his ministrations.

Zerik took another cloth, and began to perform the same service for Rhiannon. "Wait, what about Maddie?" Rhiannon asked.

Maddie grinned. "Since I got up, I get to be washed down last. By everyone."

Rhiannon giggled and closed her eyes. "Okay." She basked in Zerik's attentions, the warm cloth almost unbearably pleasurable as he brushed her breasts, between her thighs. "You know, I always thought I was oversexed or something," she said. "I mean, I love sex. A lot. But growing up, you'd think I was a nympho or something." She opened her eyes, smiled at Zerik as he ran the cloth down her thighs. "But it seems my husbands and wives like it just as much as I do."

Zerik chuckled. "Well, it's kind of an aeternan trait."

"There's a reason we have so many names for different types of *era*," Emma commented.

Rhiannon sat up. "Are all aeternans bisexual, too? Is it because we can be born in male and female bodies? In Kansas City, being bisexual made me – " she grimaced. "Weird."

Grayling frowned. "Gender, sex, and sexuality are three different things," he said.

Maddie handed Rhiannon an icy glass of water. "Sexuality is biological – nature, not nurture – though through the centuries, we've come to understand that most people are bisexual, at least to some extent." She laughed. "Some oblivi have a very hard time admitting even the tiniest attraction to someone of the same sex. They do like to see things in black and white, either, or."

Rhiannon drank deeply. The water was invigorating, after the warmth of the hot towels and heated flesh.

Zerik climbed out of the immense bed and went to the sideboard, preparing hot towels for Maddie. He glanced over his shoulder at Rhiannon, favoring her with his dazzling grin. "This particular Form," he said, indicating his own dusky naked body with the sweep of a hand, "is most satisfyingly bisexual. As Maddie said, most are. But even if I weren't, even if this body was purely heterosexual, I would still wish to make love with my husband." His gaze lingered on Grayling's sinewed form. "Because he is my best friend. Because I love him."

"Base flattery," Grayling growled. He winked at Rhiannon.

"Lie down Maddie, there's a good witch," Zerik said, returning to the bed with four fresh hot towels.

Maddie closed her eyes and leaned back into the pillows, beaming, satisfied. "You look like the cat that ate the canary," Grayling commented, as he stroked Maddie's feet with his warm towel.

As Rhiannon helped her spouses wash down Maddie's soft, voluptuous curves, she felt a wonderfully curious mix of love, the stirrings of new passion, and a kind of protectiveness, almost maternal – a desire to care for and protect her Sister.

"Basically," Zerik said, picking up the thread of the conversation, "if you get pleasure from being stroked like so – close your eyes, *varenya* – " Rhiannon closed her eyes obediently, then gasped as Zerik's fingers stroked lightly between her thighs. "Can you tell if the touch is from a man, or a woman? Is it not pleasurable regardless?"

Rhiannon shuddered deliciously at his touch, nodding.

"Now if you open your eyes, and see the face of one you love, why does gender matter?" He leaned over and kissed Rhiannon, his lips featherlight against hers. When he pulled back, he held her eyes in his deep gaze. "To reject a partner based solely on gender is, for aeternans, bad manners indeed."

"Oh, that would be rude," Emma blurted out.

"Reject a partner because you don't like who they are, because you're tired, even because of incompatible *e'drai* – but for gender alone?" Zerik shook his head. "No. For oblivi, gender is a first consideration, with all else secondary. For us, it is the last consideration, if at all."

"Bodies come and go so easily, you see," Emma chirped, her smile electric.

Graying was leisurely sliding his warm cloth between Maddie's legs, the rough terrycloth rubbing gently back and forth. She'd begun making little mewling sounds, her hips shifting restlessly against the sheet. Rhiannon felt a rush of heat pooling between her own thighs, just watching. Unable to help herself, she leaned forward and pressed her mouth to Maddie's plump breast, suckling her taut nipple, sliding her fingers to the damp flesh between Maddie's nether lips.

Maddie gasped with the pleasure of it, arching her back, opening her eyes, seizing Zerik with a heated stare. Her aura had begun to blaze. Her thought was part sigh, part growl. *"Enough talk, beloved. More era. Now."*

Rhiannon dreamed she and Emma were bound on a pyre in a forest. She'd had this dream before, but now she recognized the other women. She knew how it ended.

Rhiannon was groggy from the herbs they'd given her, unable to feel the earth, the trees, cut off from everything that she was, her strength, her e'drai. Emma was slumped forward, unconscious, cold and still, dangling from her bonds. Maddie lay on the ground in disarray, arms and legs flung wide, insensible. Like Rhiannon and Emma, she wore only her thin lawn shift, now torn and filthy. One of her breasts was exposed.

Two men in coarse brown robes stood over Maddie's body. "The witch can't stop the flames now," one sneered, kicking Maddie's ribs, hard.

"Bring the torch," said the other.

As the flames licked upward, Rhiannon cried out in agony, watching as they decapitated Maddie's unconscious form. The air, the

254

world, seemed to deflate, empty, as the last light faded from Maddie's aura. As the fire burned, at her back, Rhiannon felt Emma die, felt her soul fly from her body.

The flames licked her charred face, her eyes open and filled with blood. The pain absorbed every cell, every fiber of her being, and she opened her mouth in a silent scream that went on and on.

Rhiannon cried out, bolting awake. The bedroom was silent, moonlight soaking through the windows.

"Rhiannon," Emma whispered, lying next to her.

"Sister," Maddie said, her voice low.

Beside them, Zerik and Grayling slept.

"Are you all right?" Maddie murmured, touching her arm.

"I had a nightmare," Rhiannon said brokenly, tears coursing down her cheeks. "A memory."

"Tell us," Emma said.

She told them. Told them about dying, burning, watching and feeling them die. And the three Sisters wept together in the moonlight, remembering.

SIXTEEN

In this life, her Bryne incarnation, Rhiannon remembered the interminable Kansas City winters: naked, black tree branches clawing the grey sky, the icy dark painful, endless. Wrapped in a faded pink comforter, her nose pressed to her frosted bedroom window, she exhaled against the glass, watching as the rime retreated before her heated breath, aching for summer.

But summer, when it came, felt fleeting, transitory, ephemeral. And later, while she would remember the long, winter days with agonizing detail, her memories of summer were a blur, snatches of experience, a vivid insubstantial crazy-quilt of sunshine and dandelion fluff, the icy shock of jumping into swimming pools, flashlight ghost stories and laughter, grass cool and damp beneath her bare feet.

Most of us like to think we're higher beings, that we've risen above our animal nature. We believe that, unlike beasts, we are no longer driven by instinct. We are intelligent, self-aware. We choose, we decide, using that lovely wrinkled mass of grey matter, our marvelous evolved brains. We exercise judgment. We are conscious of our actions, our sagacity and insight giving us a deep awareness of our own condition, our own lives, our personal behavior and identity.

But animal nature lurks beneath our arrogant, ignorant perception, driving and controlling us in a thousand ways we can only begin to conceive.

It is our fundamental nature, the primitive lizard brain, which controls the basic way we process and record memory. Unless we make a conscious, sophisticated effort, happy recollections slide by in hazy pleasant focus, an agglomeration of joy, laughter, and kisses — while agony is etched in perfect, minute, excruciating detail in the mind, every moment of pain like indelible grooves in the raw, taut skin of our magnificent grey minds.

Pain is a gift from nature. Pain equates to lessons learned, survival an indication we've successfully passed the test. We remember suffering in order to avoid it.

Happiness is the trophy, but of little consequence in the grand scheme of survival of the species. We remember it only as suffering's prize, motivation, something to look forward to when we aren't busy trying not to die.

For Rhiannon, summer was its own kind of magic, the reward for surviving the endlessly dark days of winter. Each day stretched lazy and succulent, a thousand ways to divide minutes of eternal sunshine, and she tried to savor every one. But looking back, she only remembered fragments, a montage of sparkling water and sunshine, driving with the windows rolled down and the wind in her hair, laughing, endless afternoons of sun-dappled forest picnics, sandy beach towels, sticky strawberry jam children's kisses, nights overflowing with stars and promise.

Rhiannon had two lifetimes worth of unhappy memories, long bleak winter days, hurt and loneliness and danger and abuse and pain. She remembered so much unhappiness, interspersed with fleeting inconsistent impressions of peace and laughter, the little fragments of happiness filling the spaces between.

Throughout the remainder of that summer with her aeternan family, sharply aware of the transient, evanescent nature of joy, Rhiannon tried to hold on to each second with everything she had, to force the lizard brain to remember, remember. Remember perfect golden days, remember love.

She'd stop and close her eyes, trying to paint every detail of that second, that moment, that *now*, in the darkness of her mind. "Remember this," she'd whisper, holding the image behind her eyes. "Remember."

And so she hoarded her shining treasures, against the day when darkness would come again.

In the small hours of the night, Rhiannon lay with her head pillowed on Maddie's ample breasts, listening to her steady heartbeat as she slept. "I'm a monster," Rhiannon whispered aloud into the darkness, not expecting anyone to hear the painful truth resonating in her heart.

"*No,*" Maddie's thought sounded in her mind. "*You are amazing, beautiful, and powerful.*" She reached down and tipped up Rhiannon's chin, holding her eyes in the dim light. "*Power can be monstrous when misused, but you follow The Way. You just need to learn how to use your gifts again.*"

Rhiannon's eyes stung, overflowed. "Can you help me, Maddie? Can you stop me from hurting anyone?"

Her jaw set in a determined line, Madeline nodded. "*I will help you, wife. We will all protect you, and anyone else.*"

Remembering the last time she'd set foot in the Sisters' Circle, her uncontrollable power ripping a great gash in the shaking earth, doubt reflected in Rhiannon's eyes.

Maddie touched Rhiannon's cheek, wet with tears. "*I promise,*" she said, bringing her fingertips to her mouth, to lick the salty moisture, then leaning down to press her lips to Rhiannon's, sharing her tears.

One evening after dinner, Emma danced for them – *da'siao*, aeternan dance. They'd retired to the U-shaped seating area beyond the dining table, the cutwork candle-lanterns and torches outside the pavilion flickering in the summer night air.

"*Da'siao* – dance – is one aspect of *e'lain*, artistic expression particular to aeternans," Maddie explained, as Emma prepared for her performance, the skin on her shoulders gleaming peachfuzz gold in the ardent light, the skirt of her pale blue gown skimming around her ankles as she paced back and forth before the jewel-toned silk divans. She slipped off her sandals, scuffing her bare feet against the ground, her normally animated features focused inward, intent.

"Traditional *da'siao* is often performed barefoot, sometimes nude." Maddie took a sip from her wine glass. "Aeternan art forms use either *e'drai*, skills perfected through many incarnations, or artistic influences from a variety of cultures over several time periods – and often, all three."

Zerik used his silent *e'drai* to call Lyds with a thought. The bespectacled little man in his pink apron appeared quickly, carrying a broom and dustpan, plus a long, carved wooden case, which he placed almost reverently on the chaise next to Grayling. He pushed the inlaid Moroccan table off to one side, and began sweeping the area clean of pebbles and any other refuse or obstructions. Zerik sent Lyds another direct thought. *"You and Robbie are welcome to watch, if you'd like."* Flushed with pleasure, Lyds trotted back into the house to fetch Robbie. One of the Sisters performing *da'siao* was a rare treat indeed.

Rhiannon lay back against Grayling's chest on the purple and red embroidered chaise beneath the canopy, the incandescent torches rendering the area luminous, magical. Grayling's lips grazed her ear and she sighed, content.

Robbie and Lyds came to stand near the open doorway to the house, Lyds shifting back and forth on his feet, eager, his excitement palpable.

Emma finished exploring the area before the lounges with her feet, satisfied that all was smooth and clear. She looked up, her blue eyes bright, and nodded to Grayling.

Grayling kissed the top of Rhiannon's head. "I'm sorry, love, but I have to play now." He gently guided her to the lounge shared by Maddie and Zerik, settling her next to her other husband.

Zerik put an arm around Rhiannon. Maddie leaned against his left side, the older woman's head resting against his, her red hair vivid against his dark braids. Rhiannon leaned forward, alight with anticipation.

Grayling opened the ornate wood case Lyds had brought. From within a nest of quilted topaz silk, he removed his rebec, a narrow, boat-shaped stringed instrument, played with a bow. The wood gleamed with a rich, aged patina.

"Part of musical *e'lain* is using a variety of historic instruments," Zerik commented, as Grayling tuned the three-stringed rebec.

"I have carried this rebec since the 11th century, back when I first met Emma, and my *dzina*," Grayling said. "Whenever I've died, it's been passed from family member to friends, eventually stored in bank vaults. It's precious to me, and it's only fitting to use it for Emma's *da'siao*." He tightened one of the strings, plucked it, listened, smiled fondly. "The rebec sings like a woman. It is played something like a violin." Resting the instrument against his left arm, just below his chin, he stroked the strings lightly with the bow. He adjusted another peg, slid the bow along the strings, then, satisfied, nodded to Emma.

Emma's smile was brilliant, her joy effervescent as she stood barefoot before her husbands and wives. "Tonight, I celebrate the new Family growing inside me," Emma said, cradling her hand against her still-flat belly.

Zerik raised his wine glass, and the others followed suit, smiles beaming all around. "*Maghkai!*" *We fight together.* All echoed the traditional Family toast.

Emma acknowledged the honor with a regal nod, spreading her arms wide. "I give you the *da'siao* of Spava and Varenya," Emma announced. She smiled at Rhiannon. "A love story."

Emma paced to the center of the space in front of the couches, one foot poised before the other, arms out, head down, her golden curls joining with her aura like a halo.

For a few moments, all was silent, but for the sputtering of the torches, the waves roaring against the cliffs in the darkness.

Now Grayling began to play, a slow, almost mournful, tune. Emma stepped tentatively, looking over her shoulder, as though fearful.

"If the musician and the dancer work well together – and after centuries, Grayling and Emma have danced together thousands of times – their e'drai begin to harmonize, even to join, as they do in era," Zerik whispered in Rhiannon's mind.

Rhiannon gasped. She could see Emma moving through a dark forest, alone and afraid. The trees were hazy, insubstantial, but somehow there, visible. *"Grayling's music, his e'drai, creates the images flowing from the dancer's thoughts,"* Zerik murmured.

Rhiannon glanced at Grayling. His eyes, glowing faintly, were intent on Emma, hands on his rebec, his aura shimmering.

Together, he and Emma created the story of Spava and Varenya, one of the old Eternal Tales Rhiannon remembered reading as a child. The beginning of the story, in which Spava rescues Varenya from a beast in the forest, and they fall in love, was unfamiliar to Rhiannon. The end of the fairy tale was all she'd read – the story of good triumphing over evil, and love's resurrection.

Emma played all the parts with consummate skill, from the terrible bear to her lover Spava, his aura shining in the darkness of the forest. The elegant movement of her arms, her expressive hands, the way her feet pounded, slid, or fluttered on the ground, each motion seemed unique to her characters.

Then came the part of the story Rhiannon knew, the old fairy tale of evil and Light. Suddenly, she was consumed with a cold terror. Emma had sunk to the ground, curled in a fetal ball, as a newborn child. Then, rising to her feet, swaying and twisting like coiling smoke in the air, she was playing the part of a terrible demon. Her aura had changed, swirled and congealed into a horrifying blackness, roiling clouds of black and filthy grey, gashes of red the color of raw meat.

Rhiannon nearly jumped to her feet, everything within her screaming to run. Zerik's hand on her thigh, warm and reassuring, restrained her. *"It is only the dance, varenya,"* he murmured within her mind. *"She uses her air e'drai to change the appearance of her own shining aura. It is illusion, love. Only illusion."*

Sensing Rhiannon's panic, Maddie reached out and touched her arm, her thoughts reassuring. *"She plays the demon who destroyed all he touched, he who is erim. He who Spava destroys. It's only a story,*

Rhiannon." Maddie frowned with concern. *"Do you want them to stop?"*

Rhiannon shook her head mutely, her eyes on Emma with her ghastly black aura, as she danced and destroyed the world.

Rhiannon dreamed of wartime San Francisco. She dreamed of moments, fragments. Crowded into the Maisonsur with her Sisters and many members of the Dao Yin, contributing to the war effort. Their service flag in the window, with a blue star for Zerik, who was fighting with the RAF, smuggling Jews and Family to the Caistra near Zurich. Maddie's lush Victory Garden. Playing cribbage in the kitchen, the blackout curtains pulled tight against the windows. Helping Emma process scrap tin and rubber. Grayling helping to hide aeternans unlucky enough to be born into Japanese-American Forms in the Caistra in the north. Rhiannon, working with new recruits in the WAVES, teaching the girls to shoot at the Navy base on Treasure Island.

There was a girl. Her name was Georgia. Georgie. A silly, adorable, little oblivi girl with brown curls and bright eyes to match, a determined chin, and dreams of something more.

Rhiannon met her on the base. A secretary with the Chronicle, Georgie wanted to be a real hard-nosed investigative reporter, and was trying to impress the editor. She'd interviewed Rhiannon for an article on the WAVES.

They'd had too much to drink at the Jubilee, a speakeasy sort of bar full of women, with a peephole in the door. They'd staggered back to Georgie's apartment, laughing. Rhiannon didn't normally dally with oblivi, but Georgie had been deliciously insistent. "I thought all WAVES secretly liked girls," Georgie had whispered in the darkness, her hands sliding over Rhiannon's bare shoulders like a breath.

"Not all of them," Rhiannon had answered, cupping Georgie's face in her hands, pulling her mouth to hers. "But I do."

But then somehow, in the warm darkness, the dream changed, and Rhiannon was afraid.

She was late. "Wait for me," she'd told Georgie. "Don't face him alone."

Georgie had been eager, her eyes bright. "I have to get this story. My source says he's not just selling stockings and cigarettes, or ration books – he might even be dealing with the Nazis," she frowned, determined. "It's not just about me being a reporter, it's about the world."

"Don't face him alone," Rhiannon begged. A terrible foreboding felt like ice spiders crawling under her skin. It was important, so important, and she didn't know why. Couldn't say. "I can help you."

"Oh, you think you're tougher than I am?" Georgie laughed.

"Yes," Rhiannon answered. "More than you know." But she wasn't, not really.

She was late. She said she'd be there, and she was late.

The darkness shifted, growing deeper. Rhiannon was shaking uncontrollably, fear bitter and metallic on her tongue. Her back had started to hurt again, that deep ache like a steel bar under her shoulder blades.

Rhiannon was pushing open a hotel room door. He was hunched over Georgie on the floor, next to the bed. Her skirt was pushed up over her hips, her face and thighs bruised and smeared with blood, crumpled white nylon panties around one ankle, brown eyes staring empty, lifeless. Her arms were flung wide, as though in supplication.

He turned his head, his churning aura black and twisted, smiling hideous, sepulchral, intoxicated, as he absorbed the last flickering light from Georgie's body.

Rhiannon stared aghast, unable to move, his endlessly black eyes boring into hers. "Ah, my love," he murmured, reaching for her. "I thought you'd never come."

And Rhiannon started screaming, screaming mindless agony, Gehenna, screaming for almost a hundred years. Screaming until she couldn't remember anymore. Couldn't remember anything at all.

Waking abruptly, Rhiannon sat on the side of the bed, burying her face in her shaking hands, weeping with the fading memory of her own screams. The Fae spirit joined with Grayling's soul had been right. She thought she couldn't remember, but now she understood a part of her truly didn't want to remember. For good reason.

The trees forming the border of the Sisters' Circle were robust and splendid, their leaves shimmering and dancing in the sunlight and ocean air. The sentinels chosen to protect and aid the Sisters in their work were apple trees, willows, poplar and sassafras, black walnut, holly, maple, beech, fragrant cedar, strong oak, elm, ash, alder, cherry, faithful birch, hazel, and elder.

Sacred trees, all. Trees that poured energy through their roots into the ground, drinking magic from the earth, the water, the air, the fire of the sun. Trees honored for centuries, associated with Gods and Goddesses, trees with healing properties and magical associations, sacred to ancestors and old wisdom, the Sidhe and those who travel Other Paths.

On this day, their leaves and branches swayed in the Northern California salt-sea breeze, a living, gentle barricade between the world of men, and the magic of goddesses.

"I don't know if I can do this," Rhiannon mumbled, avoiding their eyes, her hands twisting in her lap, as she sat in the grass within the Sisters' Circle.

"Yes, you can," Emma said encouragingly.

The three women were sitting crosslegged in the grass, connected, touching knee to knee, forming a closed circle. Beyond them stretched the ugly gash in the earth created by Rhiannon's *e'drai*, 30 yards long, yawning deep into the heart of the cliff.

"We're going to help you control your *e'drai*," Maddie said. She looked over her shoulder at Zerik and Grayling, lounging on the chaise in the striped pavilion, deceptively relaxed.

Beside the shaded canopy, a small flame burned in Maddie's copper fire pit. Next to that, someone had placed a slate fountain, with a spiral of water four feet high, spinning down into a stone bowl.

Zerik called to Rhiannon. "I'll be here to sense what is happening, to feel the *e'drai*, the strength and control."

265

"And I'll bring in reinforcements in case of trouble," Grayling added gravely. "Whatever happens in this Circle, will stay in this circle, I assure you."

Zerik caught Maddie's eye. *"Madeline, she's got the skills and control of a neonate, and the* e'drai *of one of the most powerful aeternans ever reborn. You are sure this is the best option?"* Zerik's thought was for the *Kir* alone.

"This is the only way," she returned his thought. *"You must warn Grayling if we lose control, give him time to contact the Sidhe."*

"We'll be ready."

"Thank you for trusting me, Z."

"I know you won't fail me, varenya. Te a'behs."

From across the circle, Maddie smiled into his eyes. "Te a'behs, *my* socia. *My Consort.*"

Rhiannon watched Maddie, felt a shimmer of something along her skin, an electric whisper, knew the older woman was speaking privately to Zerik with her thoughts.

"I don't want to make a mistake," Rhiannon said. "I don't want to hurt anyone."

"You won't," Emma chirped, touching Rhiannon's knee. "We won't let you."

Rhiannon shook her head, remembering the unbelievable rush of power she'd released in this Circle. She looked at the horrible wound in the earth, undeniable evidence of the magnitude of her power, the potential for even greater destruction. "How can you know? How can you be sure you can help me?"

Maddie turned to look at her, smiling placidly. "We're witches, you know."

Rhiannon could only stare, wide-eyed.

"I'm teasing," Maddie laughed. "Well, the world might call us witches. Heaven knows, they did in the past." A shadow flitted across her face, faded, and for a moment Rhiannon remembered her dream of fire and pain. "We're just women who know a lot about growing things. If we're going to get spiritual about it, I would think we're more Druids than witches."

"What's the difference?" Rhiannon asked.

Emma laughed. "We see the connection in all things. Gods, goddesses – it's all the world, the people in the world, the trees, the plants, the earth and sky. The fire, the lava in the heart of the Earth. Energy flows through all things, so all things are connected.

"The original Druids understood that, so they tried to learn more about everything, knowing all things are a part of – and affect – everything else. Understanding math and science helps you understand childbirth. Understanding language and art allows you to connect with all people, everywhere. That kind of thing." Emma grinned. "The more you know, the more you see the connections. The more you realize how much more there is to know."

Maddie touched Rhiannon's cheek with one hand, slid her fingers through the grass with the other. "The three of us are going to join in *caih'es'drai*. It's much like when we share *e'drai* during *era*, but specific to that purpose – sharing *e'drai* during *era* is a side-effect, rather than the primary goal. Our thought is that if we can share our *e'drai*, then Emma and I can help you guide and control your gifts. You'll be able to feel our abilities and the way in which we control them, and learn from that as well."

Maddie leaned back, staring up into the azure sky, the pale clouds drifting overhead. "I think it's best, to start, if we have a basic understanding of *e'drai* itself." She took Rhiannon's hand, held her eyes with her bright blue gaze. "Like all aeternans, we have *e'drai*, gifts that come from within us. I can speak with my mind; those with like gifts can respond. Like Zerik," she nodded toward the pavilion. "But I can also read the future."

Rhiannon remembered her dreams of Maddie, and the stories they'd told after dinner, Madeline predicting the future with her *sortes*, or tea leaves. "So you can see the future?"

Maddie shook her head. "No, thank heaven. To see it is to burn with it. No, I *read* the future, in symbols, like reading a book. The problem is that, much like reading the word-symbols in a book, symbols are open to interpretation, subjective. It is my lives' work to perfect my understanding of the symbols." She looked away. "And sometimes, I see too much, feel the heat of the Story in my soul. And I weep with it."

267

Rhiannon felt a wave of pain from Maddie, and reached out, touched her arm, needing to reassure her somehow.

Maddie looked down at Rhiannon's hand, surprised, then smiled. "Don't worry for me, my love." She looked over at Zerik and Grayling, sitting quietly in the shade of the canopy, waiting.

"*E'drai* comes from the Universe, from the Gods, or just God – if that's a word that works for you. Psychic energy is spiritual energy. Spiritual energy is part of who we are, part of nature, of all things. All things have energy, the divine flowing through them. *E'drai* is something that comes natural to us. As aeternans evolve, as we live lifetime after lifetime, our *e'drai* grows, intensifies. We become more powerful." Maddie leaned forward, gesturing with her hands, elegant, expansive. "Most *e'drai* comes from within. We use our own energy, channel it, direct it, in ways dictated by our gift. So, for example, when you feel an object, touch it, learn from it, you are pulling energy from within yourself and directing it into your hand. Then, when you touch the object, you feel that energy resonate back to you in the form of information. For someone as strong and old as you are, that amount of energy expended is negligible. You don't really notice or feel the loss of that energy.

"But very powerful *e'drai* requires very strong energy. You saw what happened when Zerik caused those monks to forget. He had to pull immensely strong energy from himself, and expend it to create the desired reaction – in this case, *mirsyatun*, forgetting. Afterwards, he was exhausted, his energy almost completely depleted. This is true for most immensely powerful *e'drai*. To effect strong change, one must use powerful energy. For every action, there is an equal and opposite reaction. We only have so much energy to expend, because we are pulling that energy from ourselves."

She sighed. "So most *e'drai* comes from within us, from our own energy. But you and I, and Emma – we have special gifts. We are able to pull energy from outside of ourselves, and use that energy, direct it, create with it. Effect change. Because we pull it from beyond ourselves, pull it through us, channel it, we don't lose energy. We can effect very powerful change without tiring, without heavy loss to ourselves. Though it can be tiring to direct it."

Maddie waved a hand, and behind her, the fire flared in the pit. "My *e'drai* connects with the energy in flames." She fluttered her fingers, and the water in the slate fountain danced. "My *e'drai* connects with the flows of water as well. I am the only Sister to hold two elements."

Emma smiled, and began to hum a sweet melody. She blew gently across the palm of her hand, and Rhiannon felt her body lift from the ground, a breath of wind against her thighs and the soles of her feet as she hovered a few inches above the grass. "My *e'drai* connects with the energy in the wind, in air, in song," Emma said. "I enjoy writing because it's a challenge – I must use words and create without *e'drai*, with thought alone."

Rhiannon was relieved to feel herself gently touch the ground again.

"Your *e'drai*, Sister, is your connection with the earth. The land, the soil, the trees, all share their energy with you." Maddie touched Rhiannon's knee, her eyes kind. "This is how you healed Zerik, when you escaped from the monks. His energy was depleted. Yet he tells me he came to awareness, feeling better than he had in weeks. Came awake to see you, standing barefoot in the grass."

"I'd never done that before," Rhiannon said. "Now I understand. I just wished – wished so hard. I just wanted him to be well. And there was this green inside me, and I – " she fumbled, trying to find the words to describe what had happened. "There was green inside me, and I brought it from somewhere. I gave it to him."

Maddie smiled. "Exactly." She looked over at Zerik, in the shade of the pavilion. "*We are ready.*"

He nodded, glancing at Grayling.

Emma smiled, pressed her palms to Rhiannon's thigh, knee. "You can do this, Sister. I promise."

Rhiannon wasn't sure, but she trusted these women, more than she'd ever trusted anyone in her life. "Okay."

"First, we breathe." Maddie instructed. "Close your eyes and feel me, follow my breathing."

Rhiannon closed her eyes and listened to the sound of Maddie's breath, breathing slowly, in and out. After a moment, she realized she could not only hear Maddie's exhalations, but feel them, feel Maddie's breath inside herself. They began with a simple pattern, one deep breath in, exhale for two heartbeats. As Rhiannon became accustomed to the pattern, Maddie shifted to another, more complex, and then another.

Soon, it felt as though there was nothing but breath, nothing but that moment, these two women and the air flowing in and out, their lungs expanding and filling with the world itself, exhaling into the ground, the sky, the ocean, the flames.

Rhiannon felt herself flowing outward, her essence, her aura flowering, expanding, joining with those of Emma and Maddie. She could feel their bodies, their skin, their breath swelling in time with her own, three hearts beating in unison.

Maddie opened her eyes.

In the darkness behind her closed eyelids, Rhiannon could see what Maddie saw, see herself and Emma, breathing still, the flames of the firepit behind them, the sun shining on the grass and the encircling trees.

Maddie spoke. "We are Sisters. We Talk the world into being."

Eyes still closed, breathing in harmony with the other women, Emma spoke. "This gash in the earth heals. It is healing even now."

"The soil joins with rock, pulling together, sealing."

"The grass becomes one with the grass, until there is only unbroken meadow."

"Solid, the earth is. It comes together and bonds, rock to stone, soil to earth, stronger than before, unbroken." Maddie breathed, and Rhiannon felt her breath expand her ribs.

"Unbroken earth."

Emma sighed, breathed again. "Smooth grass stretching to the cliff's edge, always smooth, ever unbroken."

"Hard rock, dense earth, joined stronger than ever before, unshakeable."

Rhiannon opened her eyes, radiating emerald light, like her aura. "I heal the earth."

She felt the green energy now, pulling up through the earth, into her feet, her thighs, her bottom. It rushed into her body, flowing through her limbs bright and easy, the way it coursed through the trunks of the sentinel trees. The power flooded her, rushing to the crown of her head, flowing back down her spine, back down into the earth, spinning outward, connecting to all things. The earth stretched vast beneath her. Rhiannon felt Emma, Maddie, Zerik and Grayling, but this time she felt something more.

She looked at Emma, her eyes and aura shining brilliant blue-white, the energy of the air, luminous cerulean and silver, refracting into streams of rainbow light, shimmering translucent, blowing through her pores, a tempest cascading smooth and endless within her body, zephyrs of energy humming and singing in continuous song, the gale skimming outward, her blonde curls streaming around her head like a golden halo.

Shivering from the ecstatic green energy vibrating her every cell, Rhiannon looked now at Maddie. Madeline blazed like a fiery star, the energy of fire and water dancing and popping through her flesh, her aura dazzling turquoise and crimson, platinum and gold, a deluge of heat, a nimbus of boiling saffron and aquamarine swirling, gushing, licking electric through her skin, to release cascading back into the world.

"Take my hands, Sisters," Maddie sang in their minds, her voice at once crackling and fluid.

Rhiannon closed her eyes and reached out her shining veridian fingers, touched Maddie and Emma, felt their e'drai flow into hers. As one, they lay their luminous hands on the earth.

The cliff trembled as the Sisters joined their gifts, pouring their e'drai into the ground. With a wild energy, the heat of the earth below the cliff burned, rocks joining, fusing. "Good, pull in the earth now," Maddie whispered to Rhiannon. Water coursed into soil, earth and dirt shifted, connected, throbbed. Huge gouts of earth and grass rose, collapsed, joined. "My turn," Emma murmured. Air rushed outward, streaming from gaps and holes, to be filled with hot rock and cold earth. "Ah, I feel it, I understand," Rhiannon sang. Meadow and land staggered, knit together, as the weavers sewed the earth together again.

In the shade of the canopy, Zerik shuddered with the force of the power, the undeniable ecstasy as the sensation of the combined

271

energy of the three Sisters flowed through his body. *"They have control,"* he sent his thought to Grayling. *"And it is ... exquisite."*

Grayling watched the three women, faces reflecting a seraphic peace, their combined shimmering radiance dazzling, almost blinding, unbelievably beautiful, their hands pressed to the ground as the very earth swelled and came together again. "No," he said, a tear trickling down his stony cheek. *"They* are exquisite."

Late in the summer, Grayling crossed the wild meadow to the row of sentinel trees curving around the Sisters' Circle. He looked out at the stretch of grass, his memory the only evidence of the great gash in the earth that once marred the verdant cliff.

He found Zerik standing just within the trees, a fond smile on his lips, watching the three women. Grayling stopped next to his husband, following his gaze.

The Sisters were creating.

Maddie was barefoot, wearing an old tank top and a pair of outsized overalls, the pantlegs rolled up above her bare ankles. Her red hair was piled loosely on her head, tendrils curling down around her ears and the back of her neck. She was creating a fabric painting using the aeternan art form *hata'zhi*, in this case a kind of batik, a process that utilized both her water and fire *e'drai*. Sweating in the sun, she hovered over several steaming buckets of dye, fluttering back and forth between the vats to stir or prod the immersed fabric. Nearby was a wood frame, over which was stretched a large sheet of muslin. Next to that was a carefully controlled fire beneath a wide, shallow pan of molten wax.

Apparently satisfied that the dye-vats were coming along, she picked up a tjanting tool, something like a pen with a reservoir for the hot wax. Filling the tool, she began painting delicate lines onto the muslin in wax. The wax would act as a barrier for the dye, allowing different parts of the fabric to be dyed without bleeding.

Emma was sitting in the shade of the pavilion, writing. After finishing a paragraph, she looked up at her sister wives and smiled. Unconsciously, her hand strayed downward to her slightly rounded belly, and she sang a little and stroked her tummy, before returning to her pen.

Rhiannon was on the ocean side of the Circle, sculpting. She was completely nude, spattered in clay, and frowning in concentration as her hands traced slick paths through the wet clay. She seemed to be sculpting a life-size male figure. His handsome features were strong, with a large nose and chin, a firm jaw. As Grayling watched, he realized there was something very familiar about the face Rhiannon was sculpting. This was more than sculpting – this was *dia'okta*, sculpting using *e'drai, aeternan e'lain*.

He looked at Zerik, a sense of unease taking hold of him. "That looks like – "

"It is," Zerik said, without looking at him. "The incarnation from about 150 years ago, I'm thinking. Forms come and go, it's easy to forget faces. But he was always unforgettable." His smile was wry. "She said she got the idea from a dream."

Grayling frowned. "Does she know what she's doing? Does she realize?"

"No, she doesn't," Maddie's thought came to them from across the grass. *"She's learning to use her* e'drai *again. Let's see what comes of it. Leave her be."*

"Knotty-pated villianous bastard," Grayling grumbled, turning and stalking back to the house.

SEVENTEEN

Her seizure came without warning.

One moment, Rhiannon and their oldest child, Eva, were lying in the grass near the stone pools, pointing out dragons and wolves in the fat cumulus clouds, their wet bathing suits drying in the afternoon sun. But then, suddenly, Eva was gasping, shaking all over, her limbs rigid, twitching, eyes staring sightless into the sky.

Horrified, Rhiannon moved instinctively, scooping up the gangly young teenager, holding her in her lap, pressing the corner of her towel against Eva's tongue to prevent the child from biting herself, or choking. But while she moved automatically, Rhiannon's physical reaction was a calm, undiminished contrast to the torrent of panic and paralyzing fear devouring her within, leaving her gasping for breath, even as she struggled to hold the trembling child.

She glanced around wildly, but none of the family was anywhere in sight. Frantic, she looked back down at Eva, who continued to seize and pant, almost hyperventilating. She needed help. Now.

Rhiannon closed her eyes, fighting to find the necessary inner calm. She breathed deeply, distancing herself within from the thrashing child in her arms. There. The pale green wisps of energy and light, drifting slowly up through her bottom, her thighs, her feet. She opened herself to the energy, pulling it into her body with a desperate force, allowing a barely controlled flood of power to rush into the warm darkness within. As the circuit completed, the shining light cascaded back down her spine, back into the earth, and she sent roots, tendrils of energy spinning delirious and breathtaking outward into the ground in every direction.

She could feel the lawn stretching toward the house, her warm grass skin. Now, the torches biting into her soil. The earth was alive, vibrant and writhing with spiders and snails, earthworms, beetles, centipedes, ants, glowing in her capillaries and veins. Rhiannon touched the roots of the trees by the cliff, the big cottonwood carefully clutching the children's treehouse like a jewel.

Her energy spun outward, beneath the house now, around the wood and glass conservatory. *There.* Grayling. She could feel her husband's booted feet on the earth, light on her flesh, just around the front of the house. His aura blazed resplendent in the darkness of her inner vision, silver and forest green melding and twisting into a spiral of light.

Dimly, as though underwater, Rhiannon could still feel Eva in her arms, twitching and shaking. With a determined thrust of power, she sent her veridian and peat energy spinning up Grayling's ankles and legs, fusing with his aura. Gritting her teeth, she gathered her strength, pulling him toward her, toward the back of the house, toward Eva. *Help me, husband.*

Grayling was standing on the gravel front driveway, near the conservatory, when a sudden rush of light and power swelled tingling around his feet and legs. Roughly, his body jerked forward, as he felt himself forced to stumble toward the cliffs.

After several yards, Grayling found himself once again in control of his own body. He stood stunned, looking around, everywhere at once. But he didn't have long to contemplate what was happening to him, as the energy gripped his legs once more, forcing him to stagger forward again, the power undeniable, irresistible. When he was finally able to stop again, red-faced, baffled and angry, he'd nearly rounded the conservatory.

Your wife, fool. She's afraid. Your wife needs you now.

Grayling's brows raised as comprehension dawned, his anger dissolving into cold apprehension. He needed no further urging from Rhiannon. He started running.

As Grayling ran across the lawn toward Rhiannon and Eva, he saw Rhiannon open her eyes, her aura radiating blazing emerald. "Grayling," she breathed, and he felt a ripple of energy flow upward from the earth, his name a plea, a beatitude.

And then, after interminable seconds, he was beside her, dropping to his knees in the grass, his hands on their oldest daughter, her muscles still rigid and shaking. His eyes held Rhiannon's. "*Anam cara.* Don't be afraid. It will be all right."

Rhiannon was crying. "She just started having a seizure. I didn't know what to do. There was no one else. I had to pull you – I'm sorry, I – " she stammered to a halt, gulping back more tears.

"Shh," Grayling murmured, soothing. He put an arm around Rhiannon, leaving one hand on Eva's heaving chest. "It's okay. You did right." His gaze dropped to Eva, his eyes fond, somehow sad. "Her time has finally come. It is the *fis.*"

Rhiannon's brow creased in confusion. "The what?"

But just then, Eva stopped twitching and thrashing, went still. Rhiannon looked down into her face, the child's wide brown eyes suddenly aware. She smiled, her brilliant grin so reminiscent of Zerik's. "I had a dream while I was awake, Mama Rhiannon."

Eva struggled to sit up in Rhiannon's lap. "I dreamed I was a knight, with a big black horse, and a sword that had my father's name on it. And there was this big battle in the forest. It was awesome!" She turned and saw Grayling, her face alight with excitement. "Papa Grayling, I had a dream while I was awake. Is it the *fis*?"

Grayling nodded soberly. "Yes, love."

Eva was practically bouncing. "I can't wait to tell the mamas and Papa Zerik!"

Feeling somewhat shellshocked, Rhiannon looked at her husband, her eyes red, her tears drying on her cheeks. "What is this, Gray? What the hell was that?"

"*Memor'fis.* The waking dreams and visions aeternans undergo, harbinger of *Memora Magia*, the Remembering. They increase in intensity as the time for Remembering comes near."

Rhiannon sat back in the grass, stunned, recalling her desperate run down Independence Avenue when she was 13. The day she remembered being Kat Weiss, living her life. Her visions coming in waves of three, four. Falling again and again, clutching the sidewalk, shaking blindly, overcome with the force of the waking dreams. Then rising once more, running for home.

Grayling touched Eva's cheek with a gentle finger. "Our girl will be Remembering who she really is."

At dinner that night, the family seemed subdued, everyone eating in silence. Rhiannon looked around. "Why is everyone so quiet?"

Zerik offered her a gentle smile. "Eva. She'll be going through *Memora Magia* soon now."

Emma looked up from her plate, where she'd been picking at her food. "It's a happy time, but it's a sad time too. We're going to lose our little girl, and get someone else in her place."

"She'll still always have a piece of us, a portion of a lifetime that we gave her," Maddie declared. "Love and memories of us, and we of her. Whoever she becomes."

Emma nodded. "She will always be joined with the Ciatri *Dinach*." Her merry grin suddenly erupted. "Or he."

Rhiannon laughed shakily. "I hadn't thought of that." She reached for the wine, but Zerik lifted the bottle solicitously and poured her another glass. "We should explain. You probably only remember going through *Memora Magia* once."

Rhiannon snorted. "Yeah, well, once was enough."

Zerik grinned. "You've been through it hundreds of times. And yes, it is not a pleasant process." He handed her the glass of

Chardonnay. "*Memora Magia*, The Remembering, is a rite of passage all aeternans share. The process is grueling, intense, a kind of psychic childbirth."

"It comes with puberty," Emma put in. "Usually, between 11 and 14 years of age. For those of us with female Forms, it mostly happens around the time we begin menstruating."

Rhiannon looked at Emma, digesting that information. She glanced around the table. "Why? Why do we Remember then? Why are we not born remembering everything?"

The hint of a smile flickered on Grayling's lips. "Who can know the whole Story?"

"Some members of the Family spend lifetimes trying to figure out why we exist, why we are reborn, why we Remember when we do," Maddie said. "Like any academics or philosophers, they spend a great deal of time arguing with one another about whose theory has more merit." She smiled, took a sip of her wine. "So far, none has proven anything, one way or the other."

"Whatever the reason," Zerik said, "it does work out better this way. Can you imagine, being a 2-year-old, with 10 lifetimes roaming around in your head?"

Rhiannon had to laugh.

"Anyhow," Zerik continued, "Most of us have dreams of our previous lives, periodically, as we grow up. It is only when we begin to have the waking dreams, *memor'fis*, when the Remembering is at hand."

"It was terrifying, when I was a kid," Rhiannon said, staring at the candlelight flickering through her wineglass. "I didn't know what was happening to me. And it got worse – much worse."

Maddie laid a hand over hers. "I'm sorry you had to go through it alone, without anyone to help you, guide you."

"The Remembering is hard for everyone, especially neonates, or those raised by oblivi," Zerik said. "As you've experienced, it's a painful, frightening event. But those lucky enough to be born into aeternan families have somewhat different experiences."

"Mmm-hm," Emma agreed, nodding, her mouth full. She swallowed her last bit of roast chicken, smiling at Rhiannon. "For one thing," Emma said, waving her fork, "we tell our children what's coming. Prepare them for it. When they get close in age, we explain about the *fis*, the waking dreams. Tell them how they grow more intense, in preparation for *Memora Magia*."

Just then, Robbie appeared with her serving cart, and all conversation paused as she whisked away the dinner plates, leaving a tray of cheese and fruit. She left with a friendly nod.

"Mmm, apples and brie," Emma chirped, leaning forward to help herself. Grayling cast her a glance and began preparing a plate for her. "Thank you, dear," she said, taking the plate from him and patting her belly. "Babies like brie."

Grayling raised an eyebrow. "Your babies seem to."

Rhiannon laughed. Recalling a question she'd wanted to ask, she turned to Zerik. "So you tell kids about the waking dreams, but how else do you prepare children for Remembering? I mean, what else is there to say, other than, 'Hey, this is gonna suck'?"

Zerik threw back his head and laughed aloud, and the others echoed his laughter. "The Remembering is involuntary – it comes upon us and can't be denied. Our behavior becomes something that's actually instinctual."

"Like cats preparing to birth kittens," Grayling added sardonically.

Emma laughed.

"Well, it's kind of an apt description," Maddie said, her blue eyes kind as she turned to Rhiannon. "When you Remembered, where were you?"

Rhiannon closed her eyes for a moment, recalling that desperate, panicked run for home. "I was having visions over and over, three and more at a time. I was at school. I ran to my house on Forest Avenue. My room upstairs." She picked up her wineglass, and her hand trembled slightly. "I just wanted to get home. It felt like nothing else mattered."

Maddie nodded. "When *Memora Magia* is upon us, we are driven to find safe shelter. Our best guess is that we are vulnerable during the moments of Remembering, and need to feel secure, protected." She leaned back in her chair. "So, with our children, we help them choose a safe, impregnable spot ahead of time, usually when they have their first *fis*. So they know a safe place to go."

"And we give them the option of having one or all of us there with them, to help them through it." Emma added.

Rhiannon frowned. "How on earth could you help someone through it? I mean, it just happens, you just do it. No one else can Remember for you."

"We help with the chant," Grayling said.

"The words come to us, as instinctive as the need to find shelter." Zerik touched her hand, his eyes warm. "Somehow the chant helps, brings on the moment of Remembering. If others join the chant, it seems to amplify the power, the energy."

Rhiannon could still hear it, echoing in her head, the low rumble of sound, the relief when she could finally recognize the shape of the words in her mind. "*Amin'via, amin'ma*," she whispered. She looked up, into Grayling's serious gaze. "What does it mean?"

He shared his rare smile. "Remember life, Remember me."

Madeline threw herself into preparations for Eva's Remembering.

The girl was squired around the house, to make her choice of one of several rooms Maddie thought might be suitable – windowless; or high in towers with inaccessible windows; stout doors with multiple locks on the inside; rooms with thick padded carpets or large, soft beds.

Eva chose a tower room at the back of the house, facing the sea, with a wide bed and lush carpet. She asked that Madeline alone, mother of her flesh, help her through *Memora Magia*, to share in the chant. Maddie had flushed with pleasure at being chosen to help her daughter.

Eva did not have another waking dream, a *fis*, that day, or the next. Life at the Ciatri nest went on as usual – though a heightened sense of anticipation seemed to pervade the air.

At breakfast on the Saturday following Eva's first *fis*, Emma announced there would be dancing lessons for the children in the ballroom. "You should have lessons, too," she told Rhiannon, her lovely face cheerful, earnest. "Since you don't remember your lives." She added there was usually a large, formal aeternan party at the

Caistra to celebrate the Fall Equinox – and the Ciatri family was always invited. "And just before the Equinox, the Prodigies are coming to Santa Cruz. We've been looking forward to it for months."

Sipping her morning tea, Maddie looked worried. "I hope it will be safe to go to Santa Cruz, now that Rhiannon's with us."

Emma shook her head, her blonde curls bobbing. "We'll have the men with us, and besides, the Prodigies always perform in a Fairy Ring."

"What are the Prodigies?" Rhiannon asked.

"Aeternans born into unusual Forms, who are gifted with very powerful *e'drai*, for this lifetime only." Maddie smiled. "It's something like the old oblivi circus sideshows, but a thousand times better."

Rhiannon remembered Zerik suggesting that perhaps their daughter Missy might become a Prodigy one day.

"I'm sure it will be fine," Maddie said, waving a hand dismissively. "At any rate, we do have to practice dancing for the Equinox ball." She smiled at Rhiannon. "We have our own etiquette. *Politesse* and gracious manners, courtly behavior, are expected – especially at formal events." She laid a friendly hand on Rhiannon's knee. "Dancing is part of that. But we should also brush up on your other manners – appropriate use of the *anam'sal*, the *anam'ta*. Correct greetings for *Kirs*, *Kir'dinas*, and the *Kir'da*, the ruler at the national Caistra. That sort of thing."

Rhiannon must have looked as stricken as she felt, because both Emma and Maddie laughed sympathetically. "It's not that hard." Maddie said. "You'll get it. On the plus side, it's easier for you, because you're one of the Sisters, and likely you'll be one of the longest-lived Eldest present."

Emma grinned. "People will be bowing to you, not the other way around."

Rhiannon laughed nervously. "I'm not sure that makes me feel better."

Maddie put down her napkin, took Rhiannon's hands. She held her gaze, her eyes serious. "I'm not going to varnish this – you have a lot to learn. Not just courtly manners, but we're going to have to fill you in on some of the politics: who you'll be meeting, who to be careful of, who are considered allies of our *Dinach*."

Emma shook her head, pushing her chair back from the breakfast table. "No politics today, Maddie. Let's just start with dancing."

Maddie released Rhiannon's hands with a smile. "She's right. One thing at a time." Maddie looked down into her now-empty teacup. The tea leaves formed a rough hexagram, a six-pointed star. Maddie frowned, making a mental note to explore the symbols of the Story further, after dancing lessons.

Rhiannon looked up at Emma, her blonde curls bright in the morning sunlight. "What kind of dancing do I have to do? I know how to waltz." She blushed, remembering the man with eyes the color of new leaves. "I know that from my dreams."

Emma held out a hand, helping Rhiannon to her feet. "There will be modern ballroom dancing. But there will also be older dances, like a saltarello, or an allemande. And Alvar — the current *Kir'da* — is known to enjoy a vigorous galliard." Emma offered her sunny smile. "That one involves a lot of hopping, mostly." She laughed. "Plus there will be baroque dances — minuets, formal dances — and country dances like the gavotte, and then on to quadrilles, scotch reels, and waltzes, of course."

Rhiannon sighed, rubbing her forehead. "I guess I can use the exercise."

The three Sisters rounded up all of the children, except for Eva — who, nose in the air, had declared she was too grown up for such things — and headed for the ballroom. Grayling had gone to the Caistra that afternoon, to deal with Family business. He was a member of the Chorus — something like a senator, as far as Rhiannon understood — representing *Dinach* Zel'mori. Zerik, gripped by artistic inspiration, was painting in his studio.

Rhiannon loved the ballroom, the floor a broad expanse of pale, veined marble, with the aeternan *anam pratik* some 12 feet across, inlaid in gold in the center of the room, a spiral above a circle, bisected with an elongated figure eight. The shimmering gold walls were decorated with the images of birds in flight, swallows, robins, even falcons. The sweeping domed ceiling was painted the azure of a summer sky, and what seemed to be actual translucent clouds drifted lazily overhead. French doors led to a broad stone balcony facing the ocean. The room smelled of summer and promise.

On a small walnut cabinet, near the French doors, was what looked to be an antique record player, with an Edison cylinder and a huge morning glory horn, hand-painted with roses and vines. "I bought this in 1898," Maddie commented. "Grayling's converted it – it's actually connected to a huge digital music library. We can listen to anything." She smiled fondly as she flipped a switch, turning on the device. "I do love things that are both beautiful and functional."

She opened the cabinet doors, revealing a black box with a digital readout and a small glowing screen. "Let's start with something with lots of harpsichord."

For more than an hour, they danced, the children taking turns partnering with Rhiannon. There was a great deal of laughter, everyone dancing until they were out of breath, then returning to the floor again. Joshua, at 5 years old, particularly enjoyed the hopping galliard, though it was hard to induce him to stop hopping when the music ended. Young Jacob, trying so hard to be grown-up, maintained a serious demeanor, chin up, eyes grave, as he led Rhiannon through the formal allemande.

Three-year-old Missy spent most of the time gleefully spinning in circles, her wing-like arm held out perpendicular to her body, until she collapsed into a delighted, dizzy heap on the floor.

The music was loud – the three Sisters and the children were laughing, dancing in the late morning sunlight streaming in through the French doors, the atmosphere one of festivity, revelry.

But then a bell rang somewhere, loud, resonant, deep and musical. The sound echoed throughout the ballroom, above the volume of the music. Maddie and Emma looked up, suddenly alert. Even the children stilled.

"What's that?" Rhiannon asked, unaccountably nervous.

"Someone's at the gates," Emma whispered.

"Someone is trying to get to the house," Maddie added, her voice low, laced with an underlying tension. "*Zerik?*" she sent her thought outward, and all could hear it ringing in their minds.

"I hear the bell, love." Zerik's thought came back, for all to hear. *"Let's wait for the second chime."*

Maddie turned to Emma, who nodded, changing the music with a placid smile, only a slight tremor in her hand, revealing her tension. Cheerfully, she encouraged the children to continue dancing.

"What's going on?" Rhiannon asked Maddie.

Madeline looked toward the children on the dance floor. "It's probably nothing. When someone tries to come to our home, they must pass the three gates." She glanced at Rhiannon. "You remember, when you came through."

"Yes," Rhiannon nodded. "At the first gate, everything felt wrong. I had to put my hands on the gate, to make it open."

Maddie nodded. "That gate is Fae-forged. When you touch it, it feels you, tastes you. It reads who you are, and only those who are worthy are allowed to pass." She offered a slight smile. "It sometimes takes a long time, for the gate to decide if one merits entry."

Rhiannon frowned. "I got through right away."

Maddie laughed. "You are part of our *dzina*, our family. You are our wife. Of course you passed almost immediately. The gate recognized you, even if Zerik had not."

Just then, the bell rang again, sonorous, resonating throughout the house.

Emma turned away from the children, staring at Maddie. "That was too fast."

"Only family should pass so quickly," Maddie breathed, shock written on her features.

"Maybe it's Grayling," Rhiannon suggested. "You said he'd gone to the Caistra."

Maddie shook her head. "We have another route to the Caistra. Grayling has no need of passing the front gates."

"I am going to the third gate," Zerik's thought came then. *"Should this person pass the second gate, I will be there. No one can pass the third gate without one of us using the key."* He paused, and then – no doubt knowing Maddie so well – he added, *"Don't fret, wife."*

Emma glanced at Maddie, then turned her attention back to the children. "Everything's fine," she chirped. "Let's dance." The children crowded around her, oblivious to the unfolding drama.

Maddie wandered to the French doors, and Rhiannon followed her. "This doesn't happen often, does it?"

Maddie stared out blindly at the sea. "No. Most people never get as far as the first gate. They are usually lost in the sense of wrongness, the sense that they've made a wrong turn." She glanced at Rhiannon, offering a tight smile. "In most cases, if someone comes to the house, they've been invited, expected."

Rhiannon thought back to when she'd arrived at the Ciatri *dzina* with Zerik. After the first gate was the second, an illusion which seemed different to each person who viewed it. Zerik had driven right through it, despite its solid appearance. She remembered what Zerik had said, once they'd gone through. *"If we weren't supposed to go through it, we would have found ourselves back on the highway, two miles south, completely unable to remember how or why we got there."*

Maddie turned to Rhiannon, her smile a shade too bright. "No one can pass the third gate without one of us opening it for them. So it's not as though there's anything to worry about." She looked back through the windows, at the ocean beyond the cliffs.

Rhiannon remembered Zerik holding out his palm, and the shadowy *e'drai* key hovering in a golden glow above his hand.

And then the bell rang again.

Maddie turned abruptly, meeting Emma's eyes.

Rhiannon felt a strange tension overtake her, as though all of her nerve endings were somehow electrified, humming. "What are we afraid of?" she whispered.

Maddie looked back at her, and took her hand. "There is someone after you, someone *erim*, his soul and aura black. There are monks after you, The Guard. You are not safe, Sister. We protect you here." Maddie shook her head wearily. "Strangers at the gates make me nervous."

The music still blared in the vast ballroom, echoing over the marble floors. "Are we going to keep dancing?" little Melody asked plaintively. Emma smiled and touched her hair, her cheek. She looked up at Maddie, a question in her blue eyes.

The bell rang again, bright and cheerful in the midst of the loud piano music streaming from the morning-glory horn, and the speakers secreted throughout the room.

"*All is well*," came Zerik's thought, and it almost seemed to hold a note of laughter. "*Our guest is welcome, my wives.*"

Maddie took a deep breath, sighed, released it. She nodded at Emma, and the dancing began anew, as if nothing had happened. The music played brightly, and the children laughed, twirling, stomping, and hopping around the ballroom.

"Is everything okay?" Rhiannon asked, feeling bewildered.

"Apparently," Maddie answered shortly. She looked slightly irritated. "*Zerik, who are you bringing into my home?*"

Now Zerik's laughter was clear. "*An invited guest, my love.*"

Madeline frowned. "*I don't recall inviting anyone.*"

"*You weren't the one to invite him, dear.*"

For a moment, Madeline looked downright furious at Zerik's evasion. But then her eyes widened, as if in revelation. Glancing at Emma, and then Rhiannon, she walked toward the wide double doors leading to the hallway and the rest of the house.

Before she could advance more than a few steps, the doors flew open, and Zerik was there, grinning. Next to him was a tall aeternan, broad-shouldered, with black hair, touched at the temples with grey. His aura was vast, reflecting with the shimmering *fainna* of the most senior of the Eldest, misted with faint shadow.

The music shifted, and a sprightly waltz began to play.

The man looked around the room, taking in everything.

"Ah, you're dancing," he said with a soft British accent, laughing. "Of course."

He turned and cupped his hands, offering a formal *anam'sal*, first to Madeline, and then Emma. Finally he turned to Rhiannon. Grinning, he held out a hand to her. His casual smile was belied by the intensity of his gaze, and Rhiannon gasped when his eyes, the color of new leaves, met hers. "Ah, *ma moitié*. May I have this dance?"

Dinner that night was a festive affair. They dined outdoors under the striped silk pavilion, and Maddie surrounded the space with ornate Moroccan candle lanterns, and extra torches burning in the moonlit lawn beyond the tent.

Robbie and Lyds proudly presented them with a perfect Beef Wellington, embellished with three-dimensional leaves and flowers picked out in delicate, flaky pastry.

Zerik watched his family with a smile. Maddie was openly flirting with their guest, Alexander – no small wonder, they'd formed a strong bond centuries before, back in Constantinople. Emma was giggling more than usual. Grayling ate in stony silence, doing his best not to laugh during the conversation, occasionally failing. And Rhiannon – she was like a nervous schoolgirl, trying to avoid looking at Alex, only to be caught staring, quickly returning her gaze to her plate.

Their old friend looked to be in his late 30s, laugh lines around his green eyes, strong, patrician features, and a deep dimple when he smiled or laughed, which seemed to be almost always. It was a good Form, handsome, strong.

Zerik sat back in his chair, feeling pleasantly content. In retrospect, it seemed so funny, so oddly logical, that he, Grayling, and Alexander Lazarus should be here, now, that they had known each other so very long. Since that battle at the Catalaunian Fields, back in the fifth century, fighting Atilla.

They had always known each other, but had still been a millennium apart.

Zerik smiled, remembering one of their last encounters, perhaps 150 years before. They'd been at an aeternan party in the finest Regency splendor, one of those Frost Festivals the British were always having, celebrating winter. This one was in Brighton, Zerik thought.

There'd been an elaborate, formal dinner, with dancing afterward. The Family always loved a proper party. The ladies were dressed in high-waisted, diaphanous formal gowns, many so sheer the shadows of nipples could be seen. The gentlemen wore silk stockings and breeches, tailcoats and cravats.

288

Zerik and Grayling had stood together in an alcove. Rhiannon tarried with them, watching Emma and Maddie whirl about the dance floor with their respective partners — Maddie danced with Alvar Noriaki, at that time the new protégé of Edward Angelis. Emma had been with some member of the British Chorus — what was his name? It didn't matter, now.

Alexander approached them then, a dark-haired man with eyes the color of new leaves, a strong chin and large nose that somehow fit with his face. His ebony silk cutaway jacket was immaculate, his manners impeccable, his grin utterly outlaw.

"Alexander," Grayling nodded, his eyes wary.

"Gray." Alex nodded to Zerik. "Good to see you again, Zerik." He turned his fathomless green eyes to Rhiannon, and Zerik watched as she shivered involuntarily. Still intent on Rhiannon's eyes, he spoke to the men. "Gentlemen, would you mind if I danced with your wife?" He smiled at Rhiannon, a slow, warm smile like honey. "Assuming the lady would care to."

"Provided the lady wishes it," Grayling said stiffly. Zerik frowned at his husband, then offered Alex an urbane smile. "Of course."

Alex held Rhiannon's gaze, and Zerik could see she was unable to look away. "Well madam? Would you dance with me again? It's been at least 100 years."

She nodded gracefully, clearly relieved to look away from his disconcerting eyes. "I would be delighted, sir."

As Alex led her to the dance floor, Zerik nudged Grayling in the ribs. "You may as well get used to him. I think he's the Sixth."

Grayling glowered, his eyes never leaving the couple, as Alex whirled his wife gracefully across the parquet floor. "Spend eternity married to him? Not if I can help it." He shrugged in casual pretense. "Besides, she can't Choose for at least another hundred years."

Zerik laughed. "He's a good man, Gray."

Grayling shook his head. "He's *liath*, and you know it." He nodded toward the couple on the dance floor. Alex's shining aura carried the uncountable *fainna* of the Eldest — and a slight mist of shadow.

"We all have darkness within us," Zerik commented, lighting a cheroot. "If he has a bit more than most, and if she Chooses him, it's because she needs it, for some reason." He shrugged, exhaling fragrant smoke. "We are here for them. To give them what they need. And in return, they give us everything we've ever needed or wanted, and more. An equable situation, to my mind."

"Humph." Grayling folded his arms across his chest, his expression dour.

Zerik laughed, knowing it didn't matter what he or his husband thought. She would Choose when she was ready, in a century or so, when the time came.

"I don't know, Maddie," Alexander said, as they walked toward the Sisters' Circle in the moonlight. "I just thought it would be a good time to visit. I've got business at the Caistra, anyhow."

Maddie smiled, her hand tucked in the crook of his arm, her long skirts whispering around her ankles. "Ah. So it just felt right to come visit us?"

Alex laughed. "Why not?" He slanted a glance at Maddie, and though her Form was different, she was as lovely as the first day he'd met her, during that terrible plague, when they'd escaped from the city with Rhiannon.

The two crossed the line of sentinel trees, advancing into the grass of the Circle. Maddie waved a hand, and several low-burning torches flared bright, illuminating the Sisters' Circle clearly.

Maddie guided Alexander toward the cliffs, to stand before Rhiannon's sculpture, a male form shaped from clay, the facial features depicted in exquisite, loving detail. "She said she got the idea from a dream," Maddie said. "You need to know – she doesn't remember who she is."

Alex looked at the sculpture and rocked back on his heels, stunned into silence. The smooth clay face emphasized a strong chin and large nose which somehow fit with the rest of the features. It was a face he knew intimately, from long ago, a face he'd seen every day in the mirror for many, many years.

"My dear Alexander," Maddie laughed, indicating the clay form with a graceful wave, "you didn't come here by accident. Or indeed, by your own will. You weren't even invited." She turned to him, smiling. "You were summoned."

Eternal Tales: The Way

Once upon a time, the People had a great leader called Mawr. Mawr had many Gifts and tremendous magic, and Traveled the Earth and the Other Worlds.

But Mawr exalted his vast power, and that of the People. He mocked the weakness of those who forget, men who live in ignorance and oblivion. He scorned these as naught more than beasts.

Mawr gathered his Family, to live in seclusion, separate from those he believed unworthy. Yet after many Seasons, Mawr tired of the simple toil and worry of life, working grain fields, the heat of the forge. He decided to make lethian men the servants of the People, to domesticate man.

But when Mawr traveled into the world to take his slaves, three Gods appeared to him. The first grew up from the earth as a tree. The second flowed outward from the waters of the stream. The Third God blossomed from the air in an effulgent cascade of gold light. The three Gods were so beautiful to look upon, their features shining perfection, that Mawr wept and fell to his knees.

Looking down at Mawr huddled on the cold ground, the Gods laughed at the arrogance of the People. "Yea, as you compare yourselves to man, the People may seem as Gods," the First God said. "Yet one day man would hope to join the People, as he lives oblivious from one Season to the next. All have their place in the shape of the Universe, their part to play in the Story."

"The Universe is all powerful," the Second God said. "Only through the mercy and benevolence of the Gods do the People live from Season to Season."

Then the Third God spoke in anger and disdain, and Mawr trembled on the ground. "You are not much greater than man," the Third God said. "You may be as Gods in the world, but you are Lesser Gods, not more."

"For all you remember, you still know naught," The First God continued. "Be grateful for the Gifts from the Gods. But do not imagine yourselves greater than man. Humble yourself before men, for you are all that they are, only little more."

Nearly blinded by the shining beauty of the Three Gods, Mawr begged forgiveness for his conceit.

"Some brave enough might dream of something Greater," The Second God said.

The Third God laid a luminous hand on Mawr's brow. "Those who follow The Way, gathering memories of humility and joy, loving deeply, sharing the Gifts of the Universe – these may dream of becoming Greater Gods, their flesh not subject to the whim of the earth and Seasons."

In a dazzling blaze of gold light and power, the Gods dissolved into the sky and earth and water, leaving Mawr sobbing, curled chastened and repentant on the soil.

And they lived ever after.

EIGHTEEN

Taking deep, rasping breaths, Grayling blinked back the sweat dripping into his eyes. He pressed the tip of his rapier against the older man's chest. "Yield," he snarled.

The villainous ass just grinned. "Never."

And then everything happened fast, too fast. Moving with preternatural speed, Alexander slid down beneath Grayling's blade, snap-kicking Grayling in the stomach, forcing him to stagger back, gasping. With a spinning sweep kick, Grayling was on his back in the turf, and Alexander was standing over him, the tip of his sword against Grayling's throat. It had all happened in barely a second, and Alex had never once stopped his infernal grinning.

Zerik, still out of breath from the drubbing he'd received at Alexander's hands minutes before, sat in the grass at the edge of the clearing and laughed.

Chest heaving, but otherwise holding carefully still beneath Alex's blade, Grayling rolled his eyes at Zerik and scowled.

For some time, the wide forest clearing had resounded with harsh breath, grunting, laughter, growls, and the clash of steel on steel. Beyond, the forest was silent, the trees dense around the glade where the three men had been dueling.

Alex pressed the point of his rapier lightly against the tender flesh of Grayling's throat. "Answer me this, Gray," he said, conversationally, as though they were sharing urbane discourse at the dinner table. He was not at all winded. "What is your problem with me? We were friends, once. Brothers." He paused. "More."

Grayling glared into those green eyes, fortifying himself. His chest rose and fell with even regularity as he took deep breaths, trying to regain his equilibrium. "I don't have a problem with you," he bit out.

Alexander laughed with genuine amusement. "Ah. So centuries of glowering have been a sign of your profound and abiding affection."

Grayling's scowl deepened as he stared up at Alex, though when he responded, his tone was formal, entirely polite. "I have always treated you with the utmost respect, as is your due. You are the most long-lived of all Eldest I have known. You are *Kir'dina* of my *Dinach*. You are an invited guest in my home, easily passing our gates." He looked away. "And my wives adore you. Why would I have a problem with you?"

"Hmm." Alex casually leaned a bit harder on his sword, and Grayling reverted to shallower breaths, trying to avoid the point of the rapier cutting his skin. "Quite a long speech, for you. And very pretty answers, which I'm sure will please your wives." Alex's grin broadened. "But it's all just so much bullshit, isn't it?"

Zerik struggled tiredly to his feet, rubbing his forehead. "Just tell him, Gray. Lyds is doing roast beef for lunch. With those little potatoes." He sighed longingly. "Three-way dueling makes a man hungry."

The tip of Alexander's sword pierced Grayling's skin, just enough to draw a bright bead of blood, glistening ruby wet against the pale flesh of his throat. "You son of a bitch," Grayling hissed. "You know why. You're *liath*."

Alexander stepped back, removing his rapier with a flourish. "Ah, so that's all? I'm *liath* – I have tasted darkness, tainted my soul with shadow." A brief, self-deprecating smile flickered on his lips. "My every move, thought, word, and deed is now somehow questionable? The traditional aeternan prejudices are all that apply?" He offered Grayling a hand, but Gray ignored it with a glare, wearily pulling himself to his feet. "Or is it something more?" Alexander watched Grayling thoughtfully.

"No, I think that's it," Zerik interjected cheerfully. "Let's go eat."

Grayling didn't say anything, just stared steadily into Alexander's cursed green eyes.

"I think there is something more," Alex murmured. His aura flared, and he whispered a Word into the wind.

And suddenly the world went utterly silent, and very still. There had been a sound, a hum, a roar, a whisper, or perhaps nothing more than the sensation of sound, or feeling, or movement – but Grayling hadn't known it was there, until it was gone. It was as though the world was lighter, clean, brighter, in that soundless place. "What did you do, Alex?" he growled.

Alexander smiled, yet it wasn't that damned cocky grin, but instead something kind, even gentle. "I've sent Thicket Curdletree away for awhile. The Fae can't hear you, now."

"What?" Grayling was stunned.

Alex laughed at his expression. "Speak your heart, you dour bastard. Before he comes back."

Grayling turned away, to stare blindly into the dense forest. He was shaken to his core, marveling at the strange silence within, the Fae half of his soul somehow gone. "Your eyes always remind me," he whispered, unable to look at Alexander. "You're Fae."

"True," Alex said quietly. "And you are an honorable man who would never speak ill of those powerful beings who thought to gift you with a capricious fairy soul. You would never call a gift a curse." He came forward to stand close behind Grayling. "I can't help the circumstances of my birth, Grayling Sonam. But I am, and have always been, your friend." He laughed. "Whether you like it or not."

"Can you take him away forever?" Grayling turned, his characteristic stony features belied by his eyes, aching, haunted.

Alex shook his head sadly. "You're already dying, even now. You'd be *mortaetun*. You can't be reborn with half a soul, and that's all you've got left." He laid a strong hand on Grayling's shoulder. "So, your problem with me isn't a problem with me at all – it's a problem with you."

The world seemed to gasp then, and a rushing hum of energy seemed to flood through Grayling.

For a moment, I danced alone in the ancient woodland with the stars and the Sidhe. I was free.

As though waking from sleep, Zerik looked around. Grayling was standing in the center of the clearing, his silver mane luminous in the sunlight. Alex stood next to him, a hand on Grayling's shoulder. A kind of ease had somehow grown between them, in the space of a second, the murmur of the wind.

Zerik gave them his brilliant grin. "How about that roast beef, gentlemen?"

They say the King's Child touches everyone he meets.

"Eva had two more *fis* yesterday, and another this morning," Maddie said, as she and Rhiannon climbed a winding marble staircase in a tower at the back of the house. "Her time is coming soon."

Rhiannon had to smile. Maddie seemed so excited, consumed with a vibrant, joyous energy. Not just about Eva's upcoming Remembering, but simply *everything.* It was as though the whole Universe had conspired to fill Madeline with cheer – and it was infectious. She told Rhiannon how she'd been reading the Story that morning, how the symbols had been unusually, delightfully clear. In addition to signs, symbols, and portents gleaned from her fire, a rough six-pointed star had graced the bottom of her teacup, and after several more readings from clouds, cast pebbles and sortes, finally a random draw of her tarot cards had produced the sixth card of the Major Arcana – the Lovers.

While she didn't understand most of it, Maddie's obvious delight filled Rhiannon with a happiness of her own, sharing her wife's pleasure.

They reached the top of the staircase, which opened onto a wide circular room. The space featured a deep glass-tiled soaking tub with room for at least eight, broad divans covered in midnight blue celestial-patterned silk, and a small kitchen against one wall. Narrow gothic arched windows ringed the room. A carved, slender, wooden staircase led up to another room above.

"I need to get Lyds and Robbie up here right away," Maddie said. "We've got to get this room aired out, everything cleaned." Looking around the room, she began absently ticking off a list on her fingers. "We'll need lots of towels, sheets, blankets, refreshments."

"What is this place?" Rhiannon asked.

Maddie turned to her, smiling. "Come with me." She led the way up the ornate, close wood staircase, reaching up to throw back a rectangular door, like an attic hatchway set into the ceiling above the stairs. As they climbed into the room above, Rhiannon gasped.

She had noticed this tower on her first day at the Ciatri nest, standing in front of the house with Zerik, but hadn't realized, until that moment, that was where she was. "This is one of our Family rooms," Maddie said. "A very special room, for special occasions."

"An observatory," Rhiannon breathed. The room was perfectly round, the ceiling an arching split-dome above, decorated with exquisite Victorian-era paintings – clouds, angels, thousands of gold stars. Standing on the top step, Rhiannon could see the entire floor of the room had been upholstered with dense foam, nearly 3 feet thick, covered with a silk brocade sprinkled with shimmering gold stars and moons. Modern recessed lighting ringed the base of the dome, casting a warm glow on the walls and elaborate paintings.

"No, not an observatory," Maddie said. She motioned for Rhiannon to climb up onto the cushioned floor. "It's an equatorial room – an observatory without a telescope." She smiled. "Honestly, it just seemed too extravagant, having our own telescope, when so many learning institutions were going without. I think it was 1916 or '17, when we donated our equatorial telescope to Adelphi College in Brooklyn – anonymously, of course." She climbed onto the mattress and closed the hatchway, which was likewise upholstered, leaving the floor seamlessly soft. "I wanted to give it to Columbia – I've always liked that school – but they already had one." She shrugged.

"Wow," Rhiannon breathed, turning around to view the dome from every angle. The detailed old paintings on the inside of the dome and the walls were superb, the clouds so fine she thought they might drift away. "It's so beautiful."

"It's better at night," Maddie said, her smile secretive. "Watch this." She pressed a button on the wall near the hatchway, and with a groan of ancient machinery, the dome slowly peeled back, until the entire room was open to the sky.

"Aah," Rhiannon sighed. "What an amazing place."

Glowing with happiness, Maddie looked up into the early fall sky, clouds floating diaphanous against a sea of endless blue. "We will rival the stars in our brightness."

Once again, he caught her staring at him, too often. His Form was handsome, that was undeniable. He was in his late 30s, his dark hair threaded with grey at the temples, laugh lines deep around his leaf-green eyes, his nose and jaw strong, his skin tanned or naturally dark, she couldn't tell. When he spoke, his voice was deep, frequently teasing, or filled with laughter. He had a slight accent — at first, she thought it was British, but at times it seemed to have the cadence of Gaelic, or a touch of Scottish brogue.

And then he'd look at her again, grinning shamelessly. Rhiannon focused on her dinner plate with grim determination, ignoring the knowing glances from Maddie and Zerik.

After dinner, Alex invited Rhiannon to take a walk near the cliffs. She suspected the walk had been Maddie's idea, but she had no direct evidence. Alexander didn't seem to mind, as he meandered at her side with a gentle smile, his hands in the pockets of his black chinos. Rhiannon felt unaccountably nervous, uncomfortable in ways she had never experienced as a cocky, self-assured teenager in Kansas City.

They halted near the cliff edge, beyond the stone pools. She looked up at Alex's profile as he stared out at the ocean. His aura was beautiful in the moonlight, layers of shimmering *fainna*, its pale shadow somehow blending into the darkness, as though he were born of the night itself.

Rhiannon gathered her courage, curiosity overcoming awkwardness. Alex stood silently next to her, as though waiting.

"I saw a man once, he had that kind of shadow in his aura," Rhiannon said, thinking of the frightened little man at St. Michael's hospital in Kansas City. The one who was afraid of her. Who had run from her, terrified. She avoided Alex's eyes, remembering what Zerik had said about *aura'kur*, shadowed auras. It meant he was *anam'liath*, a shadowed soul. Damaged, somehow.

Alex contemplated the moonlight glittering on the water, an endlessly dancing path into the horizon. "Does it bother you?"

Rhiannon shook her head. She cleared her throat. "N-no. I guess I just want to understand it."

He turned to her, his eyes somehow bright in the dim light. "You don't know enough to hate me, to fear me, do you?"

"Do people fear you?"

"Some do, yes," he reached out, his fingertips gliding across her cheek, as a breath of the night air.

She sighed, closing her eyes briefly at his touch. There was just something about this man, who turned her insides liquid and steam, always before only in dreams.

"I believe we will all eventually become *liath*," he said quietly. "You live enough lifetimes, ultimately you will taste darkness." He smiled. "And I have lived a very, very long time."

"Zerik told me stories about people captured by The Guard. How they become *liath*." *Tortured.* She couldn't bring herself to say the word.

His laugh was short, mirthless. "Poor bastards. Can't help it." He turned away, staring blindly out to sea. "But some of us can help it, you know." His smile was bitter. "I chose darkness, for a time." He turned suddenly, gripping her shoulders with surprising urgency, his eyes searching hers. "It's what we choose afterward that matters."

She could only stare at him mutely, trapped in his gaze.

"Most aeternans are prejudiced against those of us who carry *aura'kur*. Frightened." He smiled. "And with good reason. Many choose darkness, and keep right on choosing it. Until they are *erim*, irredeemable."

As though suddenly aware of himself, he released her shoulders, straightened, took a step back. His manner was once more casual, easy. "Your husbands and wives tell me you don't remember who you are, Rhiannon."

She shivered at the sound of her name on his tongue. "No," she said. "I only remember one life before this one." She frowned at the thought of her life as Kat Weiss, her death. Pushing the thoughts away, she said, "I have had dreams about you. But they're just moments, not much more."

He grinned. "I like the thought of being in your dreams, *ma moitié*." He scratched the hair at his temple thoughtfully, as though trying to draw forth an idea or understanding. "If you remember so little, then you probably think like a neonate," he said. Before she could respond, he added, "Have you ever known a recovering alcoholic?"

Rhiannon nodded. "In my other life – incarnation. Back in New York. My Uncle Simon."

"When he was drinking, he was a different person, was he not? And after he achieved sobriety, he tried to right the wrongs he'd caused?"

"Yes," Rhiannon said, remembering how her uncle had carefully made amends to all of the family, including her grandmother and herself. She'd been a young teenager then, but she'd understood what he had been trying to do. She'd been proud of him.

Alex nodded, watching her face. "Some of us who are *liath* are rather like that. We may have embraced darkness, but we chose to walk away." He took her hand, his fingers warm against hers. "Some won't understand that. But we embrace the light, nonetheless." He grinned wryly. "I am *Kir'dina* of the Sidhe *Dinach*, House Zel'mori. The aeternan leadership is forced to accept me, whether they like it or not." His grin broadened to include a decidedly wicked glint in his eye. "I confess, it amuses me."

Rhiannon gazed up at him, his strong features, that shameless grin. "I don't care if you're *liath*. I feel like I know you. Really *know* you. Inside, I mean." She laughed self-consciously. "And I know I've known you for centuries. But I wish I could remember more than a few waltzes."

He touched her cheek. "I can try to help you remember, if you like."

An unreasonable wash of panic swamped her, and she shook her head. "My Sisters and husbands have tried. It's just not that easy."

Alexander offered her a lazy smile. "When you're ready." He tipped her chin up with a gentle finger, his lips a breath from hers. "And in the meantime, let me show you what I always dream of." He seemed to melt against her, pressing his mouth to hers, turning her blood suddenly vapor.

The dome of the equatorial room was open wide, welcoming the night. Beneath the luminous stars was a heaving, groaning, multi-limbed, single organism, moving and shifting as one, shining blinding and beautiful, sweat and limbs and mouths, fingers, soft curves and hard lines, wet and slick, hot and aching, slow gentle caresses and lapping tongues, pounding slapping thrusts and arched backs, harsh breath, moans, sighs, pleas, and delicious entreaties.

Moments – the moonlight cool on Maddie's full breast, the taut peak of her nipple shimmering with moisture, Grayling's mouth hovering, open and hot. Zerik looking up at Rhiannon from between her thighs, his mouth exquisite flame against her flesh, his eyes wild and deep. Alex sitting behind Emma, his hands covering her breasts, his lips moving against her ear, her eyes closed, flushed in serene joy.

As their auras joined as one, so, too, their gifts. Fused together in glorious light, the sharing deepened. Zerik spoke first, his sigh in Emma's mind, *"Yes ..."* and Maddie responded, sharing her thought with Grayling, *"More ..."* Their *e'drai* became part of the light, the connection, and now they were all whispering to one another, to everyone, as throats vocalized moans and sighs, minds danced with mental commentary, encouragement, demands, delight. *"Kiss me,* husband." "Touch me there." "Her face is so beautiful when he does that to her." "Yes, show me."

Rhiannon found herself lying shoulder to shoulder with Maddie, hands and fingers entwined. Emma had crawled down to lie between Rhiannon's thighs, her mouth on her sex, a finger sliding within her body, then another, and another. Rhiannon gasped and looked up to see Grayling moving behind Emma, slowly stroking her from within, his eyes feverish, jubilant, watching Rhiannon's face.

Rhiannon turned her head to see Maddie, her eyes closed, gasping with pleasure. Hovering above and inside her was Zerik, his back arched, his head thrown back, his face a mask of transcendent exultation. And behind him moved Alexander, one muscular arm wrapped around Zerik's big chest, a hand clutching Zerik's hip as Alex bore down, his mouth open, tasting, on Zerik's neck, shoulder. With every thrust, he pushed Zerik deeper into Maddie, who gasped euphoric, shuddering, soaring.

Rhiannon stared at Alexander, overcome with the sensual vision of it, almost able to feel his body, his ecstatic bliss, to feel Zerik and Maddie, even as Grayling's driving motion pushed Emma's mouth and fingers deeper, forcefully, against her own heated flesh.

As if sensing her regard, his mouth still gasping on the curve of Zerik's neck, Alex opened his eyes, looked directly at her. "*I see you,*" his thought came to her, and she knew it was for her alone.

She met his verdant eyes steadily. "*I feel you,*" she thought.

"*I know,*" his mind whispered. "*I have felt you for so long, now.*" His smile deepened, turned wicked. "*Now feel this,* ma moitié." She gasped. Suddenly, she felt his hands on her breasts, his long fingers skimming over her nipples, caressing the aereola — but his hands weren't there. His chest pressed to Zerik's back, he still had one arm wrapped pale around Zerik's dark chest, the other gripping his hip. Emma groaned abruptly, thrashing beneath Gray's slow strokes, and then Maddie cried out, opening her eyes to look down at her bare breasts, surprised as invisible fingers fondled her skin.

"Oh, I like this," Grayling's thought suffused the room, the first to understand the nature of the *e'drai* Alex was wielding. And sharing.

A frenzied intensity exploded outward, as bodies moved, mouths tasted, fingers explored, while their minds engendered more hands for touching, more tongues for licking, more ways to give, to receive, to fill, to be filled. Through Zerik's *e'drai*, the magnitude of the power rebounded and expanded in every body and mind, creating an almost unbearably sensual harmonic. The light was full and complete now, and Rhiannon couldn't tell where one person began and another ended, where her own body began or ended.

"Rhiannon," Zerik gasped aloud. "Nudge Maddie. Nudge the fire part."

Rhiannon squeezed Maddie's hand, their connection instantaneous. She found Maddie's passion, her heat and desire, red and pink and hot, and beyond that, the wild gold-red of her fire *e'drai*. Arching her back with the luscious intensity of Emma's mouth and fingers, Rhiannon grabbed Maddie's passion and fire and pushed, opened it outward, huge and aching and rich. Maddie screamed, her pleasure and the vast burning energy redoubling, her *e'drai* and Rhiannon's flaming outward in a simultaneous explosion that caught and consumed them all, crying out, their light flaring to eclipse the stars.

For a long time afterward, they lay together in a sweat-slicked pile of tangled limbs, smiling and absorbing their bodies, the moment, and each other, silent but for steadying breath. *"Te a'behs,"* someone thought, and it didn't matter who, as the words suffused the warm, fading radiance beneath the open sky.

Rain came in from the ocean in the night, a wild fall storm thrashing the rugged Northern California cliffs. In the morning, from the windows of Grayling's ground floor sitting room, Alexander watched the leaden, choppy sea, the wind whipping the branches of the sentinel trees surrounding the cliff and the Sisters' Circle.

Zerik sat in a comfortable, massive leather chair by the wide river-stone fireplace, the fire crackling bright and cheerful against the howl of the wind outside. Across the room, Grayling stood framed in a tall jagged gash which seemed ripped into the warm, carved wood paneling – the entrance to his bedroom, a cozy soft-floored cave cut into the rock, several steps down into the earth.

Grayling looked over at Maddie, curled up under a quilt on an overstuffed green velvet sofa across from the fire. "Where are my other wives?" he asked casually, casting a brief, tense glance at Alexander.

Zerik answered for her. "Emma and Rhiannon are in the kitchen with the children, I believe," he smiled. "Helping Lyds and Robbie make cupcakes."

Maddie watched Alex, his face seemingly relaxed, his manner nonchalant. But she'd known him too long. Something was bothering him.

"Alex," she said, and he turned from the window to look at her, an eyebrow raised in question. "You need to know. Her memory – there's a lot we don't understand yet. And something happened to her, back in the second oblivi World War." Maddie looked down at her hands, clenched in her lap. "There's someone after her. Someone *erim*." Maddie didn't have to specify who *she* was.

Alexander tensed, as though his whole body came suddenly aware. His face hardened, eyes glittering. "Monks, as well?"

Zerik looked at him curiously. "Yes. How did you know?"

Alex sighed, running a frustrated hand through his hair. "My coming here seemed necessary for more reasons than one. Edward Angelis and the Chorus at the British Caistra – and leaders of House Zel'mori – asked me to meet with the *Kir'da* at the Seat here." He looked at Grayling, held his gaze. "To discuss a rogue aeternan, *erim*. Daz Minoru." He shook his head. "He has become an extremely serious problem."

Maddie leaned forward, hands clenched, seized with an immediate anxiety. "You think this is the man after Rhiannon?"

Alexander's face was grim. He looked away, back at the sea, and for a moment Zerik thought he caught something in Alex's face, almost a kind of grief. "I don't know. Could be."

Zerik frowned, unable to shake the feeling that Alex knew more than he was saying.

Alex's tone was casual, though his shoulders betrayed a tension as he stared out the window. "Do you have any idea why this man is fixated on her?"

Maddie shook her head, her lips pursed. Then her eyes widened, struck with a sudden thought. "We might ask Emma. There was some unpleasantness a couple centuries ago. Something to do with an *erim* man." She cast Alex an apologetic glance. "They were in France. I was with child then, couldn't make the trip with them." She shrugged helplessly. "But it probably doesn't make sense. That was a long time ago. And there weren't any monks involved, that's certain."

"Hmm." Alex turned to look at them. "Well, over the past couple hundred years, Daz seems to have forged some kind of relationship with The Guard, the monks."

"Jesu," Grayling whispered, coming to stand behind Maddie's couch.

"But that would mean he would have to —" Zerik began, halting abruptly as Emma and Rhiannon, laughing and out of breath, ran clattering into the sitting room.

"I win!" Rhiannon cried, pink-cheeked from exertion, grinning bright-eyed at her spouses and Alex.

Emma laughed, breathing hard. "No way, you had a head start."

Clearly unaware of the tension in the room, Rhiannon looked over at Maddie, her smile electric. "That hallway is great for racing. It's so long! I want to try it with roller blades."

Emma brightened. "We should get blades for all the kids, too." Her eyes widened. "And we could skate in the ballroom!"

Rhiannon laughed in response, then glanced at Maddie, sitting on the green sofa by the fire. "Oh, yeah," she said, coming forward. She dug into the back pocket of her jeans and pulled out a small cream-colored envelope. She held it out to Maddie. "Lyds asked me to give this to you. You've got mail." She grinned broadly.

Clearing her throat, Maddie cast warning, silencing glances at the men, then pasted on a cheerful smile. She held out her hand to Rhiannon. "Let's see that, dear."

Rhiannon gave the envelope to her wife, sitting down on the couch next to her. Emma perched on the arm of Zerik's chair by the fire. "What is it?" Rhiannon asked.

"It's a formal invitation," Maddie answered absently, fingering the thick, creamy paper. The letters seemed hazy, insubstantial. Printed with *e'drai*. She passed the card over to Zerik.

"We've been invited to the Caistra, to celebrate the Fall Equinox," Zerik said.

Emma nodded at Rhiannon "I told you. They always have a big party. We should have more dancing lessons."

"There's a formal ball on the Equinox," Zerik said, scanning the invitation. "And additionally, we're invited to a special, private *erapakiv* on the eve."

Grayling glanced over at Alex.

"All of us," Zerik said, glaring at his husband. Privately, he sent Grayling a thought. *"Alexander is the senior Eldest known to the Family."* When Grayling frowned, he added, *"Someday you may live long enough to acquire a little shadow on your soul, husband. I will love you then, as I do now."*

"The Prodigies are performing earlier that week," Maddie said. She looked up at Zerik, her eyes troubled. "Do you think it's safe for us to take Rhiannon to Santa Cruz? I know the Caistra is secure, but – "

Grayling shook his head. "I don't think it's a good idea."

"We'll be there, with her," Alexander said, his tone light. "And the whole show is protected by the Fae."

"I hate to miss it," Emma said wistfully. "It's their only performance in the United States."

Zerik eyed his silver-haired husband, then shrugged. "I think we can make it work."

Grayling scowled, but said nothing further.

"This is going to be so much fun!" Emma chirped, clasping Rhiannon's hand. "First, the show, and then the Equinox."

"After we leave Santa Cruz, we should go up to the Caistra a day or two early, to get settled in, and give Alex time to conduct his business with Alvar," Maddie said.

"Actually, I'll probably try to get up the Caistra before we go," Alex put in nonchalantly, as if nothing in the world were wrong.

"Well, regardless," Maddie said. "I'd still like to go early, stop in Rockport for an afternoon, to see if we can straighten out Rhiannon's bank account."

"That might not be easy, given that she doesn't remember who she is," Alexander frowned.

Surprised, Rhiannon looked around. "I have a bank account?"

Emma giggled. "Of course you do. Now, whether you can access it is a whole different issue."

"Let's see that again, Zerik," Maddie said, reaching for the invitation. He passed it over; she read further. "Oh, this is going to be a very special *erapakiv* indeed."

"What's an *erapakiv*?" Rhiannon asked.

"Oh, it's a wonderful party!" Emma enthused. "It's a sensual dance and celebration."

"It's intensely erotic, intimate, and yet very public," Alex said, capturing Rhiannon's gaze. "It's an aeternan tradition going back hundreds of years."

"Performing will be a multi-incarnations married couple from House Niku," Maddie said, continuing to read. Her eyes widened. "And the Senti *nahyin* will be present," Maddie looked up from the invitation. "They've been touring the world. This is a rare event."

Rhiannon looked back to Maddie. "Who are they?"

"The Senti are a circle of three, like us. Together, their *e'drai* allows them to enhance feeling and experience, and broadcast those sensations to others."

Zerik's eyes widened. "They're going to enhance an *erapakiv*? With lovers from Niku, no less? That's going to be one amazing erotic party."

Alex's eyes had never left Rhiannon. "House Niku is the *Dinach* of the Flesh. They believe that since we are born of flesh, learning the secrets of the flesh are the foundation for spiritual attainment and the basis for love. Many members spend lifetimes studying *era* and pleasure in all forms." His outlaw grin erupted. "They're a lot of fun."

Emma smiled at Rhiannon. "It's polite to attend an *erapakiv* in couples. Your partner should be your initial partner for dancing and *era*; after that it's kind of a free-for-all."

Casting another glance at Alex, Grayling came around the couch, taking hold of Rhiannon's hand. "I will partner with you, *anam cara*."

Avoiding Alex's eyes, Rhiannon nodded.

Zerik, who wasn't fooled, offered to escort Emma.

"I guess that leaves you and me," Alex said, coming forward to take Maddie's hand, slowly pressing his lips to her fingers, his eyes locked with hers.

Maddie blushed. "I will look forward to it, sir."

Later that afternoon, Lyds found Eva on a staircase at the back of the house, in the throes of a terrible seizure, her muscles rigid, twitching, the crotch of her jeans soaked dark with menstrual blood. The *memor'fis* were coming in cascades of three and four now, the poor child trying with instinctive, blind desperation to make it to the tower room she'd chosen with Maddie.

The family was sent for posthaste. Rhiannon was terrified for their daughter, but her spouses seemed to know just what to do, handling the situation with a kind of efficient, calm anticipation that was somehow joyous and sad all at once.

Zerik easily scooped up the convulsing girl into his arms, carrying her swiftly up the stairs to the safe room they'd chosen. He gently laid her down on the bed, pressing a kiss to her forehead, even as Eva stared unseeing heavenward, spasms wracking her body.

Emma and Grayling followed Zerik to the bed, also kissing the lanky young girl. For a moment, Eva had a sudden respite from her seizures, her memories. Her muscles relaxed, even as she continued to shudder in the aftermath. In her brief lucidity, she threw her arms around Emma's neck. "*Te a'behs*, mama," she whispered. And then she was gripped by another *fis*, thrown back onto the wide bed in a sudden paroxysm. Her aura had begun to brighten.

Alexander stood in the doorway, watching silently.

310

"It won't be long now," Maddie said. With backward glances reflecting a mixture of love and concern, everyone but Maddie filed out of the room. They heard her throw the bolt behind them.

"The rain's stopped," Grayling said, as they descended the steps. "Let's go out on the lawn and watch the light."

They didn't have long to wait. Standing in the wet grass, looking up at the small square windows of Eva's tower room, a light began to grow, the shining aura of an aeternan in the midst of *Memora Magia*, The Remembering. The light expanded, brightened, until it was nearly blinding, a blazing, coruscating beacon streaming outward to blot out the tower, and then even the sky itself.

It went on and on, longer than Rhiannon could imagine, but exactly how long, she couldn't say. It felt huge and important and wild inside her, some part of her aching and calling out, wanting to be a part of that radiance.

Finally, the light began to dim, just a little. Rhiannon heard a loud popping sound behind her, whirling to see Alex, holding a bottle of champagne, a silver tray of glasses lying at his feet in the wet grass.

He smiled at the Ciatri family, his friends for so many long centuries. "A toast to new Family among us. To that which makes us what we are. To Remembering."

Grayling nodded, looking into Alexander's Fae green eyes. Holding his gaze, he took a glass, held it aloft. "*Maghkai.*"

Alex smiled at him. "We Fight Together."

"*Maghkai,*" they all echoed the traditional toast, drinking deeply, wiping back tears of happiness and loss, staring up at the fading radiance shining from the little windows above.

NINETEEN

Rhiannon dreamed of the Floods, the Inundation, the waters of the Nile streaming over the land in rivers like shining ribbons, flowing endless abundance amidst the green fields and carmine desert.

She was singing at a nobleman's elegant garden banquet, celebrating the Beautiful Feast of Opet, honoring Amon. It had been a long night, the party lush, the tables groaning beneath the weight of haunches of beef, roast duck and goose breast, fresh-baked breads and fruit, beer, and wine. The revelers were not inclined to leave anytime soon.

The cone of myrrh and sandalwood Rhiannon had placed on her head had long since melted into her dark braids, surrounding her with sweet fragrance. Clothed in her linen shift, damp and nearly transparent in the heat, she felt more exposed than the nude servant girls who wandered the garden with trays of honeyed figs, grapes, and pomegranates, wearing nothing but braided wigs and faience necklaces and anklets.

As she sang, undulating to the music, Rhiannon surreptitiously watched their host, Senenmut. The nobleman had the lustrous aura of

313

an aeternan – one older than herself. Quite drunk, he swaggered over to the ornate pergola next to the lotus pool where the musicians had set up their instruments. Throwing a friendly arm around Rhiannon's shoulders, he laughed. "Sing for me!" He met her gaze, the black galena and malachite paint around his dark eyes rendering him undeniably handsome, mysterious. "Sing on, little sister," he whispered.

Her accompanist, Ra-an, plucked the strings of his harp, and she sang the words to an old, long-beloved song: "Be joyous, tireless, celebrate! Man cannot take his property with him. Behold, there is not one who departs who comes back again."

"Now, that's a lie," Senenmut whispered in her ear, grinning mischievously.

He would try to come to her bed tonight, she knew then – a terrible danger for her, if they were found out – given his station, and her own. She wondered if he was as handsome within as he was without. She took a deep breath, found the Soul Magic she carried within. "My soul speaks to yours," the magic called to him. "Who are you?"

Unaware of her e'drai, Sennemut stood beside her, grinning, one arm around her bare shoulders, tapping a foot in time with the harp and the rhythmic clapping of the guests.

His soul responded to hers with a swamping wave of darkness which had yet to color his aura, a wash of black, a putrid green and red which threatened to consume the remaining gold. His soul spoke to her, the soul of one who aspired to be a God on Earth, a soul lost in power and control, ruthless, demanding, greedy, hungry. This was a man who would defy all who stood in his way. A man who would obey none, take all.

Rhiannon shrank from his touch. Oblivious, he wandered away, raising his gold cup to a laughing friend across the room. "Drink to Amon! Drink to me!"

She nodded to Ra-an and resumed singing. Outwardly composed, calm, Rhiannon felt as if her insides were trembling, her mind racing, trying to form a plan, an escape. If she could make it to the river, she could float away on the bosom of the generous Nile, to another place, another time.

314

Early in the morning, Rhiannon stood on the cliff's edge, by the narrow trail leading down to the private beach below. In the damp turf at her feet were canvas tote bags overflowing with sunscreen, water shoes, folded-limp, brightly deflated rafts and water tubes, plastic sand pails with diminutive shovels, sunglasses, water wings, and thick beach towels.

Emma and the six remaining children — for, whoever she had become, Eva was a child no more — were finishing brushing their teeth, wiggling into bathing suits. Feeling suddenly confined in the warm house, Rhiannon had escaped to the cliff, to wait.

She slipped off her sandals, her bare feet cold at first in the wet grass, warming as she breathed deeply. Her connection with the earth came naturally now, as much an extension of her understanding of the world as her vision, the taste and scent of the wind.

The day before, the clouds had been vast, heavy with impending cold and rain, hanging low over the coastline. The rain, when it came, was frigid, biting, drenching the dark redwoods, the reddish-green copses and stretches of open land, the tawny cliffs, until everything seemed washed nearly colorless into the grey sea, the brown wet sand.

When the rain finally stopped, they'd stood in the wet lawn in the fog, beneath pendulous dark clouds, watched the endless radiance of a mensaeternan in the throes of *Memora Magia*, watched as Eva lit the world with the effulgence of her memories and *e'drai*, the brilliance of that light conquering the storm, subsuming the night.

And something in that moment had called to Rhiannon, leaving her with a hunger, a yearning she couldn't name, couldn't understand.

Now, standing on the edge of the cliff, her feet connecting her to the soil, the sand below that, to the fiery heart of the earth deeper still, Rhiannon breathed deeply of the morning air. The sun was warm on her face and arms, the air after the rain fresh and sharp. The tawny-reddish cliffs seemed washed clean, the ocean vivid, reflecting the cloudless azure sky. Below, waves foamed against the damp

315

beach, strewn with clumps of seaweed and driftwood disgorged by the storm-tossed sea.

The curve of the cliff, the sweep of beach, hadn't varied; and yet this morning, in the vivid sunlight, the earth wild and solid beneath Rhiannon's feet, it seemed like she was seeing it all for the first time, different, somehow. Everything was as it had been, yet in one night the world had been transformed.

Rhiannon turned as Emma and the children approached in a noisy, excited pack, anxious to get to the beach. Rhiannon smiled, waving as she slipped on her sandals, gathering up the canvas bags of beach gear.

Emma looked beautiful in the sunlight, her hair and aura glowing golden, her face alight. "Oh, it's a perfect morning for the beach!"

"Shouldn't we wait for Maddie and Eva?" Rhiannon asked. She already knew the answer. They hadn't seen Madeline or Eva since the night before, when Eva had begun the process of *Memora Magia*.

"No sense waiting," Emma replied cheerfully. "These things can take time. They'll be down when Eva's ready."

The two women carefully picked their way down the sandy, narrow trail to the beach, each helping the younger children as they went. The oldest – Jacob, Marcus, and Melody – ran ahead, tripping and sliding, laughing.

At the beach, Rhiannon used her *e'drai* to send the clumps of seaweed and driftwood sliding along the surface of the sand, back into the sea. Emma spread out a blanket, and the children busied themselves unpacking their toys, putting on water shoes. Her aura shimmering, with a whisper of breath, Emma inflated all of the rafts and water tubes at once, plus a pair of water wings for Missy, who patiently allowed her mother to slide one over her deformed arm.

Holding 5-year-old Joshua's hand, Rhiannon waded out into the water. "It's cold," she complained, looking over her shoulder at Emma.

Emma laughed merrily. "It's September in Northern California. And our fire witch isn't here."

"Well, Joshua doesn't seem to mind," Rhiannon smiled wryly, then howled as the exuberant child splashed her from head to foot with frigid salt water.

"It's not so cold when you're all-over wet, Mama Rhiannon," Joshua explained matter-of-factly.

Casting Joshua a sour glance, Rhiannon shook her head like a wet dog, sending water flying, much to the child's delight.

After a half hour of splashing and sandcastles, Rhiannon heard a commotion on the trail. She looked up to see Robbie and Lyds toting two huge wicker picnic hampers, closely followed by Zerik, Grayling, and Alexander carrying blankets, and folding striped canvas chairs. *"Good morning, wives,"* came Zerik's thought, carrying a warmth of emotion. *"And before you chide me, Emma, we tried to help with the hampers. They wouldn't hear of it."*

Once the group made it to the beach, Lyds and Robbie deposited the baskets next to Emma. "Breakfast by the sea!" Lyds announced enthusiastically. "Take advantage of the weather while it's still nice."

"It'll be raining in a week," Robbie grumbled.

Rhiannon helped Lyds and Robbie spread out four wide blankets, while Emma and Grayling began unpacking the baskets. Zerik busied himself unfolding and setting up chairs for the adults. Meanwhile, Alex took on the formidable task of getting all of the children out of the water, or away from their sandcastles, and seated on the blankets, ready for their meal.

"He doesn't look much like he's getting them ready for breakfast," Emma said. Alex was chasing the delighted, screeching older children, grabbing them, plunging into the water. Grayling snorted.

Three-year-old Missy was completely fascinated with Alexander, and followed him with tottering steps wherever he went, as he played with the other children. Taking note of his young shadow, Alex turned and knelt in the sand, touching Missy's wing-like, deformed arm, his expression serious, his eyes gentle. "Can you fly, little bird?"

"I usta could," Missy said. "When I was uh angel."

"You still are," Alex responded, sweeping her up onto his shoulders. Missy squealed with elation. "Now you're closer to the sky, little bird," Alex said, and they both laughed as he ran down the beach, arms outstretched, flying.

By the time Emma finished unpacking their breakfast, she looked up to see all of her children sitting neatly on the blankets, hands folded in their laps, waiting quietly for their breakfast. She looked over at Alex with a mixture of surprise and suspicion on her face.

"I promised them all seahorse rides, if they behave," Alex said.

Jacob looked askance at Alex. "You can't really ride seahorses. They're small. We're way bigger," he said scornfully.

"He says, so we can," Melody huffed.

Alex smiled at her, acknowledging her defense, but holding up a hand in mock surrender. "No, no, Jacob is right. Seahorses are pretty small." He pretended to think for a moment. "I know. How about *I* be the seahorse, and you can all ride me? I think I can swim like a seahorse."

After a brief debate as to whether Alex could swim upright and curl his feet like a tail, the children agreed that Alex would be an acceptable substitute. "Real seahorses would be kind of spiky to sit on anyhow," Jacob noted.

Everyone was hungry. The wicker hampers had been filled with covered platters of omelets and sausages, fresh fruit and pastries, plus elegant silver servingware, and pale blue linen napkins.

Rhiannon looked up at the cliff, and though unable to see the house, in her mind she could still see the glowing windows of the tower where Eva had gone through *Memora Magia*. She looked over at Zerik, who was lounging on one of the blankets, sharing his omelet with their son, Charlie.

"What's taking them so long?" Rhiannon asked Zerik. She didn't need to specify who she was talking about. Maddie and Eva were surely never far from any of their thoughts that morning.

Zerik wiped his mouth with his napkin. "Actually, Maddie has been unusually silent in my mind – but I see no need to prod her. My guess is that she has her hands full." He shrugged. "Sometimes, the process of Remembering is challenging. Trying to make sense of what you're feeling afterward, integrating your previous lives and experience into this one – it can be painful, and awkward."

Rhiannon thought about her own ordeal, Remembering her life as Kat Weiss. How difficult it had been, to try to understand an adult life suddenly an intrinsic part of herself, her thoughts and memories, trapped in Megan Byrne's little 13-year-old body.

"Still, she's a medius," Alexander interjected, busily slicing an apple. He looked up at Grayling. "She's had what – nine, ten incarnations?"

"Ten," Grayling affirmed.

"So she's done this before. This will be her ninth time," Alexander said, smiling at Rhiannon. "She'll manage a bit better than a neonate might. And she's got help – she's got this *dzina*, this family, to support her. So many of us are born to oblivi families, and have to cope alone." He glanced at Missy, handed her a piece of apple. "She's damned lucky to be born into the Ciatri *Dinach*, to be forever allied with the Sisters." He beamed at Emma, who returned the smile, her cheeks pink. "To be born into any aeternan family is a blessing, but this *dzina* is special. Anyone would be deeply honored. Would that one day I might have Emma birth me, to be mother of my flesh."

Emma laughed. "You'd be a troublesome baby, I am sure."

"And an even more troublesome toddler," Grayling said gruffly, almost, but not quite hiding a smile.

Suddenly flustered, Rhiannon looked down at her plate. It seemed so strange, this talk of giving birth to one's friends or lovers. But more than that, she found herself trying to ignore the hollow ache in her chest that the talk of motherhood engendered.

Alexander glanced at her, saw too much. "Being a mother doesn't require flesh," he whispered. No one else seemed to hear. Rhiannon looked up into those green eyes, felt something soft melt within, warming her belly. She took the apple slice he held out to her, pressed the tart sweetness to her tongue.

After breakfast, Emma and Alex played with the children. Alex was busy giving his promised "seahorse" rides, while Emma dug in the sand with Jacob, who, at 10 years old, declared he was too old for seahorse rides – though he watched the other children longingly, when he thought no one was looking.

Rhiannon was content to lie on the blankets with her head in Grayling's lap, soaking up the salt air and her husband's touch, as he stroked her shoulders in lazy, gentle circles. Zerik stretched out next to them, like a big cat, basking in the morning sun.

"The sun is getting pretty high now," Zerik said. "Must be almost 10. I expect at this point, they've gotten through the worst of it." He stretched, yawned. "Eva — whoever she is — will be feeling pretty solidly herself again."

Rhiannon turned her head to look at him, shading her eyes with one hand. "How do you do that? Feel like yourself, I mean." She thought about her own experience and winced. "It took me a long, long time to feel ..." she faltered. Zerik waited. She struggled to sit up, leaned against Grayling's chest, so warm and solid. "To feel like one person again. For so long, it felt like I was two people — and one was real, and one wasn't. Or like it was maybe just my imagination."

Grayling looked down at her, his rare smile sympathetic. "It's harder for neonates. I know you aren't one — but you Remember like one."

Zerik nodded. "Without going through Remembering before, it's really hard to know who you are, to make sense of things." He looked out at the water, where Joshua splashed a few yards away in the shallows, two thin golden *fainna* defining his aura. "This will be Joshua's first Remembering, when he comes of age. It won't be easy."

"But we'll be here to help him," Grayling said. At that moment, the boy looked up at Grayling, his little face so serious, and Rhiannon could suddenly see Grayling's features, his Form, echoed in miniature in the child's face, but for blue eyes, bright, like Emma's.

"Flesh is flesh," Grayling said quietly. "Flesh comes and goes. The soul is Eternal."

Zerik nodded. "The honor, for aeternan parents, is to bring Family souls back into this world." He sat up, folding his legs in front of him, staring out at Alexander playing with the children, splashing and laughing in the water. "The children like him," he murmured.

"Everyone likes him," Grayling muttered irritably.

Zerik laughed. He looked back at Rhiannon, still reclining with regal ease against Grayling's chest, and picked up her original question. "There are many ways we re-integrate ourselves, when we Remember. I think most of us have to take time to simply go through our memories, dust them off, perhaps even re-experience them."

"You have to re-live your memories?" Rhiannon asked nervously, that familiar sense of panic welling up inside her.

Zerik reached out and stroked Rhiannon's bare leg, almost absently, his fingertips light. "We have to focus on what makes us who we are. Bodies, our Form, doesn't necessarily have much bearing on that."

"But isn't your childhood important? You spend several years with your parents, learning, growing – I mean, my childhood with Rosa still has an effect on me." She grimaced.

"That's because you're remembering like a neonate," Grayling said quietly.

Zerik nodded. "Of course your childhood in every incarnation has some effect on you – but it's only 10 or 13 years out of a couple thousand." He sighed. "The main thing is to focus on who you really are, not the experiences of a few years. Little things can help with that. When you look in the mirror, you see the flesh, the Form, of this incarnation. So things like clothes can help. The way you dress, what you see when you look in the mirror, it helps you feel like yourself again."

Rhiannon looked up at Grayling, his silver hair braided down his back, his grey clothes. "It feels like who I am," Grayling said, noticing her perusal.

She looked at Zerik, in his habitual sanded-silk shirt, his comfortable jeans. She thought of Maddie, always wearing flowing dresses and skirts that skimmed around her ankles like water, and Emma, in her empire-waist dresses that seemed so elegant – and yet so easily accommodated her growing belly.

Rhiannon laughed. "Hmm, okay. So, clothes really do make the man. Or woman."

Zerik smiled. "We are who we are, naked or otherwise. But it is true that sometimes just dressing in ways that feel familiar can help us feel more comfortable in whatever skin we happen to be in." He paused, looking at her thoughtfully. "You know, you might try that – we have a closet full of clothes for our kids, from every time period, every country, every spiritual practice. Maybe you should just pick out something, something that calls to you. It might help you remember."

Rhiannon sat up then, hugging her arms to herself, shaking her head. "I don't know about that."

"I just think – " Zerik began, but then he stopped, a faraway look in his eye. After a moment, he seemed to come back to himself. He looked at Grayling. "Maddie's coming. We should get the children and head back to the house."

"What's going on?" Rhiannon asked, as Grayling unfolded himself with perfect elegance, holding out a hand to help her to her feet.

"Maddie's bringing Eva out. To greet us." Grayling said.

Zerik looked out at the water, sending out thought. *"Emma, children. Alex. It's time to go back to the house now. We are to be formally introduced."*

"C'mon," Emma said, bustling about like a mother bird, toweling down the younger children, handing a beach towel to Alex and the older children. "Leave the blankets and hampers," she ordered Grayling, who had started to gather up their breakfast things. "We'll get them later. And tuck in your shirt, Zerik." Zerik obediently tugged at the wayward shirt-tails of his beige silk shirt. Grayling laughed, and Zerik shot him a look.

The narrow trail up the cliff only accommodated one at a time. Emma took the lead, Rhiannon following. Zerik and Grayling came next, then the children, with Alexander bringing up the rear, little Missy on his shoulders, flapping her arms like a bird, a brilliant smile lighting her chubby cheeks. Rhiannon looked back over her shoulder, and thought she caught a sense of wariness from Alex.

Rhiannon felt nervous, for no reason she could name. "What are we doing?" she whispered to Emma.

Emma glanced back at her, as she climbed the cliff trail. "This is Eva's first introduction to her *dzina* as an adult, as her true self. We will find out her Family Name, her *Praenom* and *Secunom*." Emma smiled. "Who knows, it may turn out one of us knows her already." She reached back and squeezed Rhiannon's hand. "It is a formal introduction, so manners are important. As a medius, she'll be expected to offer us – as Eldest – a formal bow. We respond with the *anam'ta*." She demonstrated by bowing her head regally to Rhiannon.

"Okay," Rhiannon said, clutching Emma's hand and returning the squeeze.

When Rhiannon reached the top of the cliff trail, just behind Emma, she could see Maddie standing a few yards away in the lawn, her red hair glowing in the morning sunlight. Standing next to her was Eva, but the girl looked far different than she had the night before. Her unruly black curls had been close-cropped to her head, almost shaved. She wore a brown, old-fashioned men's suit, including a vest, with a crisp, white tab-collar shirt and a dark blue tie. Her face was composed, serious, almost stern. No longer did she fidget and run; instead, she stood sedately at Maddie's side. Despite all that, she was still a beautiful young girl, her coffee-and-cream skin glowing warm in the sunshine, her elegant features so like both Zerik's and Maddie's.

The party from the beach straggled up to the trailhead, lining up salt-soaked wet, sandy and sunkissed to stare at Maddie and Eva.

Alex came up last, swinging Missy down from his shoulders, who offered a whining complaint. "Shh, little bird. Be a good girl, and meet your Family," Alexander whispered.

Maddie indicated Eva with a wave of her hand, her chin up proudly, her smile a shade too determined. "My *dzina*. May I present our Family, David Anthony."

She came to stand next to her Sisters, smiling encouragingly at David, once their daughter Eva.

David Anthony stood in front of Emma, offering her a precise, crisply executed formal *anam'sal*. She nodded in response, then said, "It is a pleasure to meet you, David Anthony."

"Thank you, Mama Emma," David said gravely.

He moved to Rhiannon and repeated the gesture. She responded with the *anam'ta*, nodding carefully.

Rhiannon watched as David Anthony – *Eva!* – moved down the line, formally greeting each of his parents in turn. When he came to his siblings, Emma spoke up. "Children, David Anthony is your elder." Each child performed an *anam'sal* with varying degrees of skill, receiving the *anam'ta* nod from David in return. The younger ones appeared confused, but seemed to recognize the gravity of the situation.

When he reached Missy, David performed an elegant *anam'sal*. The child was only 3, but was still an Eldest with nearly 30 *fainna*. Missy giggled. "You're funny, Eva."

David Anthony regarded her somberly, then turned to face Alexander, standing next to the little girl. David's eyes hardened, his beautiful face congealing into an ugly sneer. "I do not recognize *liath*," he hissed, and spat on the ground at Alex's feet.

Emma gasped. For a long moment, there was a horrible silence.

Maddie drew herself up to her full height, all five feet six inches of her suddenly bristling with fury, her eyes snapping fire. She marched across the lawn to stand a few feet from David. "*Naire!* Alexander passed my gates, David Anthony. He is Eldest, older than any member of this family. He is a guest at the Ciatri *dzina*." She advanced a pace, pointing her finger at the child, no longer Eva, suddenly a man. "How dare you," she snapped. "You, David Anthony, were born into my *dinach* by a whim of fortune, the Universe smiling upon you. You were child of my flesh, my heart. Your failure to show respect to this Eldest dishonors not only you, but me, and my House." And with that, she whirled around, giving David her back.

Suddenly pale, David cupped his hands, offered a perfunctory *anam'sal*, nodding his head to Alex. Then he turned and ran into the house.

Maddie burst into tears and ran toward the Sisters' Circle, Zerik close on her heels, arms outstretched, gasping mental entreaties. "*Maddie, wait, varenya.*"

Grayling stood for a moment as if stone, then turned and walked silently toward the woods behind the house.

"Well, that was fun," Alexander drawled.

Tell me about the Soul Magic. She wanted to ask. But she couldn't.

Tell me about the Soul Magic. Tell me why I can talk to someone's soul in my dreams. Tell me about Alexander's soul. But she didn't say anything.

The day after David's uncomfortable introduction to the *dzina*, Maddie was carrying on as if nothing had happened, with careful cheer.

The three women were in the Sisters' Circle, making beads for the Equinox Ball. They would leave for Rockport and the Caistra the day after the Prodigies show. "Exchanging beads is part of the tradition of Court parties," Emma had explained. "We like to make special beads, using *e'drai*."

Using her Fire *e'drai*, Maddie heated the glass and wound the glass rods around steel mandrels, while Emma inserted perfect, impossible bubbles of Air into the glass, laced with emotion – joy, happiness, peace. Maddie whispered the words with her mind, and they showed Rhiannon how to use her Earth gift to anchor the *e'drai* within the bead. With a wash of Fire *e'drai*, Maddie annealed the beads. The finished product was a shining, luminous glass bead filled with tiny glowing air bubbles. When Rhiannon held one in her hand, she heard the word *joy* echo in her mind, felt a hint of the emotion wash over her for a brief moment.

"These are so cool!" Rhiannon said, looking up in amazement.

"The exchange of beads is a tradition as old as aeternans," Maddie said. "From bone to faience, precious stones and metals, wood and glass, beads signify eternal life, power, beauty."

"Everyone brings beads to the ball," Emma said. "You wear a little purse to collect them."

"I always string mine the next day," Maddie added. "I love to look at the string of beads, to touch them and remember who gave them to me, where I was." She smiled. "Beads are the gift of memories. I suppose that has obvious significance for us."

Rhiannon gathered her courage, rolling the small iridescent bead around between her fingers. She looked up at Maddie. "Tell me about the Soul Magic," she said.

Maddie turned from the fire to look at Rhiannon. "Why do you ask?" She frowned. "Did Zerik say something to you?"

Bewildered for a moment, Rhiannon shook her head, frowning. Then her brow cleared. "Well, yeah. He mentioned something about me choosing a Consort. But that was a while ago." She flushed, trying not to think about Alex with some determination. "You know, I'm not sure I'm ready to do that. It seems like a lot of pressure."

Emma giggled behind her hand, then silenced herself, wide-eyed and grinning, at a glare from Madeline.

"But I'm not even sure what it is," Rhiannon continued. "I had a dream last night. I was in Egypt. A long, long time ago. There was a man there – he seemed all right, but then it was like I could talk to him, to his soul." She looked down at the bead in her hand. "He was a bad man."

Madeline sighed and came to stand next to Rhiannon, the fire dying behind her. "You know the Sisters carry elemental *e'drai*. Earth, air, fire, water." She looked at Emma, then back to Rhiannon. "There is one other element the Sisters share, and it is the only one which doesn't stay with us as we move into our next incarnation."

"The Soul Magic. The Soul *e'drai*," Emma said soberly.

"As far as we know, we are the only aeternans, the only *nahyin* – Circle – to have a special gift that we share with one another, from lifetime to lifetime. One of us always holds the Soul *e'drai*, but we never know which of us will receive the gift from one lifetime to the next."

"And we never know what form it will take," Emma added. "All three of us have carried it. It is a powerful gift, but it can also be a terrible burden."

Maddie waved a hand toward the silk canopy at the edge of the Sisters' Circle. "Let's sit and have some tea." Rhiannon nodded assent, and she and Emma followed Madeline to the pavilion. A pot of tea sat on the table there. Maddie laid a hand to the teapot, her aura brightening slightly, and steam curled from the spout.

As she poured each Sister a cup of tea, Maddie continued, "The most common form the Soul Magic takes is *Anam Fhios*, the Knowing Soul. All of us have experienced this *e'drai* in several lifetimes. It is the ability to see or feel the soul of another, to know their true soul."

Emma poured a dollop of milk in her cup, then leaned forward earnestly. "Sometimes the Soul Magic takes the form of *Aisling Teag M'hail*, the Dream Touch. When we carry it, we can communicate to others through dreams, touch or speak to their soul through dreaming."

Maddie nodded toward the house. "When we met Zerik, at the bazaar on the Silk Road – I held the Soul Magic then, *Anam Labhartha*, the Speaking Soul. I was able to speak directly to Zerik's soul, and my mate spoke back to me." She laid an earnest hand on

Rhiannon's. "In the dream you had, of Egypt, it sounds as though you were carrying *Anam Labhartha*."

Emma nodded. "I held *Anam Fhios* when I met Grayling. I could see his soul, see Thicket, the Fae half of his soul."

Maddie shook her head. "I'd hoped to save the discussion of Consorts for a while later, after you'd had time to adjust a bit better." She sipped her tea, looking almost embarrassed. "I was hoping you'd remember yourself first."

Emma spoke up. "And hoping Alexander – " Once again she silenced herself abruptly, after another of Maddie's warning glances.

Madeline continued, ignoring Emma. "The legends about the Sisters are clear. Every thousand years, one of us may choose a mate, a Consort. The Sister who chooses will be carrying the Soul Magic. It is said that when the last sister chooses, a new Circle will be created, a Circle of Six, which will be unbelievably powerful."

Maddie touched Rhiannon's hand. "It has been more than a thousand years since Emma Chose Grayling. You are the only Sister who has yet to Choose a Consort."

"And neither Maddie nor I are carrying the Soul Magic in this incarnation," Emma said.

"So," Maddie said, taking a deep breath, "you must be carrying the Soul Magic."

Rhiannon shook her head. "I can't see or feel anyone's soul, or talk to a soul, or send dreams."

Madeline frowned, setting down her teacup on the little table. "There can be no mistake." She looked back at Emma, then into Rhiannon's eyes. "Zerik said he sensed tremendous power in you. Your ability to connect with the Earth certainly may account for it, but I think there's something else. Something you haven't told us."

Rhiannon stood up and walked a few feet away from the canopy, finding comfort in the feel of the cool grass beneath her feet. She knew, knew what her soul could do. What she had done. "It's a terrible thing," she whispered.

"No *e'drai* is terrible. How it's used is what's important."

Rhiannon turned to look at Maddie and Emma, her Sisters who had become so dear to her, so quickly. She sat down in the grass, her face in her hands. "I think I used it for something terrible." She looked up into Maddie's face, her eyes haunted. "I killed my stepfather."

Maddie waited.

Rhiannon looked away. "He was molesting me. He was always touching me. And then he came into my room one night. He was going to ..." She stopped, took a breath. "I was just a kid," she looked at Maddie, pleading. "I bit him. I could taste his blood in my mouth. And then somehow I was inside him. I saw through his eyes, felt what he felt. It was disgusting, horrible." She shook her head, as if to shake loose the memory of those thoughts, feelings. Her face hardened and she frowned. "And so I pushed him out. Pushed everything that was him out. And then I was back in my own body, and he was lying on the floor, dead."

"The *Fola Teag M'hail*," Emma breathed, awestruck.

Maddie paled. "You carry the Blood Touch. Only once have either of us ever experienced it. Emma carried it, for a short incarnation."

Emma nodded, her normally sunny expression suddenly grave. "By tasting the blood, you can become another, join with their soul. Destroy it if you wish. Or absorb it into yourself."

"It is a breathtaking power, and requires great responsibility." Maddie looked grim.

Rhiannon tried to smile, laughed shakily. "Well, now I know we're all reincarnated. I don't have to feel so guilty about killing him now. He'll just be born into another body, right?"

Maddie shook her head. "No, honey. It's true that everyone reincarnates – at least, we think so, given that only aeternans remember – But you pushed him out of his body. You dispersed his soul. He is *mortaetun* – truly dead, his soul lost forever, never to reincarnate."

Rhiannon could only stare at her in horror.

Emma reached out a hand, as if to reassure her. "But he was *mal'neco*," Emma said. "A child molester, a demon. To send him to the winds was a kindness."

Rhiannon shook her head, suddenly overwhelmed with grief and fear. "Did you say I can absorb someone's soul?"

Maddie nodded. "The result is the same – that soul will never reincarnate again. But it is not *mortaetun*, dead. It would live within you."

Rhiannon was shaking now. "That's what he does. The man who's after me. The one who's *erim*. That's what he does. He absorbs people's souls." Stricken, she stared wild-eyed at Maddie. "You mean that's what I am? That's what I can do?"

With a sudden sense of awareness, Emma looked up then. Close by, standing amidst the Sentinel trees, she saw Alexander. His leaf-green eyes on Rhiannon, he looked so sad, as though he carried Rhiannon's sorrow, and indeed the sorrows of all the world.

TWENTY

"My lord." The page cleared his throat. *"Kir'dina* Alexander Lazarus." He held open the wide carved door to admit Alex.

Alexander sauntered casually into the office of Alvar Noriaki, *Kir'da* for the United States Caistra. The dark ruby carpet was dense and soft beneath his feet. One entire wall of the room featured windows set into the cliff face, offering a breathtaking view of the ocean and the rugged Lost Coast cliffs.

Alvar sat at the massive, gnarled-oak desk, rubbing his temples. His current Form was long and lean, bordering on skinny, an effect enhanced by his shimmering Fae-made formal long tunic and leggings. Today, his sharp features looked pale, drawn. A large, long-haired calico cat sat on the floor next to the desk, regarding Alex with emerald-eyed disinterest.

Alexander stopped before Alvar's desk, offering a brief *anam'sal*. *"Navtu,* brother." While Alvar was ruler of one of the most powerful Caistras in the world, he was also subject to Alexander, *Kir'dina* of his *Dinach,* House Zel'mori.

"*Navtu*, Alexander Lazarus." Alvar said, sitting up and brushing his long, blond hair out of his face, revealing pale, grey-green eyes. He stood stiffly, coming around the desk to press a dry, formal kiss to Alexander's cheek. "It is good to see you, Alex. It's been too long."

"I wish I were here to celebrate the Equinox and indulge in too much drink and *era*," Alex said with a smile, holding Alvar's gaze. "But you already know why I'm here, I imagine."

His jaw clenched, Alvar turned away, and Alex noticed the *Kir'da*'s hands shook slightly. From the floor, the cat leapt onto the surface of the desk, slipping past a large, ornate hourglass with black sands, picking her way delicately amongst the paperwork there, purring. Alvar reached out and stroked the cat's silky fur with long, tapered fingers.

Alex watched him take a deep breath, and when Alvar turned again to face his *Kir'dina*, he seemed visibly calmer, his cheeks taking on more color.

"Yes," Alvar said. "I know why you're here." He walked to a baroque walnut sideboard, lifting a crystal decanter. "Scotch?"

"Please."

Alvar poured two glasses, neat, handing one to Alex. They sipped the liquor in silence for a moment. Finally, Alvar spoke. "I can feel a Decision point coming, Alex."

Edward Angelis, the *Kir i'dai* – Supreme Ruler for all the Family – had sent Alexander to Alvar Noriaki for a reason. It was more than the fact that Daz Minoru was thought to be at large in the United States. There had been great argument and dissension among the dynasty leaders, and none could agree on how best to deal with Daz. So Alexander was sent to tell Alvar all they knew, to receive his suggestions and thoughts.

Alvar Noriaki's primary *e'drai* was tremendously powerful. He possessed the ability to sense when a Decision was required, and knowledge of the correct course of action – even if he did not fully understand the reasons or logic behind the determination, or have any inkling as to the final outcome. When he judged a Decision point was at hand, his action was never wrong.

It was a formidable gift, but it also meant that occasionally the leader made judgments that seemed random or nonsensical at best, dangerous and deadly at worst, decisions the rightness of which periodically appeared only on reexamination, sometimes centuries later.

And yet, while life is full of choices, the vast majority are variable, depending on constantly changing factors beyond the control of any one individual. Only rarely, then, did Alvar sense a true Decision point, a choice written in the heart of the Story.

Alex frowned. "Edward seeks your input, but not necessarily your immediate action."

Alvar shook his head. "I will offer my thoughts, but I feel a Decision, dimly, approaching me. It is my call to make." He looked up at Alex, his eyes pained. "You and Edward have involved me in this matter. I have to follow what choices, if any, speak to me. My *e'drai* can be a burden, Alex."

Alex nodded. "You'll do what's right, I have faith in that." He watched as the cat jumped down soundlessly from the desk, padding over to wind affectionately around Alvar's legs.

Alvar took a deep breath. "You've come to me about the demon, Daz Minoru. He's been in the United States for many years now." Alvar sipped his scotch. "He's been stealing souls for a long time. I have been unable to do anything." He looked up at Alex, his expression bleak. "That was a Decision made long ago. But he's started attacking Family now. There is some concern as to what will happen if he manages to absorb someone with a Sidhe soul." He shook his head. "His *e'drai* is frightening, more powerful than I've ever heard of."

"It's worse than that," Alex said grimly. "Edward has suspected – for more than a century now – that Daz has developed some kind of relationship with The Guard. We've finally been able to confirm it."

Alvar stared at him in surprise. "How is that possible? Why would *La Guardia* ever choose to align themselves with Family? We represent everything they fear."

"He can offer the monks the ultimate Honor Death. He can ensure they will be *mortaetun*, never to reincarnate, never to become aeternan." Alex shrugged, the casual gesture belied by his somber expression. "We don't know whether he destroys them, or absorbs them into himself, as he's done with others. If the latter, then he may also possess detailed knowledge of The Guard, and whatever the Dead Monks may know about us."

Alvar paced to the wall of windows, hands clasped behind his back, pensively looking out over the sheer drop to the sea. "And yet they must hate him, as they hate us. He is still aeternan, no matter what he's promised them. It must be an uneasy alliance. Perhaps we can use that, somehow."

Alexander shook his head. "There is still much we don't understand. But we do know that somehow he's ensured a steadfast loyalty amongst the *Monaco Morto*. They'd follow him to the gates of Hades and beyond." He frowned, cleared his throat. "It is said some *liath* follow him, also."

Alvar cast him a sidelong glance, his eyes apologetic.

Alex gulped the last of his scotch, setting the glass on the sideboard. "Edward thinks that to fight him, we'll have to gather a group of powerful Eldest, if we can find those with the requisite *e'drai*. Basically, manufacture a Circle, if we can."

Alvar looked up sharply. "You don't agree."

Alex turned, pretending to study a 16th century portrait of Edward Angelis hanging above the ornate sideboard. "Well, I thought I did, until I came here. But now I don't know if I can be objective anymore."

"Oh Gods," Alvar breathed, coming close. "Your woman."

"She's not my woman," Alex growled irritably. "Not for lack of trying," he grumbled under his breath. He frowned. "You see too much, Alvar."

Alvar sighed, meandering back to his desk, followed by the big calico cat. "I understand the pain of seeing the truth in a thing, while all around others are blind and need convincing." He thoughtfully stroked the animal's ears. "Somehow, she is *divya spava*. Isn't she."

Alex threw up his hands. "I don't know. Maybe." His shoulders sagged, and he looked away. "Yes," he whispered. "But she doesn't even remember who she is, Alvar. She's fearful, doesn't trust or believe in herself. She's like neonate. We can't ask it of her. She could end up *mortaetun*. Or worse."

"What's worse than having one's soul lost forever?"

Alex grimaced, looking down at his own shadowed aura. "Being aware of it."

"Hold still."

"I *am* holding still!"

Zerik laughed. "You three couldn't hold still if you were nailed down." Standing behind a large canvas on an easel, he waved a glistening paintbrush. "Maddie, your head was tilted to the left — no, just slightly — there." He nodded, looking back to his canvas, his expression intent as he daubed paint on the surface.

The three Sisters were lying beneath the broad, circular stone canopy which sheltered the tower balcony just outside of Emma's room. Preferring natural light for his art, Zerik had dragged a wide mattress onto the terrace, draping it with white linen. The intricately carved stone roof diffused the morning sunlight, while the slightest breath of air shimmered with the tinkling, rippling song of the windchimes festooning the edges of the pavilion.

Reclining together against downy pillows, the nude Sisters looked up at Zerik with sensual, heavy-lidded gazes, houris, sirens, nymphs. Maddie lay on her left side, head cradled on her outstretched arm, her flaming hair like a cloak over her shoulder. Emma was on her back, her curly blond head pillowed on Maddie's breast, while Rhiannon lay on her stomach at Emma's side, ebony curls strewn in charming disorder against Emma's pale flesh, her head resting on Emma's slightly rounded belly.

"Emma, move your hand back up against Maddie's breast," Zerik said.

"Why don't you just take a photo, and paint us from that?" Rhiannon wanted to know.

Zerik grimaced. "It's not the same. It just isn't, for some reason. Now hold still."

335

Rhiannon held still, looking soberly out into the blue sky beyond the shelter of the canopied balcony. "Where's Alex?" she asked shyly, ineffectually trying to sound casual.

"Alexander decided to go on up to the Caistra early, to have his meeting with the *Kir'da*," Maddie answered. Her voice took on a trace of bitterness. "I believe he said he was also going to the Lost and Found, to start a search for Eva's — David Anthony's — wife. They've been married for several incarnations, I'm told. David — " her voice trembled slightly. "Well, he's obviously not happy here." She sniffed, her tone abruptly becoming breezy, resolutely casual. "Anyhow, Alex wanted to get business out of the way, before the drive down to Santa Cruz for the Prodigies show."

Casting a brief, concerned glance at Maddie, Emma pasted on a bright smile. "I can't wait!" she enthused, sitting up to rest on her elbows. "This is going to be so fun!"

"Lie down, Emma," Zerik commanded. "How am I supposed to paint you women if you all keep moving around?" He winked at Rhiannon, his stern expression dissolving into his dazzling grin.

"All right," Emma muttered, flopping back down onto the mattress. "Did Grayling go with Alex?"

"No, he's gone to Eureka to rent a big van for the drive to Santa Cruz," Zerik said, his eyes focused on his work. "Our SUV just isn't enough anymore. You know, we're really going to have to buy one of those vans." He looked up over the top of his painting, a wicked glint in his eye. "Too many kids, too many wives."

Ducking as Maddie threw a pillow at him, Zerik laughed, holding his canvas steady. "Hold still," he said, automatically.

Rhiannon smiled at their play, but only half paying attention. Her cheek against the warmth of Emma's belly, she closed her eyes, as though drifting on the warm fall breeze, the delicate song of the windchimes. Her thoughts wandered on a darker path, to the afternoon in the Sister's Circle, when she'd learned she carried *Fola Teag M'hail*, the Blood Touch. The day she found out she was a murderer, a soul-stealer, no better than the *erim* man who stalked her. She *was* a monster, no matter how Maddie tried to reassure her.

"You're thinking too hard," Maddie murmured within Rhiannon's mind.

Her cheek heated against Emma's skin, Rhiannon opened her eyes. "I thought you couldn't read my thoughts," she answered aloud.

"I can't. But I can tell you're worried, Sister."

Rhiannon sighed heavily. "Okay, yeah, so I'm worried." Absently, she sifted her fingers through the dark blond curls at the apex of Emma's thighs. "I've always been different, Maddie. But now I find out I'm something else – something weird, dangerous."

"You're just special," Emma said, shifting her hips slightly at Rhiannon's touch. "Maybe you're meant for something more. Like Spava, in the fairy tale. I mean, you have power that can help you fight evil."

Rhiannon shuddered. "Just because I have the power doesn't mean I could actually do it," she said. "I'm not a hero, I'll tell you that right now. Like, what if I don't want to be special?" She frowned, closing her eyes briefly, the whole idea painful. "What would have happened if Spava had told the villagers no? That he just wanted to fish, and be left alone?"

"But the Gods chose Spava," Zerik said, looking up from his painting. "Somehow, the Gods would have ensured he would fulfill his destiny."

Rhiannon looked up at him, suddenly blinking back tears. "Whether he wanted to or not?"

Maddie spoke up. "We all follow our roles in the Story. And somehow, even without our knowing it, our destinies become our choices." She offered a small smile. "Or our choices become our destinies."

Emma reached down and stroked Rhiannon's hair. "The *s'lai*, the historians, say whenever the Family is threatened by a great evil, the Gods will send someone, *divya spava*, to fight the darkness."

"Well, I'm glad I'm not Spava," Rhiannon muttered. "I spend most of my time just fighting myself."

Maddie laughed, but over Rhiannon's head she caught Zerik's eye, giving an infinitesimal shake of her head.

Zerik tapped his paintbrush against the easel, as an orchestra conductor might rap his baton. "Now, damn it all, will everyone please *lie still*," he said, and Rhiannon could tell he was trying to tease, but it sounded overbright, affected.

Still, with a communal sigh, the three Sisters shifted as one, returning with easy, elegant perfection to their original positions, flesh pale, freckled, creamy and tawny dark against the fine linen. Frowning in concentration, Zerik once more applied his brush, the paint trailing a vivid wet path on the canvas.

Gathered together, the Ciatri *dzina* was loud even on a normal basis, but today they exceeded their own standards, as six children and six adults piled noisily into the big white rented van parked on the gravel driveway. Children crowed over window seats, others complained of having to sit next to "*her*," while the air was rent with the occasional cry of "he pinched me," and still more whining that someone was hungry or had to go to the bathroom. Adults jabbered about how best to strap luggage to the roof, who would sit with the children, where best to put the paper towels, snacks, and juice boxes, who would be in the front seat, if they would take turns driving, and if so, who would go first. Given that the *dzina* was going to a kind of circus, they certainly resembled one.

The typical noise level had increased exponentially when Grayling initially returned with the 12-passenger van – considering there were 14 adults and children to transport. An argument broke out amongst the adults. Despite dearly wanting to attend the Prodigies show, Lyds and Robbie at first offered to remain home – David Anthony had refused to attend, and the couple thought to keep him company. But the idea was immediately quashed by all five horrified parents, who expected the *anu'giao* to help manage their little horde of children while in Santa Cruz. Then Alex suggested driving down in his own car, with Rhiannon – alone – and while almost everyone, especially Maddie, seemed to think this was a stupendous idea, Grayling was furious and unusually vocal about it. Hanging out of the van doors and windows, the children supported him, offering plaintive, unsolicited opinions, making it clear they wanted "Mama Re'nannon" and Alex to ride in the back of the van with them.

In the end, unsurprisingly, Alexander got his way, and a scowling Grayling drove the van, muttering to himself.

"Is this safe?"

Alex turned to look at Rhiannon in surprise. "Of course it's safe." They had just passed through Santa Rosa, driving down highway 101 in Alexander's little green Aston Martin DB6 sports car. "I'm even doing the speed limit," he added, somewhat defensively.

Rhiannon laughed, clenching her shaking hands in her lap. "No, that's not what I meant." She looked out the side window, watching the green hills skimming by in a blur. She swallowed convulsively. "I meant, is it safe for me to be away from the house? With the monks after me, and that *erim* man?" She bit her lip. "Zerik said they wouldn't dare try anything within 100 miles of the Caistra. But we're going way south of that, aren't we?"

His eyes on the highway, Alex frowned slightly. "Yes, Santa Cruz is nearly 300 miles from the Caistra. But no one — especially me — would have allowed you to come if we didn't think it would be safe for you to do so." He glanced at Rhiannon. "For one thing, I don't think The Guard knows where you'll be. And you're going to be with your husbands and wives, and me — damned powerful aeternans, if I do say so myself." Alex looked back to the road. "It would take an *esera*, an army, of Dead Monks to take us." He reached out and laid a hand on her knee. "Besides, the Prodigies perform within a Fairy Ring, so we'll have that additional level of protection."

"A Fairy Ring," Rhiannon repeated in disbelief. "Like all those superstitions about rings of mushrooms in the grass, and fairies dancing at midnight."

Alex grinned. "Oh, they're very real. Though a Fairy Ring is more like an orb, or a bubble," he clarified. "It covers not only the ground, but the air as well, an arc of earth below. Even someone in an airplane, or viewing the area by satellite, would only see what they expect to, the oblivi world."

339

Rhiannon stared at him, frowning. "But can't the monks get into the Fairy Ring, too? I mean, if they know it's there."

Alex shook his head. "Monks may be able to see our auras, but they are still oblivi. Only those with multiple *fainna* — or those welcome in the Fae worlds — can enter a Ring. And even they have to focus on it, believe it."

"So we're going to the Fae World?"

He smiled at her bemused expression. "Not exactly," Alex said. "The Fairy Rings occupy two places at the same time, oblivi and Sidhe. I guess it's a bit like twilight — not exactly day anymore, but not quite night either. Both aeternans and Fae come and go in these kinds of Rings."

Rhiannon sat quietly for a while and digested this information, watching the highway. Then a thought occurred. "You make it sound like there's more than one type of Fairy Ring."

Alex deftly turned the steering wheel into a curve, the little car responding to his touch with effortless precision. "There are a handful of Rings like the Prodigies use, where aeternans and Fae move together. But there are hundreds of Fairy Rings throughout this world, and many others besides, in which only the Sidhe may travel, or one bearing a Fae talisman." Unconsciously, he twisted a large ring on his finger, which bore a sparkling cut stone the color of new leaves, like his eyes. "But without an escort, even one carrying a talisman is in danger of being hopelessly lost in the Fae Worlds."

Rhiannon clenched her hands together, her eyes on the gleaming ring he wore. Grayling had told her stories of what it was like to Travel between Worlds, the dangers for a Traveling soul. Risking one's soul sounded horrific, and yet the idea of Traveling with one's physical body as well seemed somehow even more disturbing, the idea of being utterly lost, body and spirit.

They drove in silence for a while, the green sports car smoothly following the turns in the road. Rhiannon kicked off her sandals and leaned back against the tan leather seat, one bare foot propped on the windowsill, her toes flexing in the air out the open window. She closed her eyes, trying to invoke a brief sense of peace, stifling the omnipresent murky fear and self-doubt.

It was a long drive, more than four hours, and having Alex all to herself was a kind of secret, tremulous pleasure. They talked of their thoughts and beliefs, dreams both tangible and ethereal, desires, pleasures, the minutia of existence. He told her his favorite color was blue, the azure shade of a flawless sky over a sugar-sand beach. He laughed sympathetically when Rhiannon told him about her dreams as a young girl, waking up with embarrassingly adult memories, aching, delicious adult passions, and no idea how to cope with any of it.

As they drove, she peeked at him when he wasn't looking, admiring his dark hair threaded with silver at the temples, his firm jaw, the way his long fingers gripped the steering wheel so surely. His whole demeanor seemed relaxed, confident, his multi-layered aura shining vivid bright despite the mist of darkness.

Alex didn't look at Rhiannon, if he could help it, because he had already memorized every line of her golden brown face, the full lips and endless brown eyes, her cascade of dark hair, her glowing aura. To look at her was to experience a kind of torment he'd felt for far too long.

"How long have I known you?" Rhiannon asked, as if reading his thoughts.

"Over 1,500 years, now," Alex answered, his eyes on the road. A look almost like pain crossed his features, and he glanced at her briefly. "I'm sorry you can't remember."

Rhiannon avoided his gaze, looking out the window. "I can remember some things. I told you before – I've had dreams about you – well, memories. And we're always dancing – in ballrooms, or country dances around bonfires. In taverns. At festivals. Everywhere."

He grinned, the dimple in his cheek evident. "Yes, we do a lot of dancing, *ma moitié*." Eyes on the highway, he reached out and touched her hand, his fingers warm, his aura blending with hers. "There will be dancing at the Equinox ball, of course. Will you dance with me?"

"Yes, I'd love to," she murmured, looking away to hide her smile.

"There may even be dancing at the Prodigies show, depending on the *e'drai* of the performers. I went to an exhibition in the 18th

341

century where they held a complete formal ball – one of the Prodigies was able to create the sound of a full orchestra with his mind. It was truly impressive."

Rhiannon turned in her seat to look at him, tucking a wayward strand of hair behind her ear. "So what exactly *is* a Prodigies show?"

Alexander laughed. "I know you don't remember who you are – but sometimes it's still hard to believe you don't know these things, that you don't remember who *we* are – your Family. The Prodigies have been world renowned performers since the early 17th century."

He explained that the Prodigies were aeternans who were born into unusual Forms, either physically or mentally disabled in some manner. "For the single lifetime in which they bear this Form, the Universe grants them tremendous power, unbelievably amazing *e'drai*," Alex said. He added that the Prodigies show had evolved over the years into something like the circus sideshows of the late 19th century, but the so-called freaks had always been celebrated, admired, appreciated.

"You mean we're going to be gawking at disabled people?" Rhiannon was horrified. "That's terrible, to stare at people with disabilities."

Alex frowned, shaking his head. "I understand why you could think so. But that's the oblivi point of view – and it's why most of the old sideshows died out." He glanced away from the road for a moment, offering Rhiannon a wry smile. "Certain uncomfortable oblivi decided it was cruel or shameful to ogle at those with physical differences, rather than honor and revere them, as Family does. They didn't understand that a good many of the oblivi freaks *enjoyed* being stared at, enjoyed being stars, having a way to make a good income. Most of all, they loved having a good life, traveling with others who saw them for who they truly were, saw beyond the physical. The freaks, the human oddities, even those able-bodied carnival talkers and others who traveled with these shows, thought more like aeternans – they saw past physical bodies, to the souls underneath."

Alex paused, passing a semitruck as he turned into a curve, then straightening out the little car. "Some aeternan Prodigies appear physically sound, but have schizophrenia or bipolar disorder, mental illnesses that bring with them great power. Others are much like the freaks of old; there are often conjoined or parasitic twins, little people and giants, people with all kinds of physical deformities – like your daughter, Missy, with her wing-like arm. But we come to gaze not at their physical bodies – though they, too, are unashamedly of interest, for all Forms are extraordinary and beautiful – but bodies are merely temporary. We come to the shows to appreciate their miraculous *e'drai*, the gifts that accompany their unique Forms. We come to gawk at the magic." He grinned. "See, they're not really freaks – they're Prodigies."

Rhiannon nodded abstractedly, staring unseeing through the windshield, remembering. Somehow, she could almost taste her stepfather's blood, metallic and hot, on her tongue. *I'm a freak*, she thought. She'd always been abnormal, weird, different. It seemed painfully ironic that amongst her new Family, the freaks weren't monsters at all, but she still was.

Santa Cruz, California, is utterly unique, almost – but not quite – Fae. At once earthy and enchanted, the town floats like a pale jewel on the edge of Monterey Bay. Dolphins dance in the cerulean waters beyond the sandy shores, and vast whales move groaning and singing through the deeps. In this sheltered beach community, Monarch butterflies have their breeding grounds, thousands fluttering brilliant mandarin and pumpkin against the luxuriant greenery. Eucalyptus trees tower over beaches, shedding golden bark, while on the lush hillsides giant redwoods soar majestically into the perfect blue sky.

Though only 70 miles south of San Francisco, and a 45-minute drive from the city of San Jose and, to the south, Monterey, Santa Cruz is somehow insulated from these places, as if not quite real, separated from the hectic world swarming by, barely touching the seaside town. Santa Cruz is a town of escape, temporary and permanent, as people from these other places, other worlds, come to elude their frenetic lives.

Santa Cruz is a college town, and the cafes are brimming with young students, passionately discussing literature, debating matters of science, sociology, lust, and other vital schools of thought. Lesbians walk down the streets, holding hands. Organic grocery stores and nude beaches abound. Men who have been cheerfully homeless since 1968 sing on streetcorners, strumming acoustic guitars decorated with rainbow stickers, while hats spangled with change lie before them on the sidewalk. The natives, those born in Santa Cruz, carry a kind of gently smug pride, unable to imagine living anywhere else.

After a four-hour drive from their nest, the Ciatri *dzina* settled into a cozy bed-and-breakfast hotel on the cliff overlooking the ocean, having booked all seven of the available rooms months before. The view of the water was spectacular, and they could hear the sea lions barking from the wooden pilings beneath the wharf. On the sands beyond was the Santa Cruz Beach Boardwalk, a colorful amusement park with a long, rich history. The curving spine and white support beams of the Giant Dipper roller coaster defined the park, arcing into the clear sky. The old wooden coaster was surrounded by vivid, colorful rides, everything from a water flume to a Ferris wheel, spinning and flying rides, carnival games, booths selling sticky sweet cotton candy and kettle corn. A great dome covered an original Looff carousel, the brightly painted jeweled horses elegant and delightful, beckoning riders to reach out for a brass ring.

The Prodigies show wasn't until 8 o'clock that night, so the *dzina* went their separate ways for the afternoon. Grayling, Zerik, and Alex rounded up the impatient children, taking them for an early trip to the Boardwalk and a game of miniature golf. Lyds and Robbie, who had agreed to help with the children during the show later that evening, took the afternoon off to meander on the path bordering the cliffs.

The three Sisters went to the Pacific Garden Mall, a tree-lined avenue of inviting shops and galleries. Their first stop was Bookshop Santa Cruz, a well-stocked independent bookstore, where Emma had agreed to sign copies of her latest romance novel, *The Pirate Who Loved Me*.

" 'The Pirate Who Loved Me' ?" Rhiannon laughed as they entered the bookstore. She flipped the book over to read the back cover. " 'Set sail for romance.' Really, Emma?"

"Her last book was titled 'Laird of my Heart,' " Maddie murmured, and Rhiannon rolled her eyes.

Emma sniffed, nose in the air. "I never claimed to write great literature. Just a damned good read with lots of sex."

"And they sell like bibles at a revival," Maddie said. "But honestly," she added with a wicked smile, "I don't think it's the 'good read' part that does it."

While Emma signed copies of her book, Maddie and Rhiannon wandered through the stacks, beautiful tall oak shelves stocked with all manner of books, from well-known authors and classics to self-published tomes by local writers. Rhiannon closed her eyes, breathing deeply. "I love the smell of new books."

The store was crowded that weekend, including many glowing aeternans undoubtedly in town for the Prodigies show. Given they were in such a public place, those aeternans who noticed the Sisters could only offer a respectful nod, the *anam'ta*. Rhiannon found it strangely comforting to be surrounded by Family in this oblivi place.

Maddie joined the lengthy line for the register, intending to buy a book on the history of the Boardwalk. "I met Arthur Looff briefly at a party, after we'd first moved to Northern California," she commented to Rhiannon. "He designed the roller coaster, in 1924, I think it was. But I never knew him well, and I certainly never knew his father – he's the one who designed the carousel." Maddie shrugged. "Anyhow, I think oblivi history is fascinating, especially when they manage to create such beautiful things in only one lifetime."

Standing in line with Maddie, Rhiannon casually looked around the store. Her attention was arrested by a man standing near the door, his back to her. He had a tall, rangy build, with a shock of sandy-blond hair. "Greg," Rhiannon breathed, wide-eyed. Unable to see his face, she couldn't be sure, but there was something about the way the man stood, his posture, his body structure, that made her almost certain she was looking at her old friend from Kansas City. Rhiannon waved a hand over her head, as if somehow that could get his attention. "Greg!" she called out, raising her voice slightly above the murmur of the crowd in the bookstore. The man didn't turn. "Greg!" she cried, louder this time.

Still, the man didn't turn, instead making for the door. Maddie turned, surprised, as Rhiannon frantically pushed through the crowd, trying to follow the man as he passed through the glass door and walked away. "Excuse me," Rhiannon murmured to a woman as she squeezed by. "Pardon me," she said to an older man as she brushed past him. Finally, she made it to the door, and running outside, looked left and right. But the man was gone.

Out of breath, Maddie appeared on the sidewalk next to Rhiannon. "What was that all about?"

"I thought I saw my friend Greg," Rhiannon said, shoulders slumped, defeated. "I guess I was wrong."

"Try not to worry about it, sweet," the older woman said, laying a comforting hand on Rhiannon's shoulder. Maddie looked up the street with her sharp blue eyes. They had to get back to their husbands. Now. She hoped Rhiannon had indeed been wrong, or else they were all in serious, deadly trouble.

Eternal Tales: The Fur Child

Once in the time almost before memory, a loving couple lived in a snug cottage on a great mountain, their door surrounded with vines of roses, their garden luxuriant. They had everything they could want, except a child of their own.

Every morning, the woman went to the top of the mountain, and every evening, her husband went to the base of the mountain, where they asked the Gods to bless them with a baby.

But for many, many years, their hopes went unanswered.

One day, on her way back down the mountain, the sorrowing wife saw a strange, black-furred creature worrying something small in its jaws. Flapping her apron, she shooed the brute away, causing it to release its prey. When she came close, the woman realized she had saved one of the Sidhe, a tiny green creature with enormous eyes and tiny, sharply pointed ears. "Ask anything of me, and you shall have it," the Fae being said.

"I want a child of my own," the woman answered.

The Fae being shook its head. "I cannot make flowers grow on stone," it said. "I will give you a Sidhe child, if you promise to care for it, no matter how it may look, or what it may do."

Eagerly, the woman promised.

"Then you shall have your babe by morning," the tiny Sidhe creature said, before vanishing amidst the meadow grasses and flowers.

The couple were up all night, so excited were they. And though they heard not a sound, at dawn they found a small bundle on the doorstep. Their joy was tempered when they pulled back the blanket, discovering a sleeping baby covered in rich silky brown fur, like a beast.

"It's a creature, grotesque," the husband whispered, horrified.

"He is our child, and we will love him anyway," the wife said firmly, carrying the baby into the cottage.

As the child grew older, he began to scratch himself as an animal would, using both hands and feet to scratch his thick brown fur. The couple used an herbal salve to soothe their son's itchy skin, slathering it over the child day and night, trying to stop the terrible scratching and itching.

"He's a demon," the husband whispered to his wife. "An ugly beast. We would have been better off without any child at all."

"No!" his wife cried, horrified. They looked to the furry child, forlornly trying to scratch itself. "I promised the Fae I would love him no matter how he looks, no matter what he does." She stared at her husband, realization dawning. "We must let him scratch, no matter how terrible his itch seems."

Her husband shook his head, dubious.

"I promised, no matter what he does, that we would love him." The wife threw away the jar of salve.

And the furred child scratched, and scratched, and scratched, until one day his mother saw a glimmer of something pale beneath the boy's fur. As he scratched, whole sections of fur tore away, revealing glistening, shining flesh beneath. By morning, the child had shed all of the silky brown fur, becoming a beautiful, exquisite Sidhe being, with glowing, smooth skin and delicate, iridescent wings, shining blonde curls and huge eyes the color of summer grasses.

The husband never doubted again, and the couple raised their beautiful son until he was ready to fly away and build a life for himself.

And they lived ever after.

TWENTY-ONE

The night midway at the Boardwalk was vibrant, fueled with a sense of excitement and anticipation. Brilliant electric lights and glossy colorful signs assailed the senses, the air filled with the scent of cinnamon and popcorn, and all around the crush of bodies as the dense crowd moved through lines for the rides, or wandered past T-shirt shops and games of chance bedecked with plush stuffed animals.

Here and there, between the rides and concessions, cement stairs led down to the wide pale beach below, the moonlight dazzling on the ocean, the odor of salt water blending with cotton candy and hot dogs. The roar of the waves crashing on the shore seemed dim against vast grinding motors running amusement rides, circus music, the gleeful shrieks and laughter of children, incessant shouting and conversation.

Dressed for a cool evening at the beach, oblivi in sweatshirts and flip-flops mingled unaware with similarly attired aeternans. To Maddie's relief, while Rhiannon surreptitiously searched the crowd, she never saw the man from the bookstore who looked so like her friend, Greg.

Near the wildly swinging Pirate Ship and Sky Glider were broad steps like bleachers, leading down to the sand, and a large concrete bandstand beyond. While performances at the Boardwalk bandstand were usually limited to the summer months, on this night a special show was planned, featuring a highly popular local band – scheduled to perform at 8 p.m.

"So while the oblivi are lining up for their show, we'll be lining up for ours," Zerik told Rhiannon. "In the confusion, no one will notice that some of the people in line vanish when we reach the sand."

Rhiannon stood gripping a metal railing, looking out at the bandstand, watching the performers and crew setting up for their show. "So, there's a Fairy Ring out there?" she asked dubiously.

Maddie nodded. "Actually, it starts at the beach at the foot of the stairs, and extends past the bandstand, near the stairs across from the Haunted Castle."

Rhiannon frowned, trying to imagine it. "It looks like there's nothing out there but sand."

Alex came up behind her, putting a warm hand on her waist. "It looks that way, but believe me, the Prodigies' crew are right out there, just as busy setting up for their show as these folks are for theirs." He glanced at Maddie, then back to Rhiannon. "Do you want to see? We could go in now. I've got a friend who's performing tonight."

Rhiannon looked uncertainly at Maddie. "Do you think it would be okay?"

Maddie waved a casual hand. "Go ahead. You're safer in the Ring anyhow."

Wearing a supremely satisfied grin, Alex tucked Rhiannon's hand in the crook of his arm, sauntering up the midway. They threaded through the crowd, past the kiddie Jet Copters and Speedway and the splendid antique carousel. Across from the Haunted Castle was a stairway and foot-wash for those coming up from the beach.

Alex halted at the top of the stairs, looking down at Rhiannon. "Okay, we're about to enter the Ring. Concentrate."

"I don't know what to concentrate on," Rhiannon answered nervously.

Alex smiled. "Just hold my hand, and say it with me. 'We're going to the show.' "

Rhiannon nodded, chanting with him obediently, "We're going to the show, we're going to the show." Intoning the words, Alex led her down the stairs to the beach below. As they stepped onto the sand, the very air shimmered around them, and Rhiannon felt as though her skin, her aura, seemed to stretch, expand for a moment.

Suddenly, the darkened oceanfront was awash in light and sound, and she was confronted by an enormous, long, oval-shaped tent, which stretched back almost to the bandstand, the roof delineated with round, bright show lights. Industrious aeternans were erecting a framework of metal poles in front of the tent, while others were hanging immense colorful banners from the completed sections of the structure. Still more shining men and women were putting the finishing touches on a broad platform next to the ticket booth, draping the wooden construct with red- and white-striped canvas, glittering with gold stars along the top edge. The tent itself rested on a carefully laid network of wood planks, raising the pavilion above the beach, and creating a solid floor over the sand.

Rhiannon stood staring, open-mouthed. At her side, Alex chuckled. "C'mon," he said, taking her hand. He led her past the partially constructed metal edifice in front of the tent, and a freshly hung banner easily eight feet across depicting a bald man called Bhava Moon, his skin glistering pale, eyes closed, and what looked like ghosts sparkling and swirling around his slender form.

In front of the tall ticket booth, a burly roustabout looked up, and seeing Alex, straightened and performed the *anam'sal*. "How can I help you, lord?" he asked, glancing at Rhiannon, then bowing to her as well.

Alex returned the bow with a nod, the *anam'ta*. "Is Tommy free?"

The man, a jovial medius with a mop of curly dark hair, grinned, indicating the tent with a grubby thumb. "Yeah, he's around back, in the cook tent. Show's not for another 45 minutes or so."

"Tommy is *liath*, like me," Alex explained to Rhiannon as they walked around behind the canvas show tent. "He spent a lifetime a prisoner of The Guard."

Rhiannon came to an abrupt stop, staring at him. "Zerik told me they do terrible things to people."

Alex nodded, his green eyes pained. "Not everyone who is *liath* lost a bit of their soul to The Guard, but many have. Tommy is a good man, but he's a bit high-strung. He believes The Guard are still after him — and who knows? He may be right. His *e'drai* is very powerful. That's alluring to The Guard." Alex reached out with gentle fingers, touching Rhiannon's cheek. "It's part of why they want you."

Rhiannon shivered at his touch, but only partly from fear.

Alex caught up her hand again. "Let's go see Tommy."

Behind the long show tent was a smaller, but nonetheless good-sized rectangular tent, with a metal ventilation pipe protruding from the canvas roof. Alex pushed back the flap. Inside was a titanic steel commercial stove, a refrigerator and freezer, and several tables, the largest with room for 12. A little, white-haired man sat with his back to them at the large table, perched on a red plastic child's booster seat, swinging his feet, and playing cribbage with a man swathed with tattoos, including his face. Both glowed with many *fainna*.

At the other end of the table, luminous with the multi-layered aura of the Eldest, sat a microcephalic man wearing a baggy magenta and tangerine floral-print dress, with a bushy tuft of hair on top of his otherwise rather pointed bald head. He was drawing pictures with crayons, smiling happily and humming to himself. As Rhiannon watched in surprise, one of the crayon images, a crudely-drawn butterfly, peeled away from the paper of its own accord, transforming into a genuine, exquisitely colored butterfly. The lustrous creature darted and danced in the air around the man's head for a minute or so, before fading into nothingness.

"15-2, 15-4, and a pair is 6," the tattooed man was saying, laying down his cards.

"19," the little man said in disgust, slapping down his cards on the table.

The tattooed man looked up, saw Alex and Rhiannon. He stood, cupping his hands and offering them the *anam'sal*.

"*Zanav tu*," Alex said, coming forward. "I'm Alexander Lazarus — Alex — here to see Tommy Akhila." He nodded toward the little man, who by this time had turned to look at the visitors. For a moment, the man froze, a look of unadulterated panic on his face.

"You," Rhiannon breathed. Alex's friend, Tommy, was the same glowing little man she'd seen in the mental ward at St. Michael's Hospital in Kansas City – it felt like a thousand years ago, now. He looked much the same: perhaps 60 years old, his leather-tanned face deeply wrinkled, his hair a frizzy cloud of white. A neonate, the man had four thin *fainna*, but he was also *liath*, a mist of darkness smeared into the gold.

Alex came forward. "*Navtu*, Tommy, it's good to see you." But at the frightened look on his friend's face as he continued to stare at Rhiannon, Alex frowned, concerned, looking quizzically from Rhiannon's shocked expression to Tommy, and back again. "Is everything all right? Have you two met?"

Flustered, Rhiannon cleared her throat, finally managing to choke out, "We were in the hospital together."

"You are friends with Alexander?" The little man asked her, his eyes sharp, suspicious, his features grim.

Rhiannon nodded. "Y-yes." Impulsively, she took a step forward, arms out, entreating, recalling that moment in the hospital when she'd finally *tried*, tried to reach out for once, tried to understand – only to frighten him off. "I won't hurt you. I would never have hurt you."

Brow furrowed, unsure of exactly what was happening, Alex put a reassuring arm around Rhiannon. "Tommy, Rhiannon is a special friend – one of the three Sisters. She's good Family."

Rhiannon looked up at Alex, grateful and yet pleading for understanding. All in a rush, the words tumbling over one another, she explained about seeing Tommy in the psych ward, how she'd tried *looking* at him, seeing the color and shape of his emotions, and how he'd been afraid, run from her. Alex squeezed her shoulder in wordless compassion.

"I can feel when someone uses *e'drai*," Tommy said gruffly, his faded blue eyes on Rhiannon. "I couldn't be sure of you. I thought you were one of *Dinach* Ano'fiarr, or working with The Guard." He shuddered, his hands turning over and over one another, a nervous habit. "I was running from

353

the monks, when they threw me in that hospital. I guess they thought I was crazy. Oblivi don't believe in Dead Monks."

Unbidden, an image burst wide in Rhiannon's mind, the bald, emaciated monk from her visit to Colma with Zerik. The eyes, black and soulless beneath the triangle tattoo, lingered for a moment before she was able to force the thought away. "I believe in monks," she whispered. "I wish I didn't."

Tommy awkwardly scrambled down from his chair, walking over to stand before Rhiannon. The little man was perhaps only 36 inches tall. He reached out and touched Rhiannon's hand, his darkened aura blending with her own shining *fainna*. "I'm sorry. I didn't know who you were." He cupped his hands in front of his belly, giving her the *anam'sal*. "It is an honor to meet the Sister."

"It's an honor to meet you, too," Rhiannon murmured, returning the gesture, blinking back tears. A moment from her entire screwed-up life, something wrong had been made right. Wiping her eyes, she glanced up at Alex. "Tommy mentioned Ano'fiarr. Aren't they one of the aeternan Houses? Why would anyone be afraid of them?"

Alex frowned. "There are those who don't believe the *liath* should live amongst others. You saw how David Anthony – Eva – responded to me. Some *dinachs* would go further than simple prejudice or segregation. They would destroy us, if they can."

Rhiannon stared at him, horrified, but Alex merely shrugged resignedly. "Not all who are shadowed walk a dark path. But ignorance is the pernicious curse of mankind, oblivi and aeternan alike. Unfortunately, you'll be experiencing aeternan politics firsthand at the Equinox Ball, at the Caistra."

Rhiannon was spared further ruminations on the Caistra, the Equinox Ball, and the nature of auras, brought back to the present by the newly eager friendship of Tommy Akhila. Tommy introduced the tattooed man, Van Asalo, an older *medius* who was the Talker for the Prodigies' show, gathering crowds and introducing acts. About 6 feet tall and well-muscled, with his *e'drai*, Van was able to speak within the minds of spectators, the way Maddie and Zerik could. Rhiannon was fascinated with his tattoos, which shifted and moved across his skin, as though alive.

Tommy walked over to the microcephalic man at the end of the table. "And this is Schlitzie. He's Eldest, but we don't know who he really is – he doesn't know himself." Tommy scratched his chin. "Near as we can figure, the brain in this Form wasn't able to process his past lives, when he went through *Memora Magia*. He's what they used to call a 'pinhead' – he's intellectually disabled. But his *e'drai* is amazing."

"Amazing, amazing," Schlitzie barked, in a perfect imitation of Tommy's gruff voice, a broad smile on his face. "I like to color," he told Rhiannon, holding up a fistful of vivid crayons. "You like to color?"

Rhiannon couldn't help but return his smile, charmed by the gregarious man in the garish dress. Another crayon butterfly peeled away from the paper on the table, fluttering into reality in the air.

"Schlitzie works with Tilly Nadhari – she's Eldest, has schizophrenia." Tommy said. "She helps make his ideas and thoughts more substantial, blends them with her own hallucinations." He smiled. "You'll see at the show."

Alex pulled up a chair and chatted with Van and Tommy, who resumed their cribbage game, laughing and teasing, exchanging mock insults. Schlitzie returned to coloring, singing nonsense songs to himself, butterflies and dragonflies occasionally rising up from the paper to skim and dart around his head.

Rhiannon sat next to Alex, not really contributing to the conversation, but quietly basking in a tremulous sense of belonging. She watched these unique people, different even amongst aeternans, yet so naturally accepting of one another. And while Rhiannon still thought of herself as a monster, even here, somehow the words "freak" and "weird" suddenly seemed honorifics.

A few minutes before the show was set to begin, Rhiannon and Alex met the rest of the family at the foot of the staircase near the Haunted Castle. The *dzina* entered the Fairy Ring at the end of the long banner line in front of the tent. The metal structure was decorated with enormous, beautifully hand-painted banners advertising the unusual delights and Prodigies exhibited within.

Rhiannon looked at a banner depicting an aeternan called Nur Izo, with skin like an alligator, his painted Form surrounded by images of flames and towering shards of ice. The next banner showed ethereally lovely dark-skinned conjoined twin women, clad in flowing Roman tunics and beribboned stolas, their smiles gentle as they stood amid a Fae forest alive with painted elves, deer, and flowers.

The wide bally platform stood in front of the banner line, next to the ticket booth and entrance to the show tent. Van Asalo stood on the platform, gesticulating broadly, shouting out with his mind, gathering the tip, encouraging and enticing the crowd. He wore only a leather breechclout, the better to show off his magnificently tattooed body. He was tattooed from his bare feet to his face, his skin a wild, twisting melange of color and line. Rhiannon looked closer at a ship tattooed on Van's chest, delighted to see it shift and rock, the vivid blue waves and whitecaps washing against the wooden hull.

Grinning and waving his arms, pointing into the assembled multitude or at one of the gorgeous banners, Van sent his artful patter into the thoughts of those aeternans gathered around his platform, or just entering the Fairy Ring at either end of the banner line. *"Live, the profoundly powerful Prodigies, for your enjoyment, edification, education, and aesthetic approval, aeternans gifted with exquisite e'drai, unlike any you have ever seen on any stage, in this lifetime or any other. My Family, I am honored to present the most magical and magnificent Prodigies – here you will see Monte Emmett, an aeternan born without arms or legs, move a 600-pound truck engine block through the air using only his magnificent mind. Inside this tent, you'll see the bewitching twins, Aleia and Saffron, sing like angels, their song engendering enchanting visions in the very air itself."*

A dark-bearded woman in a flowing green gown stepped up onto the bally platform, cradling a terracotta pot, the soil sprouting a single small green leaf. Without looking around, Van stretched out his hand, putting his arm around the woman as she came forward. *"My Family, this is Ceres Zi, who grows not only a lush beard on her lovely face, but flowers, vines, trees, all manner of greenery, with only a touch of her powerful hand!"*

The woman set the pot down on the platform, her aura flaring refulgent gold as she reached out with a gentle finger to caress the leaf growing in the rich earth. Instantly, a vine began to grow, wreathed with leaves and pale pink flowers, the vine becoming thicker and thicker, spiraling upward to wind around the metal poles supporting the banners. Standing in the crowd, Rhiannon sighed as she felt a delicious wash of green energy.

Quite a mass of luminous aeternans was congregating around the platform now, chattering and laughing, listening to Van. A giant man came through the tent flap behind the ticket booth, easily stepping up onto the makeshift stage. An older medius with perhaps 15 *fainna*, he was at least 7 feet tall, lanky, dressed in ornately embroidered circus-style attire – leggings and a sleeveless shirt in vibrant yellow and swirling red designs, spangled with sequins. His red leather boots were nothing short of enormous.

Van was calling out within the minds of the assemblage. *"My Family, I present Humberto Alberik, massive, monumental, the giant Human Magnet with the Magic Touch! With his exceptional* e'drai, *he can attract any object, give you a phenomenal, portentous perspective!"* Offering his broad grin and a sweeping gesture, Van pointed at the giant man. *"Show these folks what I'm talking about, Humby."*

The gigantic man smiled and closed his eyes, spreading his arms wide. His aura grew incandescent, blazing outward. Suddenly, there was a commotion in the crowd, women squealing, men crying out in surprise. Watches, bracelets, necklaces, even purses and wallets inexorably pulled free from their owners, slicing through the air to cling to the chest, arms, and legs of the giant Humberto Alberik, the Human Magnet. The man's aura flared even brighter, and for a moment, those in front of the stage found themselves seemingly standing high on the platform above, seeing themselves on the sand below, through Humberto's viewpoint, their eyes wide, jaws slack. The unique perspective lasted only a second or two, and then all were back within their own minds, discerning the world through their own eyes, laughing and jabbering in excitement.

"Even more wonders, marvels and miracles await you in the Prodigies tent," Van called out. *"Come to the platform to collect your*

belongings, folks, and step up to the ticket booth for your chance to experience the phenomenal Prodigies, aeternans with exceptional e'drai unlike any you've ever seen before, in this life or any other. Live, on the stage in the big tent! Prepare to be awed and amazed! Step right up! It's show time, Family – show time!"

"Let's go," Emma said, flushed with excitement. "I want to be up front." Catching hold of Rhiannon's hand, she began weaving through the crowd toward the ticket booth. The rest of the *dzina* followed, trying to walk quickly in the sand, while Lyds and Robbie herded the children, most sticky-faced with cotton candy.

Rhiannon clutched Emma's hand, laughing, trying to keep up. Glancing to her left, she caught sight of a man wearing a black hooded sweatshirt, the hood pulled up over his head, leaving his face in shadow. There was something unnameable about the man that made her shiver, a stab of ice in her chest. "Emma," she hissed urgently. But by the time Emma turned, the man was gone, lost in the crush of shining aeternans pressing their way to the ticket booth.

"What is it?" Emma asked, concerned.

Rhiannon looked around, every muscle still tense, cold. "Nothing," she muttered. She didn't even know why the man had bothered her so intensely, couldn't find words to explain what she herself didn't understand. She pasted on a resolute smile. "It's nothing."

Looking worried, Emma nodded slowly. "If you say so."

After they got their tickets, the family was funneled with the rest of the crowd into the big tent. Recalling low-rent traveling carnivals from both of her remembered lifetimes, the Prodigies tent was nothing like Rhiannon expected. Polished oak boards made up the floor, miraculously smooth and clean of sand. "Could use cleaning *e'drai* like that at our house, like to say," Robbie muttered from behind Rhiannon, and Maddie, next to her, laughed.

Rows of bleachers were arranged in a semi-circle around two-thirds of the tent, facing a curtain stretched across the final third of the space, and in the center, a broad, raised stage. The bleachers were surprisingly elegant, long boards of polished cherrywood supported by iron filigree legs, which, Rhiannon reasoned, must fold against the wood for travel. The seats and hinged back supports were padded with plum velvet, embroidered in gold thread.

The raised stage platform, and the wood boards on the surrounding floor, were adorned with elegant, thick rugs, artistically woven with lifelike images of flowers, unicorns, trees, birds, and deer. The entire ceiling of the tent was draped in generous folds of deep turquoise satin, appliqued with shimmering gold and silver stars, the fabric cascading down to cover the canvas walls behind the bleachers.

The heavy, deep purple velvet curtain crossed behind the stage, glittering with delicate embroidery in gold. On either side of the raised platform were tall silvery tripods, each bearing a golden firebowl, the flames flickering and dancing. Small, round, old-fashioned show lights were placed all around the edge of the stage. Finally, directly above the center of the platform was an enormous, outrageous chandelier of iridescent glass in shades of yellow, gold, and red, featuring hundreds of sparkling glass twists and spirals, seemingly frozen in the act of exploding outward.

Glowing aeternans were pressing into the space, talking excitedly, laughing. Emma, through sheer cheerful determination, managed to stake out a wide stretch of bleacher seats in the front row, and Rhiannon and Maddie helped organize the children and get them seated with Lyds and Robbie. Alex had finagled a seat next to Rhiannon, while Zerik and Grayling sat on the other side with Maddie and Emma. Emma was practically bouncing in her seat, as excited as the children.

"Is there gonna be a Prodigy like Missy?" Charlie asked loudly, squirming on the bleachers and rhythmically kicking the ornate railing separating the bleachers from the show floor.

"Probably not exactly like Missy, no," Maddie told the child. "But you'll like the show, anyway, I promise. Now do try to sit still, dear."

"I want more cotton candy," Joshua whispered to Robbie, who shushed him.

"I'm a Pro'gee," 3-year-old Missy announced, waving her sharply-clawed, wing-like arm.

"I believe you are, my love," Zerik replied, leaning over to kiss the child on top of her curly head.

Smiling at the children, Rhiannon happened to look up, across the tent. She jerked back, as though slapped. There, in the middle of the bleachers, amidst the shining aeternans, was the strange man she'd seen before, the black hooded sweatshirt pulled over his head, his face hidden. She shivered. She was still unable to put her finger on what exactly about the man disturbed her so deeply. He sat hunched over in his seat, his arms clenched close in his lap, as though trying to avoid touching the Family on either side. For a moment, there was a glimmer of light in his hands, a reflection from the stage lights.

Rhiannon glanced at Alex, then back to the hooded man. She bit her lip, debating whether to say anything to Alex or not. There was nothing really wrong with the man, she reasoned. All of the aeternans present were dressed in casual beach clothes, sweatshirts, shorts, and the like. Perhaps the man was simply cold, pulling his hood up. It was a fall night at the beach, after all. But what if he was hiding, keeping his identity a secret? What if ... Rhiannon shook her head, frustrated with herself. "What if" indeed. What if she was just imagining things? She decided she was just conjuring danger where there was none, shaking off her inner chill.

Abruptly, the lights in the tent were extinguished, leaving only the burning firebowls on either side of the stage. The throng of aeternans grew silent, watching the flames, waiting. "My Family," came the voice of Van Asalo in their collective minds, "The Prodigies."

Antiquated jazz music from the early part of the 20th century swelled. The lamps around the stage and the chandelier above gradually illuminated, revealing Schlitzie downstage, chortling and dancing wildly to the music in his baggy flowered dress. His aura, with the endless *fainna* of the Eldest, gleamed faintly lucent. A few feet upstage, a woman stood behind him, with blond hair flowing in soft curls nearly to her waist. She wore a white floor-length gown, eyes closed, her hands folded neatly before her. Finally, behind the lovely blonde, the bearded woman, Ceres Zi, stood against the purple curtain, holding two flowerpots.

Van's voice echoed in their minds once more. *"Please honor Ceres Zi, the bearded woman whose touch is like song to plants, Tilly*

Nadhari, schizophrenic artist, and the microcephalic visionary, Schlitzie."

Ceres Zi's aura blossomed, glowing dazzling as she touched the plant within one of the flowerpots. At once, 10 vines spiraled outward, twining up into the air, surrounding the back of the stage with dense greenery glimmering in the light of the firebowls. Fuchsia flowers popped open on the vines, tiny blossoms at first, becoming larger and larger. Now, with her shining fingers, Ceres touched the budding leaf in the second flowerpot. At once, a small tree sprouted, growing taller and thicker with every moment, a profusion of leaves bursting forth on its branches. When the tree reached a height of nearly 8 feet, small oranges began to appear on the branches, growing larger in the passing seconds until the fruit was full and ripe.

The giant man, Humberto Alberik, came through the purple curtain, and with his help, Ceres Zi picked the fragrant oranges, tossing them into the delighted crowd. The sturdy tree had produced enough fruit for everyone present, and when all of the oranges had been picked, Humberto bowed, exiting the stage. The audience clapped appreciatively, and the bearded woman gravely offered the *anam'sal*, before backing off the stage into the gap in the curtain, leaving the rich flowering vines and the orange tree behind, embellishing the stage.

The music continued to play, the buoyant strains of Bix Beiderbecke's *Clarinet Marmalade* fueling Schlitzie's eccentric, barely controlled dance. As he danced, flailing his arms, his aura swelled, radiating outward. Behind him, the blond woman, Tilly Nadhari, opened her eyes, spreading her arms, her hands and fingers splayed outward as her aura, too, began to shine, swelling to a shimmering radiance. "I see what isn't there," she said, her voice gentle, mellifluous. "I see people, I hear voices, born of my gift, my mind."

Schlitzie's dance grew faster, agitated, his multi-layered aura blazing.

"I see what Schlitzie sees, and my visions speak Truth aloud." She smiled. "The visions are hallucination, illusion. But the Truth is not – it is born from the pages of the Story itself."

The woman reached out and put a hand on Schlitzie's shoulder, and he stopped dancing abruptly. Their auras fused where they touched, a vivid coruscation. "I see angels, Tilly," Schlitzie announced, an indefatigable, winsome smile on his face.

"I see them, too," she answered, her voice like a sigh. Her aura flared brighter still, luminescent. And suddenly, the air was filled with the hallucination of angels. Twenty, then thirty celestial beings, utterly nude, their faces exquisite, beautiful to behold, colossal feathered wings sprouting from between their shoulder blades as they flew, dizzying, skimming and diving throughout the tent. One stopped, poised in the air close to a woman in the audience. "The son you bear will be Eldest," the creature murmured. The woman pulled back in surprise, her face reflecting joy as she clutched her full, rounded stomach.

Another angel flew near a dark-haired man sitting at the top of the bleachers, just above Rhiannon's *dzina*. The angel pointed at the man, its beautiful face suddenly terrible to behold. "What you have done is wrong. Your soul tempts shadow." The man turned white, his face reflecting horror and shame.

The angels glided sublime and bewildering through the air, whispering Truth to those chosen. At last, one hovered before Rhiannon, its flapping wings pulling in great draughts of air, and she shrunk back, afraid of what the being might say. "You must trust your feelings about everything but yourself," the angel whispered. "You are glorious," it added, before diving off into the air toward the stage. Shaken, Rhiannon could only stare, watching the creature's flight, unable to fully absorb the Truth the being had imparted.

After a few more minutes, Schlitzie, still dancing to the vintage jazz music, began to flail his arms around. "Butterflies," he called out joyfully. "I like butterflies, Tilly," he said to the blonde woman standing behind him on the stage, her aura blazing.

"I like butterflies, too," she murmured. In a flash, the angels swimming through the air became fluttering butterflies, Blue Morphos, red-orange Monarchs, enormous black, yellow and green Goliath Birdwings, multicolored Painted Ladies, and Ulysses butterflies with their beautiful iridescent blue-green wings. The audience sighed at the lovely *e'drai*.

Tilly Nadhari came forward, and reaching into the bosom of her gown, she pulled out a handful of beads, which she threw into the audience, the aeternans laughing and scrambling to catch these glittering souvenirs of her performance.

Now, Tilly took Schlitzie's hand, the vibrancy of her aura beginning to dissipate. The butterflies gradually faded as if into mist, and the blond woman gently led a chuckling Schlitzie from the stage, through the purple velvet curtain. As they exited, the lights in the tent faded to darkness once again, leaving only the burning firebowls glowing on either side of the stage, while the music continued.

Without warning, a narrow tower of flame nearly 9 feet high appeared in the center of the stage, the searing heat so intense that those in the front row of the bleachers, including Rhiannon, could feel the heat on their skin. "Ah," Maddie sighed, and Rhiannon knew her Sister could feel the energy of the flames, just as she had experienced the green energy during Ceres Zi's performance.

"*My Family,*" came the voice of Van Asalo in their minds once again, while the flames continued to burn. "*We now present Nur Izo, with his alligator flesh, master of fire and ice, and Monte Emmett, e'drai levitationist and Prodigy extraordinaire.*"

From the center of the flames, Rhiannon could see the dark figure of a man appear. As she watched, he stepped unharmed from the fire, which died down and vanished as he attained the stage. Dressed only in close-fitting gold shorts embroidered with red dragons, the man's skin had been greased, slick and shining. He had ichthyosis, his skin like an alligator's, rough and cracked. With a flourish of his hand, two garishly dressed stage-hands rolled a cushioned divan onto the stage, bearing another man, Monte Emmett. Monte's Form had neither arms nor legs, but he carried the powerful, many-layered aura of the Eldest, shining splendid, radiant.

Together, the two men created a wondrous performance, as Monte lifted Nur Izo into the air to float above his head, where Nur created marvels with flame and ice. His exquisite aura blazing, Monte lifted a truck engine, and even whole sections of the audience sitting in the bleachers, to squeals of dismay and delight.

Glancing across the tent, Rhiannon was startled to discover the strange man in the hooded sweatshirt was gone. The show forgotten, she looked around, deeply uncomfortable, while the rest of the audience was focused on the miraculous performance of the Prodigies.

"What is it?" Alex whispered, next to her. Sometimes she was sure he could read her mind.

"Nothing," she whispered back, trying to still her shaking hands in her lap. It was nothing, after all, wasn't it? *"Trust your feelings about everything but yourself,"* the hallucinatory angel had said. And then she realized what had been bothering her about the strange man all along. It was more than the hooded sweatshirt, like she'd seen under leather jackets in Colma. No, she understood now. The man had only had one *fainna*, one thin band of light around his body. Oblivi. In this place. In the Fairy Ring.

Rhiannon gripped Alex's hand, suddenly panicked. "I don't know how he got here," she hissed. "But I think I saw a Dead Monk."

TWENTY-TWO

"That's not possible," Alex said, keeping his voice low, his words belied by the worry etched on his features. "A Dead Monk could never get into a Ring. They're oblivi." But he sounded as though he was trying to convince himself, as well as Rhiannon.

Rhiannon frowned, staring down at the ever-clean, polished oak flooring, recalling the man in the hooded sweatshirt, the way he pulled his arms close in his lap as though to avoid touching others, a momentary glimmer of light on his clenched hand. She gasped, looking up at Alex in wonder. "A talisman. You said anyone could travel into a Fairy Ring if they had a Fae talisman."

Alex glanced involuntarily at the big ring on his own hand. "It's still not possible. No Fae would ever just give a monk a talisman." He grimaced, rubbing his forehead, his eyes suddenly bleak. "Not willingly."

"Shh!" Maddie hissed, leaning forward to look at Rhiannon and Alex with a disapproving frown. "What are you two mumbling about? You're missing the show!"

Rhiannon opened her mouth to respond, but Alex whispered hurriedly, "It's nothing." He looked back at Rhiannon, lowering his voice still further, until she had to lean close to understand the words, his lips at her ear. "If this is true, and there is a monk here, it could cause a terrible panic. In this crowded tent, it could be deadly. Every aeternan lives in fear of the monks." He glanced around the tent, then caught and held her gaze. "I'm going to go look for him. Stay here with your *dzina*."

"No, I'm going with you!" Rhiannon said, determined, trying to be quiet.

"The hell you are," Alex snapped. "Stay here where you're safe." He took a steadying breath, gripping her hand urgently, his leaf-green eyes searching hers, intent. "Please, Rhiannon. Please stay here. I don't want anything to happen to you."

Something in his eyes warmed her inside, and she nodded wordlessly, accepting his decree.

And then he was gone, moving with the same silent, breathtaking speed Zerik had used in the cemetery in Colma.

Rhiannon tried to focus, return her attention to the Prodigies show. Worrying, she told herself, wouldn't matter or help.

Fortunately, it was easy to become distracted. Aura blazing, Monte Emmett levitated the large divan on which he reclined, so he hovered several feet in the air above the stage. With a brilliant smile, he floated serenely through the gap in the curtain, to the deafening applause of the audience. Nur Izo had thrown handfuls of golden-red beads into the crowd, each with a perpetually burning flame within, before he, too, exited the stage in a tremendous coruscation of fire, the assemblage momentarily awash in heat.

Once again, the lights went down, leaving only the burning firebowls on either side of the stage, their light flickering and dancing. Rhiannon shivered, looking around the tent, trying to spot the man in the hooded sweatshirt, or, failing that, Alex. But the light was dim, and Rhiannon could barely make out the sea of smiling, excited faces, let alone differentiate one from another.

"*My Family,*" came Van's voice. "*The Prodigies are proud to present the bipolar brilliance of Bhava Moon, ghost talker, and the exceptional e'drai of Tommy Akhila — he who makes things whole.*"

The audience applauded as the lights gradually came up. Standing at the forward edge of the platform stood the little man Rhiannon had met – and befriended at last – Tommy Akhila. He wore a close-fitting sleeveless suit of silver, inscribed with whorls and swirls of gold sequins, standing in front of a vividly painted trunk in shades of purple, gold, and green. Van Asalo, splendid in his tattoos, stood next to Tommy, looking gargantuan next to the little man. Behind them was the pale, bald Bhava Moon, his lanky form bearing the shining aura of the Eldest, clothed in a simple blue silk robe. He stood next to a red velvet upholstered gilt chair. Smiling briefly at the applause, he closed his eyes, hands folded before him in an attitude of waiting.

"*We'll be needing some volunteers from the audience for this portion of the show,*" Van's thought rang out. "*Does anyone here have something which is broken – a watch, a piece of jewelry, an electronic device?*" Van paused. "*Or perhaps a broken heart, a broken spirit?*" He gestured broadly, smiling. "*Please, please come forward, come on down to the platform. Don't be shy, folks. The Prodigies welcome you.*"

At first one or two, then a few more aeternans stepped down from the bleachers, coming to stand on the gorgeously woven rug just below the stage. "I've got a broken watch," one man called out, holding aloft an antique gold pocket watch. "I've had it since my last incarnation, but it stopped working a few years back."

Van Asalo reached down and took the watch, examining it carefully. "*Are these your initials on the back?*" The man nodded, and Van sighed. "*I don't know, Tommy,*" he said to the little man, showing him the watch. "*Doesn't look broken enough to me,*" he added casually. Tommy smiled, shaking his head, his hair glowing white in the stage lights. Van whipped out a square of embroidered silk, dropping the watch into it, then deftly tied the bundle. Then, from the trunk behind Tommy, he pulled out a sledgehammer. Wide-eyed in horror, the owner of the watch screamed, "No!" But it was too late. Van cheerfully pounded the silk bundle containing the watch, several times, his muscles bulging as he slammed the hammer as hard as he could. Whistling a bright tune, he untied the fabric, showing the audience the glittering gold fragments of the watch. *"That's more like it,"* Van said, nodding sagely.

The man who owned the watch simply stood there, stunned, as Van carefully sifted the contents of the silk bundle into Tommy's waiting hands. Now Tommy folded closed his cupped hands around the shards of the watch, looking down in concentration at his interlaced fingers, his aura flaring outward, shimmering luminous despite the haze of shadow. The audience sat in hushed expectancy for no more than a minute, when finally Tommy looked up shyly, slowly opening his little hands. There was the watch, whole and complete. Tommy reached down and handed it back to the awestruck owner, who cried out, "Those are my initials! It's ticking! It works again!" The crowd applauded enthusiastically.

One by one, aeternans came up to Van and Tommy, bringing various broken trinkets, jewelry, hand-held computers and phones. And with each one, Van gleefully found new and interesting ways to even further destroy that which was already broken, from crushing to burning and melting, all to the horrified delight of the owners and the audience.

Rhiannon's favorite moment came, however, when Van simply broke an egg into Tommy's cupped hands, the glistening yellow yolk sliding against his stubby fingers. After a few moments, his aura glowing radiant, Tommy carefully opened his hands, his pale blue eyes timidly exultant, a perfect, whole egg resting in his palms.

The next aeternan to approach the stage was a woman in a pale green T-shirt and jeans, a neonate with only three *fainna*. When Van held out his hand for her broken object, she shook her head. "I don't have anything like that," she said quietly. "You asked for broken hearts, broken spirits." She looked up at him, a glitter of tears in her eyes, her chin up, defiant in her grief. "Well, that's how I feel."

"Ah," Van murmured in their minds. *"This is a different case altogether. What is your name, madam?"*

"Caroline. Caroline Cynthia."

Van bowed, offering her the *anam'sal*. *"Will you join Bhava Moon onstage, Caroline?"*

When the woman nodded mutely, a stagehand appeared from the darkness, pushing a bright purple and red painted wooden staircase on wheels, which he fitted to the side of the stage. Van reached out a hand and helped the lady up the stairs, where she stood blinking in the stage lights, looking nervous, twisting the edge of her green T-shirt with her fingers.

"*Prodigies always have some sort of difference about their physical Form,*" Van announced to the crowd. "*With Prodigies, such as Monte Emmett, or even with our friend Tommy here, these differences are apparent. But in some cases, as with Tilly Nadhari, who is schizophrenic, the physical differences may be harder to see.*" Van waved an arm expressively behind him, indicating the pale, bald man. "*Bhava Moon has bipolar disorder, an illness that manifests itself in emotion. And his unique e'drai allows him to see and feel emotion as if ghosts, speaking to them, sharing them with others.*"

Van bowed, taking the hand of the woman, Caroline, leading her to the red velvet-upholstered gilt chair and helping her to be seated. "*My Family. I present Bhava Moon.*"

Tommy and Van went to stand quietly before the curtain. The blue silk-robed Bhava Moon slowly walked behind the chair where Caroline sat nervously.

Rhiannon looked away for a moment, certain she'd seen a flash of movement in the crowd to her right, but neither Alex nor the man in the hooded sweatshirt was there. She twisted her hands in her lap, suddenly overcome with guilt. She'd been so certain, but now Rhiannon had begun to think she'd imagined things, sending Alex on a pointless chore.

But then Rhiannon was startled when Bhava Moon, standing onstage behind the seated aeternan, Caroline, pointed at Emma, sitting next to Maddie. "You. Sister. Please rise." The man's voice was deep and rich, commanding. Looking around with her sunny smile, Emma stood, straightening her pink sundress.

The man pointed to two more people in the bleachers, first a man, and then a woman across the tent, asking them to stand in their places amid the audience. "Please wait, for now. I appreciate your patience," Bhava Moon intoned gravely, offering each the *anam'sal*.

Then the man returned his attention to Caroline, placing his hands on her shoulders, closing his eyes and breathing deeply. His extensive aura glimmered, the uncountable fainna beginning to glow brighter, expand. At first, the woman looked troubled, fidgeting in the red-velvet chair, but suddenly she went still, her eyes closed, her face becoming composed, placid. As Bhava Moon's aura flared incandescent, a sheer white mist began to coalesce around Caroline, rapidly growing more substantial.

Bhava Moon raised his hands, pulling the translucent mist from Caroline's form, gathering it with his long, pale fingers to writhe and twist around his body, a spirit, a ghost. His features clenched as if in terrible pain, and with a rasping bellow, he threw out his hands, the white mist exploding wide, slamming outward into the audience, the assembled aeternans. Suddenly, every member of the crowd was overcome, consumed with a terrible feeling of agony and loss, pain, suffering, heartache, and grief. Many wept openly, while others clutched their sides, heads down, utterly lost in the tremendous anguish. Rhiannon cried as if she would never stop, tears flowing unchecked down her cheeks, swamped with Caroline's horrible sadness. The suffering continued unabated for what seemed an eternity.

"Enough," murmured Bhava Moon, tears trickling from his eyes. He pointed once more to Emma and the other two aeternans he'd asked to stand amidst the crowd earlier. "Share your joy with us," he said, at once a plea and a command. Throwing out a hand, he began pulling a pale mist from all three standing aeternans. Rhiannon saw Emma gasp, fumble behind her, reaching back to clutch the bleachers for support. Back arched, a shimmering gold mist extruded from her chest, streaming toward the stage, where Bhava Moon clutched it to himself, gathering it up with the effulgent light from the other two aeternans, spinning it into a gleaming golden ball alive with whorls and spirals of power.

Finally, he threw out his arms, the brilliant gold energy expanding instantly, flowing back outward from his fingertips, melting into the assemblage. Caroline, sitting in the gilt chair, cried out. "You are born of joy," Bhava Moon announced, tears still wet on his face.

Rhiannon sighed as the blissful energy consumed her whole being, her earlier weeping grief transformed. Throughout the audience, all around, she heard exclamations of exultation, euphoria. Abruptly, an image of Alex filled her mind, his tousled hair, his green eyes, and happiness swelled. She watched in awe as, onstage, Caroline shook with the force of the gold energy, her three *fainna* radiant, exquisite. She leapt to her feet, impulsively embracing the bald Bhava Moon. "I am whole again," she said, wonder in her voice.

Van Asalo came forward, his face suffused with gladness. "*This way, Caroline.*" He carefully helped the woman down the stairs, returning her to her seat in the audience. Bhava Moon pulled a handful of beads from his blue silk robes, tossing them into the crowd. Rhiannon caught one; it was a translucent blue, and when she held it, she could feel a breath of emotion, happiness, a lightness of spirit.

With a placid *anam'sal*, Bhava Moon exited the stage, followed by Tommy and Van, to exuberant applause. As they left, the lights went down, once again leaving only the burning firebowls to illuminate the space. Rhiannon could just make out the other members of the audience, some still crying, this time with happiness, others laughing, still more holding one another, embracing. The lights remained down for quite some time, allowing the crowd to gather their emotions, to regain some sense of detachment.

Rhiannon had never expected anything like this, when her *dzina* brought her to the Prodigies show. She had thought to watch performances, not become part of them. She thought not only of the grief and joy Bhava Moon had shared with her, but also of Tilly Nadhari and Schlitzie, and the angels who spoke Truth. Maddie looked over at Rhiannon, her sharp eyes missing nothing. She laid a warm hand on Rhiannon's knee. "A Prodigies performance can change people," she whispered. "But almost always for the better."

Just then, Alex slid into his seat next to Rhiannon. He moved with startling silence and speed; she hadn't even seen him coming. She smiled, glad to see him. Looking up at Alex with questioning eyes, he shook his head regretfully. "Nothing," he whispered. "I couldn't find anything, not a sign." He looked kindly into her eyes. "It's like he didn't exist."

A spark of anger cooled her happiness. "But he did," she hissed. "I saw him. In a black sweatshirt."

371

Alex put a calming hand on her shoulder. "I believe you. Really I do. But whoever he was, he's gone now."

Rhiannon looked away, torn. "I don't know, maybe I was wrong." She stared at the flickering flames for a moment, then looked back to him. "But if I'm right, then he'll be back, Alex."

Alex nodded, putting an arm around her shoulders, and she leaned into his warmth. "No matter what happens, I'll be right here," he said. And she wanted so much to believe him, defying her own darkness, her internal demons.

On the stage, behind the orange tree and the twisting vines left by Ceres Zi, lights were gradually coming up, illuminating the greenery and bright flowers. Birdsong trilled as if from nowhere, and while the stage lights remained dim, the chandelier overhead brightened, lighting the stage with a kind of glimmering softness.

"*My Family*," came Van's voice, "*We give you Aleia Marie and Saffron Lahara.*"

Two women glided onto the stage, every movement gentle, perfectly choreographed, as they moved in elegant synchronicity, dark brown arms around each other's shoulders. Dressed like Greek goddesses, they wore flowing stolas tied with glittering gold ribbon, the hems of their gowns bejeweled with sparkling emeralds and rubies.

They halted center stage, and only then did Rhiannon realize that these women were conjoined twins, connected at the waist, sharing flesh. Both were medius, a little more than 10 glowing *fainna* defining their auras. Their features were almost identical; they had perfect brown skin and ebony hair falling in tight ringlets.

The woman on Rhiannon's left raised her voice in breathtaking, delicate wordless song, her aura brightening. Floating above her head appeared a lustrous, translucent parchment banner, which read "Aleia" in flowery, old-fashioned script.

Now the twin on the right began to sing, her voice high and pure and sweet, her aura flaring as a second hazy paper banner appeared drifting over her head, reading "Saffron," in smooth elegant calligraphy.

Heads bowed, the sisters grew silent, and the banners evaporated. Overhead, the twisting, spiraling gold and red chandelier dimmed, until only the shape of the fixture seemed warmed from within. The stage lights glowed softly, illuminating the orange tree and twisting vines.

"*Welcome to the forest of the Fae,*" came Van Asalo's voice from somewhere, everywhere.

Aleia began singing, an exquisite, ethereal song, light and shining, yet somehow deep and powerful. The radiant aura around both women surged, blazing outward. All around the assembled aeternans, the blurry, indistinct image of grass and flowers sprouted. As Saffron joined her high, rare voice to that of her twin, the grass at once appeared to become solid, substantial, daisies and violets sprinkled throughout. The bleachers became a curving hillock of grassy earth, the aeternans sitting in the meadow, watching the joined sisters singing. Rhiannon heard Emma sigh, overcome with a rush of air energy, just as Rhiannon had felt the green earth energy earlier, and Maddie Nur Izo's flames. Rhiannon reached down with her fingers, feeling the cherrywood boards of the bleachers, but while she could feel reality, her eyes spoke only of illusion, the gently curving grassy hills.

Now the sisters' voices rang higher, stronger, and the meadow grass sprouted everywhere, until the stage and carpeted area all around blossomed with greenery and flowers, the twins standing on a hill before the assemblage. Trees grew up on either side of the women, producing flowers and fruit, plums, apples, pink cherry blossoms, and dripping fuchsia. Robins, bluebirds, chickadees, and all manner of birds appeared on the branches, singing and taking flight into the air around the hill, skimming over the curving hillocks where the audience sat spellbound.

The trees sprouted with breathtaking speed, growing taller and taller, branches spreading like growing crystals, until the entire ceiling of the tent was filled with leaves and boughs, warm golden light filtering through the maze of limbs and greenery, a forest in truth. The air was redolent with the scent of leaves and grass, growing things, earth, the perfume of sweet fruit, night-blooming jasmine and violets, roses and summer wine.

Saffron raised her voice, a mesmerizing song, and the shadow of a spotted doe appeared in the grass behind her. Aleia's voice joined her sister's in perfect harmony, and the deer became real, solid, hesitantly picking its way through the tall grass.

As the song progressed, each twin sang half of the whole, each working with the other to bring more visions to life, painting reality with their song. First birds and deer, then elves and fairies, the air alive with the glittering, fluttering lights of tiny fairies and fireflies throughout the space above the curving hillock. Elves danced on the grassy knoll below the watching aeternans, little creatures with bodies brown and knobby like twigs, cavorting in the grass, turning somersaults, spinning joyous and dizzy in a fairy circle.

Now, a giant furred creature moved through the tent, its stilt-like legs more than 20 feet long, crossing from the low hills to the larger knoll, walking slowly and carefully through the blossoming forest, great glistening black hooves stepping gently amid the fireflies, the bright grasses and flowers. Overhead, Rhiannon could see the beast's great pink belly covered in pale fur, turgid rosy nipples hanging low.

Throughout, the two women sang, their voices deliciously rich, blending together in perfect harmony, sweet and strong, their combined auras burning, dazzling. And though Rhiannon knew she was feeding the twins with her imagination, there could be no doubt this perfect forest was nothing more than exquisite illusion, real to all of her senses but touch, as she could still feel the cushioned bleachers beneath her fingers.

And now Van Asalo's voice was heard once again within the minds of the aeternans. *"My Family, at the last, I give you Jadira Tirion, oracle."*

From between the trees and vines at the back of the grassy knoll, a woman walked forward, her aura that of the Eldest. Her features were Asian, her hair like a curtain of black silk. Dressed in a sleeveless, sheer pink flowing gown gathered at the waist with a white ribbon, it took a moment for Rhiannon to realize that Jadira Tirion had no arms, merely gently rounded buds where her arms might have been. The woman was barefoot, stepping slowly, delicate and lissome, through the meadow grass and flowers, smiling gently, past the still wordlessly singing forms of Aleia and Saffron. At last, she came to stand at the edge of the hill, the edge of what was once the stage, before the twins' skillful illusion.

The twins stepped backward with harmonious grace, until they came to stand near Ceres Zi's orange tree, and, Rhiannon realized, somewhere beneath their illusion was the purple velvet stage curtain. Their song became softer, now deep and low, and gradually the visions of trees, grass, deer, and flowers, even the dancing fireflies and fairy lights began to diminish, growing brumous, insubstantial.

Two teenage girls clad in short white togas came through the web of illusion, at once branches and stage curtain, parting reality with a lithe wave of their arms, dancing, spinning, coming forward to the edge of what was now a stage once more. With the stage lights blooming, the two girls, both with short blond curls, halted next to Jadira Tirion. Reaching down to the edge of the stage, one lifted what appeared to be a large silver bowl lined with soft fabric, while the other picked up three lengths of some kind of silvery pipe. Afterward, they came to stand on either side of Jadira, waiting.

As Aleia and Saffron continued to sing softly, the visual world of the audience still faintly illusion and nearly reality, Jadira raised her voice to the assemblage. "I see into the burning heart of the Story itself," she said. "And I am wounded by it, scarred. With every day, I grow mad with it. Please, take what I have now, while I am still able to share it with you."

Maddie gasped, her hand flying to her mouth, and Rhiannon looked over at her with concern. "Are you all right?" she whispered.

Maddie nodded, her eyes glistening. "Sybils are rare these days," she whispered back, choking back her tears. "She must suffer terribly."

Zerik put an arm around Maddie, and she leaned against him, brushing away her tears with the back of her hand, her eyes on Jadira Tirion.

"Our proximity to the San Andreas fault line is why the Prodigies have chosen to perform in this place," came the voice of Van Asalo. "The rift in the earth speaks to Jadira Tirion, as it did to her sybil ancestresses."

The two girls in white togas came forward. One handed the padded bowl-like structure to the other, who began deftly using the objects to construct a kind of three-legged stool, a tripod. The first

375

went to the front of the stage, throwing open a small trapdoor. Light poured forth from below, gleaming blue and silver, while the gap emitted steaming wisps of vapor, which rapidly grew in volume, becoming great clouds.

The girl with the tripod stepped forward, carefully placing the object over the trapdoor, the stool barely visible in the thick haze of mist curling and twisting upward. Now, the two girls helped guide the armless Jadira Tirion onto the tripod, settling her seat in the cushioned bowl, gently brushing back her silky black hair. Jadira, somehow at once smiling and yet grave, gracefully folded her legs before her, cross-legged on the tripod. She closed her eyes, breathing deeply of the vapor, her aura blooming until her slight frame was encompassed with a stunning, multi-layered radiance, the surrounding miasma rendering her ablaze in a paroxysm of light.

Jadira took one deep breath, then another, and another. Suddenly, her body began to shake, spasms taking over her legs, her torso, her head jerking back. The two girls in togas rushed forward to hold the woman's shoulders, to steady her on the tripod above the light and mist. The audience had grown utterly silent, waiting for the words of prophecy only a true sybil could engender.

As the twin sisters Aleia and Saffron continued to sing softly low near the curtain, Jadira's head suddenly snapped forward, her eyes open wide, glowing like golden fire. She spoke, her voice deep and resonating throughout the space. "Death," she called out, her body shaking with another tremor. "Death, in the sand, death by the water, mortaetun, never to be reborn, reborn nonetheless. Your leaders have kept your eyes shadowed. A demon prowls amongst Family, bewitching oblivi, aeternan and Fae alike, stealing souls, and none are safe."

There was a collective cry of consternation from the assembled aeternans, all looking to one another in fear and dismay. His face grim, Alex reached out and squeezed Rhiannon's hand, who watched Jadira Tirion in horror. Unlike the confused and frightened aeternans around her, Rhiannon knew what the oracle spoke of, and while she didn't know the full meaning of the prophecy, she knew enough to be very, very afraid.

And then, into the terrified, panicked murmur of voices, a man called out from the audience. "What of *divya spava*?" From the other side of the tent, another cried out, "Yes! What about Spava?"

Jadira took another deep breath, breathing in the flowing vapor, her body suddenly wracked with spasms once again. The two girls in togas steadied her, their hands gentle. The oracle spoke once more, her breath labored, her voice deep. "The Gods will always fulfill their promise in time of great suffering. *Divya spava* has come."

There was a great flurry of excitement throughout the tent, muttering, whispering. "But who?" called out yet another aeternan. "Who is *divya spava*? Where can we find him?"

But the oracle slumped forward, insensible, into the waiting arms of the two teenage girls. The performance was over.

The backstage area in the Prodigies tent was nothing short of total chaos. And yet it was a controlled chaos, the madness of the cogs of a well-oiled machine, the lunacy of a perfectly executed, organized ant hill. Performers changed out of costumes, costumers standing by to mend tears or trims if necessary, otherwise carefully packing the beautiful fabrics. Roustabouts worked to break down the bleachers, lighting rigs and other apparatus, folding soft goods, including rolling up banners, moving equipment, knocking down and packing up the cook tent, breaking down the bally platform and banner infrastructure, preparing to break down the main top, rounding up props and all the little odds and ends that needed to be packed before the Prodigies show moved on.

Rhiannon, Alex, and Grayling made it past the security creature (a brown furred Fae Being with a startling number of teeth), with two of the Ciatri children in tow, 3-year-old Missy and Marcus, age 8. The little Traveler held Grayling's hand shyly, looking everywhere with big grey eyes much like his father's. Marcus wanted to meet Schlitzie and Tilly Nadhari. Their portion of the show, featuring the flying angels and butterflies, had made a tremendous impression on Marcus. Missy, however, wanted to see Tommy Akhila. "The man what makes fings all better," she said.

Maddie, Emma, and Zerik, along with Lyds and Robbie, had taken the other children out of the Fairy Ring, to ride on the Jet Copters on the Boardwalk ("And get some more cotton candy, puh-leeeze?" Joshua asked plaintively.).

Backstage, Alex approached his shadowed friend Tommy, who stood next to Ceres Zi's orange tree, which had been carefully brought from the stage. "What are you going to do with that?" Alex asked.

Tommy grinned. "Plant it in the rift in the sand. Leave the oblivi something to wonder about."

Alex laughed. "I hope you don't mind, Tommy, but Missy and Marcus here wanted to meet you." Alex and Grayling came closer, holding the children's hands. Rhiannon stood back, her smile wan, still absorbed in Jadira Tirion's performance, the words of the oracle haunting. She shook herself, almost laughing. She probably wasn't the only aeternan to leave the Prodigies show feeling distressed. Of course, she had more right to, but who could know that?

"Of course, I love to meet kids," Tommy responded to Alex with a laugh. "Always nice to meet people my size." He patted Missy's curly head. "Or shorter."

Tommy introduced Marcus to Tilly Nadhari, and the child stared starry-eyed at the woman, completely impressed. When she winked at him, little Marcus actually blushed. As the havoc of the show breakdown raged around them, Tilly looked over at the little white-haired *liath* man. "Take a break, Tommy," Tilly said. "Sit with Schlitzie and your friends. I'll deal with your part of the breakdown."

Tommy nodded. "Thanks, Til. Get Humby to help you with my trunk," he said. Tilly nodded, waving a friendly goodbye to Marcus, who turned pink again, looking down with a timid smile.

Van Asalo approached wearing his wide grin, and in short order, he, Alex and Grayling were deep in conversation about Jadira Tirion, the oracle, and her method of connecting with the Universe. "Many oracles have used fumes and vapors to trigger their *e'drai*," Van said, with a shrug. "There's Delphi, of course. Almost without exception, the vapors come from deep in the earth, at or near a fault line. We've tapped into the San Andreas fault for this show — our next performance is in New Zealand, on the Awatere fault."

The children had begun to fidget, and Tommy looked at Rhiannon, suggesting they go color with Schlitzie, while Van offered to take Alex and Grayling down under the stage, to see the pit they'd dug down into the fault rift, whence came the curling vapors and steam that fed the *e'drai* of Jadira Tirion.

At Alex's questioning glance, Rhiannon forced a smile. "Go on, we'll be fine."

Within a few minutes, Rhiannon sat at a weathered wood table with Tommy, Schlitzie, and the two children, Rhiannon talking shyly with Tommy while the children colored butterflies with Schlitzie, squealing with delight as their creations took wing.

But Rhiannon was restless. She thought of the man with the hooded sweatshirt, and then the prophecy of Jadira Tirion, shuddering at the idea of a demon moving throughout all worlds, aeternan, oblivi and even Fae, the latter she barely understood. Unable to carry on polite conversation, she got up from the table and went to stand at the rear tent flap, looking out into the night. Tommy came to stand silently beside her. The cook tent had already been broken down, the sand where it stood swept clean and smooth. Off to the right, Rhiannon could see the bandstand, the oblivi concert still in progress, loud guitars and drums and screaming fans nearly drowning out the crash of the waves on the beach.

And there, amidst the noise, confusion and anarchy of the oblivi band and the Prodigies backstage show breakdown, Rhiannon felt a horrible icy shiver run up the back of her neck. She turned, slowly, slowly, knowing what she would see, terrified, unwilling to believe what she already felt, deep and hard and cold within.

The man in the hooded sweatshirt stood not 20 feet away, holding an ugly, heavy black gun, trained on Tommy Akhila. Rhiannon stared in horror as the man pushed back his hood, revealing a bald head, a blue-black triangle tattoo between his eyebrows. A ring glittered on his pinky finger, the stone vibrant green, the color of

Alex's eyes. While his gun was trained on Tommy, the monk's eyes were on Rhiannon, gazing hungrily at her features. "Rhiannon," he croaked, his sibilant voice hideous, ecstatic. Rhiannon realized in that moment the monk hadn't known she was here, in Santa Cruz, at the Prodigies show. But he knew now.

Tommy looked up, saw the monk, his eyes widening in unalloyed terror. In a blind panic, he pushed through the tent flap, running into the night, his little legs churning in the sand. With a disturbing, sickening wink at Rhiannon, the monk ran after him. Schlitzie squealed, and Rhiannon knew he had watched the entire event. "Tommy!" he cried happily, jumping up, pushing through the back of the tent, running after the little man.

"No!" Rhiannon cried. "Schlitzie, no!" Worse, her own children, Missy and Marcus, leapt to their feet, running through the gap in the tent after Schlitzie, giggling, thinking it a splendid game. "No!" Rhiannon screamed. "No, Missy, Marcus, no!"

She couldn't even call Alex and Grayling, her mind silent. And it felt like the world was coming to an end, and she was alone, helpless.

And then she remembered. She was a monster.

Clenching her fists, resolute, Rhiannon ran.

Twenty-Three

Running was slow, almost painful, digging into the sand, shoving back the tent flap, diving gasping into the crisp night air. The blaring noise from the bandstand to her right drowned out Rhiannon's voice as she called desperately for her children, for Schlitzie and Tommy.

It seemed the harder she tried to run, the greater the resistance. Frustrated with her slow progress, Rhiannon kicked off her sandals, her bare feet lunging through the cold sand, past where the Prodigies' cook tent once stood.

All at once, the air shimmered around her, and she was overcome with a strange sensation, as if her skin and aura were stretching, expanding, then seeming to snap back around her body with a faintly audible popping sound. Rhiannon realized she'd gone through the other side of the Fairy Ring, returning to the oblivi world. The world of The Guard, and the Dead Monks.

Don't panic, don't panic, she whispered to herself. Panting, Rhiannon looked around the beach, trying to discern her family in the darkness beyond the amusement park. She figured the monk would force Tommy away from the cacophonous oblivi bandstand and the witnesses there. Rhiannon looked to her left, away from the beach concert, breathing deeply. She closed her eyes briefly, trying to calm herself, pushing down her fear, the breath-stealing sense of dread.

Without warning, her feet grew wonderfully warm in the numbing cold sand, and with a rush she felt the familiar green earth energy drifting up through the soles of her bare feet, a vibrant jade mist.

That minor flush of power was a kind of revelation, and she grasped at the strength so easily forgotten in the face of her fears. Clenching her fists, her terror translated to a righteous anger, a vehement, fervid urge to use her *e'drai*, to use it to gain control, to hurt, to stop anyone who would dare touch her or anyone she loved. She thought of Missy and Marcus, Tommy and Schlitzie, and felt a wash of horror commingled with rage, the need for action imperative, dire. She recalled the monk she'd seen in the tent, his eyes fathomless pools of cold blackness, his ghastly smile. Gritting her teeth, she fought the sense of urgency, remembering what she'd learned with Maddie and Zerik in the Sisters' Circle – that a minute in the endless darkness within was merely a second in the world beyond her body. She had time. Time to gather her defenses. Her weapons.

Shuddering, ruthlessly suppressing her fury, she closed her eyes, forcing herself to breathe slowly, deeply, in through the nose, out through the mouth, the way she had with her Sisters in the Circle on the cliff. In the vast, warm darkness within herself, she caught up the wisps of pale green energy, flowing upward in spirals of mist, growing dense as she absorbed more and more, called it up into herself. The peridot and citron vapor became shining dark-green clouds, thickening, filling her body and soul. Her aura blazed brilliant, luminescent, as the power flowed up her legs, through her belly and breasts, pounding through her heart, sliding down to her fingertips and up to the crown of her head, and then shimmering back down her spine, back into the earth, until she had become a living, burning circuit of light and viridescent power.

Rhiannon caught her breath at the strength of the potent energy and power, exultant, furious, vital. She opened her eyes, her aura dazzling, eyes glowing emerald in the darkness with the force of her *e'drai* and unremembered centuries of accumulating, increasing prowess.

She glanced at her bare feet, reaching out with the green energy to touch the sand, knitting the tiny grains tightly together with only the barest thought, until instead of wading ankle-deep in mushy sand, she was standing on a smooth, solid surface, the sand beneath her feet grown firm.

Looking away from the bandstand to the dark beach beyond, Rhiannon started to run. She held the green energy within, continually pulling it up through the earth and sending it radiating back down again in a perfect orbit. This time she wasn't digging helplessly into the soft sand, but running barefoot hard and fast on unyielding stone, faster than anyone on a beach could ever run, the sand conforming to her *e'drai* as she moved, her perfect solid footprints collapsing into loose grains behind her.

Instinctively, she ran away from people, oblivi and aeternan, away from the Prodigies tent invisible within the Fairy Ring, away from the bandstand and the amusement park, toward the water and the cliffs beyond, where the broad San Lorenzo River joined the sea.

Finally, just ahead, she saw a man standing in the sand, his bald head reflecting in the moonlight, a chunky black gun in his hand. Her breath caught in her throat when she realized he was pointing the gun at the children, huddled at his feet. Marcus was kneeling in the sand, looking up at the man, sobbing, holding Missy close in his lap. The monk was smiling, a delighted, sick thing, and sensing Rhiannon's presence, he turned to look at her, his eyes fathomless black pools, nightmarish.

"Mama," Marcus choked out.

Rhiannon's inner fury roared, uncontrollable, wild, as she held the monk's stygian gaze. "Don't fuck with monsters," she snarled, throwing out her hand, her fingers splayed as she directed her *e'drai* at the man. The earth shuddered, groaning, the sand suddenly gaping wide, a great hole opening beneath the monk's feet. He screamed, high and piercing, dropping the gun as the ground swallowed him, futilely grasping for purchase in the grainy sand, scrabbling with his arms and clawing fingers, until at last the sand filled his gasping mouth, his horrified eyes, and he was gone, buried beneath the earth.

Rhiannon didn't spare the monk another thought. She ran forward, collapsing in the sand next to the children, cradling them in her arms, kissing their beloved faces over and over. They'd grown so precious to her. "My babies," she whispered, tears of relief running down her cheeks. "You're safe, you're safe now."

Either unaffected or unaware of what had happened, little Missy smiled up at Rhiannon. "You glow pretty green, Mama Re'nannon," the child announced, looking at Rhiannon's luminous aura.

"Schlitzie fell down," Marcus said, his eyes huge, sorrowful. "He won't get up."

Rhiannon raised her head to look beyond the children, toward the sea. There was a great still lump in the sand, silhouetted black against the moonlight on the water. A breeze ruffled thin fabric draping the motionless figure. "Oh, God," Rhiannon murmured.

"Stay here," she told the children, coming to her feet. In only a few steps she reached Schlitzie's side. The man had been shot in the throat with three darts, two with red fletches, one with blue. He had died with his cheerful smile on his face, his eyes staring empty and lifeless out to sea.

Rhiannon clenched her hands, tears flowing freely for the loss of the beautiful, simple man, who'd seen angels and butterflies with his gentle soul. She knew he was Eldest and would come back to the world with a new Form, probably one that could process and Remember this life and all those that came before, but she grieved nonetheless.

She stared at the monk's darts buried in Schlitzie's throat. It had taken three darts to kill him. Rhiannon remembered Zerik explaining about monks and their tranquilizer darts, how each dart generally held a carefully measured amount of chemical tranquilizer, based on the body weight of the intended victim. He'd added that too much of the chemicals could kill. Then a thought struck her, the obvious staring her in the face as a cold trickle of ice slithered down her spine. Schlitzie had been killed by two different kinds of darts – and further, the monk she'd buried was not the hooded man she'd seen in the Prodigies tent. More than one Dead Monk was hunting on the beach tonight.

Stifling a fresh sense of panic, she turned and ran back to the children. "I have to find Tommy," she told them. "But it's not safe out here for you kids." Rhiannon forced a smile. "I'm going to find Papa Grayling and bring him here to get you, okay?"

"What if another bad man comes?" Marcus wanted to know.

"Well, how about if I build a sandcastle, so he can't find you," Rhiannon said resolutely, trying to soothe the child's fears, as well as her own. She closed her eyes, connecting with the glowing earth energy, reviving the emerald inner circuit. When she opened her eyes again, they glowed with power, and she threw her hands up into the air. Sand followed, great vertical slides of it, surrounding Rhiannon and the children with a blast of power. The sand flowed thick and high, finally resolving into solid walls of crenellated stone, a castle in truth some 12 feet high and wide, open to the sky above.

Safe within the sandstone walls, Rhiannon closed her eyes once more, the green energy flowing up through her body and down her spine, back into the earth, this time sending out twisting roots, tendrils of earth energy spinning swift beneath the sand, toward the Fairy Ring. The earth below the sand was cold, alive, sluggish, the ragged seagrasses electric in her skin. As her *e'drai* crossed into the Ring from below, she felt a shiver of returning power, a jolt of energy as her roots spiraled and spread outward, searching for Grayling's aura, his unique energetic signature, as she had on the day Eva experienced her first *Fis*, when Rhiannon was so desperate to find help.

Ah. There he was. Her *socia*, Grayling. Rhiannon could feel him, smell the sweet tang of Fae and man, could see his soul with her inner *e'drai* vision, a brilliant twisting viridian and silver, his feet dug in the sand, into her skin, her flesh. Taking a deep, determined breath, Rhiannon gathered the green energy, pulling it into her chest to throb with the weight of her heart, before sending out a great bolus of power, spiraling down through her roots at whirlwind electric speed and up Grayling's ankles and legs, fusing with his aura in a blast of energy as she pulled him toward her, toward the beach and the giant sandcastle she'd built to protect their children.

Consumed with a cold wrath, fists clenched, Alex ran. He ran barefoot with breathtaking, unnatural speed, down near the water's edge where the sand was firmest, the surf sliding up to caress the beach in shimmering sheets of hissing silver foam, moonlight sparkling on the wet sand. The beauty of the scene somehow made the horror of the moment worse.

Alex and Grayling had been backstage at the Prodigies show, still talking with the tattooed Van Asalo, when suddenly Grayling had been gripped with a powerful energy, a green haze merging with his own aura, pulling his legs forward, toward the back of the tent and the beach beyond. Surprise and shock on Grayling's face had evolved quickly into wide-eyed understanding. He'd experienced this before. As he was pulled helplessly toward the tent flap, Grayling looked back at Alex. "Rhiannon," he said simply, fear in his silver eyes.

They'd run then, leaving Van gaping behind them, through the tent flap and out into the cool, crisp fall air, beyond the Fairy Ring and the blaring oblivi band. Grayling was the first to spot the enormous sandcastle a half-mile down the beach, the crenellated walls stark against the moonlit sky.

Rhiannon was gone. She'd left behind the two Ciatri children, safe within the sandstone structure.

"How do we get them out?" Grayling wondered, touching the rock-hard sand walls.

"Try *e'drai*," Alex said, tension lining his features.

At the first notes of Grayling's *e'drai* song, the castle collapsed harmlessly to a heap of fine grains. Freed, the children ran to their father, clutching his legs. "Mama Re'nannon put a bad man under the sand," Missy said cheerfully.

Alex nodded grimly toward the water, and Grayling followed his gaze, to Schlitzie's body lying in the sand.

"I've got to get the kids out of here," Grayling said, his expression flinty. That Alex would go after Rhiannon, and Tommy and whoever might be out there, stalking them, was unspoken, expected. "I'll be back," Grayling added, knowing full well that by then, it could be too late.

Alex clasped hands with him briefly, their eyes meeting, for once in perfect agreement. And then Alex ran, ran like he never had before, fury and panic swelling within until he gasped with it, breathing the emotion like air itself, running on the beautiful moonlit beach.

She didn't want to kill him, if she could help it. She didn't want to be a monster, but she was ready nonetheless, the viridian energy swirling up through her body, down into the earth, ready to be called, to be used however she saw fit. Still, she didn't want him to die, not like the first one, screaming in panic, drowning in sand. When she'd seen that gun trained on the children, she'd lost all sense of reason. But killing them, killing this one, wouldn't do any good. He would only come back, wearing another face, another life.

His back to her, the monk hadn't sensed her yet, his eyes on Tommy Akhila, the little man terrified, standing trapped against the heavy rocks at the base of the cliffs. Tommy's eyes flicked to Rhiannon and she shook her head slightly, willing him to look away, before the monk realized she was there.

But then the monk turned, swinging his hand around – the one that held the chunky black gun. Pointing it at her. He was the man she'd seen in the Prodigies show, the monk in the hooded sweatshirt. He smiled at her, a horrifying, ghastly smile, his eyes glacial. "Rhiannon," he hissed, and her blood turned to ice. "The one I serve will reward me." His voice was a hideously ecstatic susurration.

Rhiannon froze. She knew who he spoke of, the *erim* man who hunted her, handsome as sin, with thick waves of black hair touched with silver, and eyes that held death itself in their depths, hell bound in his gaze. The man who could steal souls with a touch. And she couldn't move, breath stolen, frozen in her breast, her eyes on the black gun and the monk.

Before she was able to recover, to rouse her frozen will, gather her *e'drai*, the monk shot her.

Yet as he pulled the trigger, aiming for her throat, Tommy ran up from behind, tackling the monk around the knees. The shot went wild, but the blue-fletched tranquilizer dart struck Rhiannon in the leg, and she hit the ground hard. An icy sensation flowed from her upper thigh, turning her blood cold, and she gulped, wheezing, gripping the dart and tearing it painfully from her flesh, throwing it into the sand with shaking hands. The green *e'drai* drained back into the earth, all of her power gone. She was no longer a monster, but helpless, shivering until her teeth chattered, weak, lost.

Shuddering, she pulled her arms over her head, the algid, bone-chilling feeling of the tranquilizer spreading through her body. The monk laughed, a terrible, ugly sound, and she could hear Tommy weeping.

But then a voice came out of the dark, from the beach behind Rhiannon. The voice was familiar, deeply so, but different, unlike anything she'd ever heard. The voice offered a single word, an order, a command. No, more than that. A compulsion. Not a word, but a Word.

And the Word was "Run."

Without hesitation, his hideous features utterly terrified, the monk dropped his gun. And he ran.

The numbing sensation flowing through her blood, her skin, Rhiannon couldn't move anymore, couldn't turn her head to see who had saved her. But then she felt him, kneeling in the sand next to her, his hand gentle on her cheek. Alex. Of course, it would be Alex.

"Rhiannon," he whispered, his lips brushing her cheek, pushing back her ebony hair that she might stare up into the endless stars, his face hovering so close to hers. "That dart was weighted for Tommy," Alex said, his aura still effulgent, splendid after using his *e'drai*. "You won't die. But you're going to feel pretty bad for a while."

But she didn't feel bad at all. She was going back to her Sisters. She felt like she was floating, cold and soft on an endless sea. And when Alex picked her up, holding her close to the warmth of his chest, safe in his arms, for some reason she thought maybe being a monster didn't matter anymore.

Alex's little green Aston-Martin sped north up Highway 1, smoothly following every curve, his hands confident on the wheel. He looked over at the passenger seat. Rhiannon was curled up on the tan leather, her feet bare, her head resting on the window as she gazed out at the passing forest and moonlit cliffs. Alex glanced into the rearview mirror, a small satisfied smile curving his lips when he saw Zerik following behind him in the big white passenger van with the rest of the family.

Santa Cruz was more than 200 miles behind them, and Alex felt some measure of peace for the first time in many long, appalling hours that night. In a short time, they'd be back at the Ciatri nest, the whole *dzina* home and safe.

When Alex had carried Rhiannon back through the Fairy Ring to the Prodigies' tent, closely followed by Tommy Akhila, he'd found the Sisters waiting for him, Zerik and Grayling hovering. "Rhiannon," Maddie wept, running forward, gently pressing her hand to Rhiannon's forehead, her throat. She looked up at Alex, her eyes shimmering. "Tranquilizer?" she whispered.

"Yes," Alex said, laying Rhiannon down on one of the silk-covered divans used in the show. He carefully brushed her long black curls out of her face.

"She took the tranquilizer meant for me," Tommy said gravely. He looked haggard. "They were trying to take me back."

"Sister, are you all right?" Maddie knelt next to the couch, squeezing Rhiannon's hand. She glanced over her shoulder. "Someone get her some water."

Rhiannon nodded wearily. "I'm okay, Maddie." She met Emma's eyes, read the concern there. "Sister." She was starting to feel better – certainly not capable of running a marathon, or indeed even standing, but she was starting to feel more alert, less cold inside. Tommy brought her a glass of water and she drank thirstily. The water was refreshing, reviving.

Alex glanced at the Sisters, then looked at Zerik and Grayling, his eyes cold, hard. "It was a *dha*. Rhiannon killed one monk before we got there – sucked him down into the earth."

Rhiannon winced, holding her breath without even realizing it, waiting for the horrified murmurs, the shocked expressions from those she loved. They never came. She had proven she was an abomination, yet her family seemed to take it with equanimity.

Zerik, watching her face, saw too much, her guilt, shame, and fear stamped on her features. He sent a whisper into her mind. *"You killed a devil that murdered Family hundreds of times over, hunting aeternans just to torture them until they become* liath *or die. A creature who would happily turn you over to the* erim *man that hunts you. Don't feel guilty for what you've done,* varenya. *Not for a second."*

Rhiannon looked up at Zerik gratefully. "He was pointing that gun at the children, at Marcus and Missy," she whispered hoarsely. "I lost my mind, I couldn't think. I just had to stop him, to make him stop."

"Of course you did," Emma said firmly. "I would have done the same."

"Pointing a gun at our children? I would have burned him from the inside out," Maddie growled.

"Are the children safe now?" Rhiannon asked, raising a weak hand to touch Emma's cheek.

"They're with Lyds and Robbie, at the van," Grayling answered. "Robbie's keeping them hidden with her *e'drai*."

"We've got to get them – and you – out of here," Maddie added. "Who would have thought monks could strike at a Prodigies show? We have to get back home, all of us. Close to the Caistra. The monks won't dare attack us there."

Alex leaned down to take Rhiannon's pulse. After a few seconds, he nodded, looking satisfied. "Since they were after Tommy, the darts had enough tranquilizer to take him down – not enough to kill." His eyes went bleak. "Well, one dart wasn't enough to kill."

Rhiannon choked back a sob, looking away.

By this time, many of the Prodigies, stagehands, and roustabouts had gathered around. "Tommy!" The giant, Humberto Alberik, was so delighted to see Tommy that he swooped the little man up in his arms, perching Tommy on his shoulder.

"I'm so glad you're safe, Tommy," said one of the twins, Aleia. Her sister, Saffron, reflected the sentiment.

"We heard there were monks," said Bhava Moon, concern etched on his features.

"The Sister took a dart meant for me," Tommy said. "I got him around the legs," he added with some pride.

All the Prodigies and stagehands were shaking Tommy's hand, Van Asalo clapping him on the back. Alex looked away, his face grim.

Everyone tried to congratulate Rhiannon as well, but she couldn't bear the celebration, tears in her eyes, knowing that in this case, with joy came terrible grief.

"Wait," said Tilly Nadhari, the schizophrenic woman who worked with Schlitzie. There was an ache in her voice, as if she already knew the truth. "Where's Schlitzie?" She glanced at an empty table nearby, the surface strewn with bright crayons.

Alex rubbed his forehead, his face pained. He looked around from face to face, from Van Asalo to Jadira Tirion and Ceres Zi. Finally, he eyes caught Tilly's. He held her gaze, and the woman put a fist to her mouth with a choking sound. She could see the torment in his eyes, and he knew she could feel it. "I'm sorry Tilly," Alex murmured. "Schlitzie – the monks – he took three darts. He's dead."

"No!" Tilly cried out, running for the tent flap, closely followed by Van, Humberto, Tommy and Bhava Moon, and most of the other Prodigies. Tilly's agony combined with her unstable e'drai, her aura blazing out of control. The very air seemed to burst open, a flock of angels exploding forth to fly into the air above the mourning Prodigies, weeping, horrible soulful cries for the lost microcephalic man.

"Oh, Gods," Emma whispered, clutching her hand to her belly, as though to protect her child from the wave of suffering, the death of an innocent.

Rhiannon wasn't able to rise from the couch. She cried helplessly, unable to do more, wanting to do something, anything."I think Schlitzie protected the children," she told her Sisters and husbands, gulping back tears. "I don't know how I know, but I think he did. He died, and they were safe."

Grayling looked at Rhiannon, his silver gaze flinty. "I know you want to help these people, somehow, but you aren't safe here anymore. We have to get out of here." He looked at his family. "After I made sure the children were safe, I came back to help Alex. I caught the monk as he ran from Alex's compulsion."

"Gods, Grayling!" Maddie gasped. "He could have hurt you, too."

Grayling took Maddie's hand, smiling wryly. "Well, he didn't. He was very intent on running as fast as he could. We fought, and I pulled this from his hand, before he ran away." He held up an object, a large, silvery white ring, sparkling with a stone the color of spring grass. Grayling dropped the ring into Alex's palm. "They know Rhiannon is here now."

Alex's eyes grew shadowed as he studied the ring. "It is a Fae talisman – the only way the monk could have entered the Fairy Ring – though I can't say for sure who it originally belonged to. I'd have to take it to the seat of House Zel'mori, or possibly back to the Fae Lands to find out." He glanced at Rhiannon, then at Grayling. "You're right. We have to go." His gaze turned to Maddie. "Is there anything you can do to help get the tranquilizer out of her system?"

"Sort of," Maddie answered. She looked at Emma, and together the Sisters laid hands on Rhiannon. "We can't pull the chemical out of her blood. It will have to work its way through," Maddie said regretfully. "But we can help her feel more conscious, awake."

The Sisters' auras flared bright, incandescent, until finally so brilliant they seemed to glow from within. Rhiannon sighed, feeling the warmth of their *e'drai* flowing into her limbs, pulsing through her heart, her head. When at last they removed their hands, Rhiannon wasn't sure she could walk yet, but she felt more alert, invigorated, vibrant.

Zerik frowned, watching his wives, then looked around at Grayling and Alex. "Let's get back home."

"The sooner the better," Gray added.

Alex nodded grim agreement. "I'll carry her."

The Prodigies returned as Alex was lifting Rhiannon into his arms. They were crying and singing, carrying Schlitzie's body, draped in his bright magenta and orange floral dress. The flock of Tilly's solemn-eyed angels hovered as they carried the body into the tent, and Rhiannon saw Schlitzie's vacant eyes, his frozen cheerful smile. Cradled in his hands was a dead, golden-orange Monarch butterfly.

As they left through the front of the tent, Rhiannon felt as though her own heart was weeping, listening to the Prodigies, singing and wailing, crying for the loss of one of their own, *varenya* Schlitzie, beloved to all.

After a couple of hours on the road, the tranquilizer had worn off completely, though Rhiannon was left feeling weary, perhaps a little lost. Maybe, she thought, her feelings were less because of the tranquilizer and more because of the madness the day had wrought, from the exquisite beauty of the Prodigies show to the nightmare afterward.

As Alex drove the little car with calm self-assurance through the twists and turns of Highway 1, Rhiannon thought how glad she would be to get back to the Ciatri nest, to the home that had come to feel so much her own in such a short time, a place of peace and sanctuary. Home meant Maddie and Emma, once nothing more than the yearning dreams of a young girl in Kansas City, now real and flesh, precious Sisters, lovers, friends. They had given her children when she could have none, as though birthed from a fairy tale, the little beings made flesh and real, hers in truth.

Rhiannon slipped off her sandals, curling up in the passenger seat, watching the night stream by. She closed her eyes briefly, thinking of Zerik and Grayling, their endless kindness and support, exulting in their profoundly sensual touch – Zerik so sure, slow and tempting; Grayling intense, passionate.

Beyond the car window, the waves crashed on the beach, shimmering beautiful in the moonlight. They would be home soon, close enough to the Caistra that she wouldn't have to be afraid anymore. The thought of the upcoming party at the Caistra to celebrate the Equinox was exciting and perhaps a little worrisome all at once. She wasn't sure she was ready for a formal aeternan event. But she reminded herself, no one had any serious expectations of her, at any rate. And with her wives, husbands, and Alex around her, she would be all right. Safe.

To have such a family for her own, every childhood dream come true, was still almost unbelievable. Rhiannon wished she could remember the lost centuries of those she loved, remember who she was, the yearning like an ache in her soul.

She shifted in her seat, thinking of Schlitzie, the Eldest who didn't know who he was, filled with joy, dancing and laughing amid the flutter of butterflies. He'd saved her children, she knew it. Rhiannon could still feel that moment, Marcus and Missy precious in her arms, alive and beautiful. Maybe she was like Schlitzie, an Eldest who didn't know who she was, but was trying to learn, trying to understand. To remember.

With a shudder, she recalled how it felt to use her powerful earth *e'drai* to destroy the monk who would hurt her children, who hunted Tommy – and her, too. She knew the monk who shot her in the leg would surely tell the *erim* man who hunted her. He would know where she was. She grimaced, remembering the demon's face as he killed the blond woman in Kansas City, the dark mask of ecstasy as he absorbed a soul into his own, taking such pleasure not only in the horrific death itself, but knowing she was watching. He performed murder for her benefit.

Rhiannon shook her head, looking out the window at the moonlit forest, the winding road heading home. Megan Byrne was gone; the insecure young woman who'd fled Kansas City with her friend Greg, trying to find herself, trying to run from herself at the same time. She was still afraid. The true monster stalked her, and she didn't even know who she really was.

But despite the fears and challenges, she felt stronger. She was surrounded with love and family. She was weird, a freak, a goddess, powerful. Tough.

Wounded. Broken.

But like the day she first found her family, met Zerik in Topeka, she was ready to try. She shook inwardly with the force of the thought. But she would try.

Rhiannon looked up as Alex reached over and took her hand, savoring the warmth of his touch, as his aura blended with her own. Smiling, they drove north, into the night.

GLOSSARY

Aeternan, aeternans – (pronounced "EH-ternan") Casual, everyday term for the immortal minds that are the Family, analogous to "human," or "humans." Those Who Do Not Forget; Those Who Are Reborn. The people who are reborn to remember. SEE ALSO MENSAETERNA, FAMILY.

Aisling Teag M'hail – (pronounced "ah-shling-tee-ug-mwale") Literal translation, "the Dream Touch" in Irish Gaelic. Soul magic sometimes held by one of the three Sisters. Wielder has the ability to communicate to another's soul through dreaming.

Amin'via, amin'ma – "Remember life, remember me," a ritual chant recited during the process of remembering oneself, usually at puberty, The Remembering. SEE ALSO MEMORA MAGIA.

An'via'lach – "The Way of Life," or simply "The Way." A particularly aeternan spiritual belief system, encompassing reincarnation, Druidry, and Fae notions. A positive concept that all life has purpose, that all life is connected energy which can be moved and controlled with *e'drai* and Fae gifts. The dogmatic religion, *An'via'lach'morta,* or *An'vilamort,* ("The Way of Life and Death") tries to codify The Way, to control it. Many members of this religious organization espouse the superiority of aeternans over oblivi and even Fae. *Dinach* An'via is dedicated to the spiritual pursuit of The Way. Some members are part of *An'vilamort,* others follow a more loosely based spiritual practice. Many members of *Dinach* Ano'fiarr are aligned with *Dinach* An'via, though their members and those believing in their spiritual tenets can be found in all of the Houses.

Anam – Soul.

Anam'sal – Formal greeting to an Eldest before speaking. Propriety dictates Eldest must speak first, or initiate contact with younger aeternans. Younger aeternans can indicate a desire to speak to an Eldest by performing the *anam'sal.* Left hand is held against the belly, palm up; right hand cups over the left – tips of right fingers touch heel of left hand. Thus, hands are cupped as though holding something within, resting against the belly. This is accompanied by a bow of the head or even a physical bow from the waist. The cupped hands symbolize the body holding that which cannot be held, the soul.

Anam'ta – Bowing one's head in acknowledgment of another aeternan, usually from a distance. Also an appropriate response to an *anam'sal,* especially from an Eldest to medius or neonate. Acceptable substitution for the *anam'sal* when acknowledging an Eldest publically.

Anamcaillte – (pronounced "ah-nom-kyle-tuh") Literally, "lost soul," refers to those who go mad after too many lifetimes.

Anam Cara – Soul mate. Can be deeply romantic, or refer to a true friend.

Anam Fhios – (pronounced "ah-nom-iss") Literal translation, "the Knowing Soul" in Irish Gaelic. Soul magic sometimes held by one of

396

the three Sisters. Wielder has the ability to see/feel the soul of another, thus knowing their true soul. Most common permutation of the soul gift.

Anam Labhartha – (pronounced "ah-nom-low-her-tuh") Literal translation, "the Speaking Soul" in Irish Gaelic. Soul magic sometimes held by one of the three Sisters. Wielder has the ability to speak directly to the soul of another.
Anam'liath – (Also called simply *liath*) Shadow Souls. Aeternans who have embraced darkness on some level, generally a negative term; there is much prejudice against the *liath*. See also Aura'kur, The Grey.

Anam pratik – Or *pratik* (pronounced "prah-TEEK"). The soul symbol, the symbol of the Family. A small spiral sitting above a larger circle. An elongated figure eight runs from top to bottom, bisecting the circle. The spiral represents the cycle, life beginning, ending, and beginning anew. The larger circle represents the unending nature of the aeternan soul, the open circle also representing psychic gifts or *e'drai*, the open mind, and the open third eye. The elongated figure eight is an infinity symbol on its side, representing the eternal soul, an empty (or conversely, full) hourglass whose sands can never run out. The symbol became standard in the 14th century; prior to that, images of a phoenix, or the ourobouros (a snake consuming its own tail, in a circle) were often used. These older symbols are sometimes still seen among Eldest Family members, primarily in decorative uses.

Anam'spava – Formal bow given to one who is thought to be Spava, or the chosen Sword of the Gods with which to fight evil for the Family. Rarely used. The left hand is held against the belly, palm up, cupped slightly; the right hand is then placed across the left, palm facing left, fingertips pointing forward, like a sword crossing the left palm. The head is then bowed.

Anu'giao – (pronounced "AHnu-gee-ow") Indentured. Refers to those aeternans who choose to indenture themselves to other aeternans, to learn and amass fortune.

Arali – (pronounced "uh-RAW-lee") The netherworld, the between world, little understood. The place humans go between incarnations.

Aura – The glowing light that surrounds all living beings. SEE ALSO FAINNA.

Aura'kur – Dark or shadowed aura. SEE ALSO ANAM'LIATH, THE GREY.

Caistra – (pronounced "KAI-stra") or Family Seat (or "the Seat"). Each country has a Caistra, an administrative/governmental location that also acts as home to any Family member who chooses to live there. Caistras can be as small as a single estate or as large as a huge complex, which may even include a small town, such as Rockport, California, in the United States.

Caih'es'drai – (pronounced "KY-ess-dry") A breathing meditation to join and share *e'drai*, a non-sexual ritual. SEE ALSO ERA'CAIH'ES'DRAI, A SEXUAL VERSION OF THE SAME.

Chorus – the Senate at each Seat, comprised of 21 aeternans, each representing one of the 21 *dinachs* or Houses. They have the power to overrule the Kir'da.

Cor'phae – (pronounced "COR-fae") Individual members of the Chorus; leaders who represent their respective *dinachs*, but are not *Kir'dinas*.

Dahmon – The foundation laws of the Family, Just Laws.

Dao Yin (Order of) – (pronounced "DOW-yin") Those who work formally for the betterment of the Family. Includes the Seekers, those who have Gifts which can be used to find neonates or lost Family members, and the Protectors. Protectors are those who rescue Family members from untenable situations (such as slavery), but are also a kind of police force, an elite fighting group; soldiers. Originally founded to protect women, who were most often of lower social orders. As anyone could be born female, these Forms must be cared for and protected. Founded by the House of Spava (the Spava Dinach) In 1ˢᵗ and 2ⁿᵈ centuries AD, the Dao Yin were originally Spava traders.

De'drai – Doctors and scholars who specialize in the study of *e'drai*.

Dead Monk – SEE GUARD, THE.

Dha – A hunting pair of Dead Monks. SEE GUARD, THE.

Dinach – Dynasty. Refers to Family Dynasties, or Houses. There are 21 in all. Powerful or historically important houses are as follows:

House of Aliona. (Pronounced AH-lee-oh-na) *Dinach* of the Song. Aeternans dedicated to the arts, particularly aeternan arts, *e'lain*.

House of An'via. *Dinach* of the Way. The spiritual and religious class. They actively fight with/seek control over the Caistras and governmental systems. There are good people in the House, but many are corrupt, and the House is splintered and divided – one of the few things that has kept them from obtaining total power.

House of Ano'fiarr. *Dinach* of the Superiors. Great businessmen, leaders, and monsters claim House Ano'fiarr, traditionally supporting the dominion of aeternans over oblivi, to the point of being Gods. Daz Minoru is from House Ano'fiarr.

The Chaos. Not exactly a House, as no formal organization. Anarchists and libertarians, believing every man for himself. Many of the Grey loosely identify with Chaos.

House of Ciatri. *Dinach* of the Circle. The Sisters.

House of Duine. *Dinach* of Man. Dedicated to the service of oblivi, usually take a vow of poverty. Humility of the flesh, knowing all are born human and oblivi first.

House of Lein'ceal. (Pronounced LEE-in-CE-ahl) *Dinach* of the Storytellers. Members of House Lein'ceal are scholars, doctors, sociologists, the *De'drai* (those doctors/scholars who specialize in the study of *e'drai*), the *M'nach* (those who study spirituality in all forms, attempting to place aeternans in various spiritual and religious practices and belief systems, or construct new concepts), and Historians (the S'lai). Their libraries often evolve into homes for various Caistras around the world.

House of Ma'ka. *Dinach* of the Mother. Those in this house believe in the superiority of women, noting that all beings are born of woman, worshiping the Goddess.

House of Niku. *Dinach* of the Flesh. Dedicated to the idea that we are born of the flesh, and learning the secrets of the flesh are the foundation for spiritual attainment and the basis for love. Members focus on pleasure, and gratification. Many spend lifetimes studying the various aspects of *era* in all its forms.

House of Spava. *Dinach* of the Sword. Founders of the Order of the Dao Yin. Zerik Nicolau and Edward Angelis are from House Spava.

House of Thamas. *Dinach* of the Thamas, or simply The Thamas. Naia (Inanna Morrigan) is the *Kir'dina* of the Thamas. Dedicated to serving all mankind, including oblivi, recognizing oblivi as future aeternans. Specially dedicated to the annihilation of *mal'neco*, child predators.

House of Zel'mori. *Dinach* of the Sidhe. Aeternans with direct line or connection to the Fae. Grayling Sonam and Alvar Noriaki are of House Zel'mori; Alexander Lazarus is *Kir'dina*.

Divya Spava – An aeternan reborn as the chosen Sword of the Gods, born to fight evil for the Family. Considered the reincarnation of the original, fairy-tale Spava. Rare. Divya Spava is recognized and shown respect with the anam'spava, a formal bow. See anam'spava.

Divya Varenya – "heavenly beloved." A more formal way of addressing one's lover.

The Dynasty War — A short but bloody war amongst the Dynasties in the 14th century, leading to the formation of the Family bank and the modern structure of the Chorus, with 21 senators each representing a *dinach* at each Caistra. Additionally, each *dinach* has a seat on the board of the bank; all possess equal shares. The *Kir'dina* of each house tend to be the board members, but not always.

Dzina – (pronounced "Zena") Individual family groupings within the larger Family structure; individual *dzinas* sometimes choose to name themselves (such as the Ciatri *dzina*), but others do not. (ex.: "I have to get home to my *dzina* or I'll be later for dinner." Or "I've got five husbands and two wives in my *dzina*.")

E'drai – Psychic gift, power. Formal names for *e'drai* generally start with the modifier "Drai'." Gifts are defined by one or more of the following categories, with the primary *e'drai* first, followed by secondary or modifying *e'drai:*

Ali'hsa – Closing
Apira – Opening
Audiro – Listening
Co'gi – Thinking
Crea'si – Creating
Dar'itae – Giving (or Sharing)
Eman'v'la – Releasing
Engi'ka – Doing
Era'feli – Pleasuring (sexual)
Exi'kai – Destroying
Felis'ta – Pleasuring (non-sexual)
Intra'yur – Entering
Jai'lu – Exposing
Loqui'su – Speaking

Lu'yir – Traveling
M'ido – Moving
Mal'hai – Hurting
Memor'ki – Remembering
Mirsyat'al – Forgetting
Mor'tia – Killing
Natura – Of Nature, of the Universe
O'dni – Smelling
Pro'kan – Pushing
Relin'e'kai – Leaving
Sana'chi – Healing
Sentia – Feeling (or Sensing)
Shi'in – Tasting
Sidhe – All Things Fey
Sien'dao – Knowing
Sin'kan – Of Emotion
Som'ni – Dreaming
T'accia – Taking
Tacti – Touching
Tiran'la – Pulling
Transforma – Transforming, Changing
Uso'ta – Of Lies
V'sio – Seeing
Ver'e'thea – Of Truth
Yaz'hi – Suppressing

For example, Rhiannon is able to feel another's feelings and desires, and "nudge" them to follow a certain feeling. Thus, her *e'drai* would be called *drai'tacti'sentia'pro'kan*, or simply the less formal *tacti'sentia'pro'kan*. No phrases or terms exist that can exactly describe every individual type of *e'drai*, so another aeternan with a somewhat different gift may still describe it the same way. Daz Minoru's primary *e'drai* could thus be called *drai'tacti't'accia*, or *tacti't'accia*, or to be very specific, *tacti'anam't'accia* – he who steals souls with a touch.

E'lain – Aeternan arts, including art, music, or dance – any form of creative expression, but always unique to aeternan life:

> **Agear'niom** – (pronounced "AH-jeer-nee-ahm) theater, acting
> **Ceol'dea** – (pronounced "see-OLE-DEE-ah") music
> **Da'siao** – (pronounced "DA-see-ow") dance
> **Dia'okta** – (pronounced "dee-uh-OKE-tuh") sculpting
> **Hata'zhi** – (pronounced "hah-tah-ZEE") weaving and textiles
> **P'en'tura** – (pronounced "puh-EN-too-ruh") painting
> **S'lai'kaznia**– (pronounced "suh-LY-kahz-nee-uh") writing,
> storytelling

Eldest – Aeternans who have lived more than 20 lifetimes, and have much power. Always capitalized, out of respect (unlike neonate or medius). The word is both singular and plural. About one in one thousand aeternans are Eldest.

Era – lovemaking

> **Era'acor** – lovemaking to seal a contract or agreement
> **Era'amin** – lovemaking to aid in remembering
> **Era'anam** – lovemaking with a soul mate
> **Era'bron** – lovemaking to soothe grief, sorrow, or loss
> **Era'cahres** – lovemaking with someone you love, a friend
>
> **Era'caih'es'drai** – a breathing meditation ritual performed during lovemaking, with a strong focus on ritual and joining *e'drai,* sexual pleasure secondary
>
> **Era'com** – anal lovemaking
>
> **Era'd'ana** – "kinky" or "dirty" lovemaking, based on current decade, country and culture norms

Era'dr'noch – lovemaking to say goodbye for many years, or forever

Era'dr'noch'ikai – public or ritual lovemaking to say goodbye, often at a *mortpakiv*

Era'd'mal – sexual intercourse with evil intent or cruelty, evil in the heart or soul

Era'dia – lovemaking for a spiritual purpose

Era'duri – lovemaking from a distance, whether using *e'drai*, or modern technology

Era'e'drai – lovemaking which uses or enhances a psychic Gift

Era'e'lain – lovemaking as art, or to aid in creating an artistic work, often as part of *e'lain*.

Era'e'lente – lovemaking very slowly, often taking hours or even days

Era'e'soku – lovemaking in a hurry; a "quickie"

Era'f'hia – lovemaking for a personal gain or a motive

Era'famil – lovemaking with one's husbands and/or wives, in a group

Era'i'tao – lovemaking to practice the art of trust, a psychological power exchange

Era'i'yasu – lovemaking to heal

Era'liath – lovemaking with one whose soul is shadowed, the *anam'liath*

Era'magh – lovemaking before a battle or war, or in order to build power

Era'mani – lovemaking using one's hands and fingers

Era'mirsyati – lovemaking to aid in forgetting

Era'morta – lovemaking to die, or to kill with love

Era'nour – lovemaking with food, edible substances

Era'o'cahres – masturbation with someone you love, or a friend

Era'onan – lovemaking with oneself, masturbation

Era'plures – lovemaking with a group, not necessarily spouses

Era'pochva – vaginal lovemaking

Era'qui – lovemaking without penetration (male or female)

Era'sal – lovemaking to say hello, to be friendly

Era'sidhe – lovemaking with the Fae. Considered very dangerous.

Era'slua – lovemaking with a group of 20 or more

Era'spra – lovemaking for fun

Era't'adh – silent lovemaking, avoiding any sound

Era't'jonu – lovemaking to celebrate reuniting

Era't'nev – lovemaking while angry, or while in the middle of an argument

Era't'ran – lovemaking loudly, freely making natural noise and/or speaking, to arouse

Era't'sil – lovemaking to teach or learn lovemaking skills
Era't'stom – oral lovemaking

Era'tau – lovemaking to be watched, or to watch
(exhibitionistic or voyeuristic)

Era'tau'kai – lovemaking in front of an audience of 10 or
more, ritual or otherwise

Era'tias – lovemaking to say "thank you" or to show gratitude

Era'y'vani – lovemaking while under the influence of alcohol,
drugs, or *e'drai* power

Era'y'thos – lovemaking to make up after a disagreement
Era'zi – selfish lovemaking

Erapakiv – A bacchanalia, a sensual celebration, a feast for the senses. Generally includes some sort of *era'tau'kai*, a performance. Traditionally held on equinoxes, or Beltane.

Erim – Enemy, destruction, hostile, evil ("He is *erim*.")

Esera – An army of Dead Monks. Very rare, unimaginably dangerous. SEE GUARD.

Eternal Tales – Fairy tales that have been passed down, diluted, or changed over centuries, based on the lives of Family members, or often taken from The Books, the ancient prophecies of the sybils. Aeternans know there is a heart of truth at the bottom of old tales embroidered over time. SEE SYBIL.

Fainna – (Pronounced "FIE-nah"). The rings in one's aura, each representing a lifetime lived. Eldest have at least 20 *fainna*, neonates have 2-5 *fainna*, medius 6-19.

Family — Term is at once singular, plural, and collective. ("He is Family"; "They're Family"; "I'm a member of the Family.") Refers to those known as the mensaeterna ("eternal mind"), or aeternans, the next stage of human evolution. Those Who Do Not Forget. It is believed that all humans will eventually evolve and become Family — that all humans already have many lives, but aeternans begin to remember those lives — and in so doing, acquire *e'drai* — and with each lifetime, their power and strength increases. SEE ALSO MENSAETERNA, AETERNAN.

Family Name — also called Name. SEE PRAENOM, SECUNOM.

Family Seat (or "the Seat") — SEE CAISTRA.

Fae — of Faerie. The Sidhe ("shee").

Farewell — Traditional farewell exchange: "May your death be gentle." The response (sometimes used alone): "Die kindly." In other words, "we may not meet again in this incarnation, may your transition to the next be painless."

Fis — (pronounced "fees") SEE MEMOR'FIS.

Fola Teag M'hail — (pronounced "full-ah-teeug-mwail") The taste of blood, literally "bloodtouch" in Irish Gaelic. Legendary soul magic sometimes held by one of the three Sisters.

Form — One's physical body ("Oh, you have a nice Form this time! You look great!" or "His Form is Japanese-American."). Refers purely to physical appearance, which is transitory for aeternans.

Gestu — (pronounced "jess-too"). I hear, I understand.

Gift — psychic ability, power. SEE ALSO E'DRAI.

Grey, The – A highly secretive group of *anam'liath*, or *liath*, who have chosen to live outside of the Family and the Chorus system. While these aeternans have embraced darkness on some level, they have also chosen to follow the Light. They keep their activities secret, as there is much prejudice against the *liath*. See also *anam'liath*, *aura'kur*.

Guard, the – ("La Guardia") A secret society dating back to the 15th century, started by the Catholic church and La Banca Guardiano, to watch and study the Family. Organized in cells, like a terrorist group. In recent centuries, the Guard has taken to darker methods of studying the Family.

> **Unita** – individual cell
> **Priest, Soldato** – Called Priest or Soldier. Greg's rank, low on the ladder
>
> **Bishop, Capitano** – superior officer in each cell
> **Cardinal, Generale** – Bishops report to Cardinals.
>
> **Arcivescovo, Archbishop** – Cardinals report to Archbishop, leader of the Guard
>
> **The Dead Monks, Monaco Morto** – Monks travel various Dioceses, similar to the SS, making reports directly to the Archbishop. Generally, they can see auras, and sacrifice their lives and souls to avoid becoming mensaeterna in the next life. They are the darkest side of The Guard. They generally hunt alone. Very rarely, when hunting powerful immortals, they work in pairs, a *"dha."* Only once in 1500 years have the monks gathered together to form an *"esera,"* an army. They keep their heads shaved, often wear brown, and have a black, inverted triangle tattooed on their foreheads, between and

just above the eyes – to cover the third eye; the triangle symbolizes the black monk's hood, and their rejection of *e'drai*.

Historian – ("S'lai") Family members who have spent centuries studying Family histories, committing stories to memory, documenting and cataloging stories. Much of Family lore is based on oral traditions and storytelling. Historians-in-Training are called *"Neo's'lai."*

Homo Oblivia – Those Who Forget. The oblivi. Mortals.

Kir – "Ruler." Name for head of the household in individual dzinas, or those who run a Maisonsur.

Kir'da – "Great Ruler." Name for head of the Family at each country's Caistra. The current *Kir'da* in the United States is Alvar Noriaki.

Kir'dina – "Dynasty Ruler." Name for the head of the respective dynastic Houses.

Kir i'dai – "Supreme Ruler." Name for head of the Family worldwide, including a role as CEO of the Family Dynasty Bank. The current worldwide *Kir i'dai* is Edward Angelis, who originally started the Caistra system.

Kir i'sar – "Spiritual Ruler." Name for the spiritual head associated with House An'via, *Dinach* of the Way.

La Banca Famiglia Dinastia – Literally, "The Family Dynasty Bank." Founded in the 15th century; currently centered in Switzerland. The board of directors is held in equal share by the 21 dinachs or Houses, represented by their individual *Kir'dinas* (who may also be *Kir'da* at one of the worldwide Caistras). The CEO is always the *Kir i'dai*.

La Banca Guardiano – Literally, "The Guardian Bank." The Guard was formed in the 16th century by a privately-owned bank, in competition with the Family bank (La Banca Famiglia Dinastia, The Family Dynasty Bank; based in modern-day Switzerland). The Guard's bank was founded by Augustin di Paxiti in Florence in 1492. The bank was called Paxiti Guardiano Banca, now simply La Banca Guardiano, or Guardian Bank. Augustin was closely tied to the Medicis.

M'nach – Those who study spirituality in all forms, attempting to place aeternans in various spiritual and religious practices and belief systems, or construct new concepts.

Maghkai (pronounced "Mahg-KIE") – we fight together, a battle cry, a reassurance, a celebration, sometimes used as a toast.

Maisonsur ("Safehouse") – Most larger cities offer a Safehouse, the *Maisonsur*, as a refuge for Family members in trouble, or a place for visiting Family to stay. Members of the Dao Yin often live in the local Safehouse while doing their work.

Mal'nichot – any sexual behavior or contact with one who is unwilling, including animals and children.

Mal'neco – Pedophile, child molester, demon.
Mal'viol – Rape.

Medius – "Middle children" – not yet Eldest, no longer neonate. The word is both singular and plural. Medius have 6-19 *fainna*.

Memor'fis – (pronounced "memor-fees") The increasing, cascading visions/memories one has prior to Memora Magia (also simply "*fis*").

Memora Magia – The Remembering; literally, "The Great Remembering." To be born in the mind, describing the process of remembering oneself, generally in puberty. See also amin'via, amin'ma and memor'fis.

410

Mensaeterna – "Eternal Mind." More formal, collective term for aeternans, much as one might call a group of humans "homo sapiens" or "the human race." The immortal minds that are the Family; Those Who Do Not Forget; Those Who Are Reborn. The people who are reborn to remember. SEE ALSO AETERNAN, AETERNANS, FAMILY.

Mirsyati – To forget. Past tense: *mirsyatun*.

Mortaetun – Dead forever. One who is *mortaetun* will not be reincarnated. Their soul is lost.

Mortas – A *nahyin* or circle; a group of three or more aeternans who together, and only together, can kill painlessly with a touch. They are much like priests or priestesses, and study many years, taking solemn vows to use their power for the good of the people.

Mortpakiv – A celebration of a Family member's life, usually terminally ill, culminating in a publicly viewed suicide or assisted killing.

Mortpakiv'as'lathair – A posthumous celebration of a Family member's life, akin to a joyous wake.

Naire – Expletive: Shame! Gaelic.

Name – SEE FAMILY NAME.

Nahyin – A sacred circle, whether ceremonial (physical in nature) or referring to a group of aeternans with joined *e'drai* (such as the *Mortas*, the Senti, or also the Sisters, among others).

Navtu – Informal greeting, diminutive of *zanav tu*.

Neo's'lai – SEE HISTORIAN.

Neonate – Someone new to the Family, usually refers to those who remember only one past life, though all those with 2-5 *fainna* are called neonate.

Nest – The home of individual *dzinas* in English-speaking countries. A family home.

Ni'aeterna – Mythical beings, the aeternan equivalent to a fairy tale. Also called Greater Gods. *Ni'aeterna* are supposedly aeternans who do not die, their flesh as eternal as their minds. Some believe if one's *e'drai* becomes powerful enough, it will keep the flesh young and alive forever.

Nu'sar – A non-gender specific term for aeternan priests, priestesses, monks, nuns, ministers, any kind of religious person, in any *dinach* or belief system. Singular and plural.

Oblivi – Those Who Forget. Homo oblivia. Mortals.

Order of the Dao Yin – SEE DAO YIN (ORDER OF).

Pesti'era – Sexually transmitted disease.

Praenom – The first of two names which identify an aeternan within the Family over multiple lifetimes. The first name, the Praenom, is how one is called, one's Primary Name usually taken from the first lifetime in which an aeternan Remembers; the second name, the Secunom, defines and differentiates from others with the same Praenom, and is sometimes, but not always, taken from one's second incarnation. One uses the birth last name in each lifetime to identify or label one's various incarnations ("That was back in my "Smith" incarnation.").

Pratik – SEE ANAM PRATIK.

Remembering, The – To be born in the mind, describing the process of remembering oneself in puberty. See also *Memora Magia*; *amin'via, amin'ma*; and *memor'fis*.

S'lai — SEE HISTORIAN.

Safehouse — SEE MAISONSUR.

Seat — SEE FAMILY SEAT.

Secunom — The second of two names which identify an aeternan within the Family over multiple lifetimes. The first name, the Praenom, is how one is called, one's Primary Name usually taken from the first lifetime in which an aeternan Remembers; the second name, the Secunom, defines and differentiates from others with the same Praenom, and is sometimes, but not always, taken from one's second incarnation. One uses the birth last name in each lifetime to identify or label one's various incarnations ("That was back in my "Smith" incarnation.").

Sidhe – (pronounced "shee"). The Faerie. The Fae.

Socia – (pronounced "so-shuh"). Partner, spouse. Singular and plural. Not gender specific. Gender specific terms generally taken from one's current culture.
Spava – The Sword, usually referring to a person or a Family protector, not an actual weapon. Also the name of one of the oldest and strongest Family *dinachs* or dynasties, the House of Spava, or the House of the Sword. Some say the original mythical Spava founded the dynasty.

Sybil – Ancient soothsayers, seers, prophetesses, almost always female. Many were aeternan. Their prophecies are contained in the secret, sacred documents known as the Books. Many sybils were insane, driven mad by the undiluted Story flowing through their minds.

Te a'behs – (pronounced "tay-ah-bess"). I love you.

Thamas, The – One of the oldest Family *dinachs* or dynasties, the House of Thamas. An elite group of prostitutes, nuns, and highly trained assassins. They hunt the The Guard, but are also dedicated to killing child predators – they can see the predilection in auras. They are ruthless killers, skilled lovers.

Vahs'da – A particularly foul profane word.

Varenya – Beloved, a less formal term.

Ver'seah – Sometimes known to oblivi as Ley lines, magical and energetic lines connecting fairy rings and sacred sites throughout the planet. Sidhe beings and those with Fae talismans can Travel the fairy rings on the *ver'seah* lines.

Vosha'ni – An orgasm shared through the fusing of auras and *e'drai*.

Way, The – SEE AN'VIA'LACH.

Zanav tu – Formal greeting, (usually run together as one word – zah-nahv- TOO) meaning literally "know you" or "I know you." Can be shortened to the informal "*navtu*," much as oblivi say "hi" instead of "hello."

Zhu'kir – Lord or Ruler without affiliation to dinach or country, (one word: zoo-keer), often used as an honorific for Daz Minoru by his minions

CPSIA information can be obtained at www.ICGtesting.com
Printed in the USA
LVOW07s0725290615

444076LV00013B/3/P